WITHDRAWN

⑤ LAID-BACK CAMP contents

W9-CKD-431

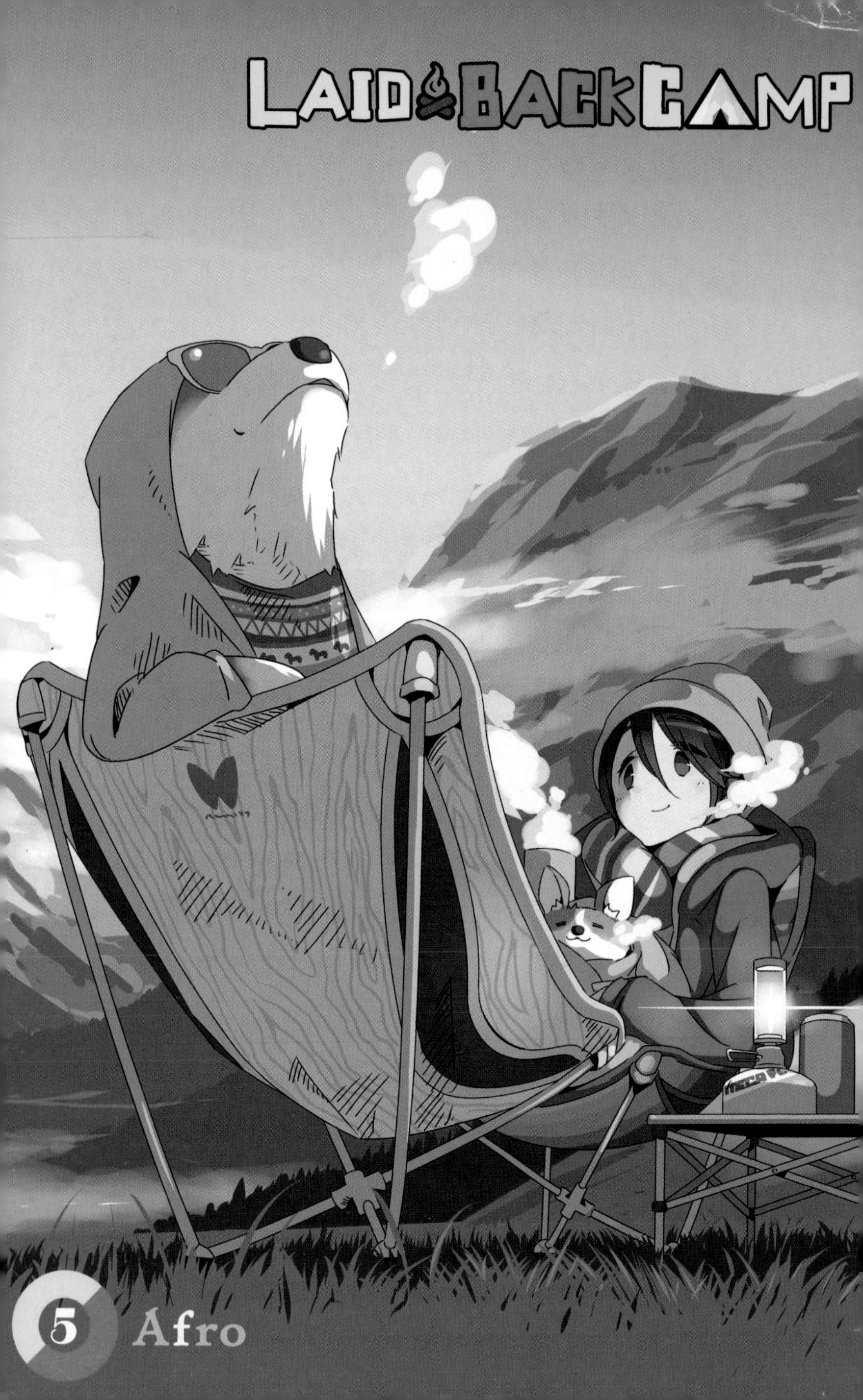
LAID BACK CAMP
5
Afro

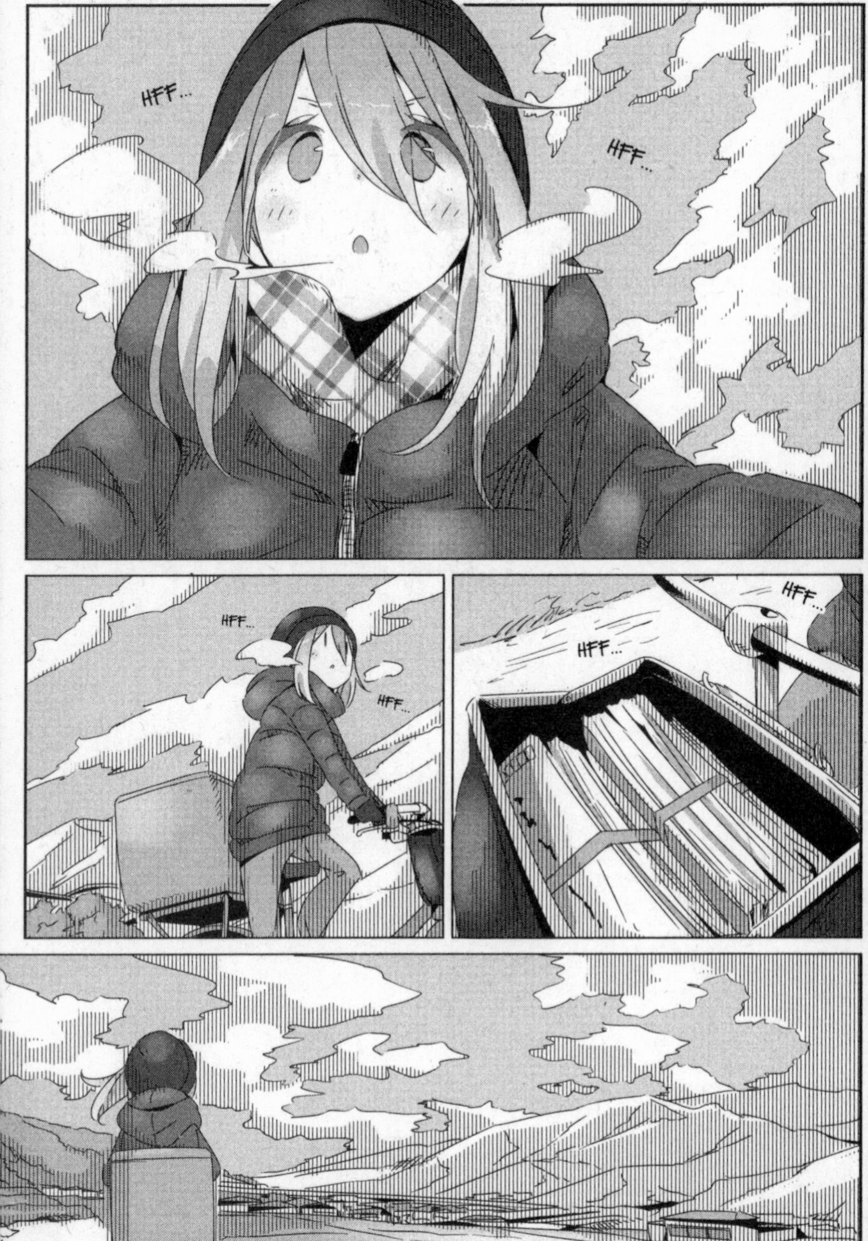
HFF...
HFF...
HFF...
HFF...
HFF...
HFF...

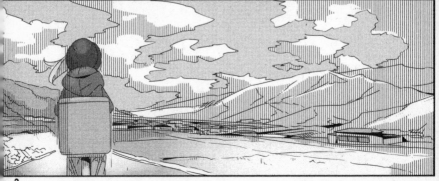

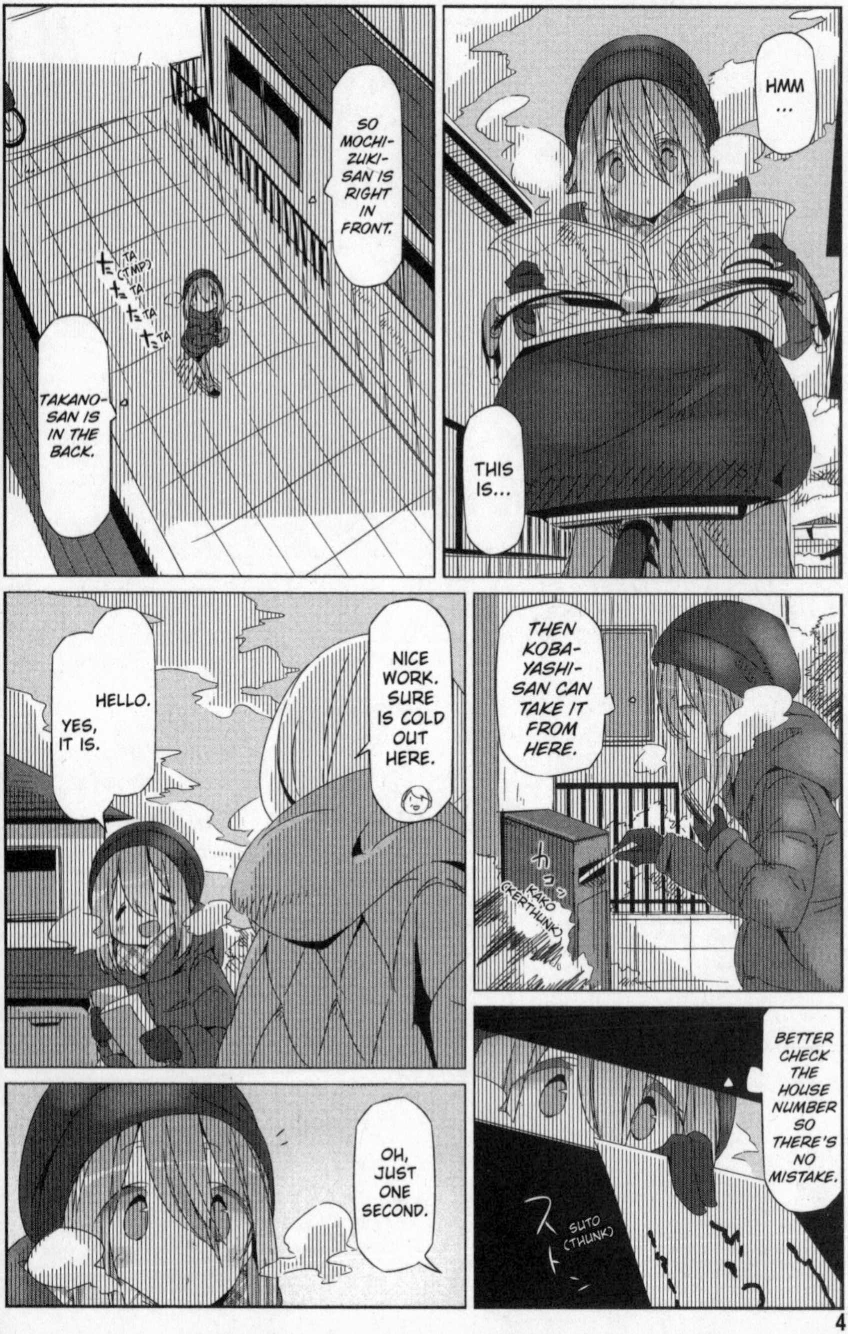
HMM...
THIS IS...
SO MOCHIZUKI-SAN IS RIGHT IN FRONT.
TA (TMP) TA TA TA
TAKANO-SAN IS IN THE BACK.
THEN KOBAYASHI-SAN CAN TAKE IT FROM HERE.
KAKO (KERTHUNK)
NICE WORK. SURE IS COLD OUT HERE.
HELLO.
YES, IT IS.
BETTER CHECK THE HOUSE NUMBER SO THERE'S NO MISTAKE.
SUTO (THUNK)
OH, JUST ONE SECOND.

BOTTLE: KYOTO HIROKAWA PARK TEA

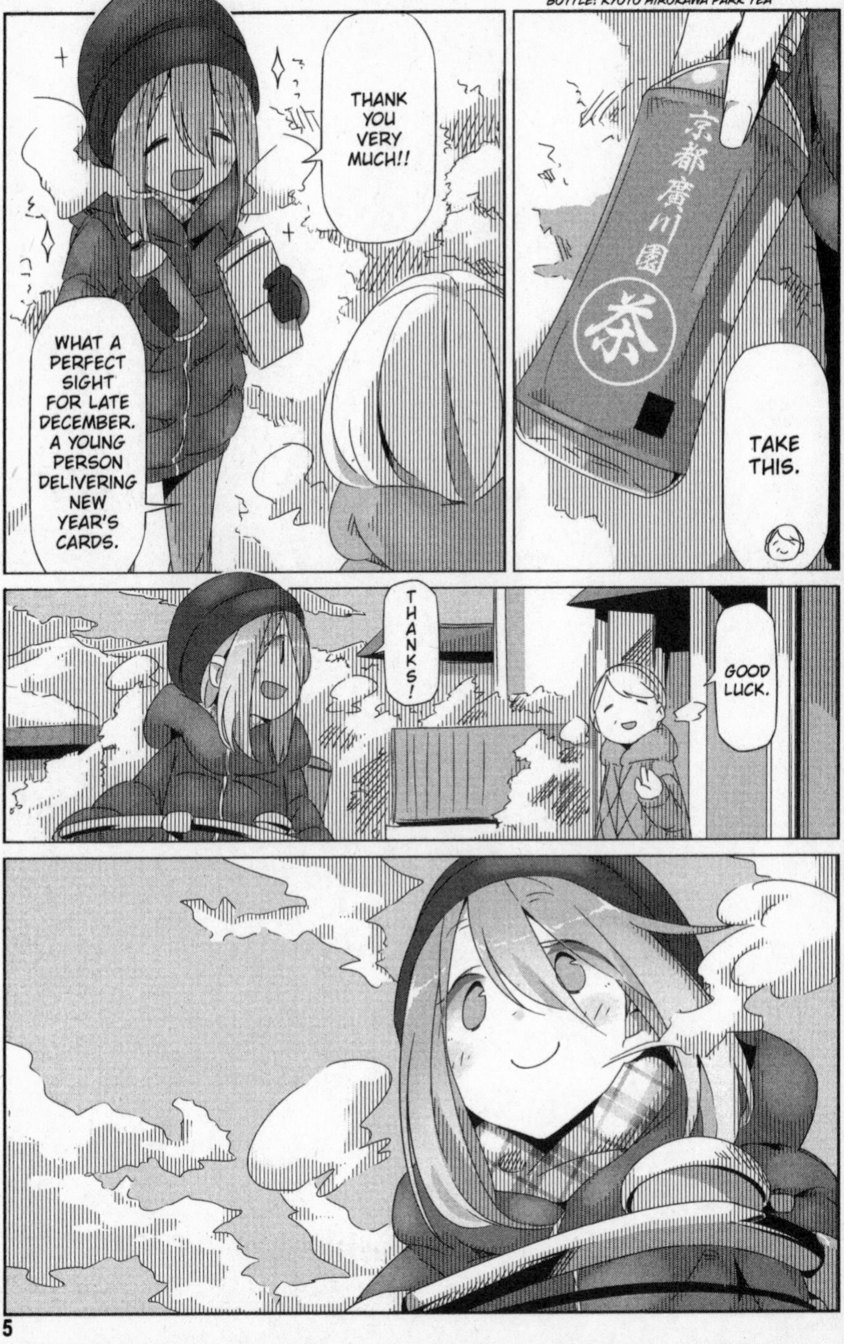
京都廣川園
茶
TAKE THIS.
THANK YOU VERY MUCH!!
WHAT A PERFECT SIGHT FOR LATE DECEMBER. A YOUNG PERSON DELIVERING NEW YEAR'S CARDS.
GOOD LUCK.
THANKS!

CHAPTER 24 DECEMBER WORK AND EVERYONE'S DAYS OFF

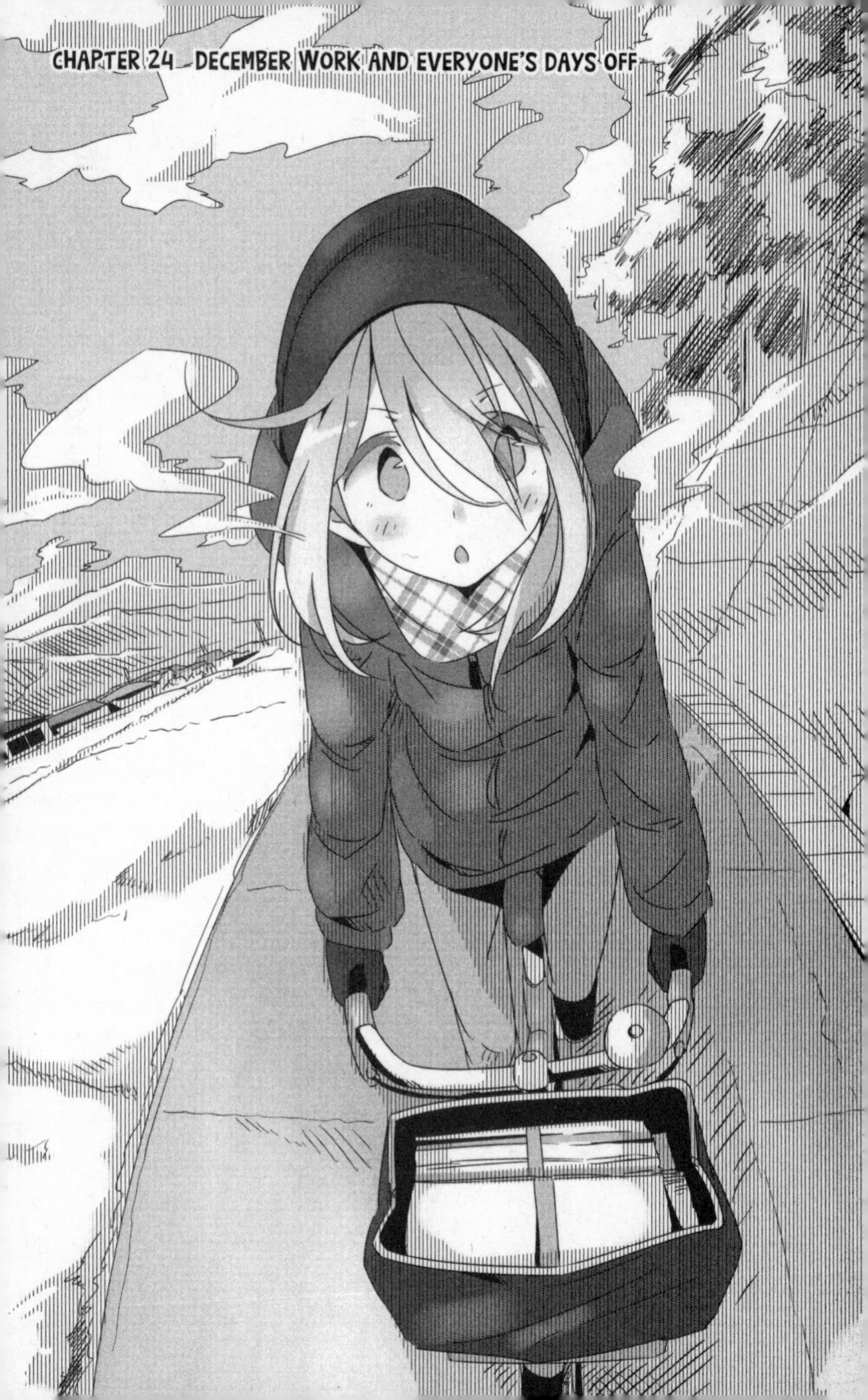

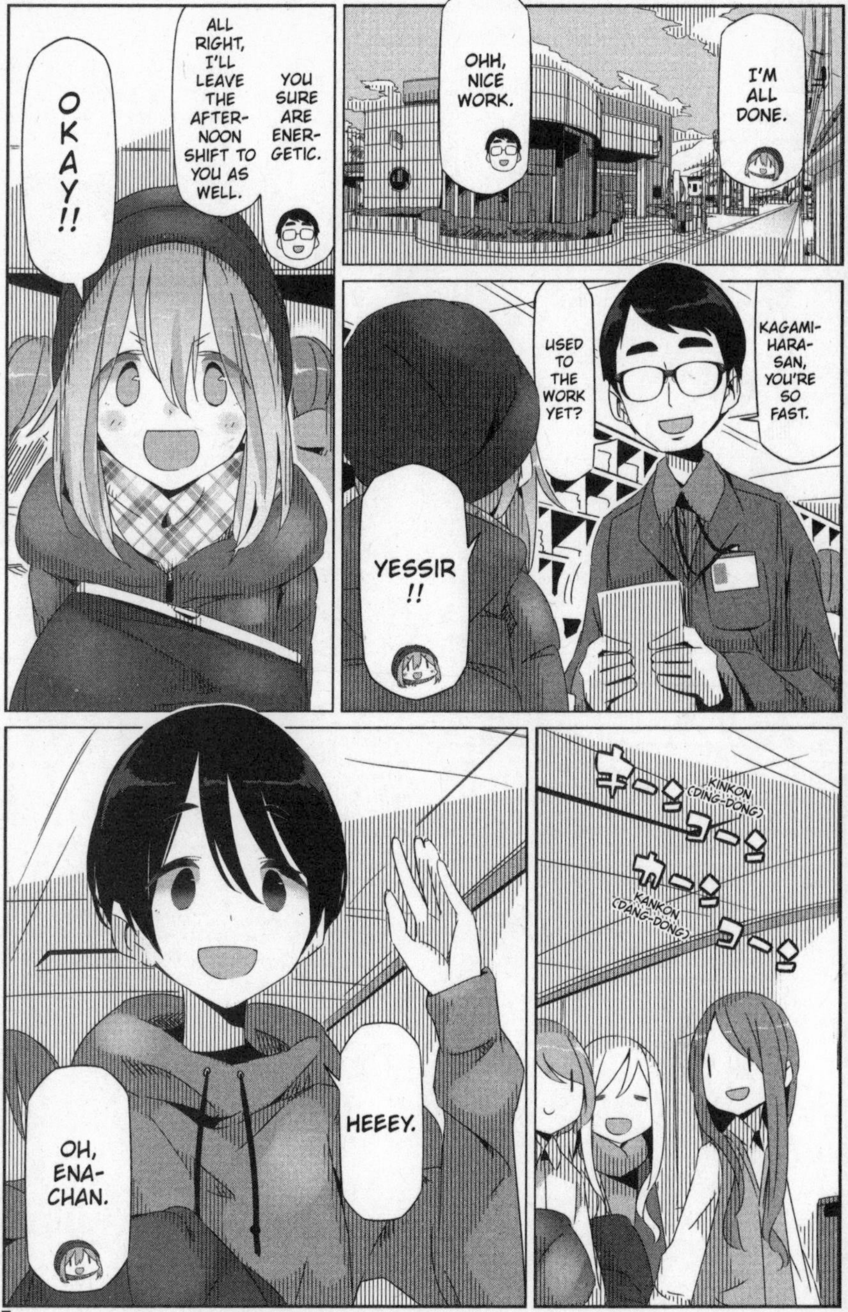
I'M ALL DONE.
OHH, NICE WORK.
KAGAMIHARA-SAN, YOU'RE SO FAST.
USED TO THE WORK YET?
YESSIR!!
YOU SURE ARE ENERGETIC.
ALL RIGHT, I'LL LEAVE THE AFTERNOON SHIFT TO YOU AS WELL.
OKAY!!
KINKON (DING-DONG)
KANKON (DANG-DONG)
HEEEY.
OH, ENA-CHAN.

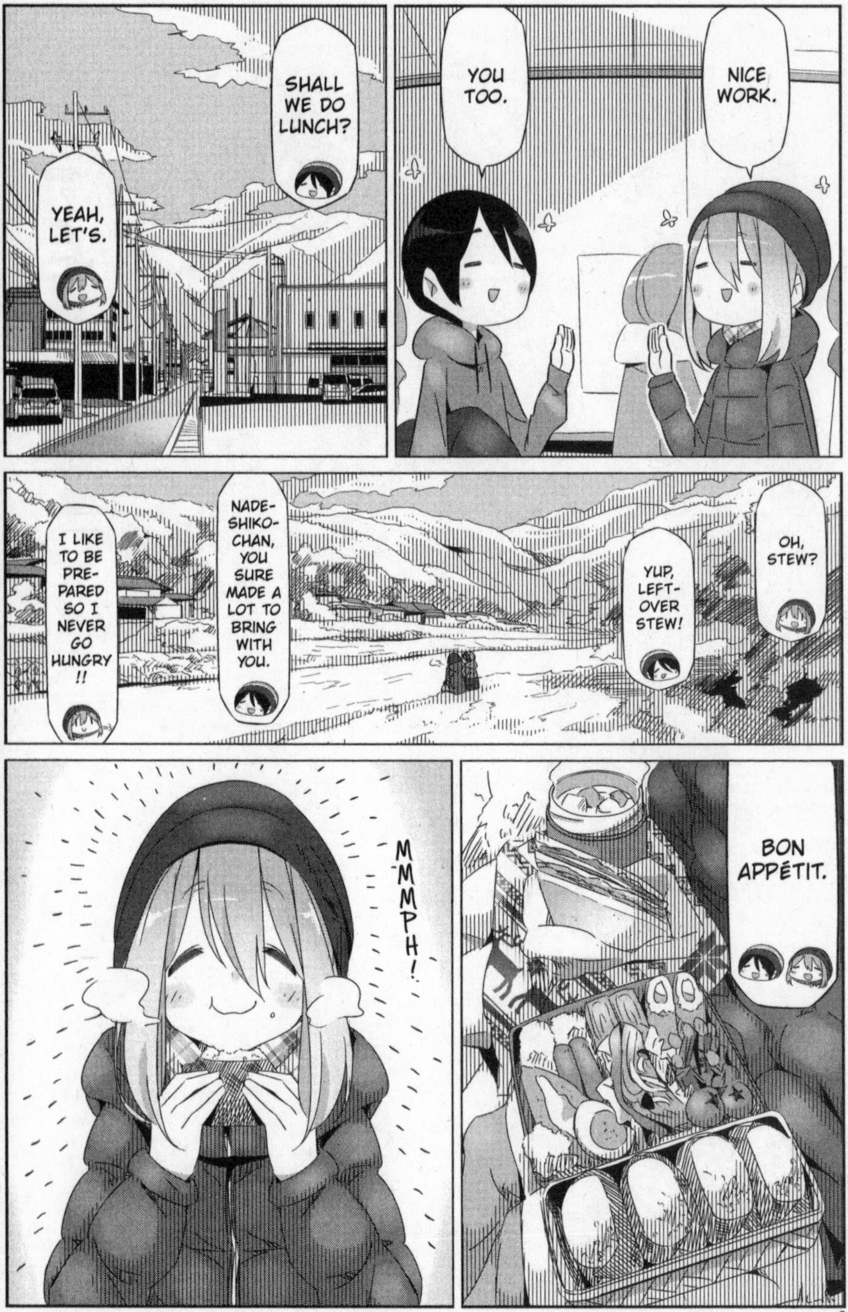
NICE WORK.
YOU TOO.
SHALL WE DO LUNCH?
YEAH, LET'S.
OH, STEW?
YUP, LEFTOVER STEW!
NADESHIKO-CHAN, YOU SURE MADE A LOT TO BRING WITH YOU.
I LIKE TO BE PREPARED SO I NEVER GO HUNGRY!!
BON APPÉTIT.
MMMPH!

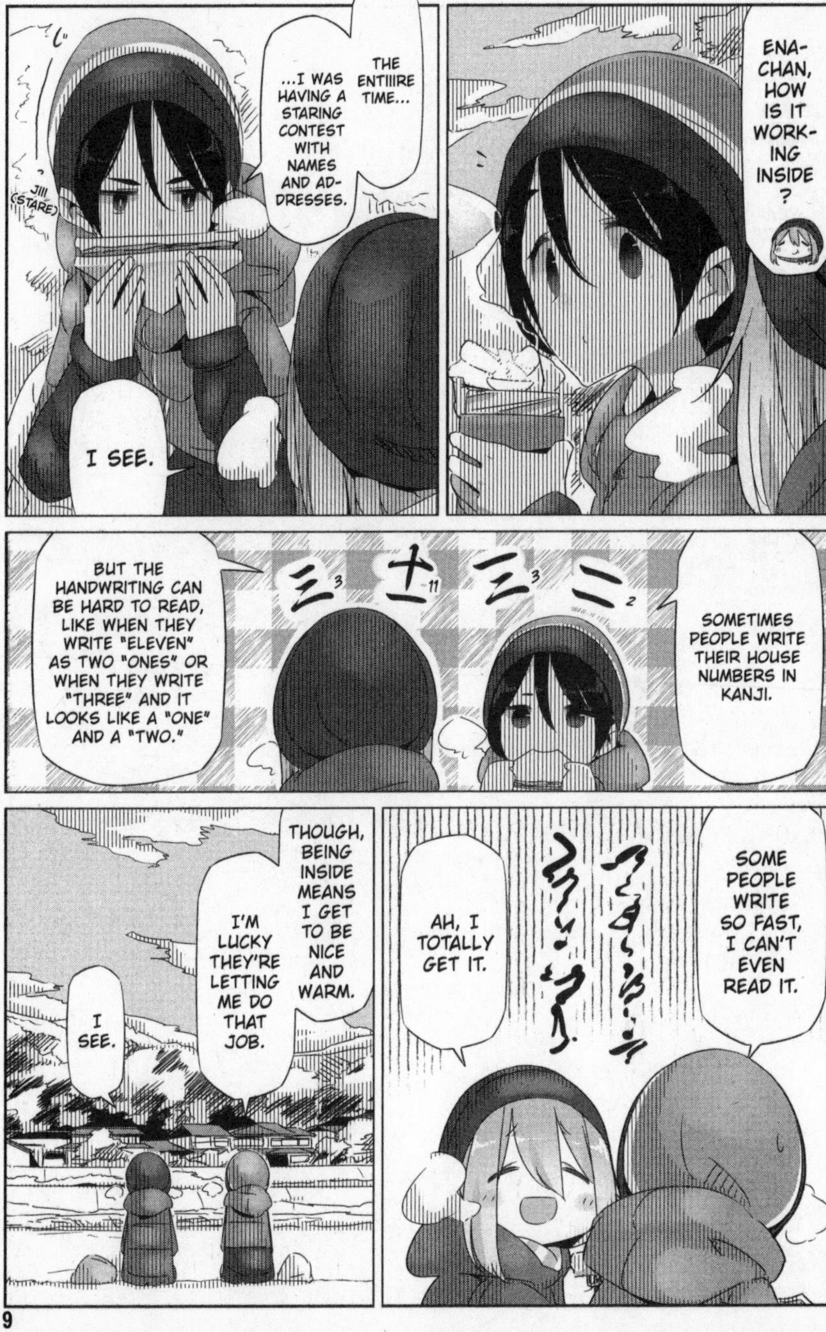
ENA-CHAN, HOW IS IT WORKING INSIDE?
THE ENTIIIRE TIME...
...I WAS HAVING A STARING CONTEST WITH NAMES AND ADDRESSES.
JIII (STARE)
I SEE.
SOMETIMES PEOPLE WRITE THEIR HOUSE NUMBERS IN KANJI.
BUT THE HANDWRITING CAN BE HARD TO READ, LIKE WHEN THEY WRITE "ELEVEN" AS TWO "ONES" OR WHEN THEY WRITE "THREE" AND IT LOOKS LIKE A "ONE" AND A "TWO."
SOME PEOPLE WRITE SO FAST, I CAN'T EVEN READ IT.
AH, I TOTALLY GET IT.
THOUGH, BEING INSIDE MEANS I GET TO BE NICE AND WARM.
I'M LUCKY THEY'RE LETTING ME DO THAT JOB.
I SEE.

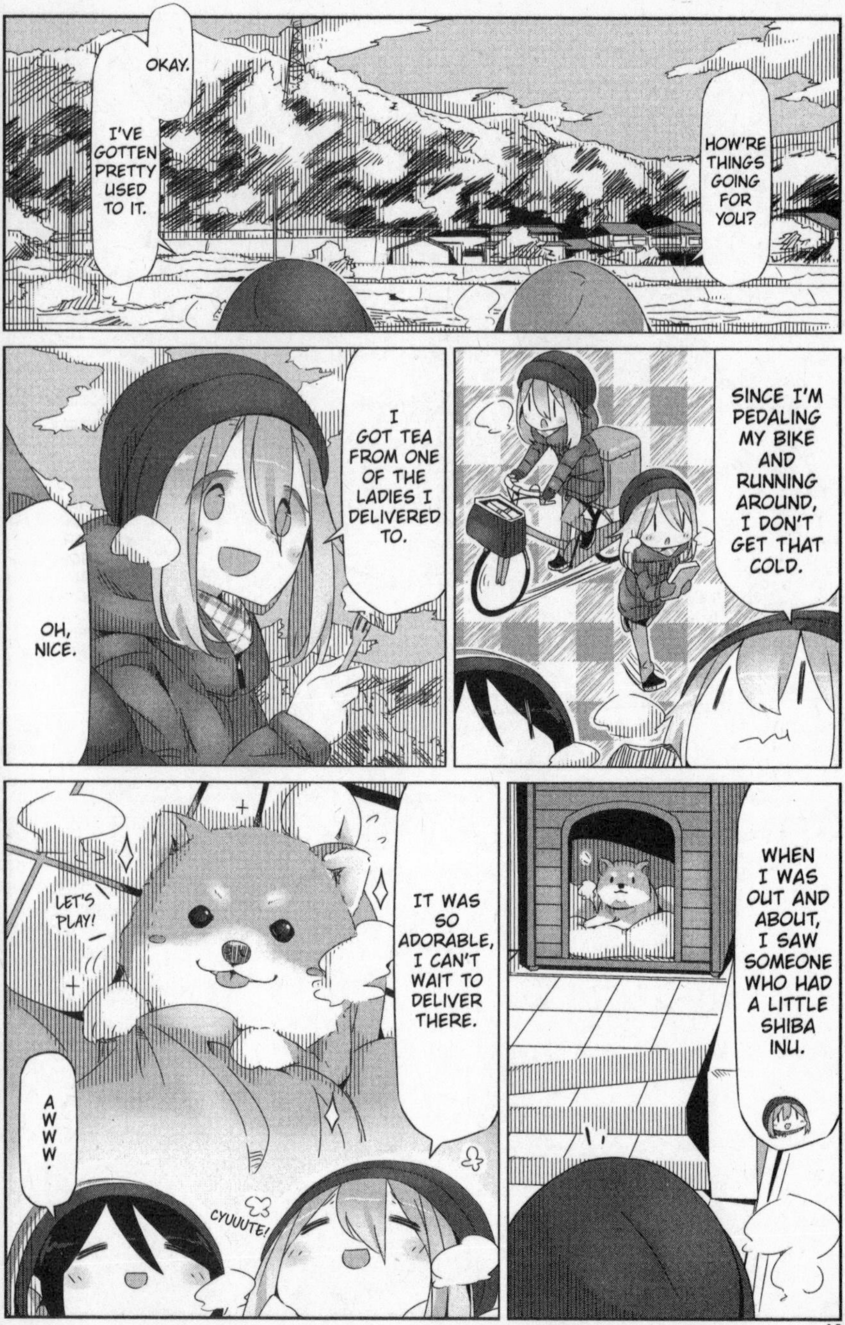
HOW'RE THINGS GOING FOR YOU?
OKAY.
I'VE GOTTEN PRETTY USED TO IT.
SINCE I'M PEDALING MY BIKE AND RUNNING AROUND, I DON'T GET THAT COLD.
I GOT TEA FROM ONE OF THE LADIES I DELIVERED TO.
OH, NICE.
WHEN I WAS OUT AND ABOUT, I SAW SOMEONE WHO HAD A LITTLE SHIBA INU.
IT WAS SO ADORABLE, I CAN'T WAIT TO DELIVER THERE.
LET'S PLAY!
CYUUUTE!
AWWW.

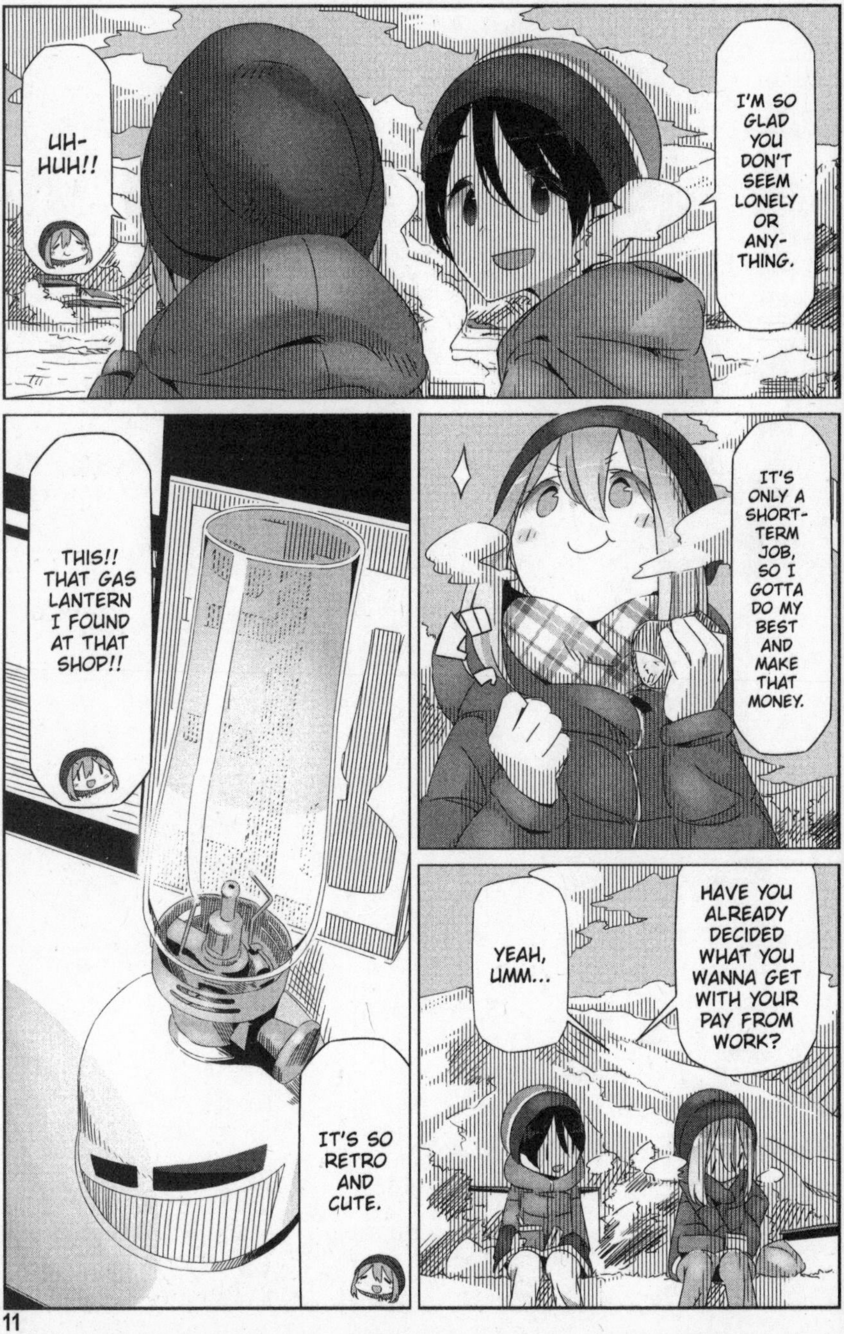
I'M SO GLAD YOU DON'T SEEM LONELY OR ANY-THING.
UH-HUH!!
IT'S ONLY A SHORT-TERM JOB, SO I GOTTA DO MY BEST AND MAKE THAT MONEY.
HAVE YOU ALREADY DECIDED WHAT YOU WANNA GET WITH YOUR PAY FROM WORK?
YEAH, UMM...
THIS!! THAT GAS LANTERN I FOUND AT THAT SHOP!!
IT'S SO RETRO AND CUTE.

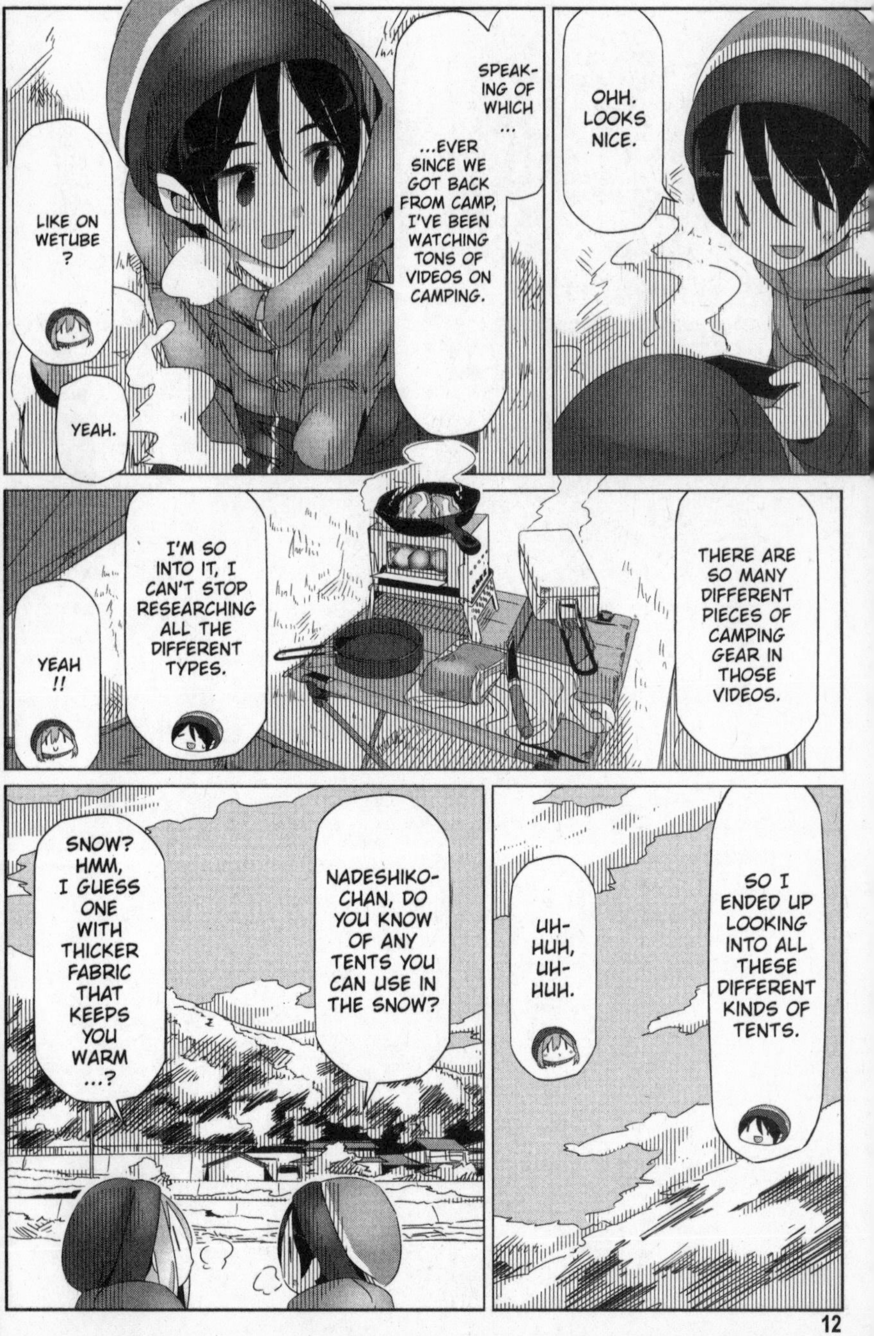
OHH. LOOKS NICE.
SPEAKING OF WHICH...
...EVER SINCE WE GOT BACK FROM CAMP, I'VE BEEN WATCHING TONS OF VIDEOS ON CAMPING.
LIKE ON WETUBE?
YEAH.
THERE ARE SO MANY DIFFERENT PIECES OF CAMPING GEAR IN THOSE VIDEOS.
I'M SO INTO IT, I CAN'T STOP RESEARCHING ALL THE DIFFERENT TYPES.
YEAH!!
SO I ENDED UP LOOKING INTO ALL THESE DIFFERENT KINDS OF TENTS.
UH-HUH, UH-HUH.
NADESHIKO-CHAN, DO YOU KNOW OF ANY TENTS YOU CAN USE IN THE SNOW?
SNOW? HMM, I GUESS ONE WITH THICKER FABRIC THAT KEEPS YOU WARM...?

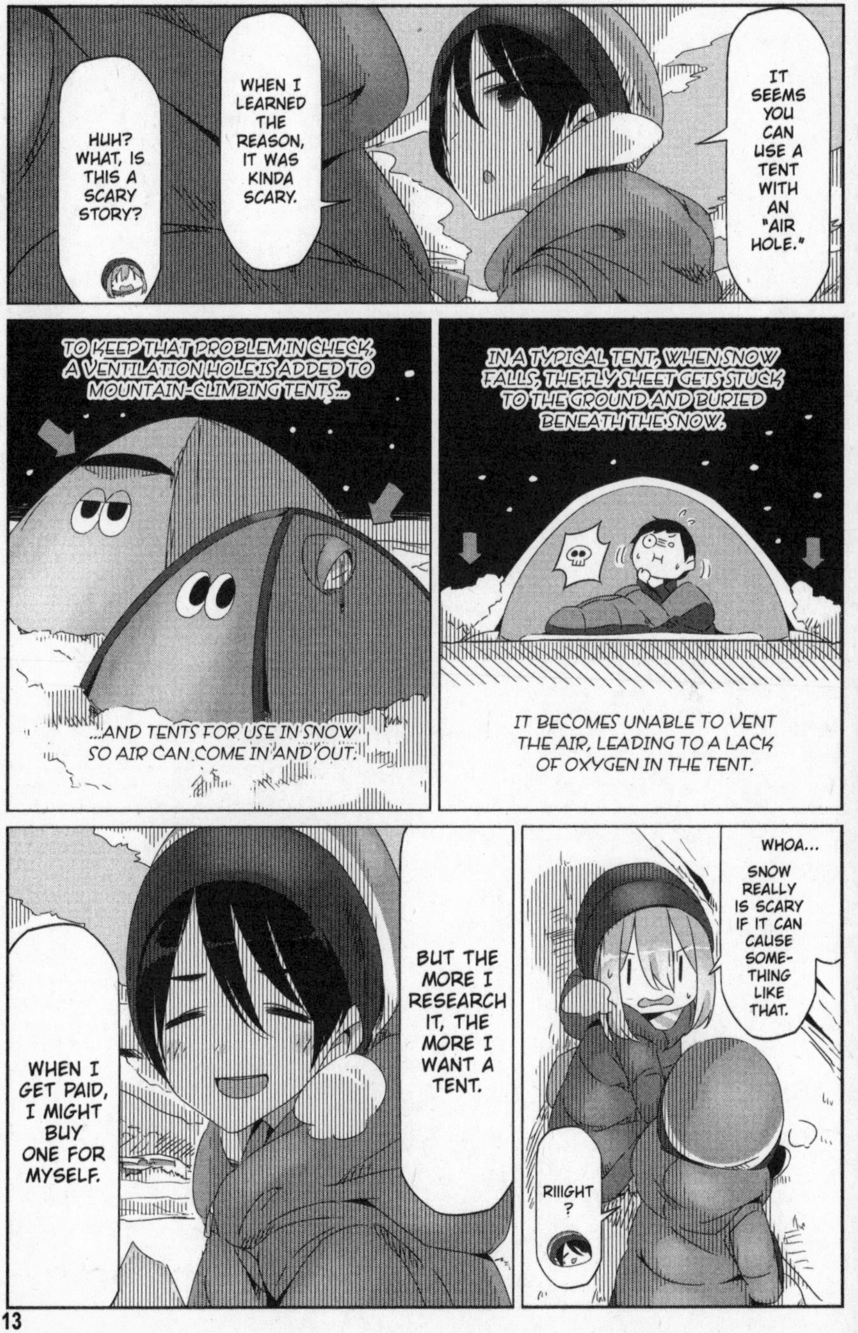
IT SEEMS YOU CAN USE A TENT WITH AN "AIR HOLE."
WHEN I LEARNED THE REASON, IT WAS KINDA SCARY.
HUH? WHAT, IS THIS A SCARY STORY?
IN A TYPICAL TENT, WHEN SNOW FALLS, THE FLY SHEET GETS STUCK TO THE GROUND AND BURIED BENEATH THE SNOW.
IT BECOMES UNABLE TO VENT THE AIR, LEADING TO A LACK OF OXYGEN IN THE TENT.
TO KEEP THAT PROBLEM IN CHECK, A VENTILATION HOLE IS ADDED TO MOUNTAIN-CLIMBING TENTS...
...AND TENTS FOR USE IN SNOW SO AIR CAN COME IN AND OUT.
WHOA...
SNOW REALLY IS SCARY IF IT CAN CAUSE SOME-THING LIKE THAT.
RIIIGHT?
BUT THE MORE I RESEARCH IT, THE MORE I WANT A TENT.
WHEN I GET PAID, I MIGHT BUY ONE FOR MYSELF.

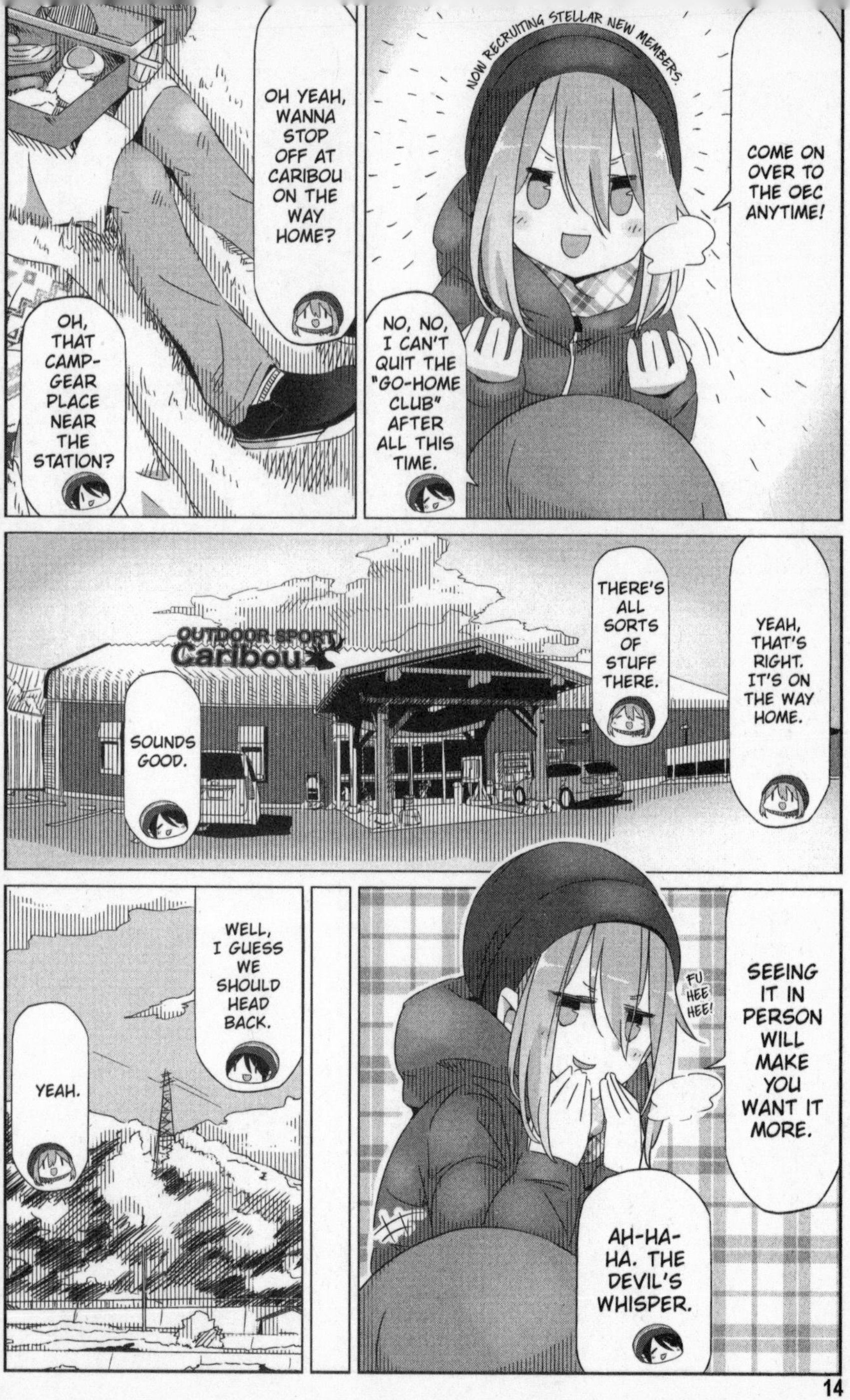
NOW RECRUITING STELLAR NEW MEMBERS.
COME ON OVER TO THE OEC ANYTIME!
NO, NO, I CAN'T QUIT THE "GO-HOME CLUB" AFTER ALL THIS TIME.
OH YEAH, WANNA STOP OFF AT CARIBOU ON THE WAY HOME?
OH, THAT CAMP-GEAR PLACE NEAR THE STATION?
YEAH, THAT'S RIGHT. IT'S ON THE WAY HOME.
THERE'S ALL SORTS OF STUFF THERE.
OUTDOOR SPORT Caribou
SOUNDS GOOD.
SEEING IT IN PERSON WILL MAKE YOU WANT IT MORE.
FU HEE HEE!
AH-HA-HA. THE DEVIL'S WHISPER.
WELL, I GUESS WE SHOULD HEAD BACK.
YEAH.

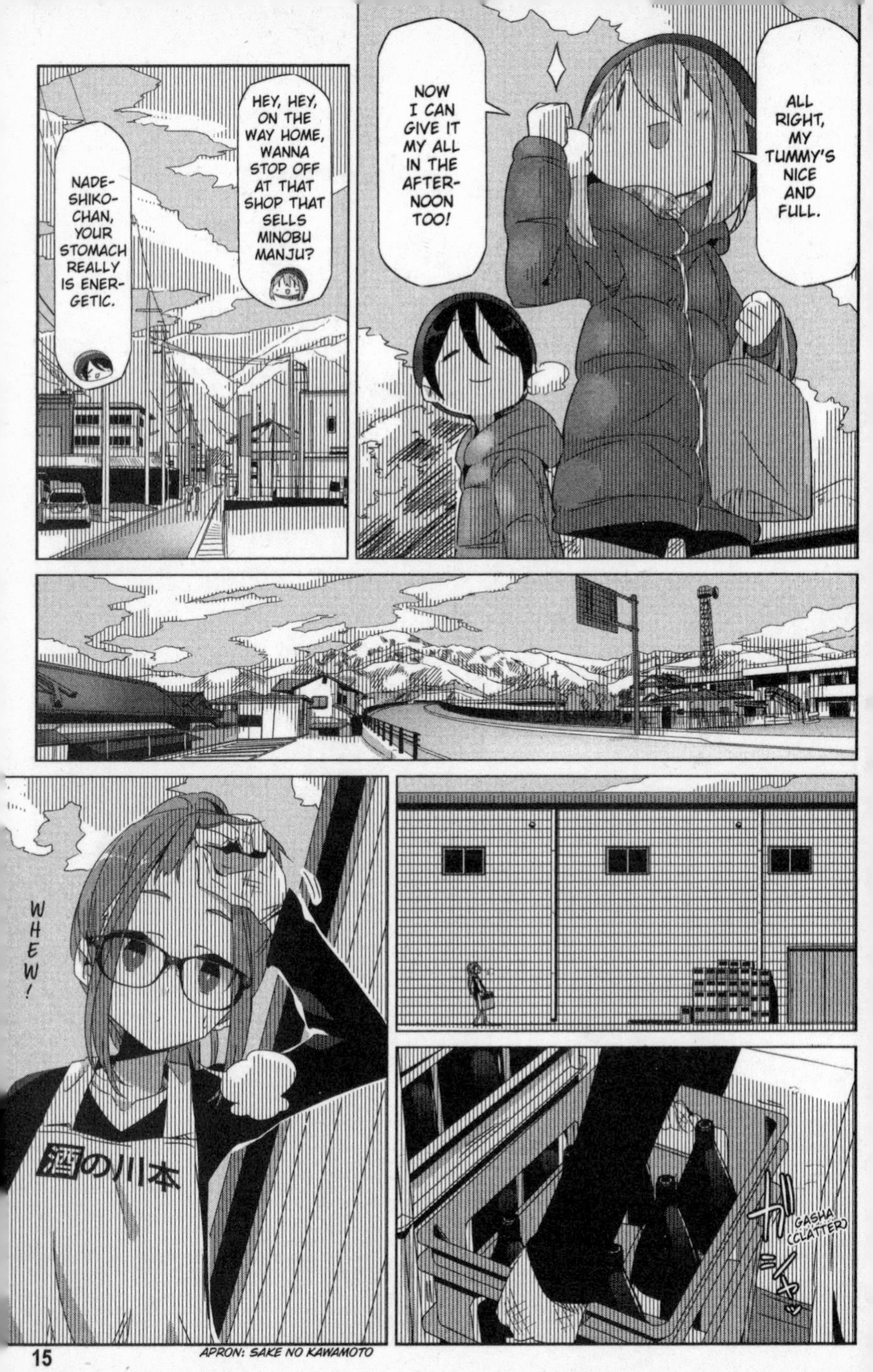
ALL RIGHT, MY TUMMY'S NICE AND FULL.
NOW I CAN GIVE IT MY ALL IN THE AFTER-NOON TOO!
HEY, HEY, ON THE WAY HOME, WANNA STOP OFF AT THAT SHOP THAT SELLS MINOBU MANJU?
NADE-SHIKO-CHAN, YOUR STOMACH REALLY IS ENER-GETIC.
ガシャ
GASHA (CLATTER)
WHEW!
酒の川本

APRON: SAKE NO KAWAMOTO

SIGN: SAKE NO KAWAMOTO MINOBU STORE

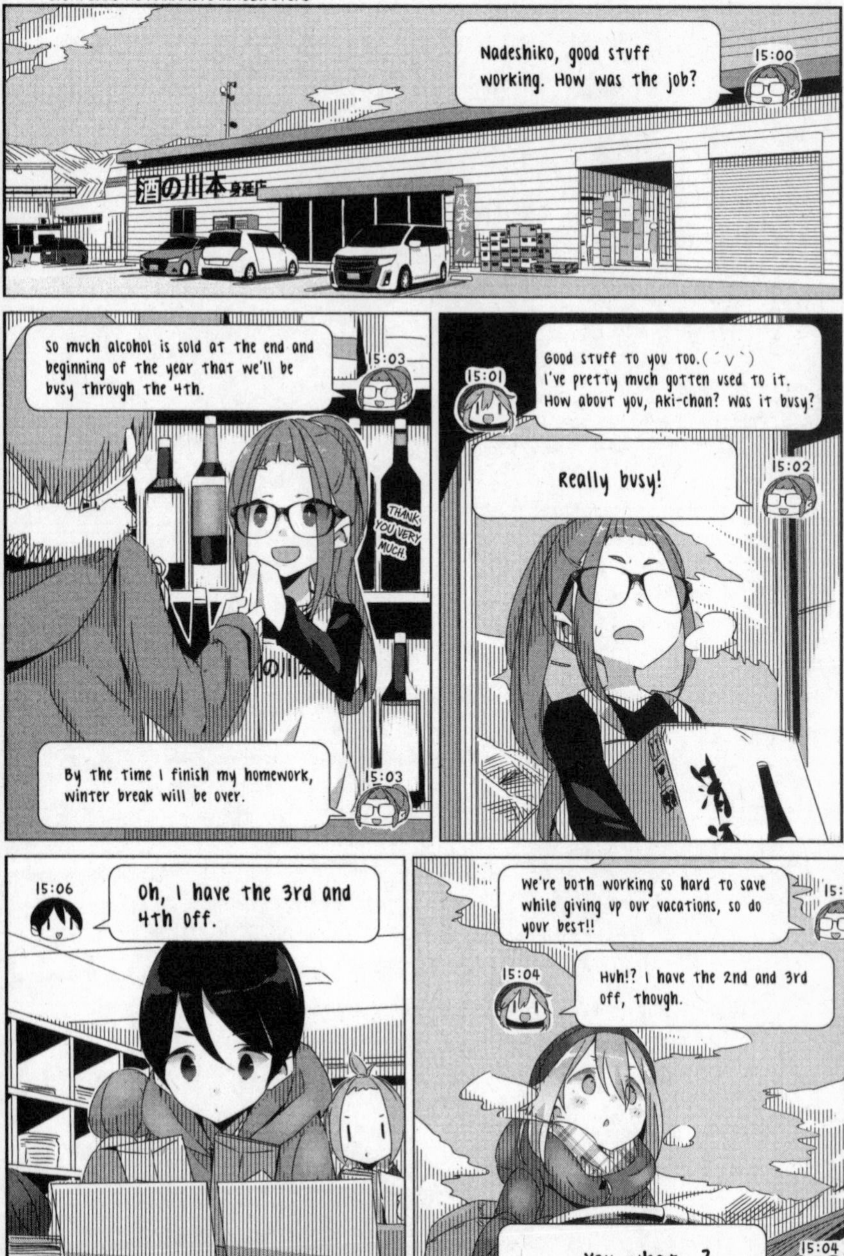
15:00
Nadeshiko, good stuff working. How was the job?
酒の川本 身延店
15:01
Good stuff to you too. (´v`)
I've pretty much gotten used to it.
How about you, Aki-chan? Was it busy?
15:02
Really busy!
15:03
So much alcohol is sold at the end and beginning of the year that we'll be busy through the 4th.
THANK YOU VERY MUCH.
15:03
By the time I finish my homework, winter break will be over.
15:04
We're both working so hard to save while giving up our vacations, so do your best!!
15:04
Huh!? I have the 2nd and 3rd off, though.
15:04
...You what...?
15:06
Oh, I have the 3rd and 4th off.

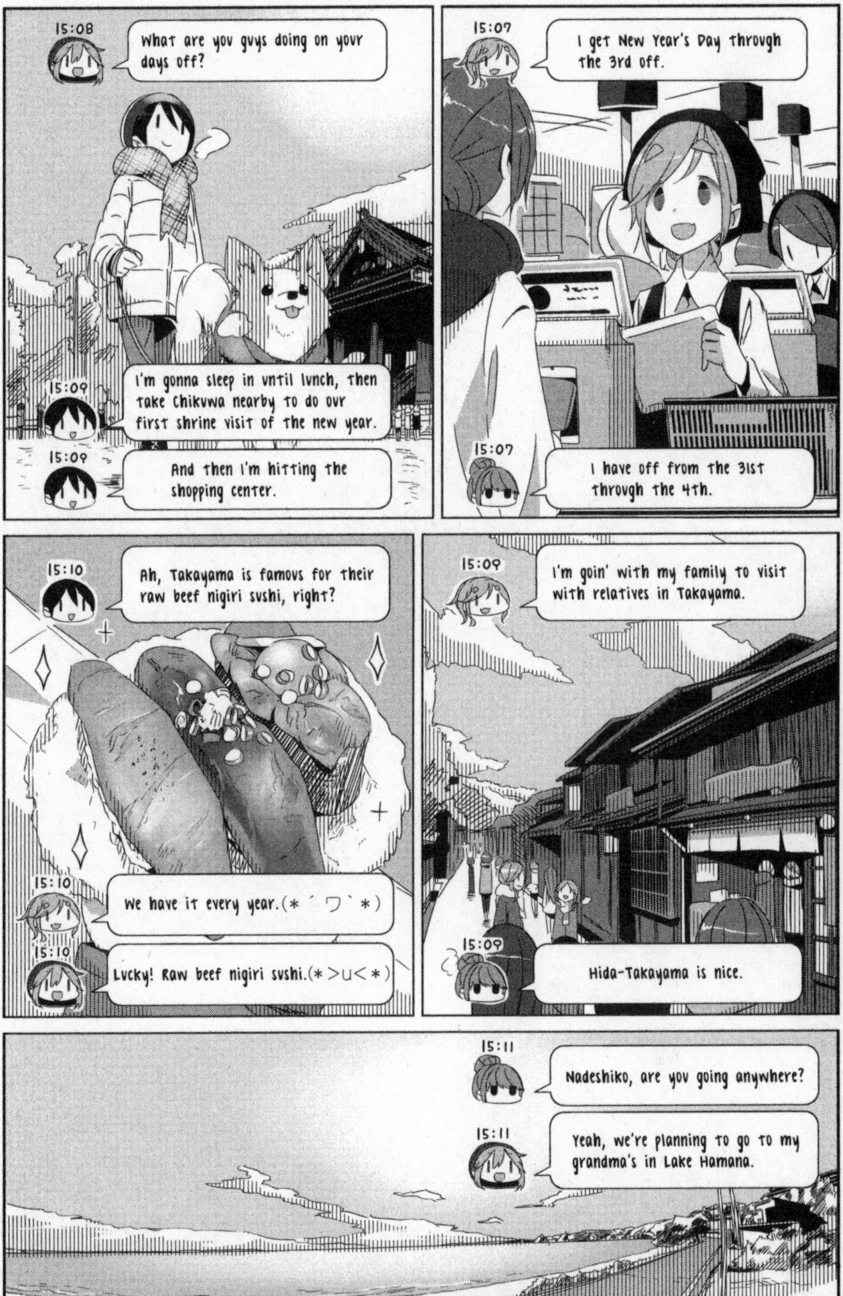
15:07
I get New Year's Day through the 3rd off.
15:07
I have off from the 31st through the 4th.
15:08
What are you guys doing on your days off?
15:09
I'm gonna sleep in until lunch, then take Chikuwa nearby to do our first shrine visit of the new year.
15:09
And then I'm hitting the shopping center.
15:09
I'm goin' with my family to visit with relatives in Takayama.
15:09
Hida-Takayama is nice.
15:10
Ah, Takayama is famous for their raw beef nigiri sushi, right?
15:10
We have it every year.(*´ワ`*)
15:10
Lucky! Raw beef nigiri sushi.(*>u<*)
15:11
Nadeshiko, are you going anywhere?
15:11
Yeah, we're planning to go to my grandma's in Lake Hamana.

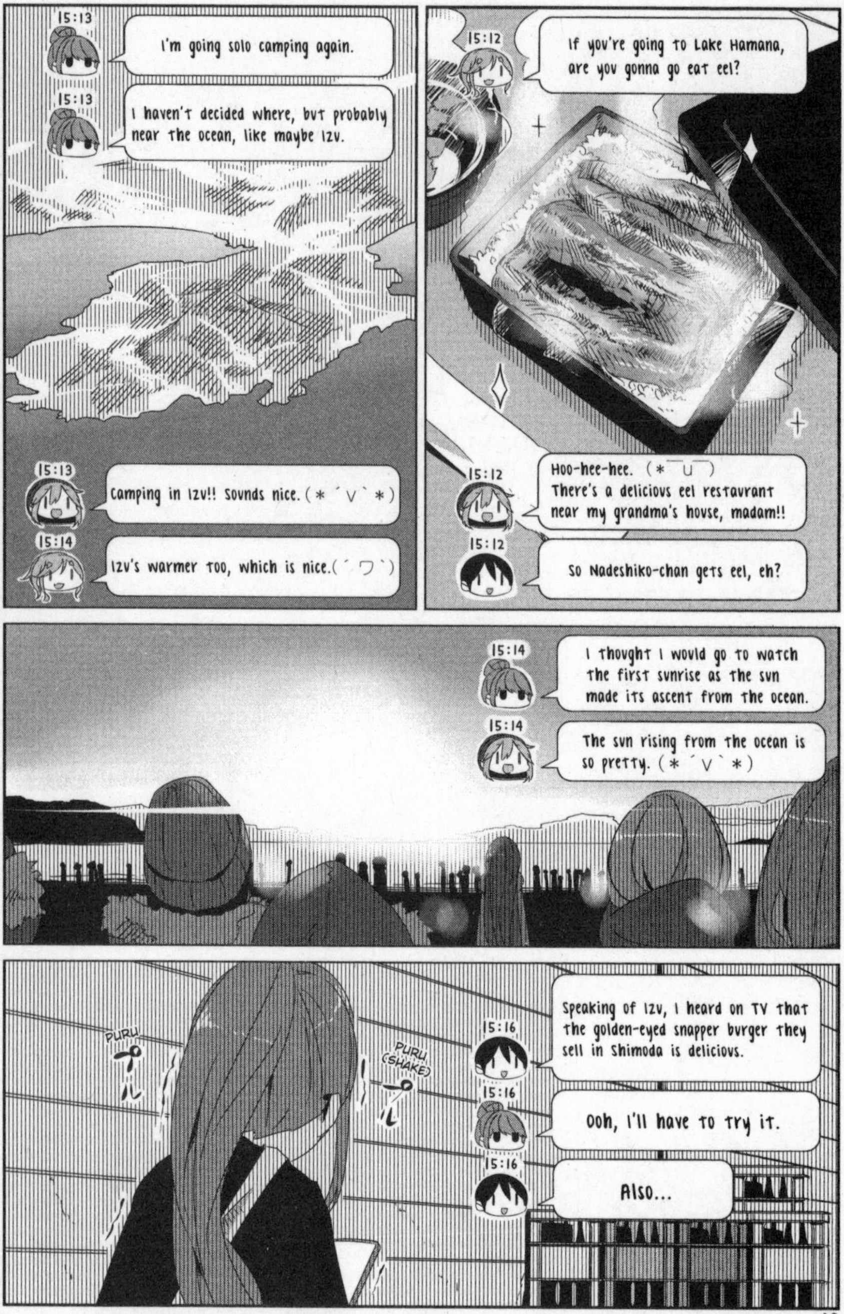
15:12
If you're going to Lake Hamana, are you gonna go eat eel?
15:12
Hoo-hee-hee. (*￣u￣) There's a delicious eel restaurant near my grandma's house, madam!!
15:12
So Nadeshiko-chan gets eel, eh?
15:13
I'm going solo camping again.
15:13
I haven't decided where, but probably near the ocean, like maybe Izu.
15:13
Camping in Izu!! Sounds nice. (*´∨`*)
15:14
Izu's warmer too, which is nice.(´ワ`)
15:14
I thought I would go to watch the first sunrise as the sun made its ascent from the ocean.
15:14
The sun rising from the ocean is so pretty. (*´∨`*)
15:16
Speaking of Izu, I heard on TV that the golden-eyed snapper burger they sell in Shimoda is delicious.
PURU (SHAKE)
PURU
15:16
Ooh, I'll have to try it.
15:16
Also...

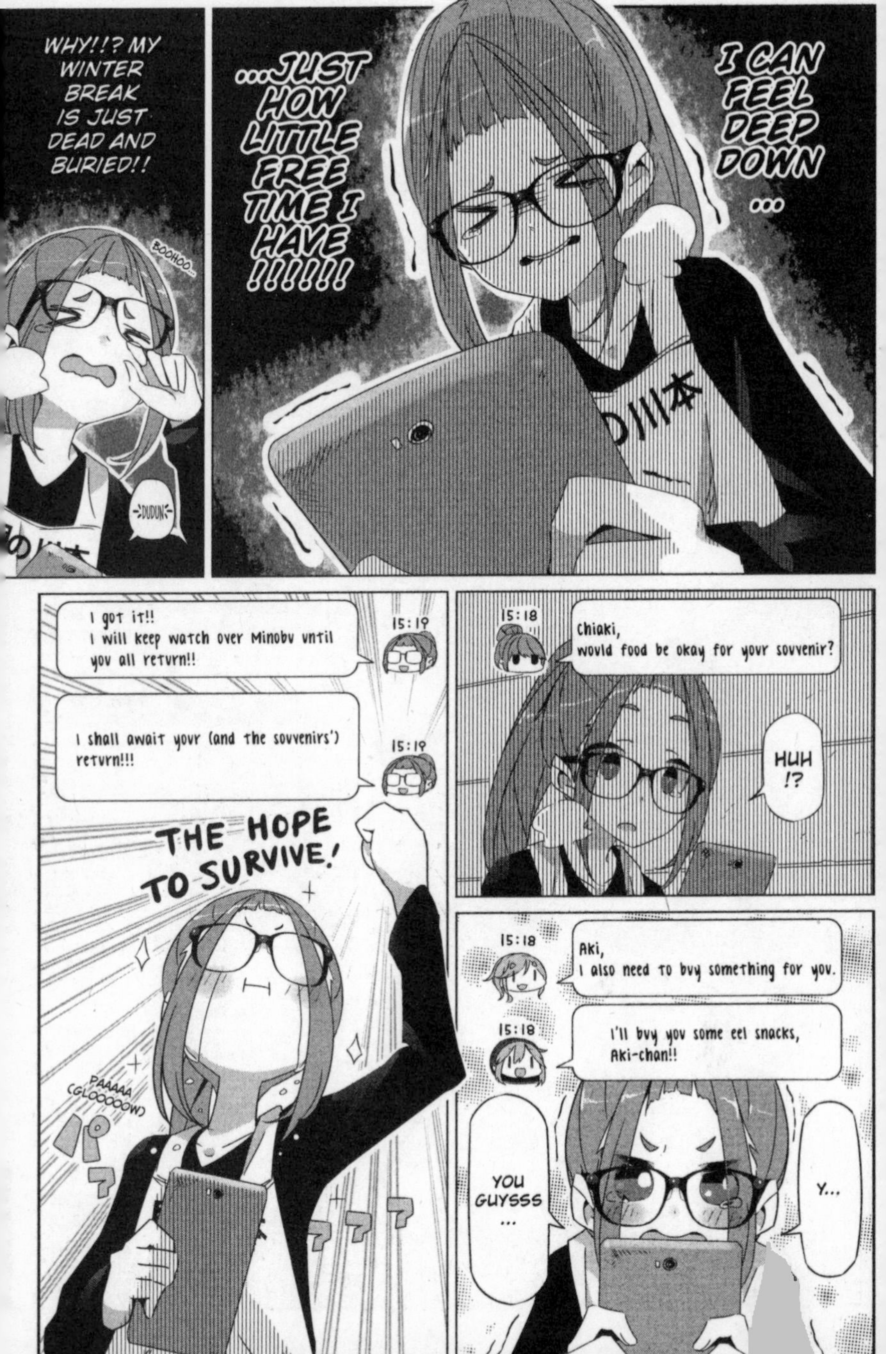
I CAN FEEL DEEP DOWN...
...JUST HOW LITTLE FREE TIME I HAVE!!!!!!
WHY!!? MY WINTER BREAK IS JUST DEAD AND BURIED!!
BOOHOO...
DUDUN
15:18
Chiaki, would food be okay for your souvenir?
HUH!?
15:18
Aki, I also need to buy something for you.
15:18
I'll buy you some eel snacks, Aki-chan!!
Y...
YOU GUYSSS...
15:19
I got it!! I will keep watch over Minobu until you all return!!
15:19
I shall await your (and the souvenirs') return!!!
THE HOPE TO SURVIVE!
PAAAAA (GLOOOOOW)

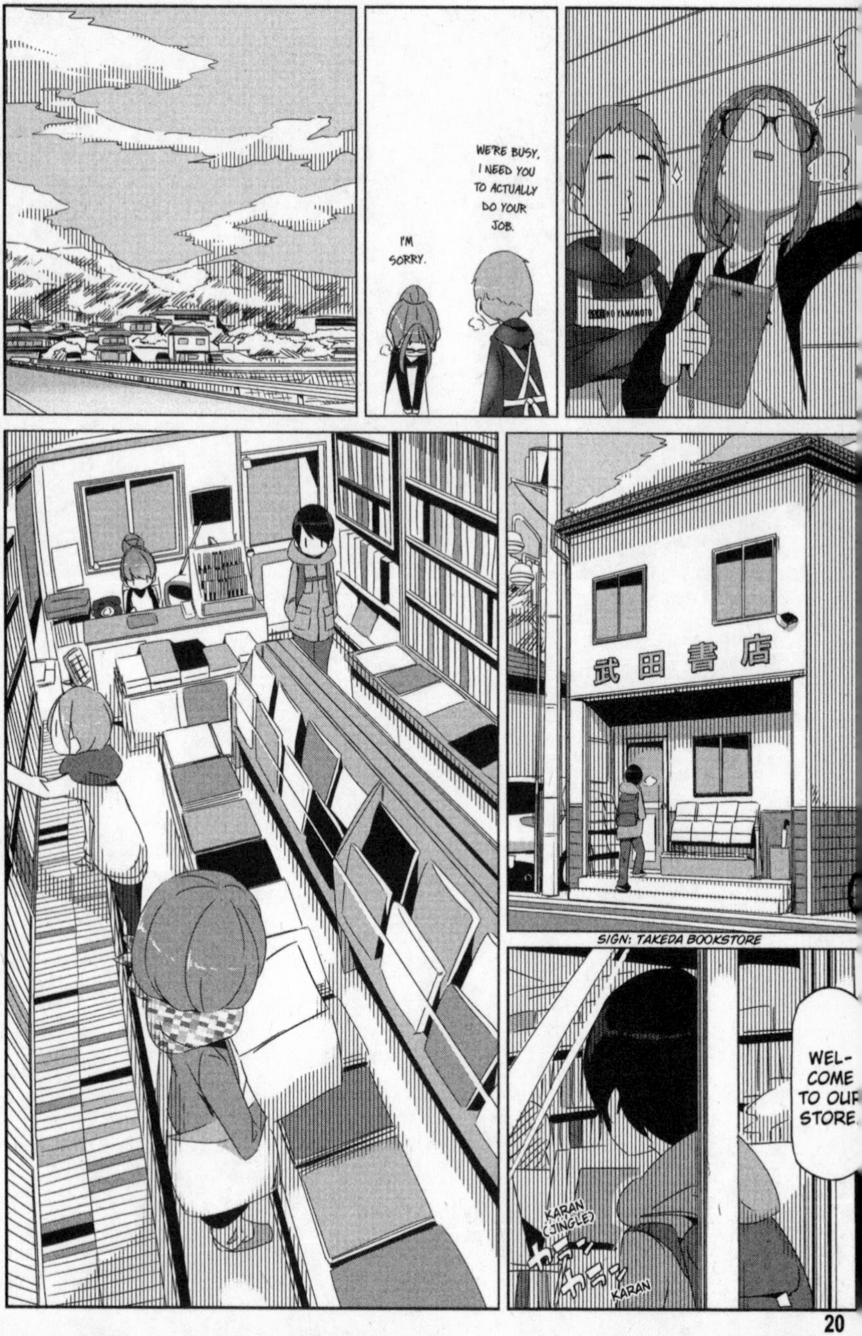
WE'RE BUSY, I NEED YOU TO ACTUALLY DO YOUR JOB.
I'M SORRY.
武田書店
SIGN: TAKEDA BOOKSTORE
WEL-COME TO OUR STORE.
KARAN (JINGLE)
KARAN

I SHOULD HEAD THROUGH NUMAZU TO NISHI-IZU.

IZU IZU IZU IZU IZU IZU IZU IZU IZU IZU IZU IZU IZU IZU IZU IZU IZU IZU IZU IZU IZU IZU IZU IZU IZU IZU IZU IZU IZU IZU IZU IZU IZU IZU IZU IZU IZU IZU IZU IZU IZ

IZU.

IZU, IZU.

ZUI, ZUI.

MAYBE I SHOULD GO THROUGH IZUNO-KUNI AND TURN OFF AT ITOH...

EXCUSE ME, I'D LIKE TO BUY THIS, PLEASE.

MMN... I CAN'T DECIDE.

NAH, GOING RIGHT IN AND OUT OF AMAGI...

...AND HITTING MINAMI-IZU DOESN'T SOUND SO BAD.

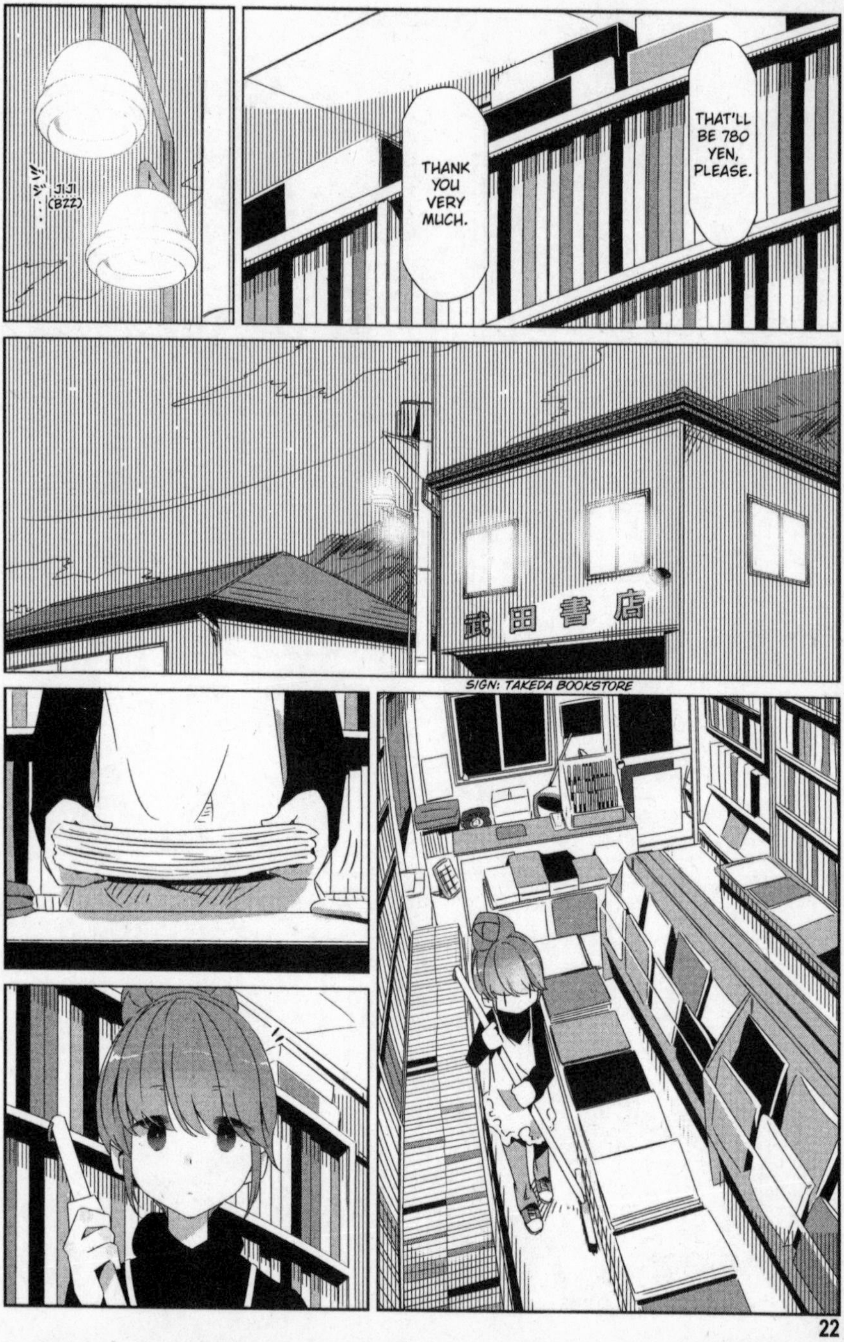
THAT'LL BE 780 YEN, PLEASE.
THANK YOU VERY MUCH.
ジジ…
JIJI (BZZ)
武田書店
SIGN: TAKEDA BOOKSTORE

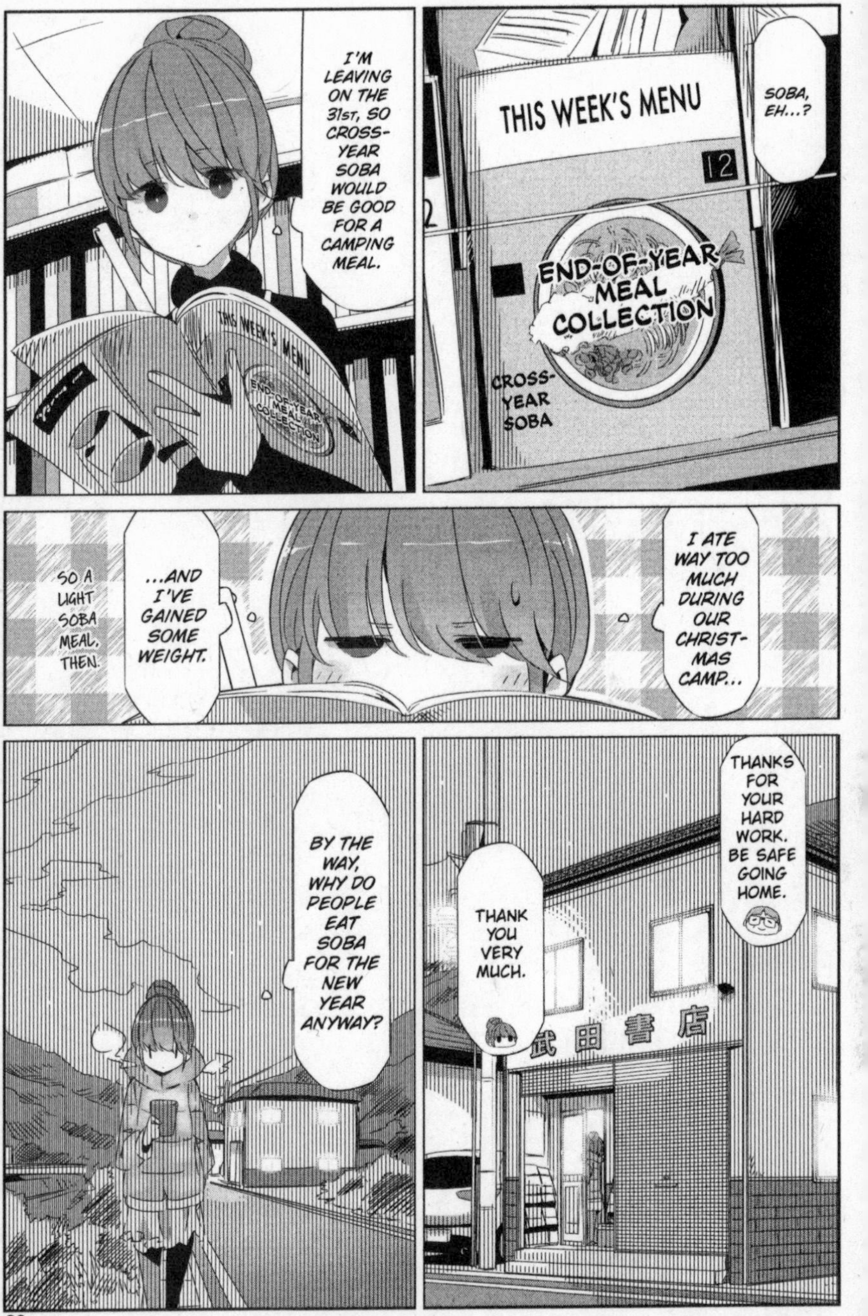
SOBA, EH...?
THIS WEEK'S MENU
12
END-OF-YEAR MEAL COLLECTION
CROSS-YEAR SOBA
I'M LEAVING ON THE 31st, SO CROSS-YEAR SOBA WOULD BE GOOD FOR A CAMPING MEAL.
THIS WEEK'S MENU
END-OF-YEAR MEAL COLLECTION
I ATE WAY TOO MUCH DURING OUR CHRISTMAS CAMP...
...AND I'VE GAINED SOME WEIGHT.
SO A LIGHT SOBA MEAL, THEN.
THANKS FOR YOUR HARD WORK. BE SAFE GOING HOME.
THANK YOU VERY MUCH.
武田書店
BY THE WAY, WHY DO PEOPLE EAT SOBA FOR THE NEW YEAR ANYWAY?

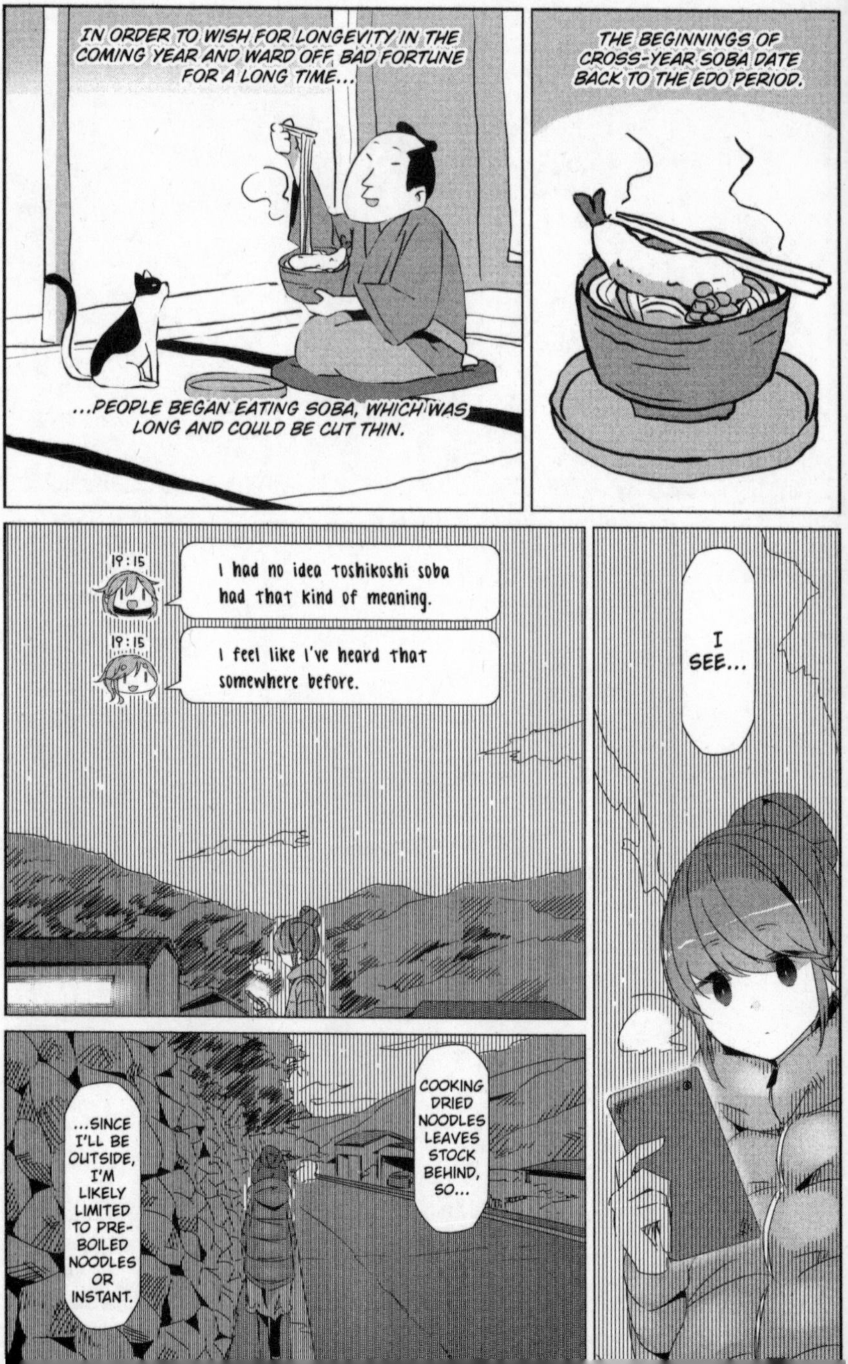
THE BEGINNINGS OF CROSS-YEAR SOBA DATE BACK TO THE EDO PERIOD.
IN ORDER TO WISH FOR LONGEVITY IN THE COMING YEAR AND WARD OFF BAD FORTUNE FOR A LONG TIME...
...PEOPLE BEGAN EATING SOBA, WHICH WAS LONG AND COULD BE CUT THIN.
I SEE...
19:15
I had no idea toshikoshi soba had that kind of meaning.
19:15
I feel like I've heard that somewhere before.
COOKING DRIED NOODLES LEAVES STOCK BEHIND, SO...
...SINCE I'LL BE OUTSIDE, I'M LIKELY LIMITED TO PRE-BOILED NOODLES OR INSTANT.

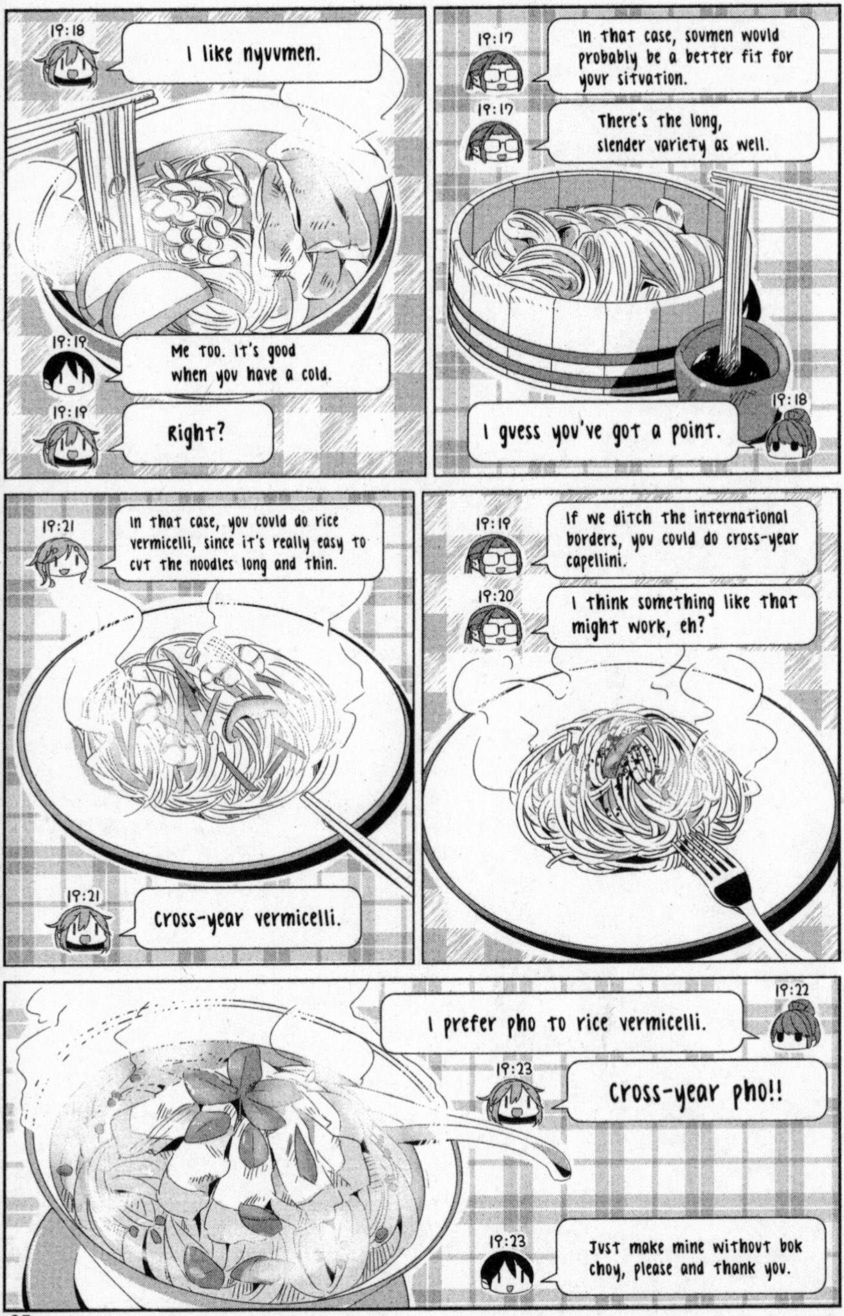
19:17
In that case, soumen would probably be a better fit for your situation.
19:17
There's the long, slender variety as well.
19:18
I guess you've got a point.
19:18
I like nyuumen.
19:19
Me too. It's good when you have a cold.
19:19
Right?
19:19
If we ditch the international borders, you could do cross-year capellini.
19:20
I think something like that might work, eh?
19:21
In that case, you could do rice vermicelli, since it's really easy to cut the noodles long and thin.
19:21
Cross-year vermicelli.
19:22
I prefer pho to rice vermicelli.
19:23
Cross-year pho!!
19:23
Just make mine without bok choy, please and thank you.

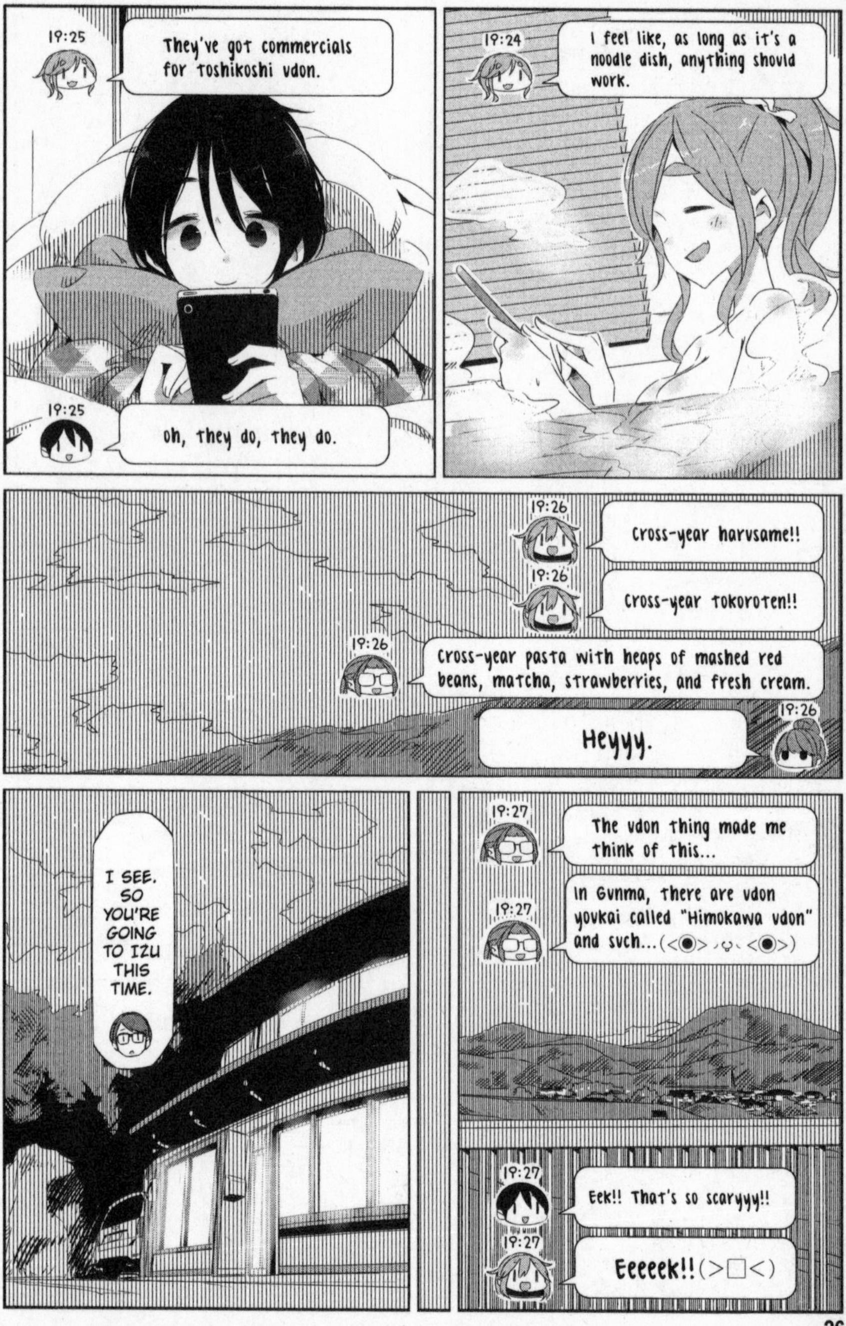
19:24
I feel like, as long as it's a noodle dish, anything should work.
19:25
They've got commercials for toshikoshi udon.
19:25
Oh, they do, they do.
19:26
Cross-year harusame!!
19:26
Cross-year tokoroten!!
19:26
Cross-year pasta with heaps of mashed red beans, matcha, strawberries, and fresh cream.
19:26
Heyyy.
19:27
The udon thing made me think of this...
19:27
In Gunma, there are udon youkai called "Himokawa udon" and such...(<◉>◞౪◟<◉>)
19:27
Eek!! That's so scaryyy!!
19:27
Eeeeek!!(>□<)
I SEE. SO YOU'RE GOING TO IZU THIS TIME.

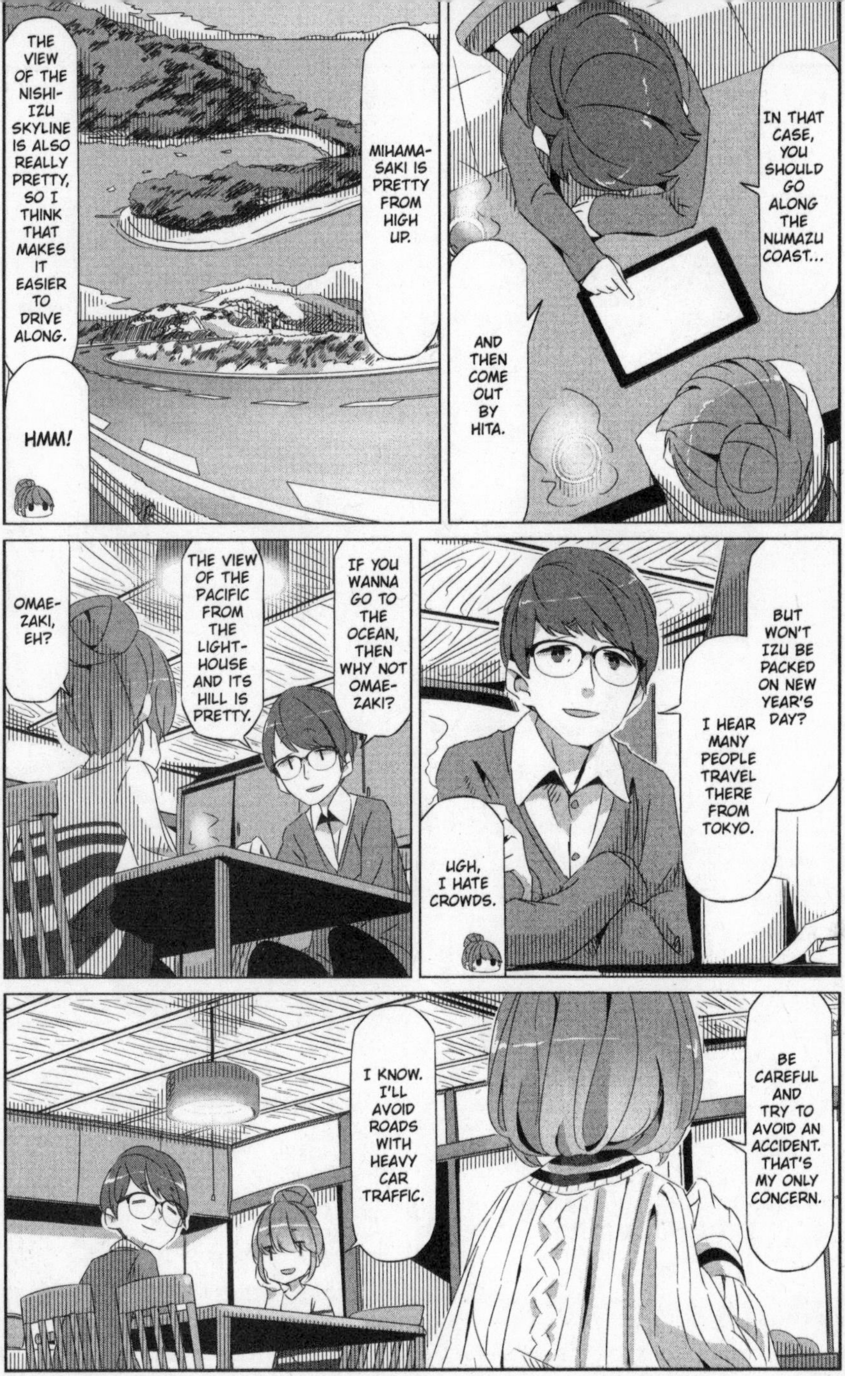
IN THAT CASE, YOU SHOULD GO ALONG THE NUMAZU COAST...
AND THEN COME OUT BY HITA.
MIHAMA-SAKI IS PRETTY FROM HIGH UP.
THE VIEW OF THE NISHI-IZU SKYLINE IS ALSO REALLY PRETTY, SO I THINK THAT MAKES IT EASIER TO DRIVE ALONG.
HMM!
BUT WON'T IZU BE PACKED ON NEW YEAR'S DAY?
I HEAR MANY PEOPLE TRAVEL THERE FROM TOKYO.
UGH, I HATE CROWDS.
IF YOU WANNA GO TO THE OCEAN, THEN WHY NOT OMAE-ZAKI?
THE VIEW OF THE PACIFIC FROM THE LIGHT-HOUSE AND ITS HILL IS PRETTY.
OMAE-ZAKI, EH?
BE CAREFUL AND TRY TO AVOID AN ACCIDENT. THAT'S MY ONLY CONCERN.
I KNOW. I'LL AVOID ROADS WITH HEAVY CAR TRAFFIC.

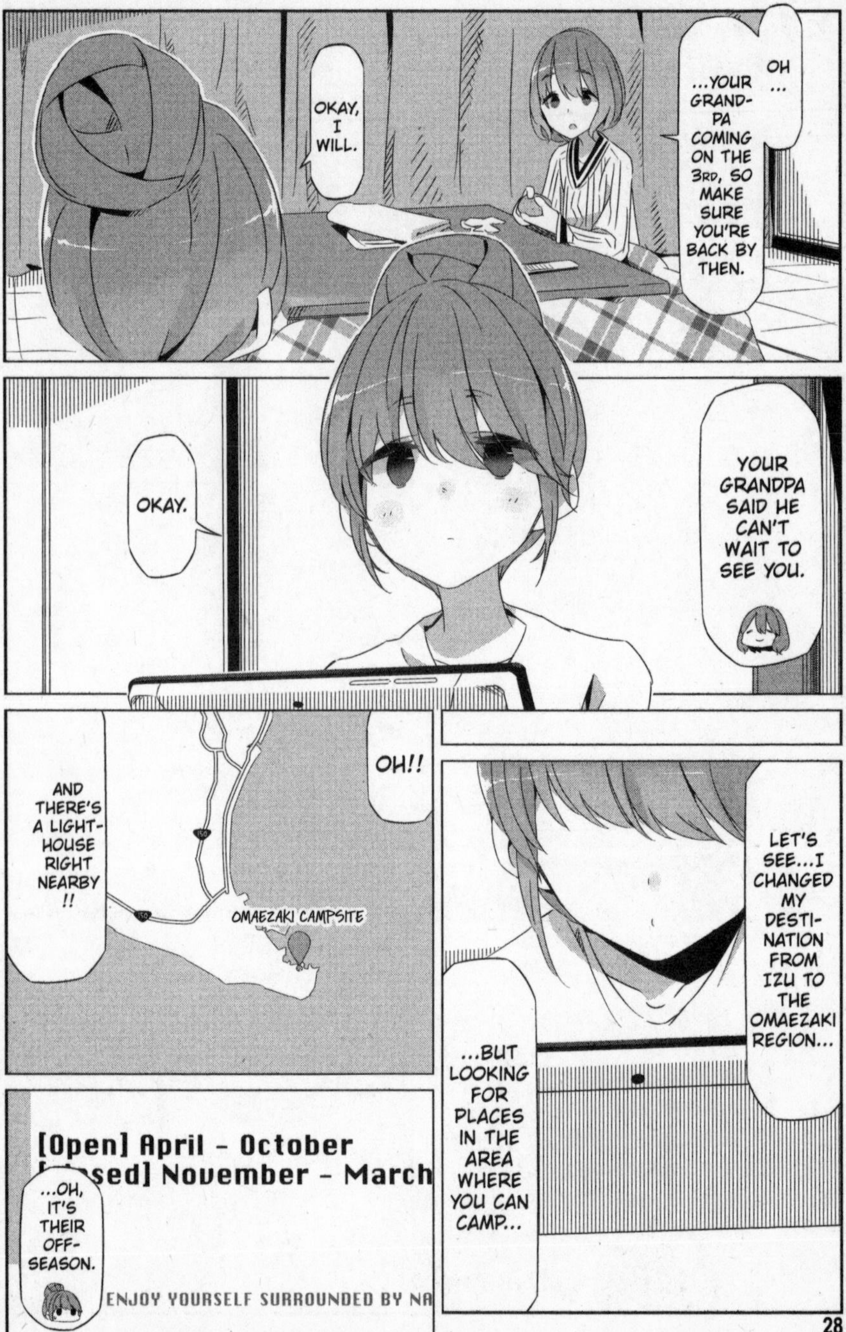
OH ...
...YOUR GRANDPA COMING ON THE 3RD, SO MAKE SURE YOU'RE BACK BY THEN.
OKAY, I WILL.
YOUR GRANDPA SAID HE CAN'T WAIT TO SEE YOU.
OKAY.
LET'S SEE...I CHANGED MY DESTINATION FROM IZU TO THE OMAEZAKI REGION...
...BUT LOOKING FOR PLACES IN THE AREA WHERE YOU CAN CAMP...
OH!!
AND THERE'S A LIGHTHOUSE RIGHT NEARBY!!
OMAEZAKI CAMPSITE
150
[Open] April - October
sed] November - March
...OH, IT'S THEIR OFF-SEASON.
ENJOY YOURSELF SURROUNDED BY NA

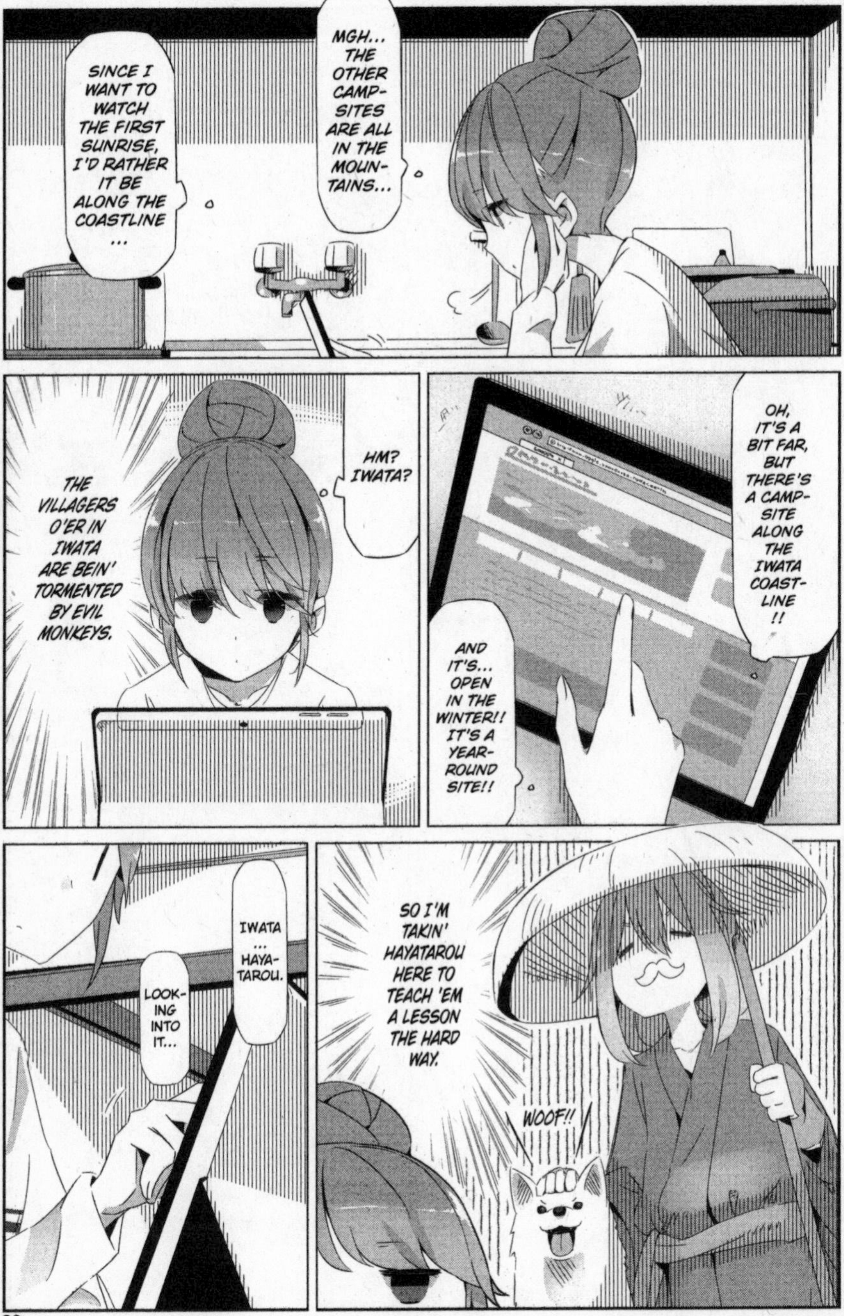
MGH... THE OTHER CAMPSITES ARE ALL IN THE MOUNTAINS...
SINCE I WANT TO WATCH THE FIRST SUNRISE, I'D RATHER IT BE ALONG THE COASTLINE...
OH, IT'S A BIT FAR, BUT THERE'S A CAMPSITE ALONG THE IWATA COASTLINE!!
AND IT'S... OPEN IN THE WINTER!! IT'S A YEAR-ROUND SITE!!
HM? IWATA?
THE VILLAGERS O'ER IN IWATA ARE BEIN' TORMENTED BY EVIL MONKEYS.
SO I'M TAKIN' HAYATAROU HERE TO TEACH 'EM A LESSON THE HARD WAY.
WOOF!!
IWATA... HAYATAROU.
LOOKING INTO IT...

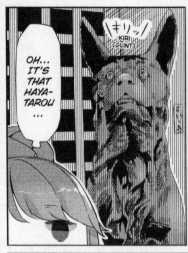

THE "GHOST DOG SHIPPEITAROU" IS REVERED AT MITSUKE-TENJIN IN IWATA CITY.
SHIPPEITAROU IS FRIENDS WITH "GHOST DOG HAYATAROU" IN KOMAGANE.
キリッ
KIRI (GLINT)
OH... IT'S THAT HAYA-TAROU...
AND WITHIN MITSUKE-TENJIN...,
...THEY ACTUALLY HAVE A REAL LIFE SHIPPEITAROU, THE THIRD IN HIS LINE.
WOOF!
THE THIRD
I CAN GO SEE...
...A GHOST DOG...
ALL RIGHT.
I GUESS I'M GOING TO ANOTHER TEMPLE TO VISIT A DOG.

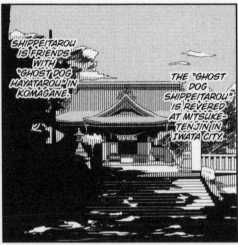

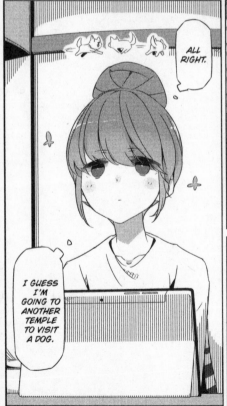

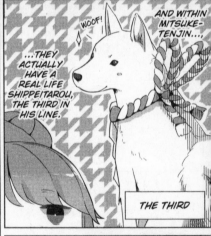

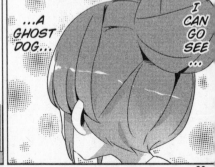

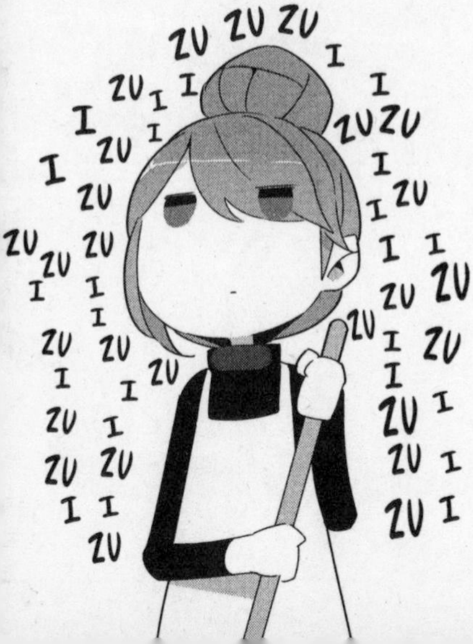
ZU ZU ZU
I
ZU I I
I ZU ZU
I ZU
I ZU
ZU ZU
ZU ZU I
ZU I I
ZU ZU I ZU
I I ZU
ZU I ZU I
ZU ZU I
ZU ZU I
I I ZU I
ZU

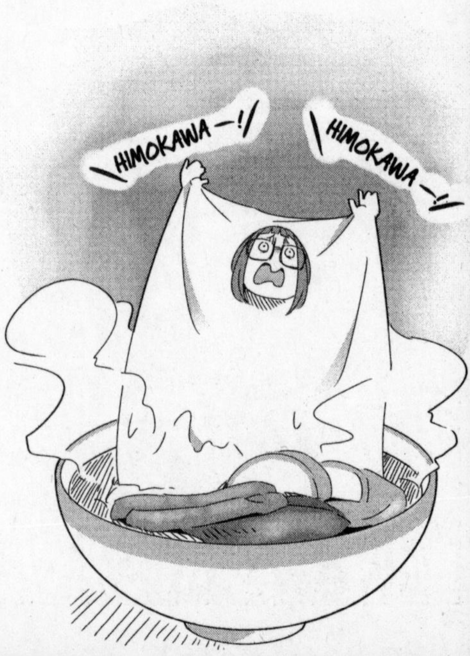
HIMOKAWA—!!
HIMOKAWA—!!

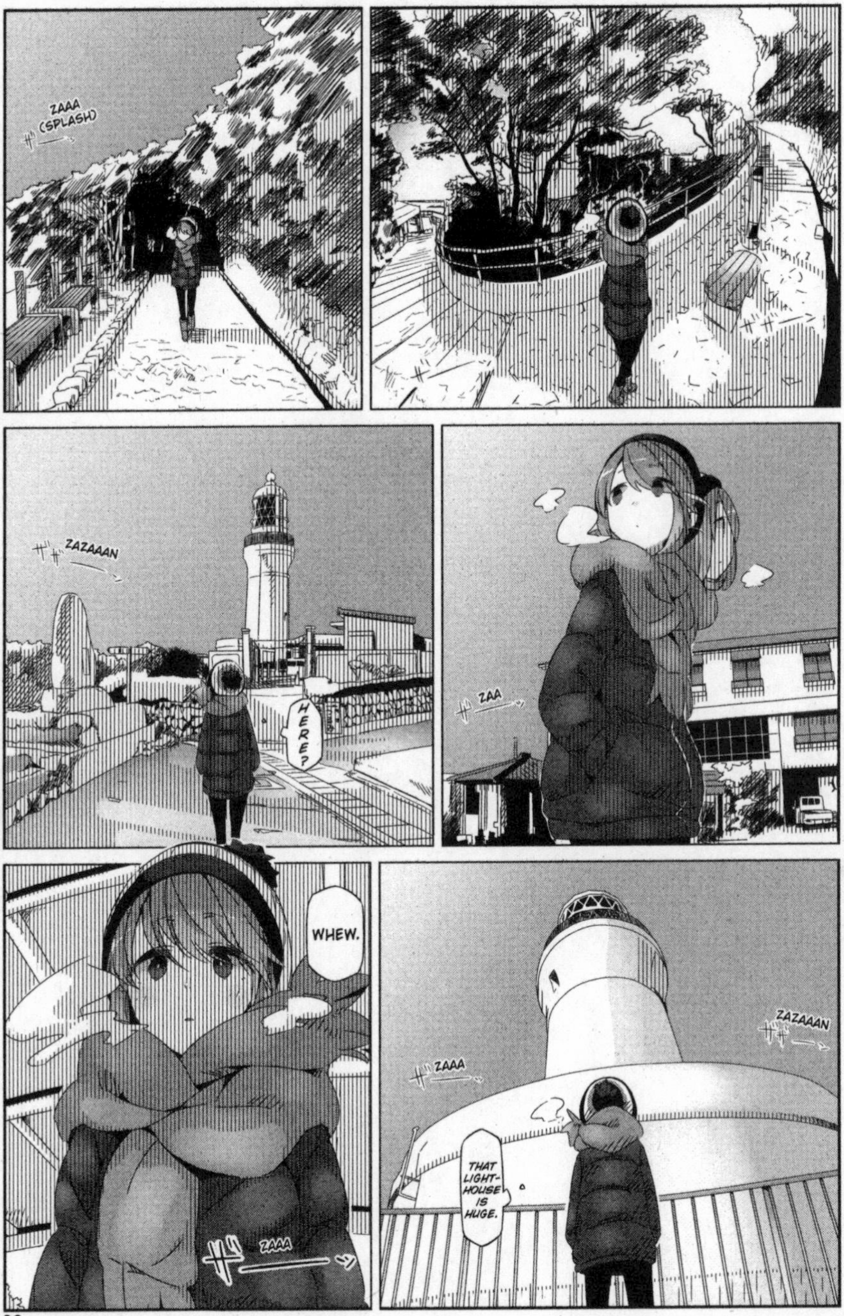
ZAAA (SPLASH)
ZAA
ZAZAAAN
HERE?
ZAZAAAN
ZAAA
THAT LIGHT-HOUSE IS HUGE.
WHEW.
ZAAA

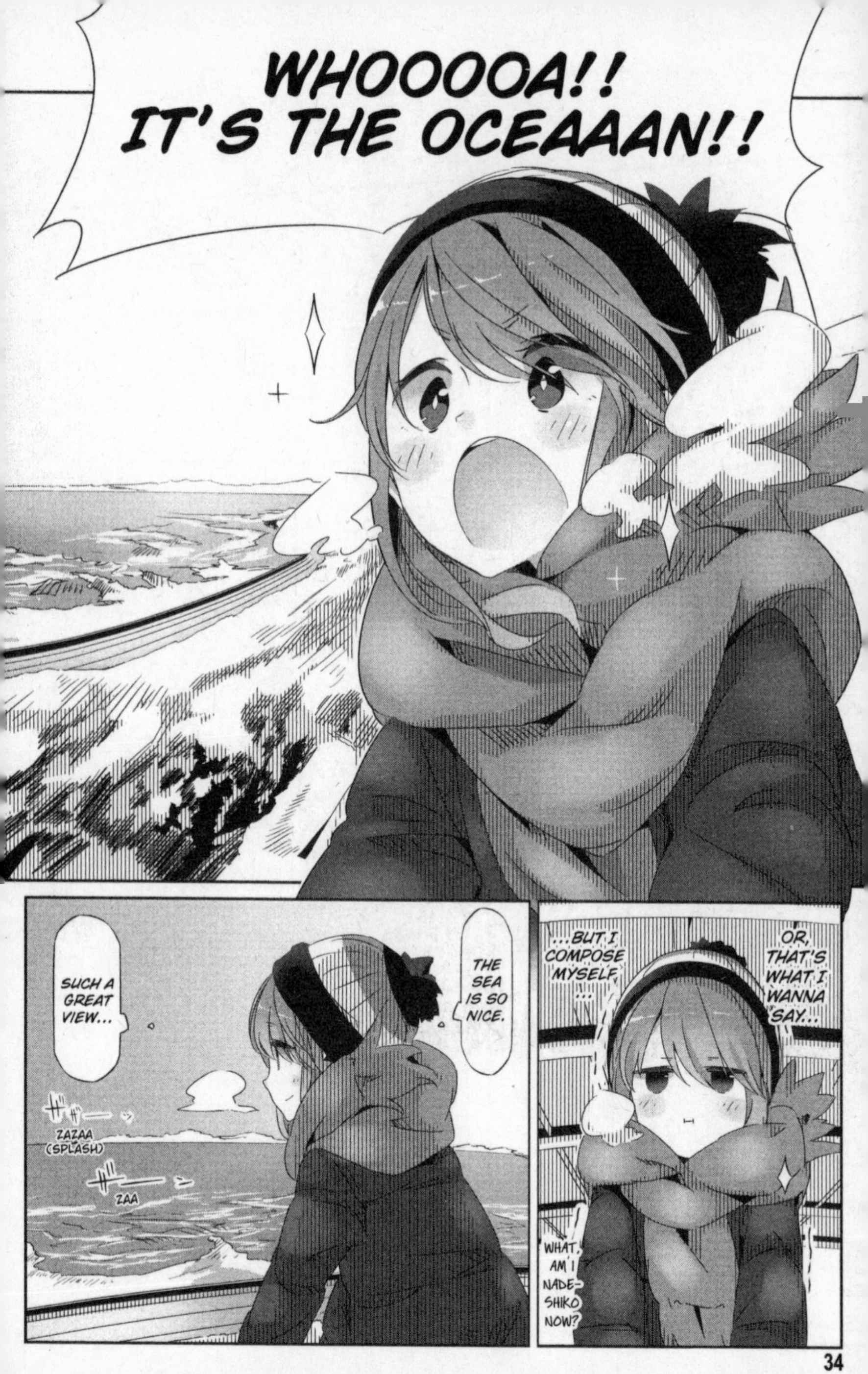
WHOOOOA!! IT'S THE OCEAAAN!!
OR, THAT'S WHAT I WANNA SAY...
...BUT I COMPOSE MYSELF...
WHAT, AM I NADE-SHIKO NOW?
THE SEA IS SO NICE.
SUCH A GREAT VIEW...
ZAZAA (SPLASH)
ZAA

Chapter 25 SOLO-CAMPING GIRL ON NEW YEAR'S EVE

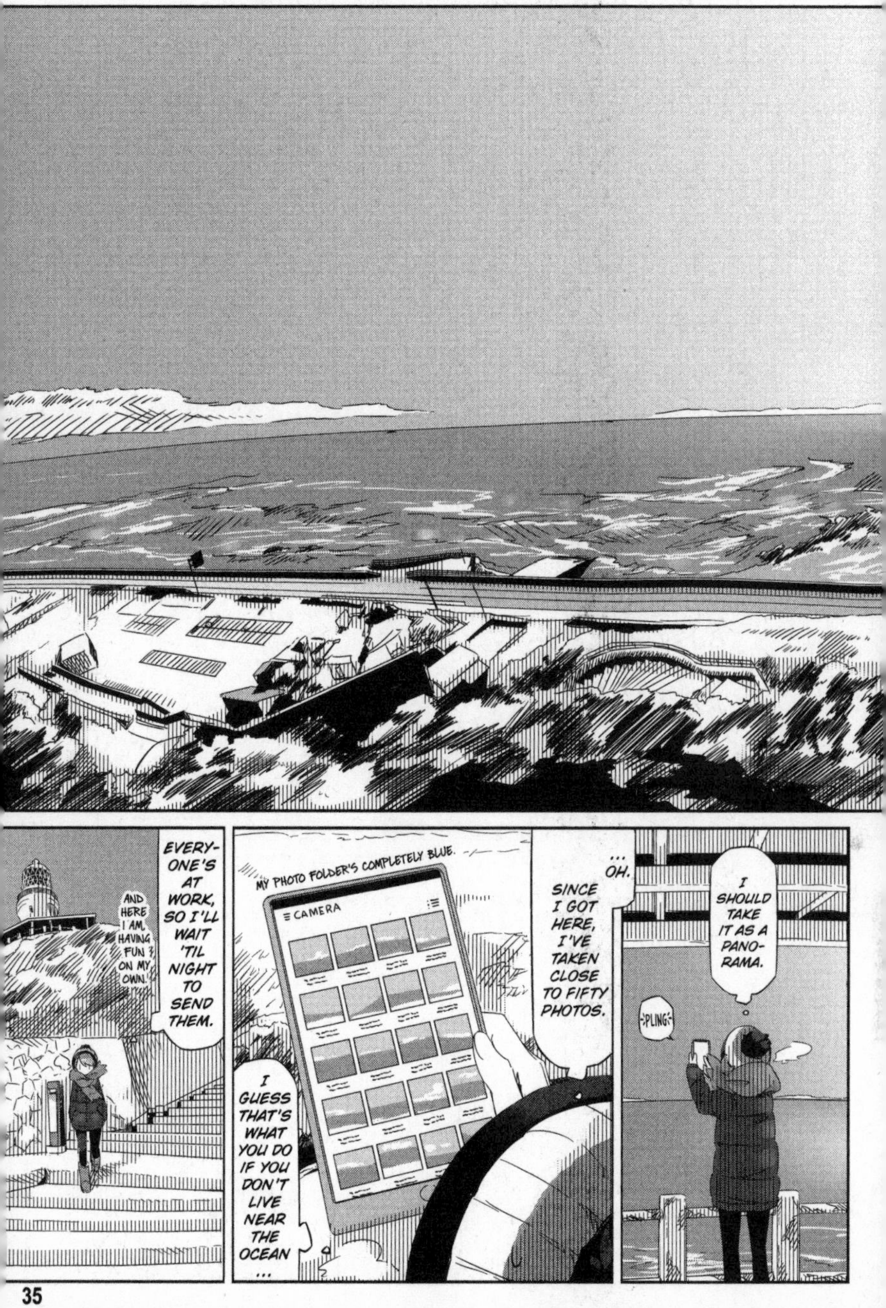
I SHOULD TAKE IT AS A PANO-RAMA.
PLING
...OH.
SINCE I GOT HERE, I'VE TAKEN CLOSE TO FIFTY PHOTOS.
MY PHOTO FOLDER'S COMPLETELY BLUE.
CAMERA
I GUESS THAT'S WHAT YOU DO IF YOU DON'T LIVE NEAR THE OCEAN...
EVERY-ONE'S AT WORK, SO I'LL WAIT 'TIL NIGHT TO SEND THEM.
AND HERE I AM, HAVING FUN ON MY OWN.

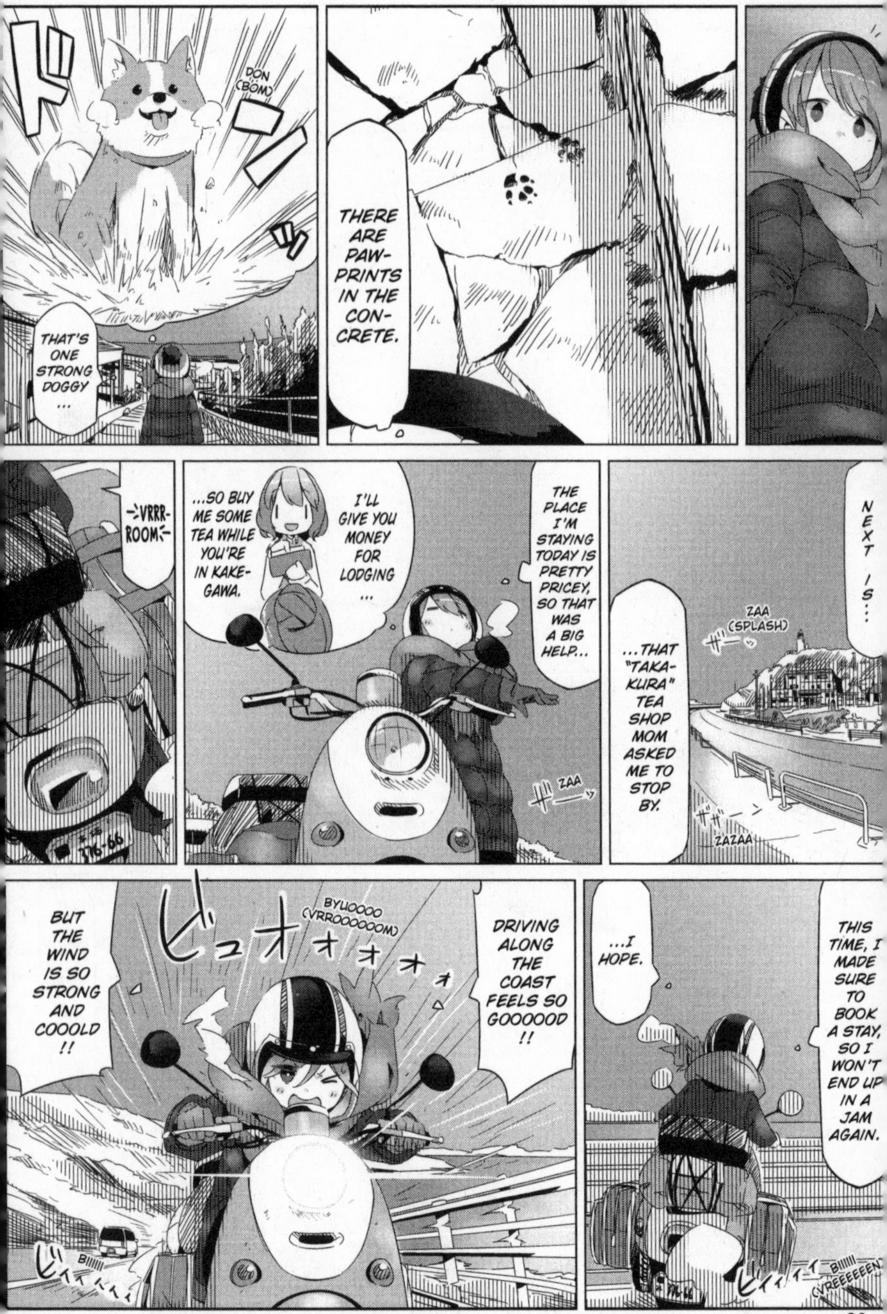
THERE ARE PAW-PRINTS IN THE CONCRETE.
DON (BOM)
THAT'S ONE STRONG DOGGY ...
NEXT IS...
ZAA (SPLASH)
...THAT "TAKAKURA" TEA SHOP MOM ASKED ME TO STOP BY.
ZAZAA
THE PLACE I'M STAYING TODAY IS PRETTY PRICEY, SO THAT WAS A BIG HELP...
I'LL GIVE YOU MONEY FOR LODGING ...
...SO BUY ME SOME TEA WHILE YOU'RE IN KAKE-GAWA.
ZAA
VRRR-ROOM
THIS TIME, I MADE SURE TO BOOK A STAY, SO I WON'T END UP IN A JAM AGAIN.
...I HOPE.
BIIIIII (VREEEEEEN)
DRIVING ALONG THE COAST FEELS SO GOOOOOD !!
BYUOOOO (VRROOOOOOM)
BUT THE WIND IS SO STRONG AND COOOLD !!
BIIIIII

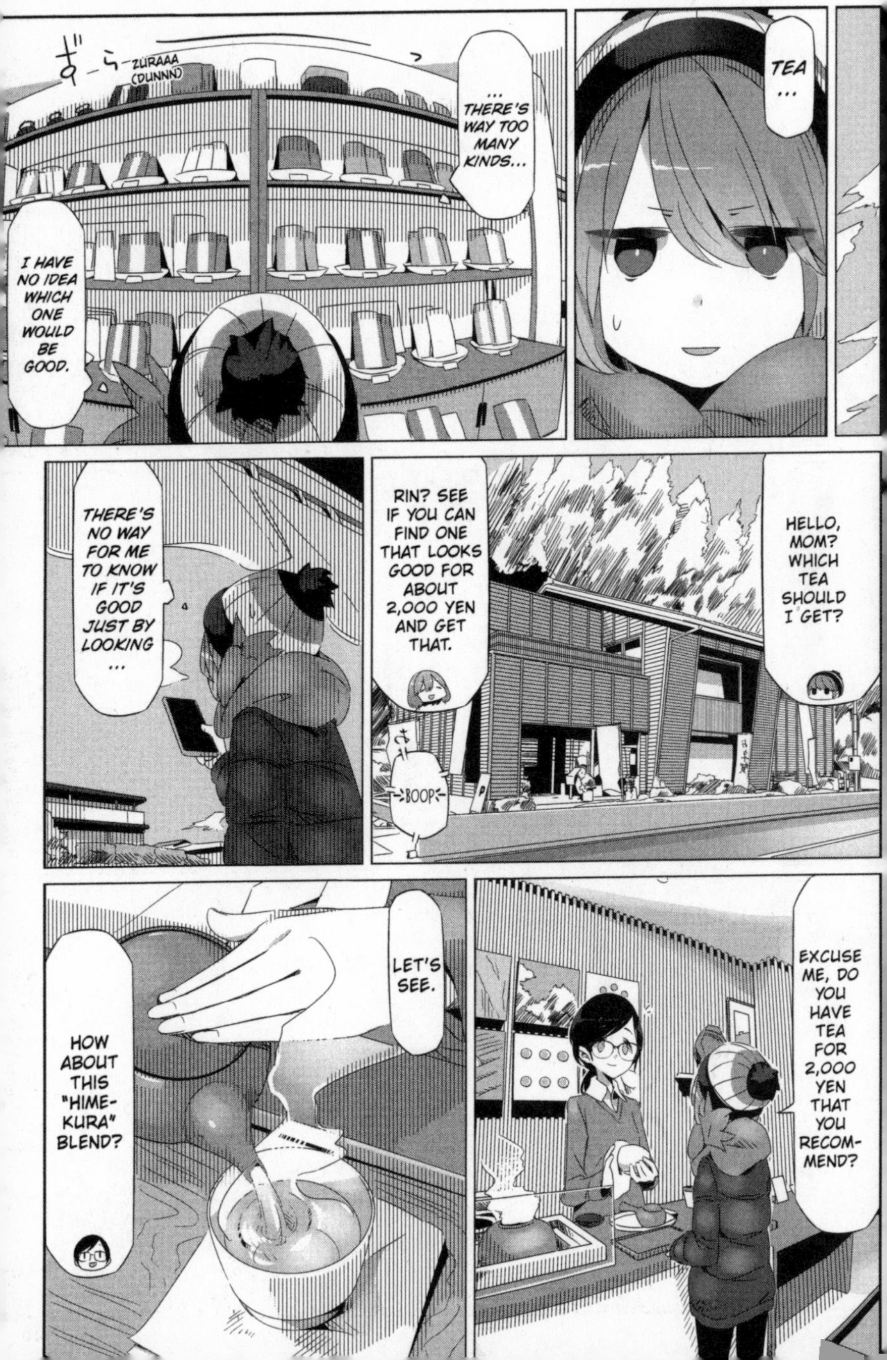
TEA ...
ずら ZURAAA (DUNNN)
... THERE'S WAY TOO MANY KINDS...
I HAVE NO IDEA WHICH ONE WOULD BE GOOD.
HELLO, MOM? WHICH TEA SHOULD I GET?
RIN? SEE IF YOU CAN FIND ONE THAT LOOKS GOOD FOR ABOUT 2,000 YEN AND GET THAT.
BOOP
THERE'S NO WAY FOR ME TO KNOW IF IT'S GOOD JUST BY LOOKING ...
EXCUSE ME, DO YOU HAVE TEA FOR 2,000 YEN THAT YOU RECOMMEND?
LET'S SEE.
HOW ABOUT THIS "HIME-KURA" BLEND?

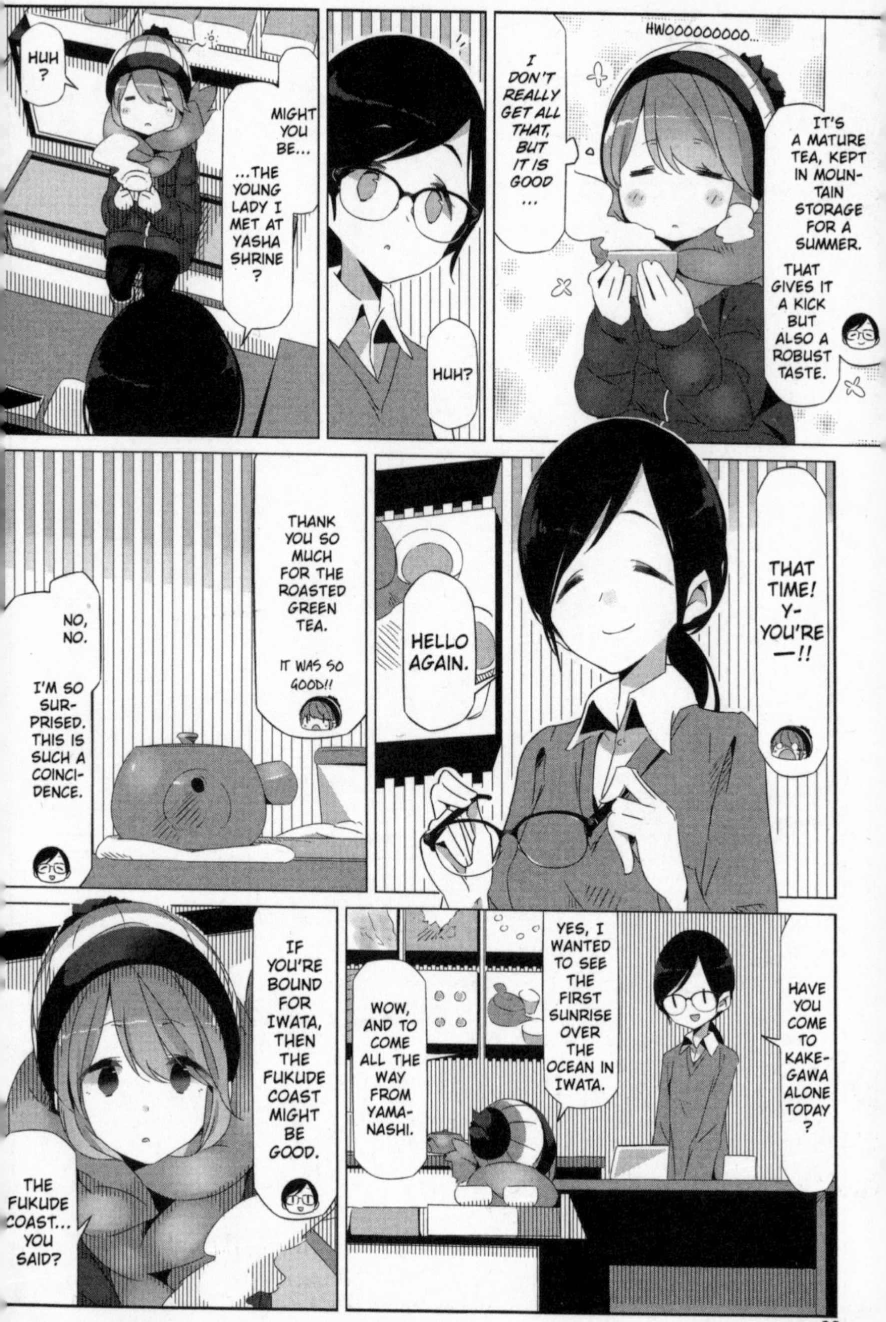
HWOOOOOOOOO...
IT'S A MATURE TEA, KEPT IN MOUNTAIN STORAGE FOR A SUMMER.
THAT GIVES IT A KICK BUT ALSO A ROBUST TASTE.
I DON'T REALLY GET ALL THAT, BUT IT IS GOOD...
HUH?
MIGHT YOU BE...
...THE YOUNG LADY I MET AT YASHA SHRINE?
HUH?
THAT TIME! Y-YOU'RE—!!
HELLO AGAIN.
THANK YOU SO MUCH FOR THE ROASTED GREEN TEA.
IT WAS SO GOOD!!
NO, NO.
I'M SO SURPRISED. THIS IS SUCH A COINCIDENCE.
HAVE YOU COME TO KAKEGAWA ALONE TODAY?
YES, I WANTED TO SEE THE FIRST SUNRISE OVER THE OCEAN IN IWATA.
WOW, AND TO COME ALL THE WAY FROM YAMANASHI.
IF YOU'RE BOUND FOR IWATA, THEN THE FUKUDE COAST MIGHT BE GOOD.
THE FUKUDE COAST... YOU SAID?

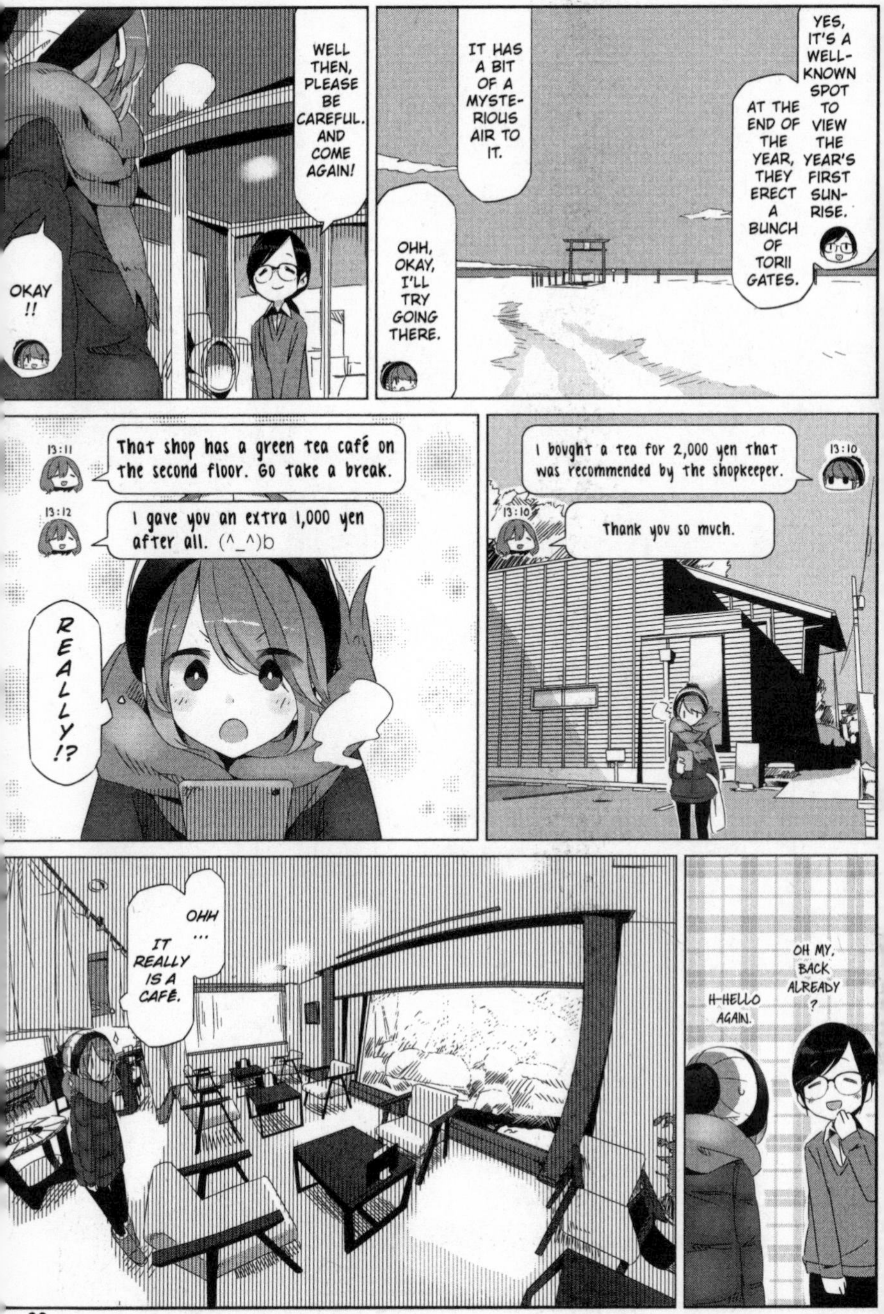
YES, IT'S A WELL-KNOWN SPOT TO VIEW THE YEAR'S FIRST SUNRISE.
AT THE END OF THE YEAR, THEY ERECT A BUNCH OF TORII GATES.
IT HAS A BIT OF A MYSTERIOUS AIR TO IT.
OHH, OKAY, I'LL TRY GOING THERE.
WELL THEN, PLEASE BE CAREFUL. AND COME AGAIN!
OKAY !!
13:10
I bought a tea for 2,000 yen that was recommended by the shopkeeper.
13:10
Thank you so much.
13:11
That shop has a green tea café on the second floor. Go take a break.
13:12
I gave you an extra 1,000 yen after all. (^_^)b
REALLY!?
OH MY, BACK ALREADY ?
H-HELLO AGAIN.
OHH ... IT REALLY IS A CAFÉ.

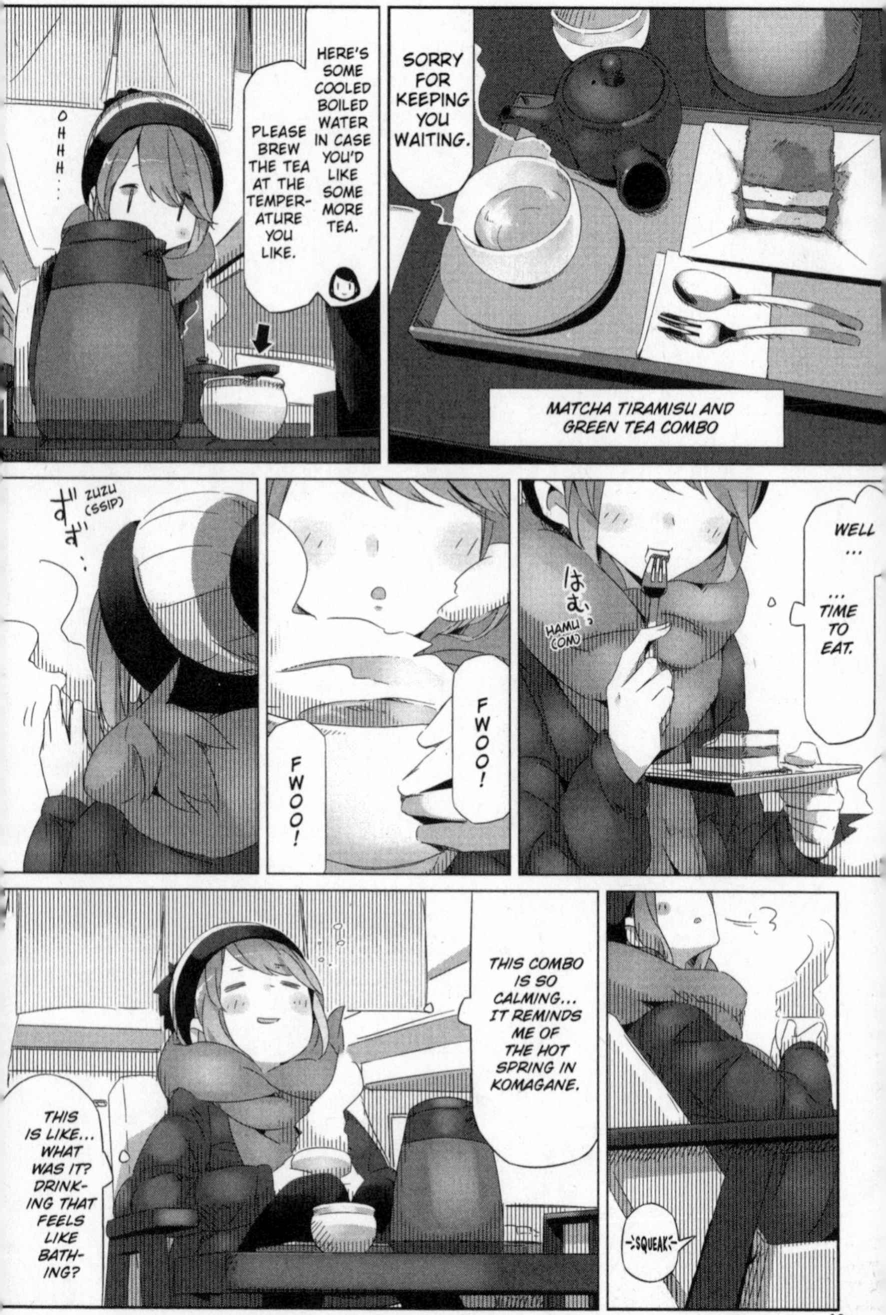

SORRY FOR KEEPING YOU WAITING.
MATCHA TIRAMISU AND GREEN TEA COMBO
HERE'S SOME COOLED BOILED WATER IN CASE YOU'D LIKE SOME MORE TEA.
PLEASE BREW THE TEA AT THE TEMPER-ATURE YOU LIKE.
OHHH...
WELL...
...TIME TO EAT.
はむっ
HAMU (OM)
FWOO!
FWOO!
ずず…
ZUZU (SSIP)
-SQUEAK-
THIS COMBO IS SO CALMING... IT REMINDS ME OF THE HOT SPRING IN KOMAGANE.
THIS IS LIKE... WHAT WAS IT? DRINK-ING THAT FEELS LIKE BATH-ING?

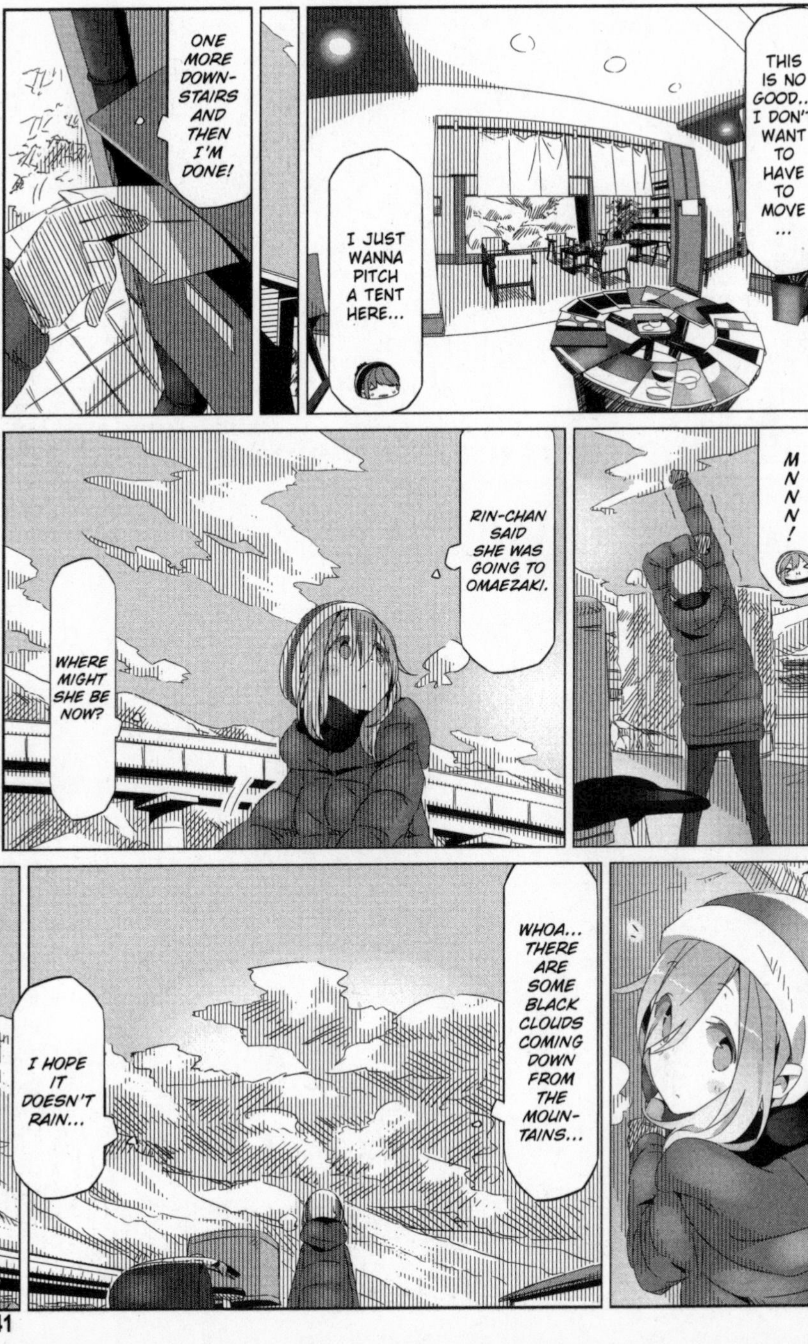
THIS IS NO GOOD... I DON'T WANT TO HAVE TO MOVE...
I JUST WANNA PITCH A TENT HERE...
ONE MORE DOWN-STAIRS AND THEN I'M DONE!
MNNN!
RIN-CHAN SAID SHE WAS GOING TO OMAEZAKI.
WHERE MIGHT SHE BE NOW?
WHOA... THERE ARE SOME BLACK CLOUDS COMING DOWN FROM THE MOUN-TAINS...
I HOPE IT DOESN'T RAIN...

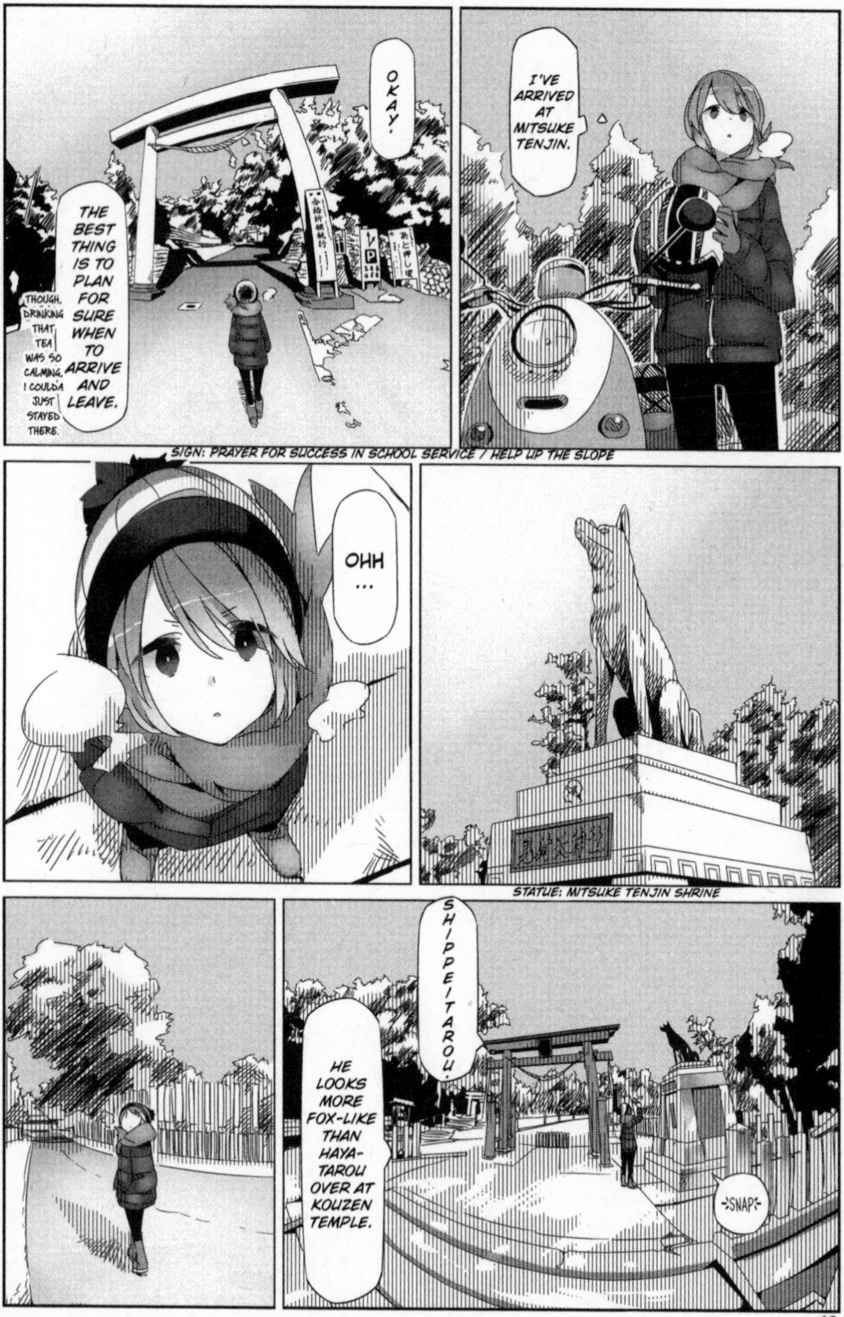
I'VE ARRIVED AT MITSUKE TENJIN.
OKAY.
THE BEST THING IS TO PLAN FOR SURE WHEN TO ARRIVE AND LEAVE.
THOUGH, DRINKING THAT TEA WAS SO CALMING, I COULDA JUST STAYED THERE.
SIGN: PRAYER FOR SUCCESS IN SCHOOL SERVICE / HELP UP THE SLOPE
STATUE: MITSUKE TENJIN SHRINE
OHH ...
SHIPPEITAROU.
HE LOOKS MORE FOX-LIKE THAN HAYATAROU OVER AT KOUZEN TEMPLE.
SNAP

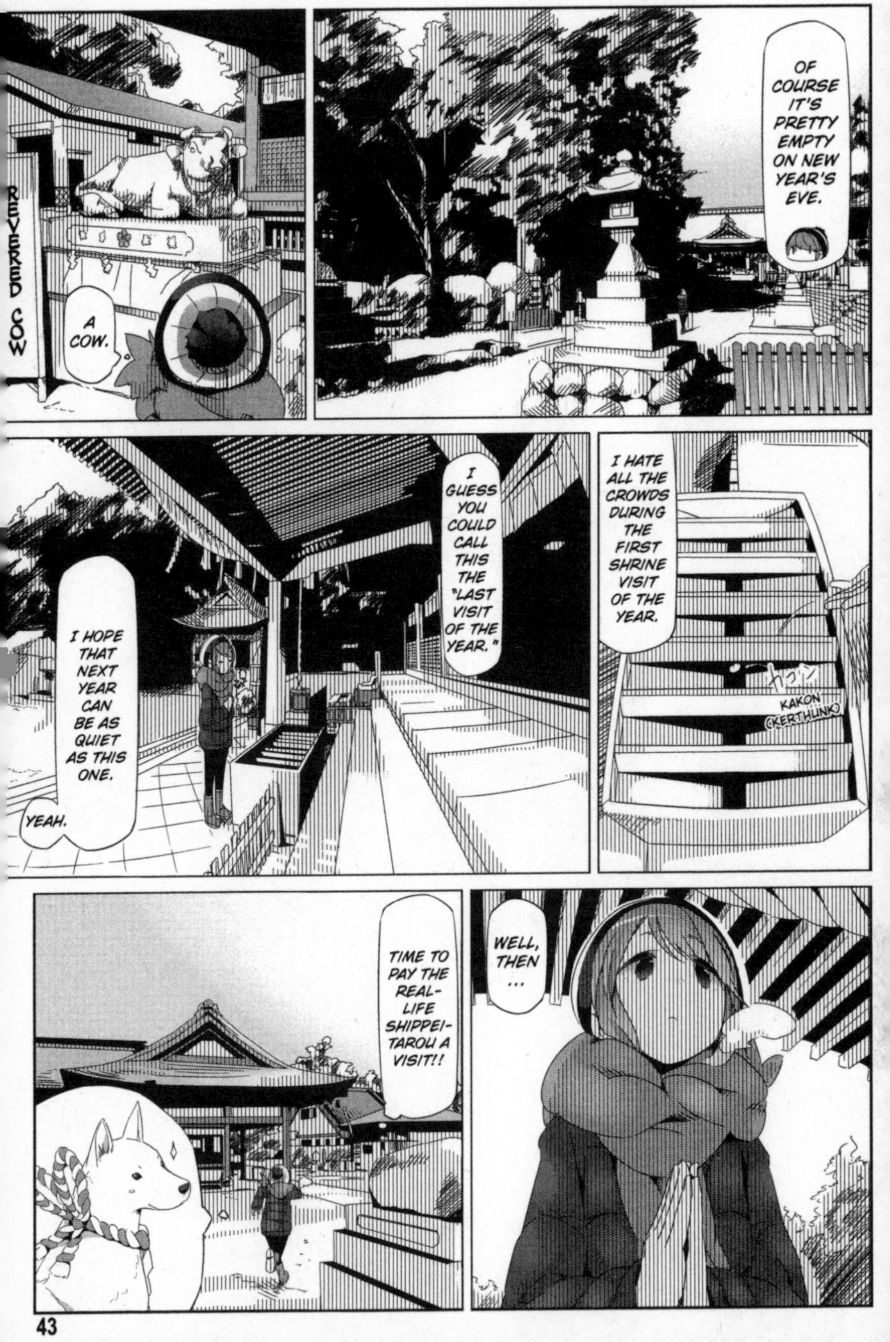
OF COURSE IT'S PRETTY EMPTY ON NEW YEAR'S EVE.
REVERED COW
A COW.
I HATE ALL THE CROWDS DURING THE FIRST SHRINE VISIT OF THE YEAR.
カコン
KAKON (KERTHLINK)
I GUESS YOU COULD CALL THIS THE "LAST VISIT OF THE YEAR."
I HOPE THAT NEXT YEAR CAN BE AS QUIET AS THIS ONE.
YEAH.
WELL, THEN ...
TIME TO PAY THE REAL-LIFE SHIPPEI-TAROU A VISIT!!

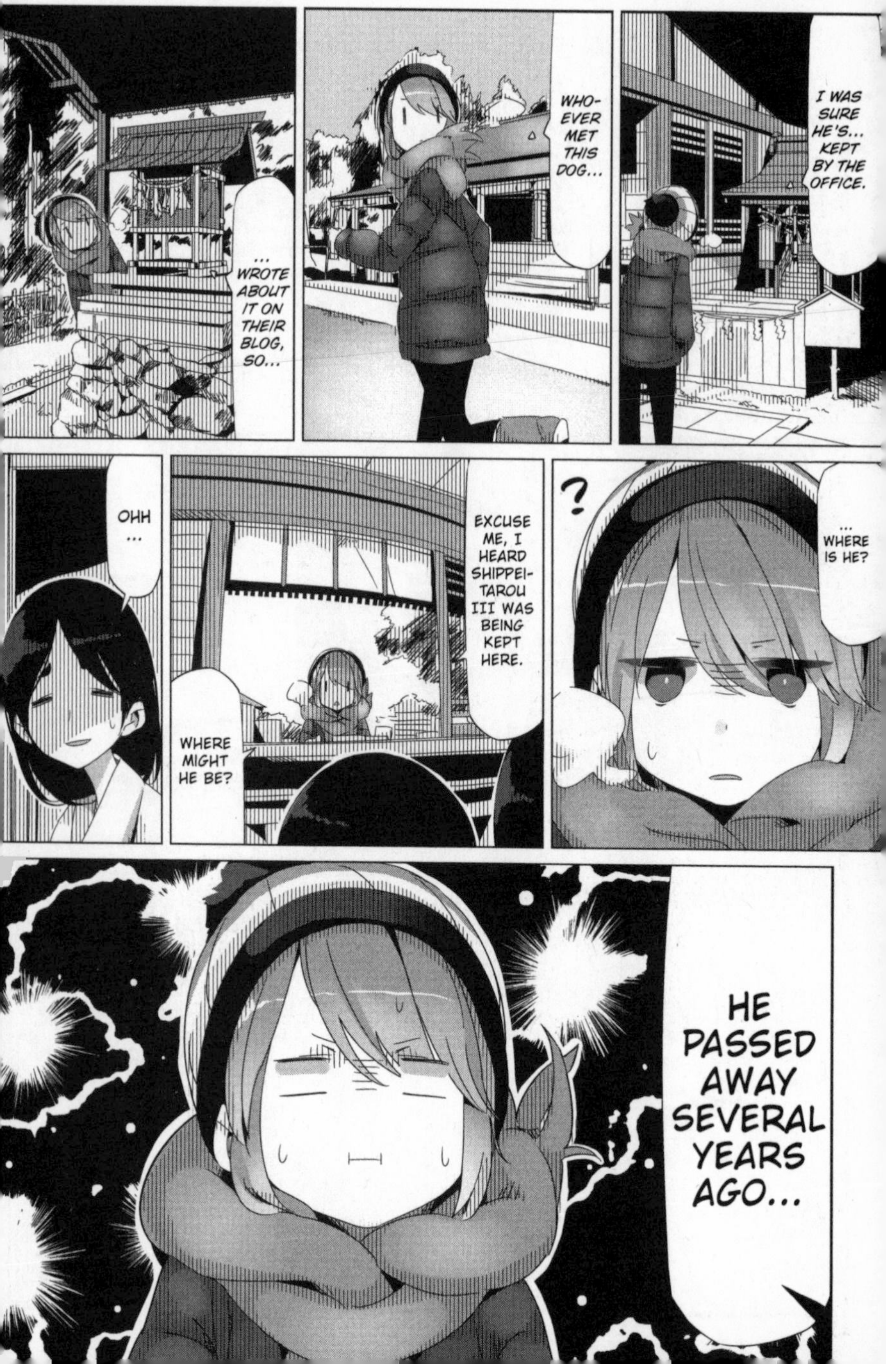
I WAS SURE HE'S... KEPT BY THE OFFICE.
WHO-EVER MET THIS DOG...
...WROTE ABOUT IT ON THEIR BLOG, SO...
?
...WHERE IS HE?
EXCUSE ME, I HEARD SHIPPEI-TAROU III WAS BEING KEPT HERE.
WHERE MIGHT HE BE?
OHH ...
HE PASSED AWAY SEVERAL YEARS AGO...

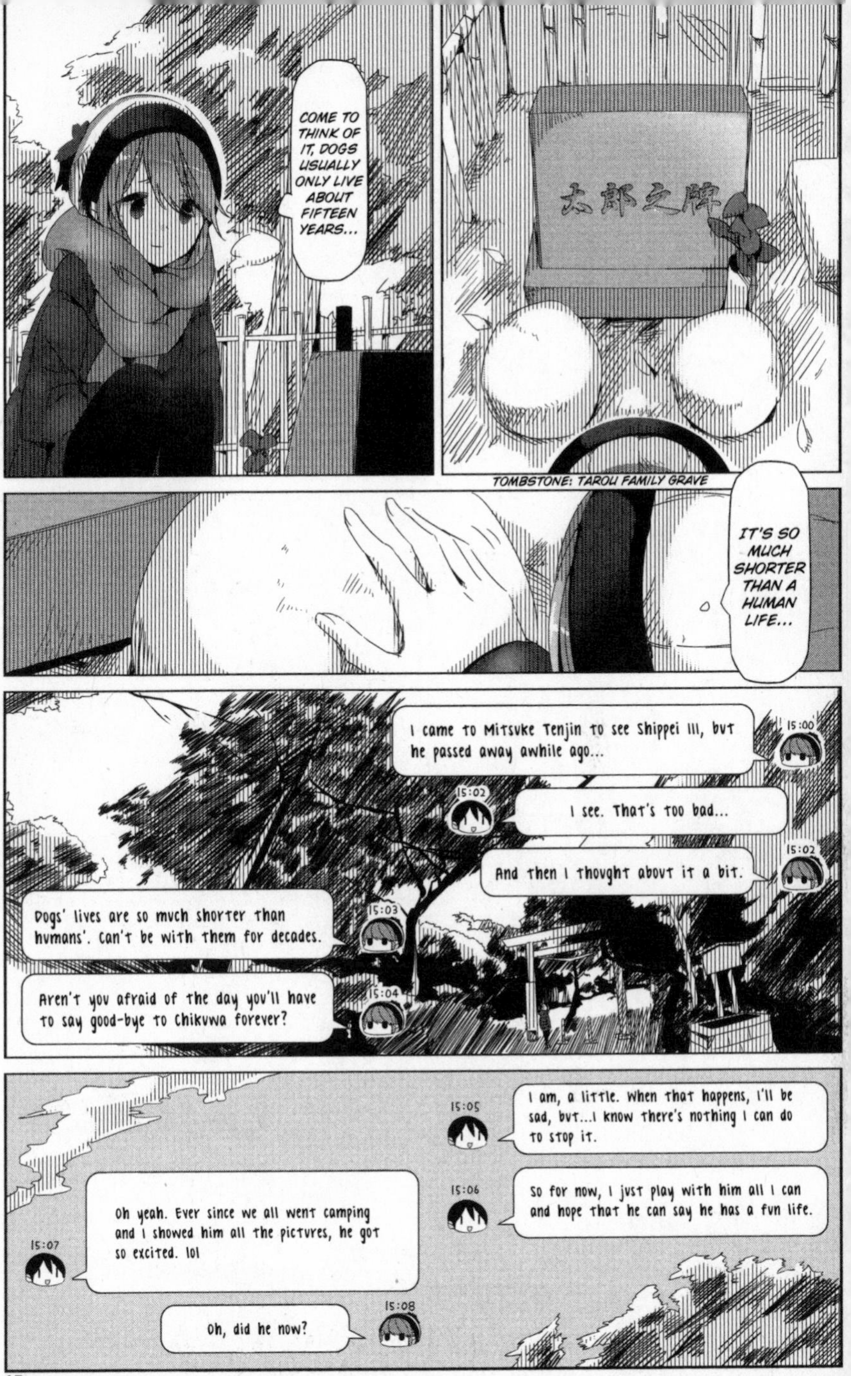
TOMBSTONE: TAROU FAMILY GRAVE
COME TO THINK OF IT, DOGS USUALLY ONLY LIVE ABOUT FIFTEEN YEARS...
IT'S SO MUCH SHORTER THAN A HUMAN LIFE...
15:00
I came to Mitsuke Tenjin to see Shippei III, but he passed away awhile ago...
15:02
I see. That's too bad...
15:02
And then I thought about it a bit.
15:03
Dogs' lives are so much shorter than humans'. Can't be with them for decades.
15:04
Aren't you afraid of the day you'll have to say good-bye to Chikuwa forever?
15:05
I am, a little. When that happens, I'll be sad, but...I know there's nothing I can do to stop it.
15:06
So for now, I just play with him all I can and hope that he can say he has a fun life.
15:07
Oh yeah. Ever since we all went camping and I showed him all the pictures, he got so excited. lol
15:08
Oh, did he now?

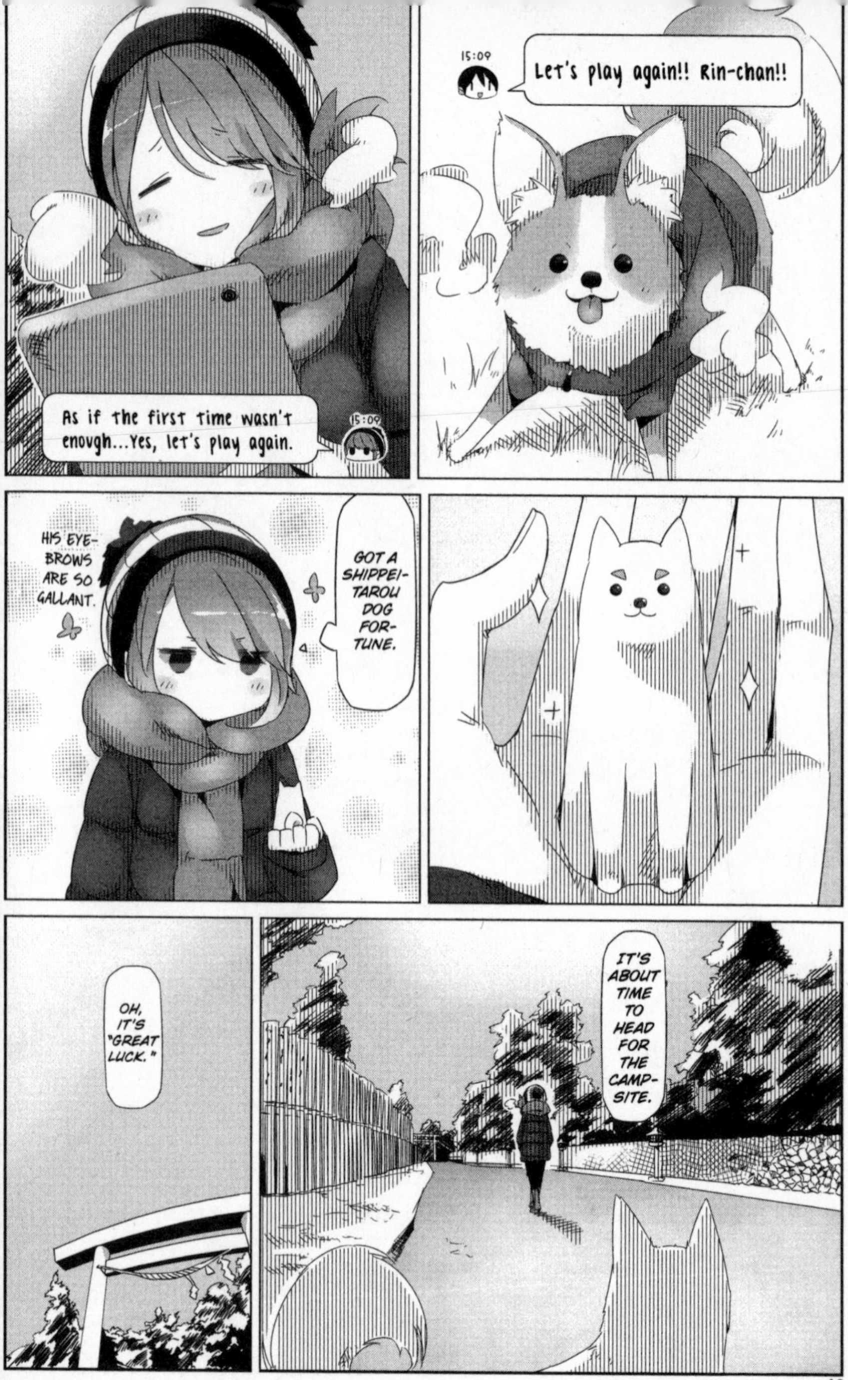
15:09
Let's play again!! Rin-chan!!
15:09
As if the first time wasn't enough...Yes, let's play again.
GOT A SHIPPEI-TAROU DOG FORTUNE.
HIS EYEBROWS ARE SO GALLANT.
IT'S ABOUT TIME TO HEAD FOR THE CAMPSITE.
OH, IT'S "GREAT LUCK."

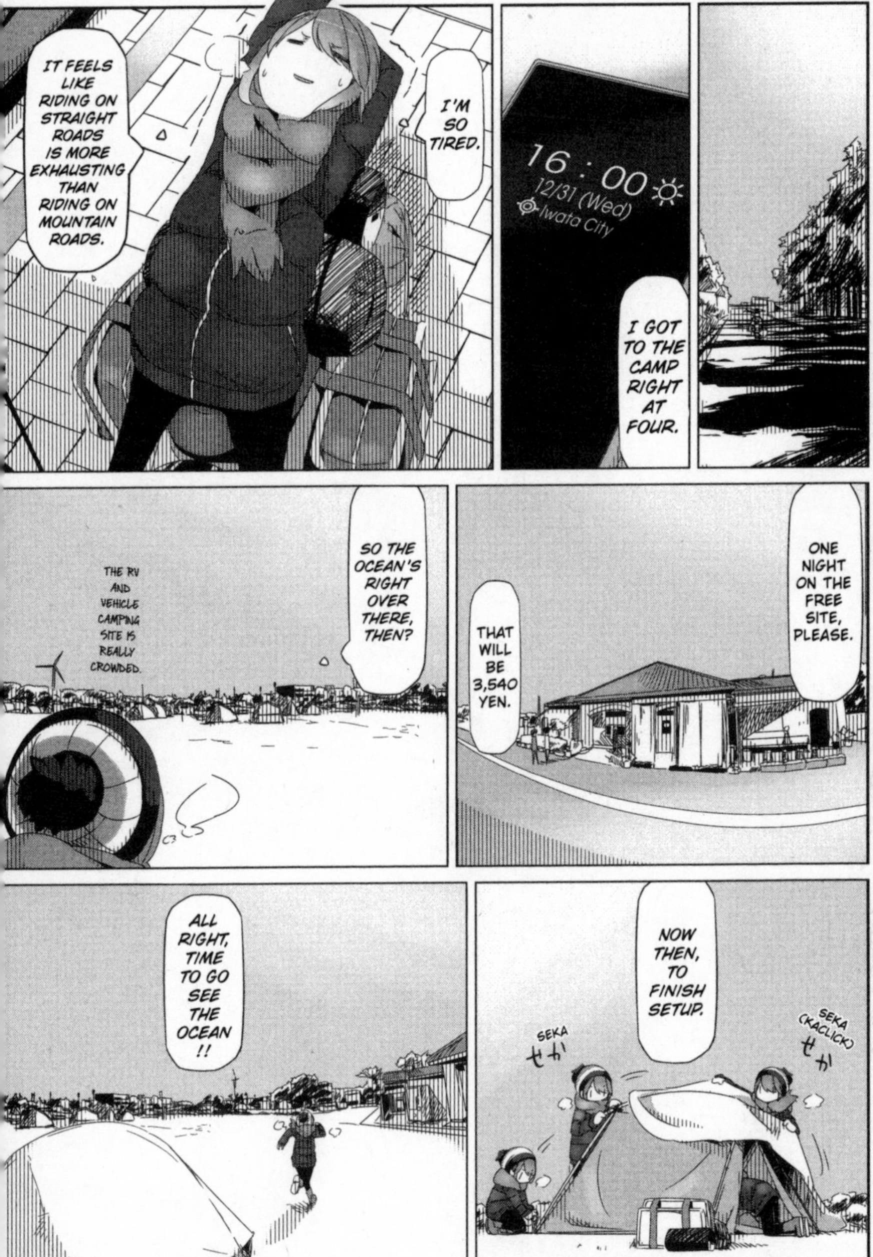
16:00
12/31 (Wed)
Iwata City
I GOT TO THE CAMP RIGHT AT FOUR.
I'M SO TIRED.
IT FEELS LIKE RIDING ON STRAIGHT ROADS IS MORE EXHAUSTING THAN RIDING ON MOUNTAIN ROADS.
ONE NIGHT ON THE FREE SITE, PLEASE.
THAT WILL BE 3,540 YEN.
SO THE OCEAN'S RIGHT OVER THERE, THEN?
THE RV AND VEHICLE CAMPING SITE IS REALLY CROWDED.
NOW THEN, TO FINISH SETUP.
SEKA (KACLICK)
せか
SEKA
せか
ALL RIGHT, TIME TO GO SEE THE OCEAN!!

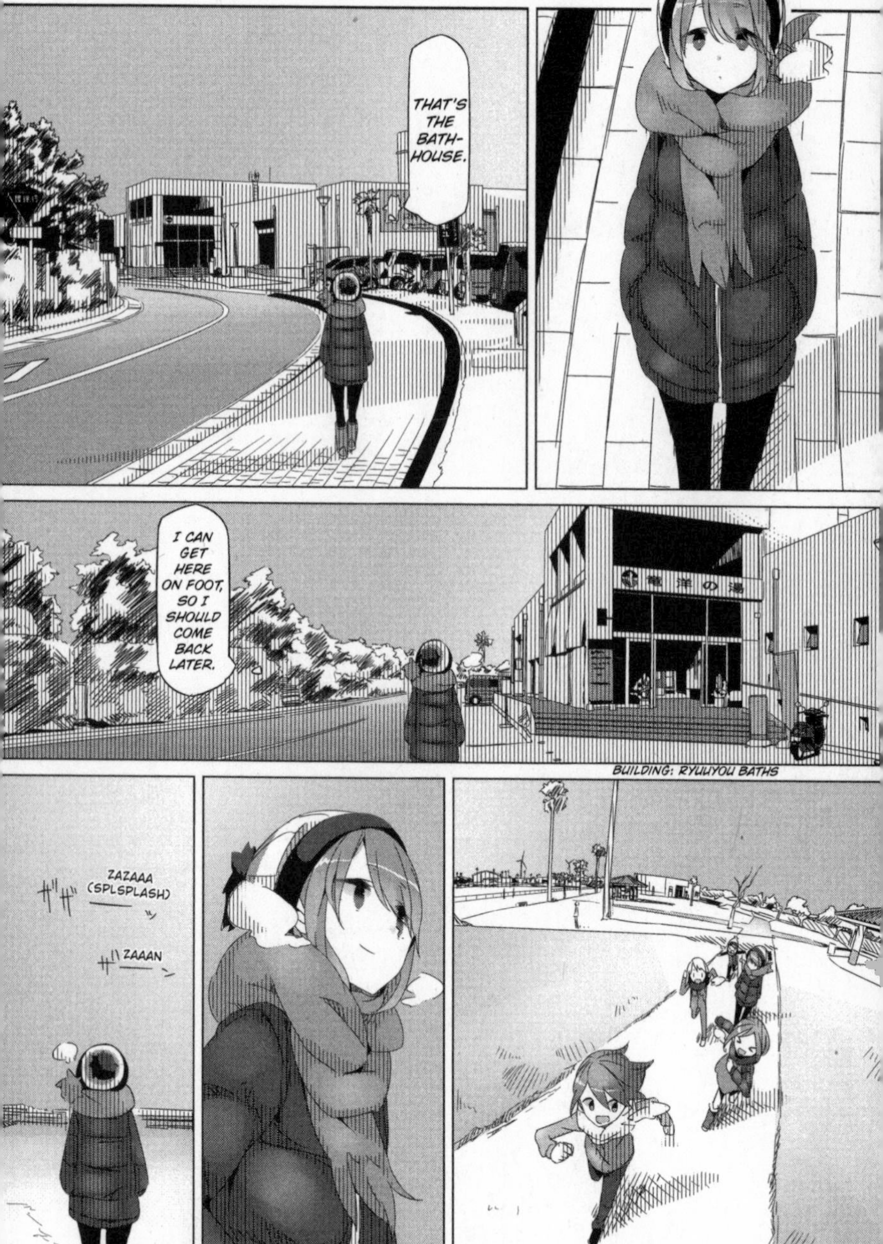
THAT'S THE BATH-HOUSE.
I CAN GET HERE ON FOOT, SO I SHOULD COME BACK LATER.
龍洋の湯
BUILDING: RYUUYOU BATHS
ZAZAAA (SPLSPLASH)
ZAAAN

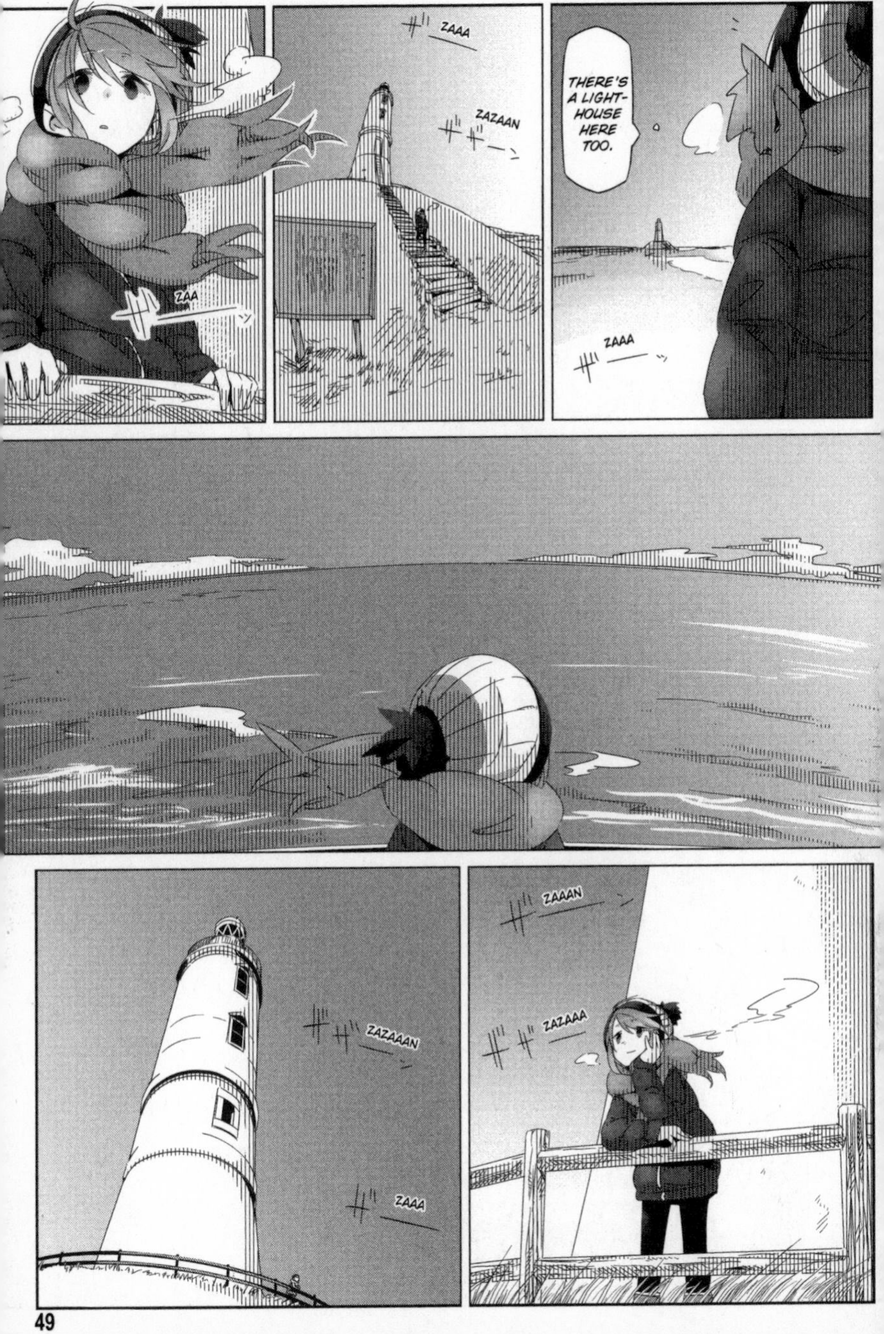
THERE'S A LIGHT-HOUSE HERE TOO.
ZAAA
ZAAA
ZAZAAN
ZAA
ZAAAN
ZAZAAA
ZAZAAAN
ZAAA

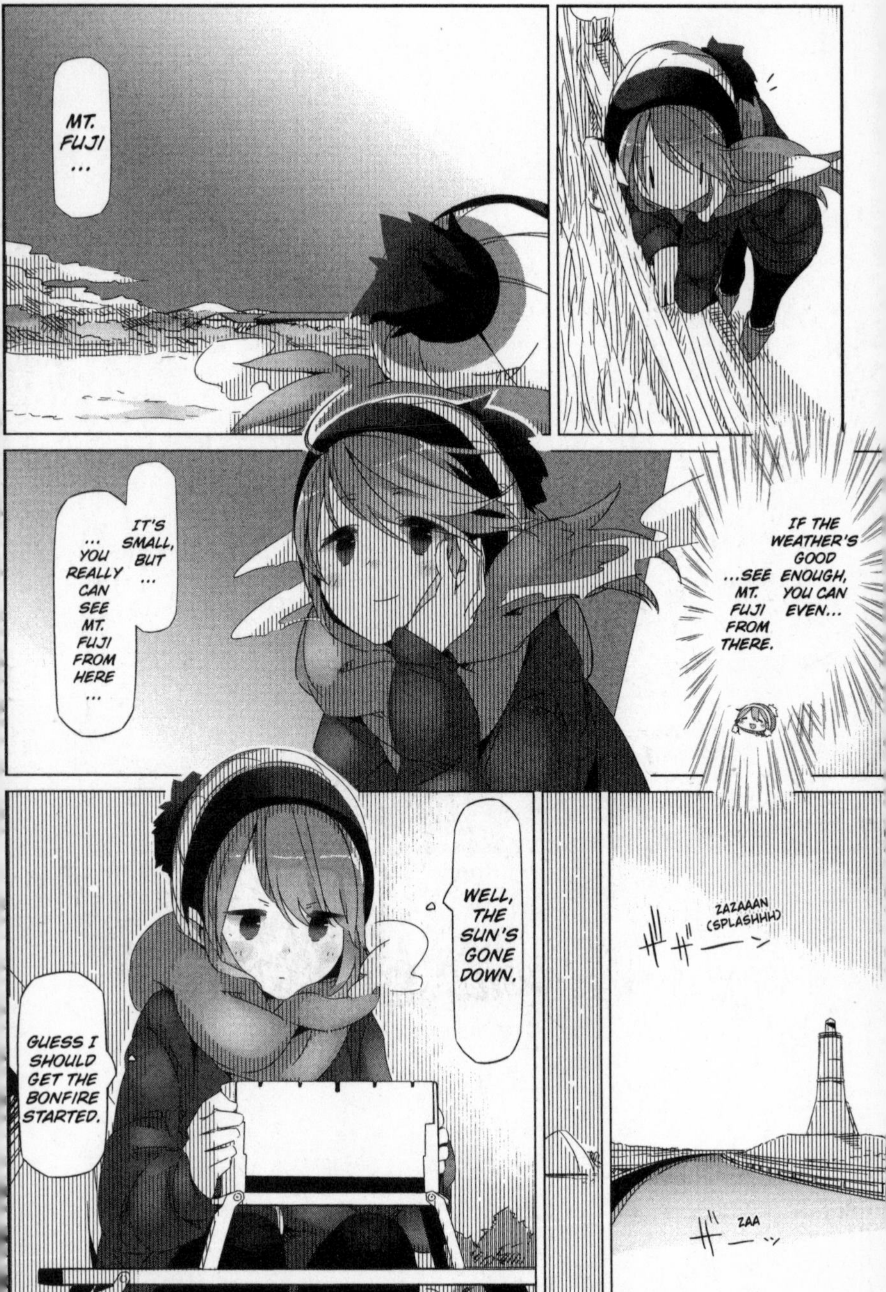
MT. FUJI ...
IF THE WEATHER'S GOOD ENOUGH, YOU CAN EVEN...
...SEE MT. FUJI FROM THERE.
IT'S SMALL, BUT ...
... YOU REALLY CAN SEE MT. FUJI FROM HERE ...
ZAZAAAN (SPLASHHH)
ZAA
WELL, THE SUN'S GONE DOWN.
GUESS I SHOULD GET THE BONFIRE STARTED.

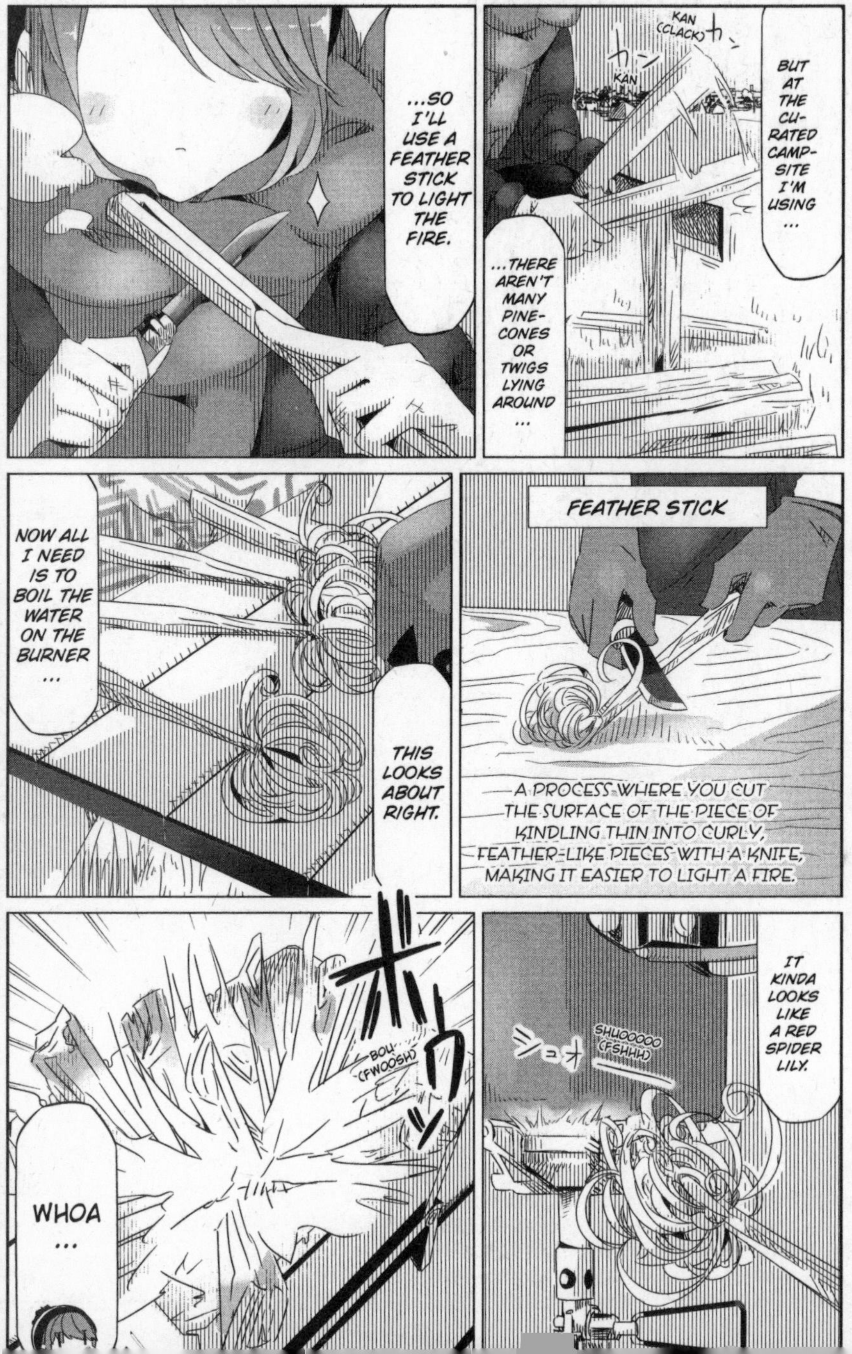
KAN (CLACK)
KAN
BUT AT THE CURATED CAMPSITE I'M USING...
...THERE AREN'T MANY PINECONES OR TWIGS LYING AROUND...
...SO I'LL USE A FEATHER STICK TO LIGHT THE FIRE.
FEATHER STICK
A PROCESS WHERE YOU CUT THE SURFACE OF THE PIECE OF KINDLING THIN INTO CURLY, FEATHER-LIKE PIECES WITH A KNIFE, MAKING IT EASIER TO LIGHT A FIRE.
THIS LOOKS ABOUT RIGHT.
NOW ALL I NEED IS TO BOIL THE WATER ON THE BURNER...
IT KINDA LOOKS LIKE A RED SPIDER LILY.
SHUOOOOO (FSHHH)
BOU (FWOOSH)
WHOA...

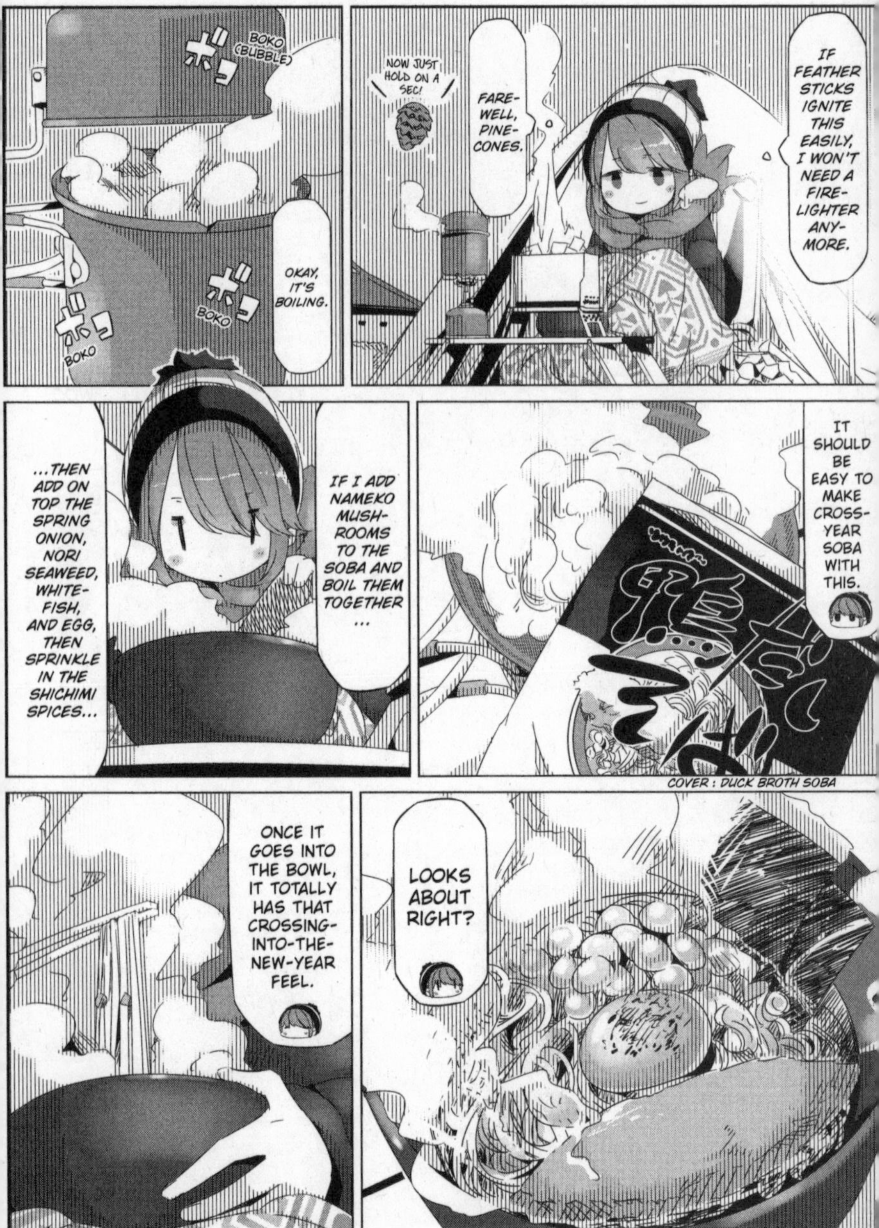
IF FEATHER STICKS IGNITE THIS EASILY, I WON'T NEED A FIRELIGHTER ANYMORE.
FAREWELL, PINECONES.
NOW JUST HOLD ON A SEC!
BOKO (BUBBLE)
BOKO
BOKO
OKAY, IT'S BOILING.
IT SHOULD BE EASY TO MAKE CROSS-YEAR SOBA WITH THIS.
COVER : DUCK BROTH SOBA
IF I ADD NAMEKO MUSHROOMS TO THE SOBA AND BOIL THEM TOGETHER...
...THEN ADD ON TOP THE SPRING ONION, NORI SEAWEED, WHITEFISH, AND EGG, THEN SPRINKLE IN THE SHICHIMI SPICES...
LOOKS ABOUT RIGHT?
DUCK BROTH NAMEKO SOBA
ONCE IT GOES INTO THE BOWL, IT TOTALLY HAS THAT CROSSING-INTO-THE-NEW-YEAR FEEL.

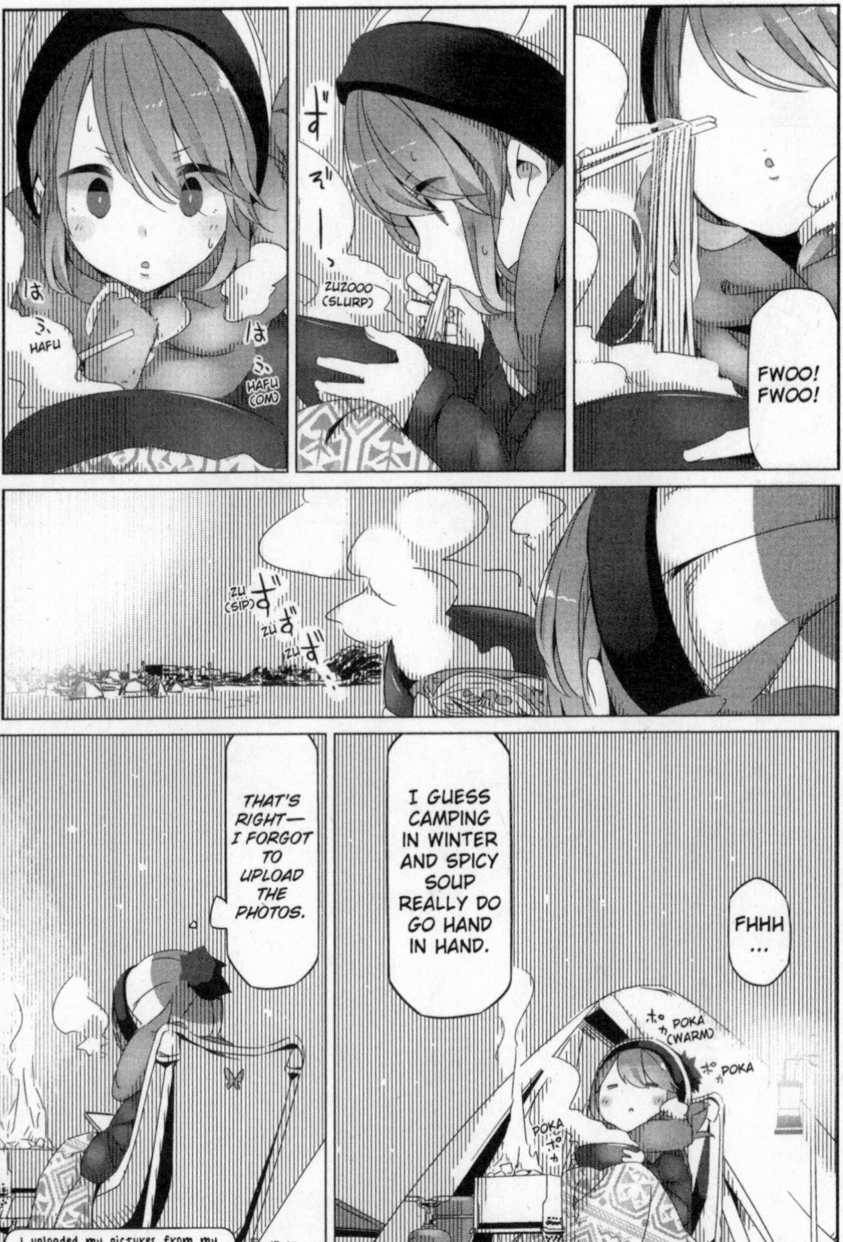
FWOO! FWOO!
ずずーっ
ZUZOOO (SLURP)
はふ、
HAFU
はふ
HAFU (OM)
ず
ZU (SIP)
ず
ZU
ず
ZU
FHHH...
I GUESS CAMPING IN WINTER AND SPICY SOUP REALLY DO GO HAND IN HAND.
ポカ
POKA (WARM)
ポカ
POKA
ポカ
POKA
THAT'S RIGHT— I FORGOT TO UPLOAD THE PHOTOS.
I uploaded my pictures from my New Year's Eve solo camp. http://vmm2/oa
17:40

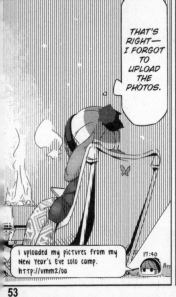

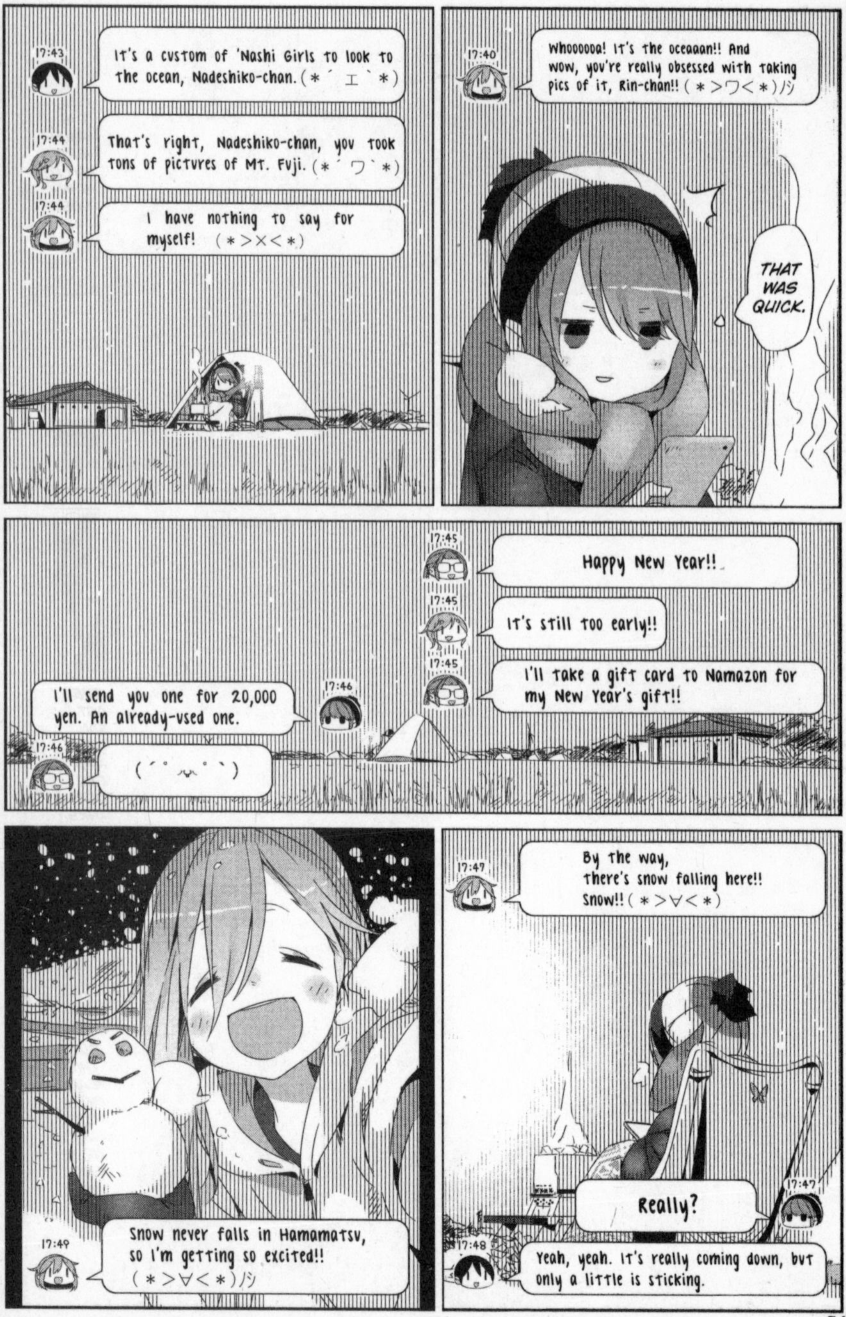
17:40
Whoooooa! It's the oceaaan!! And wow, you're really obsessed with taking pics of it, Rin-chan!! (＊>ワ<＊)ﾉｼ
THAT WAS QUICK.
17:43
It's a custom of 'Nashi Girls to look to the ocean, Nadeshiko-chan. (＊´ェ`＊)
17:44
That's right, Nadeshiko-chan, you took tons of pictures of Mt. Fuji. (＊´ワ`＊)
17:44
I have nothing to say for myself! (＊>×<＊)
17:45
Happy New Year!!
17:45
It's still too early!!
17:45
I'll take a gift card to Namazon for my New Year's gift!!
17:46
I'll send you one for 20,000 yen. An already-used one.
17:46
(´゜ω゜`)
17:47
By the way, there's snow falling here!! Snow!! (＊>∀<＊)
17:47
Really?
17:48
Yeah, yeah. It's really coming down, but only a little is sticking.
17:49
Snow never falls in Hamamatsu, so I'm getting so excited!! (＊>∀<＊)ﾉｼ

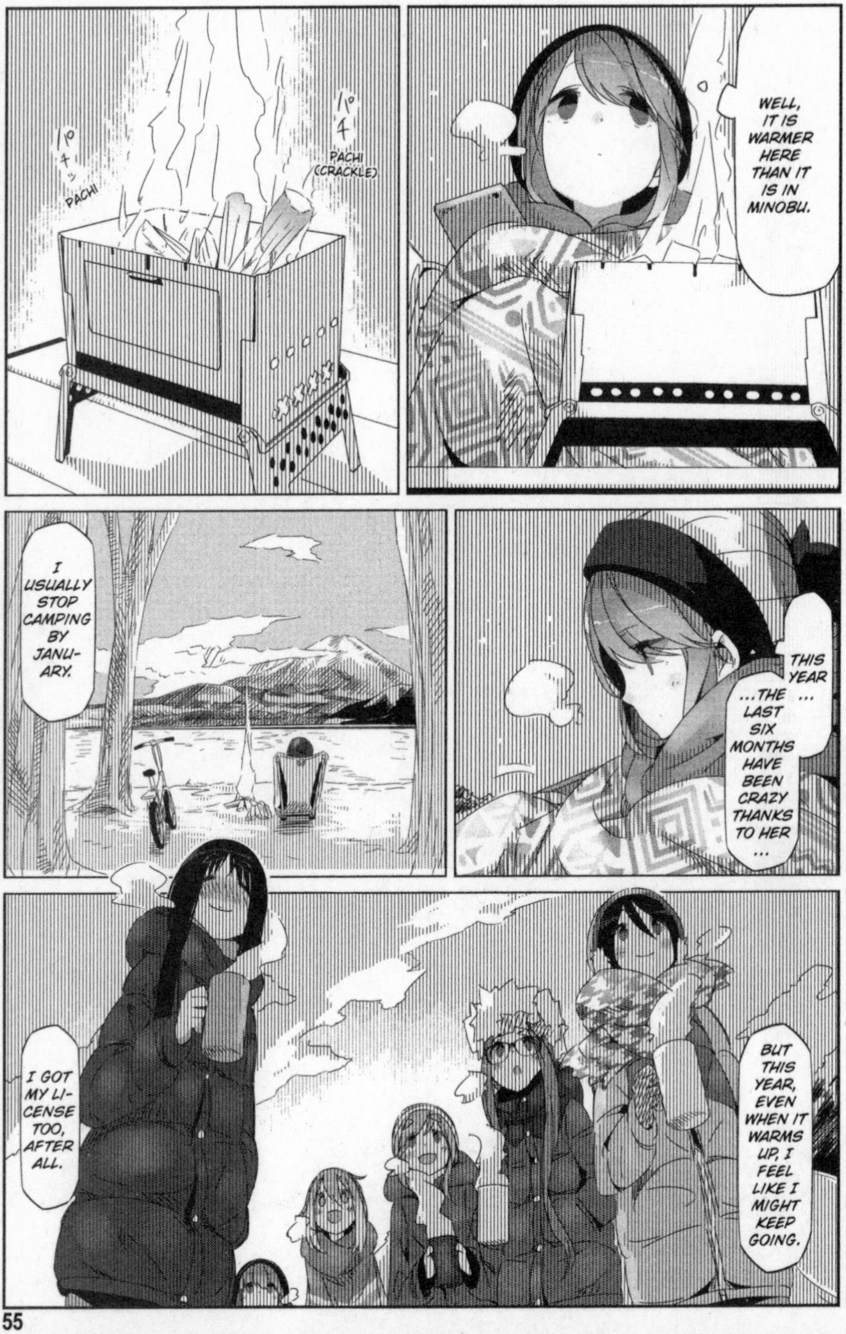
WELL, IT IS WARMER HERE THAN IT IS IN MINOBU.
パチ
PACHI (CRACKLE)
パチッ
PACHI
THIS YEAR ...
...THE LAST SIX MONTHS HAVE BEEN CRAZY THANKS TO HER ...
I USUALLY STOP CAMPING BY JANUARY.
BUT THIS YEAR, EVEN WHEN IT WARMS UP, I FEEL LIKE I MIGHT KEEP GOING.
I GOT MY LICENSE TOO, AFTER ALL.

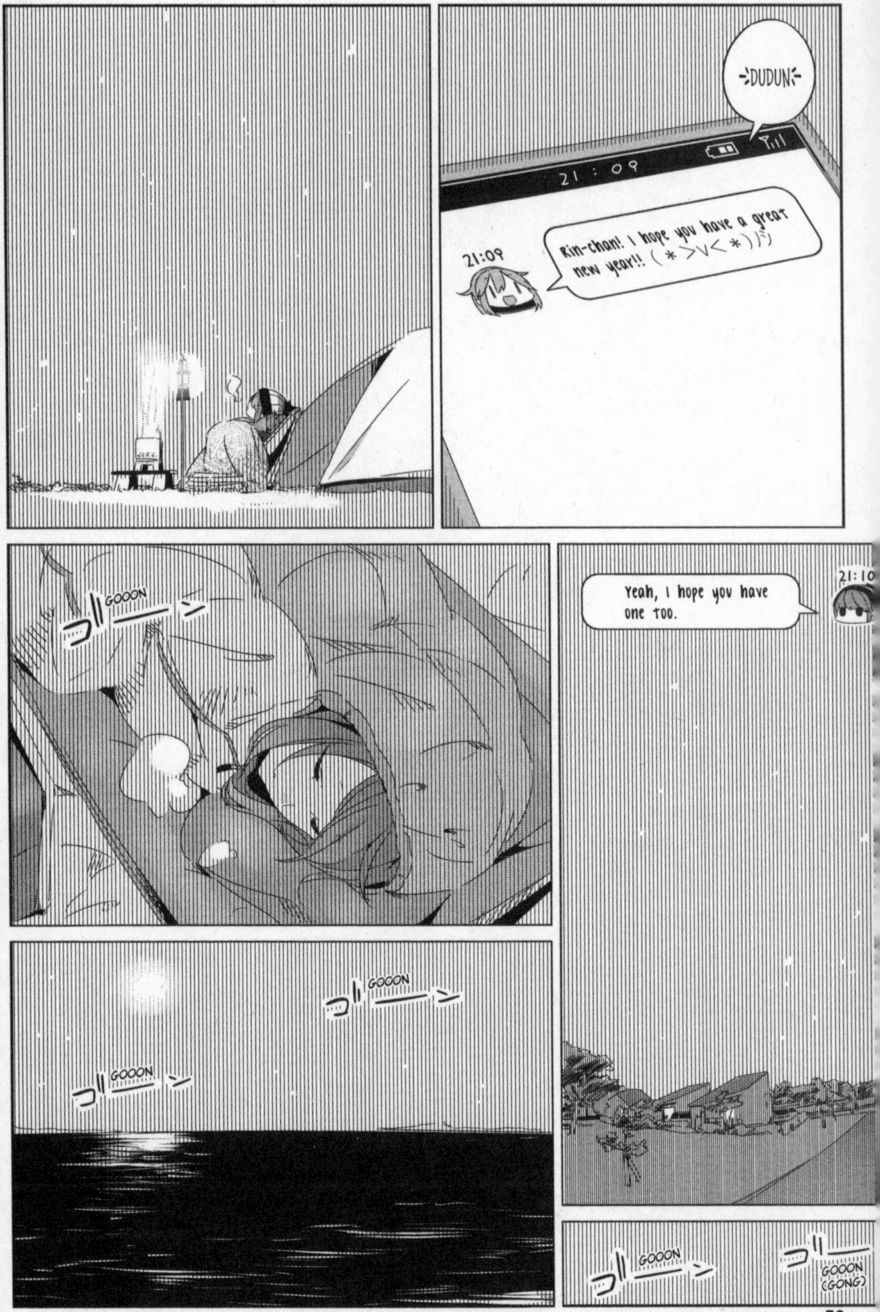
DUDUN
21:09
21:09
Rin-chan! I hope you have a great new year!! (*>v<*)ﾉｼ
21:10
Yeah, I hope you have one too.
GOOON
GOOON
GOOON
GOOON
GOOON (GONG)

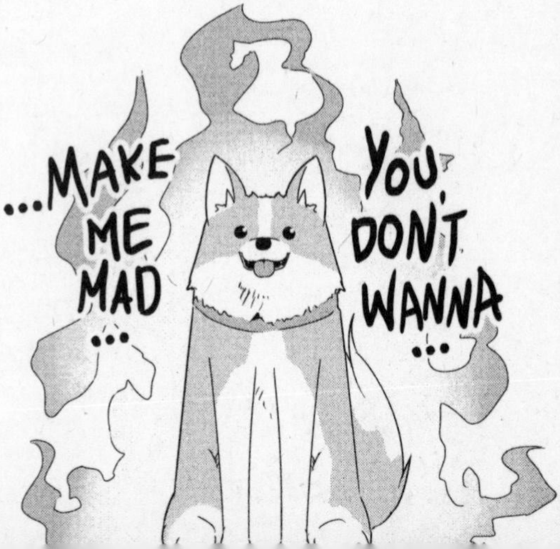
YOU DON'T WANNA...
...MAKE ME MAD...

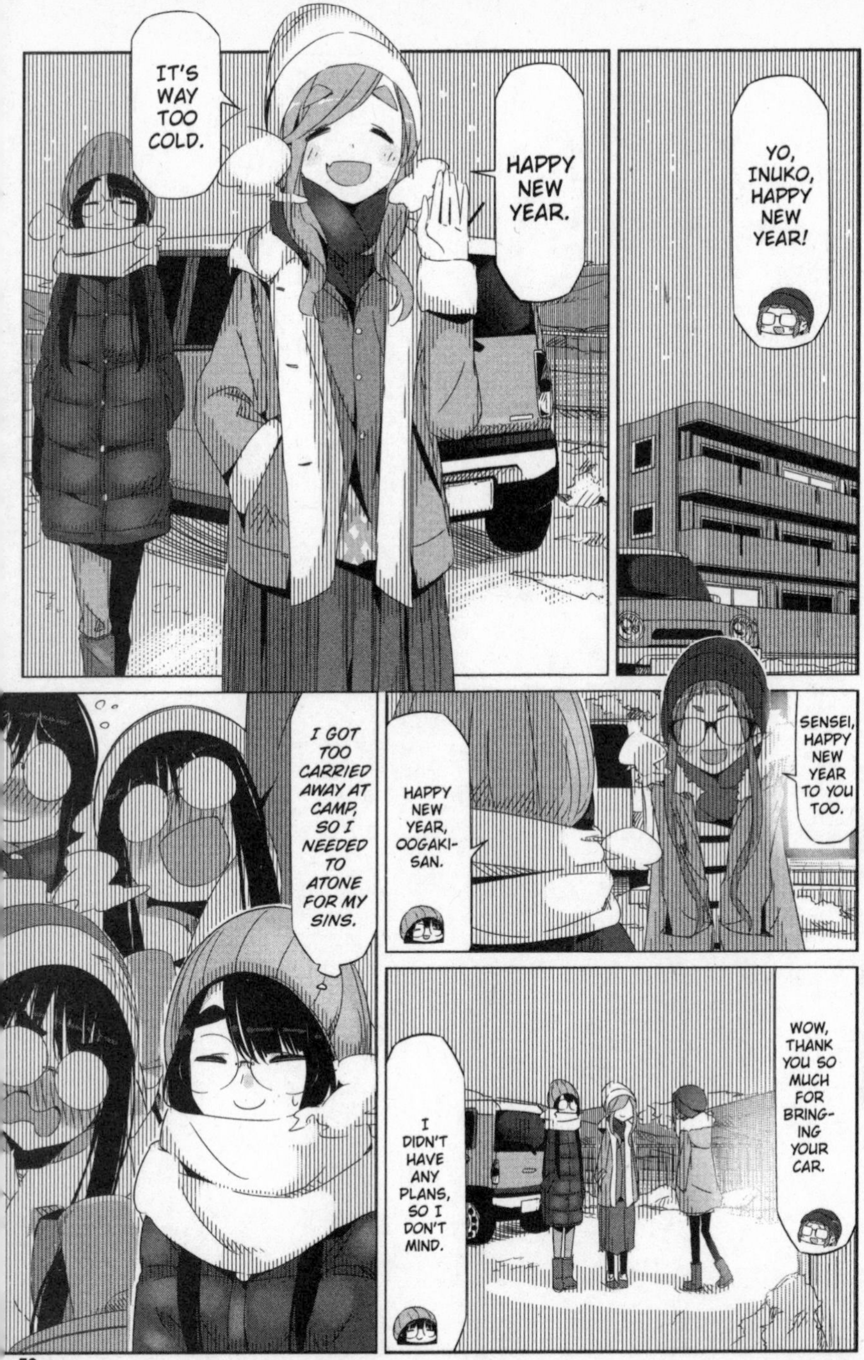
YO, INUKO, HAPPY NEW YEAR!
HAPPY NEW YEAR.
IT'S WAY TOO COLD.
SENSEI, HAPPY NEW YEAR TO YOU TOO.
HAPPY NEW YEAR, OOGAKI-SAN.
WOW, THANK YOU SO MUCH FOR BRINGING YOUR CAR.
I DIDN'T HAVE ANY PLANS, SO I DON'T MIND.
I GOT TOO CARRIED AWAY AT CAMP, SO I NEEDED TO ATONE FOR MY SINS.

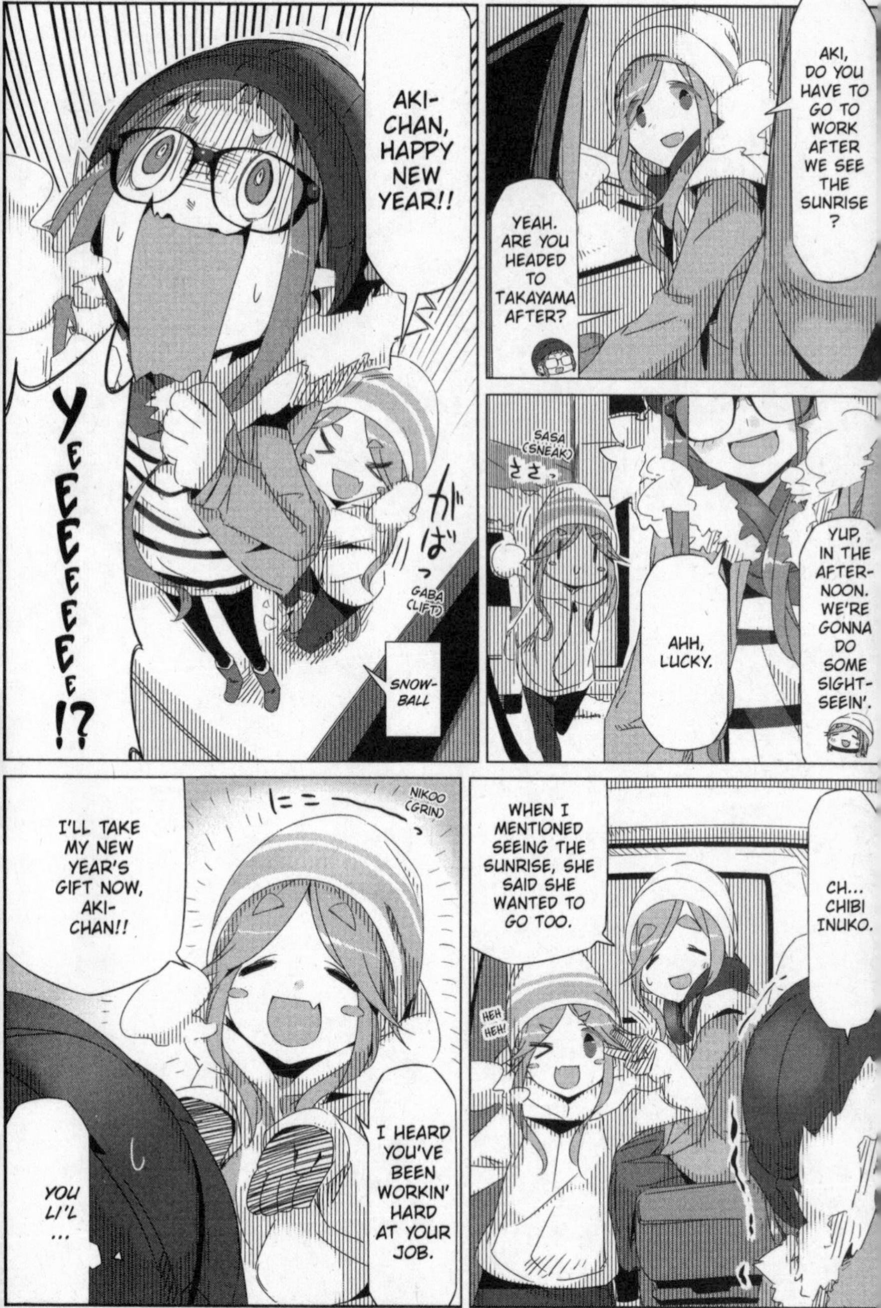
AKI, DO YOU HAVE TO GO TO WORK AFTER WE SEE THE SUNRISE?
YEAH. ARE YOU HEADED TO TAKAYAMA AFTER?
ささっ
SASA (SNEAK)
YUP, IN THE AFTERNOON. WE'RE GONNA DO SOME SIGHT-SEEIN'.
AHH, LUCKY.
AKI-CHAN, HAPPY NEW YEAR!!
がばっ
GABA (LIFT)
SNOW-BALL
YEEEEEEEE!?
CH... CHIBI INUKO.
WHEN I MENTIONED SEEING THE SUNRISE, SHE SAID SHE WANTED TO GO TOO.
HEH HEH!
にこーっ
NIKOO (GRIN)
I'LL TAKE MY NEW YEAR'S GIFT NOW, AKI-CHAN!!
I HEARD YOU'VE BEEN WORKIN' HARD AT YOUR JOB.
YOU LI'L...

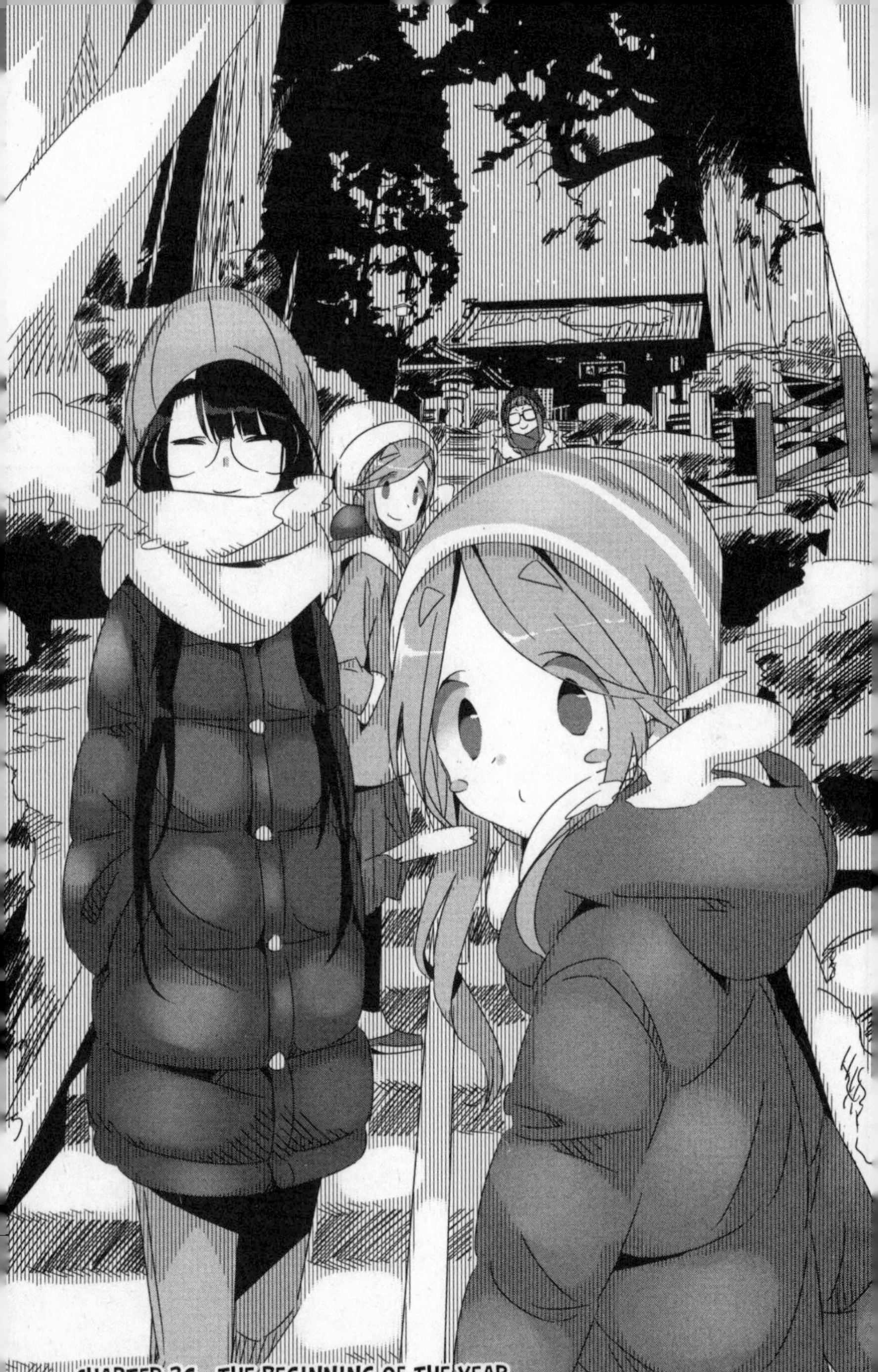

CHAPTER 26 THE BEGINNING OF THE YEAR

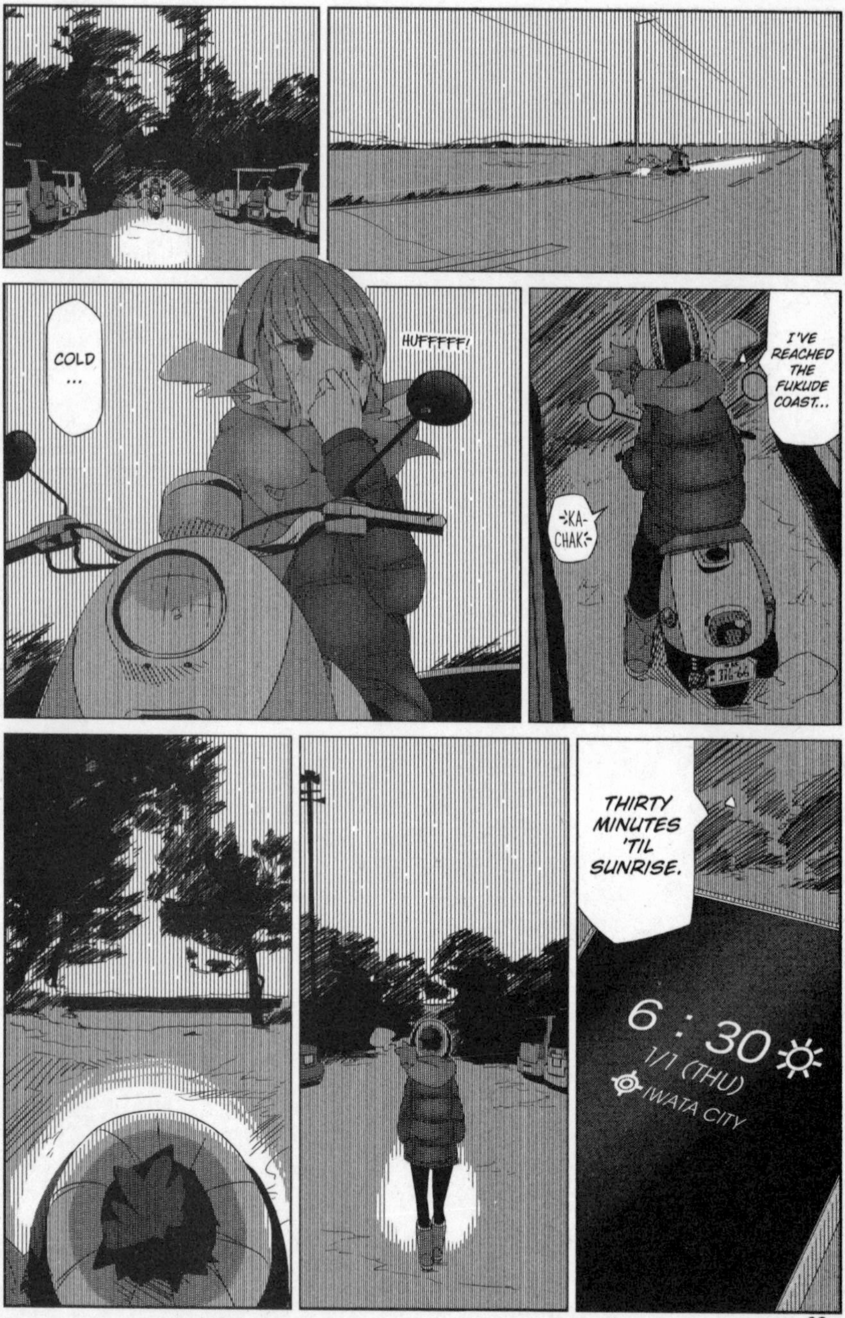
I'VE REACHED THE FUKUDE COAST...
-KA-CHAK-
HUFFFFF!
COLD ...
THIRTY MINUTES 'TIL SUNRISE.
6 : 30
1/1 (THU)
IWATA CITY

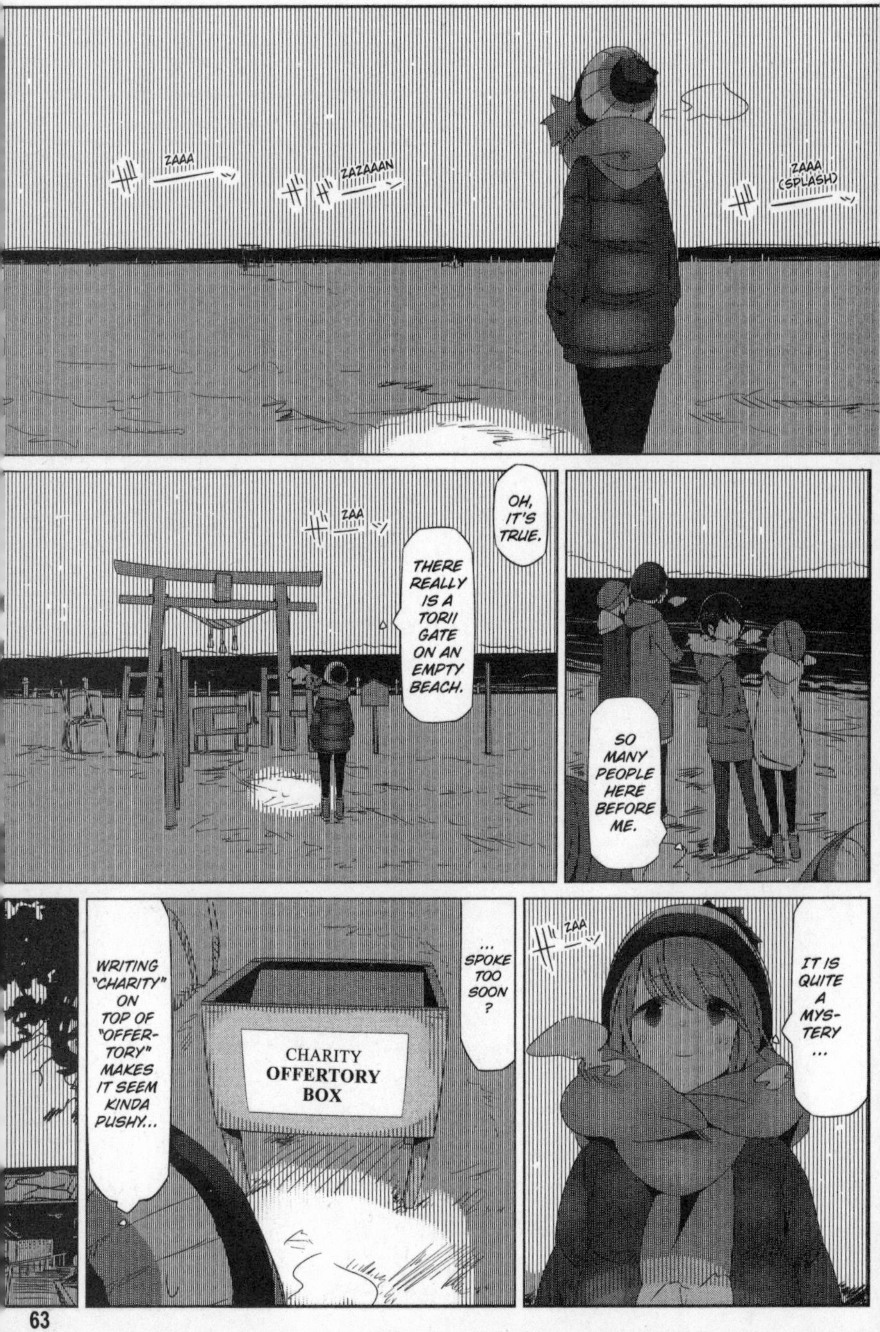
ZAAA (SPLASH)
ZAZAAAN
ZAAA
SO MANY PEOPLE HERE BEFORE ME.
OH, IT'S TRUE.
THERE REALLY IS A TORII GATE ON AN EMPTY BEACH.
ZAA
ZAA
IT IS QUITE A MYSTERY...
...SPOKE TOO SOON?
CHARITY OFFERTORY BOX
WRITING "CHARITY" ON TOP OF "OFFERTORY" MAKES IT SEEM KINDA PUSHY...

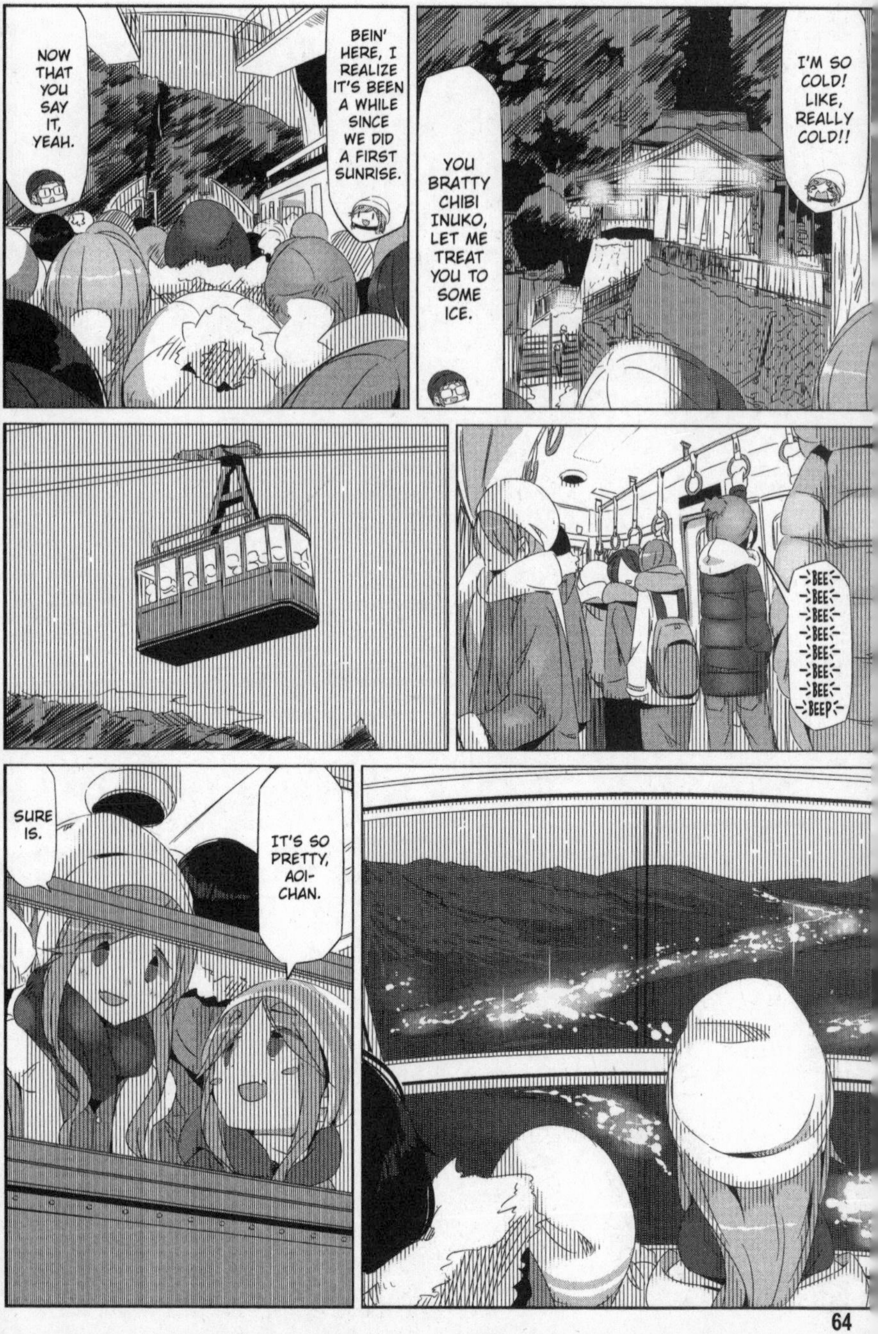
I'M SO COLD! LIKE, REALLY COLD!!
YOU BRATTY CHIBI INUKO, LET ME TREAT YOU TO SOME ICE.
BEIN' HERE, I REALIZE IT'S BEEN A WHILE SINCE WE DID A FIRST SUNRISE.
NOW THAT YOU SAY IT, YEAH.
BEE BEE BEE BEE BEE BEE BEE BEEP
IT'S SO PRETTY, AOI-CHAN.
SURE IS.

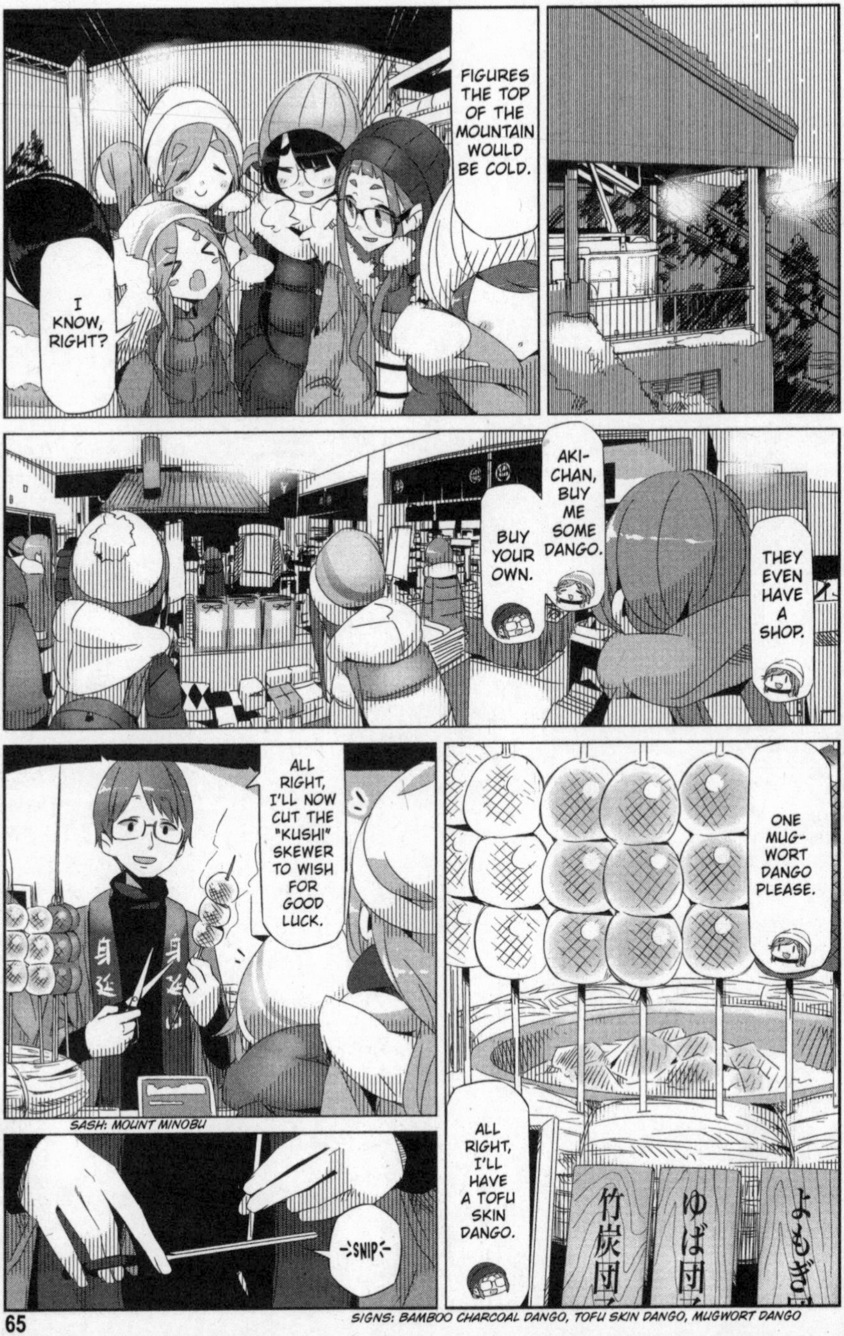
FIGURES THE TOP OF THE MOUNTAIN WOULD BE COLD.
I KNOW, RIGHT?
THEY EVEN HAVE A SHOP.
AKI-CHAN, BUY ME SOME DANGO.
BUY YOUR OWN.
ONE MUG-WORT DANGO PLEASE.
ALL RIGHT, I'LL HAVE A TOFU SKIN DANGO.
よもぎ
ゆば団
竹炭団
ALL RIGHT, I'LL NOW CUT THE "KUSHI" SKEWER TO WISH FOR GOOD LUCK.
SNIP

SASH: MOUNT MINOBU

SIGNS: BAMBOO CHARCOAL DANGO, TOFU SKIN DANGO, MUGWORT DANGO

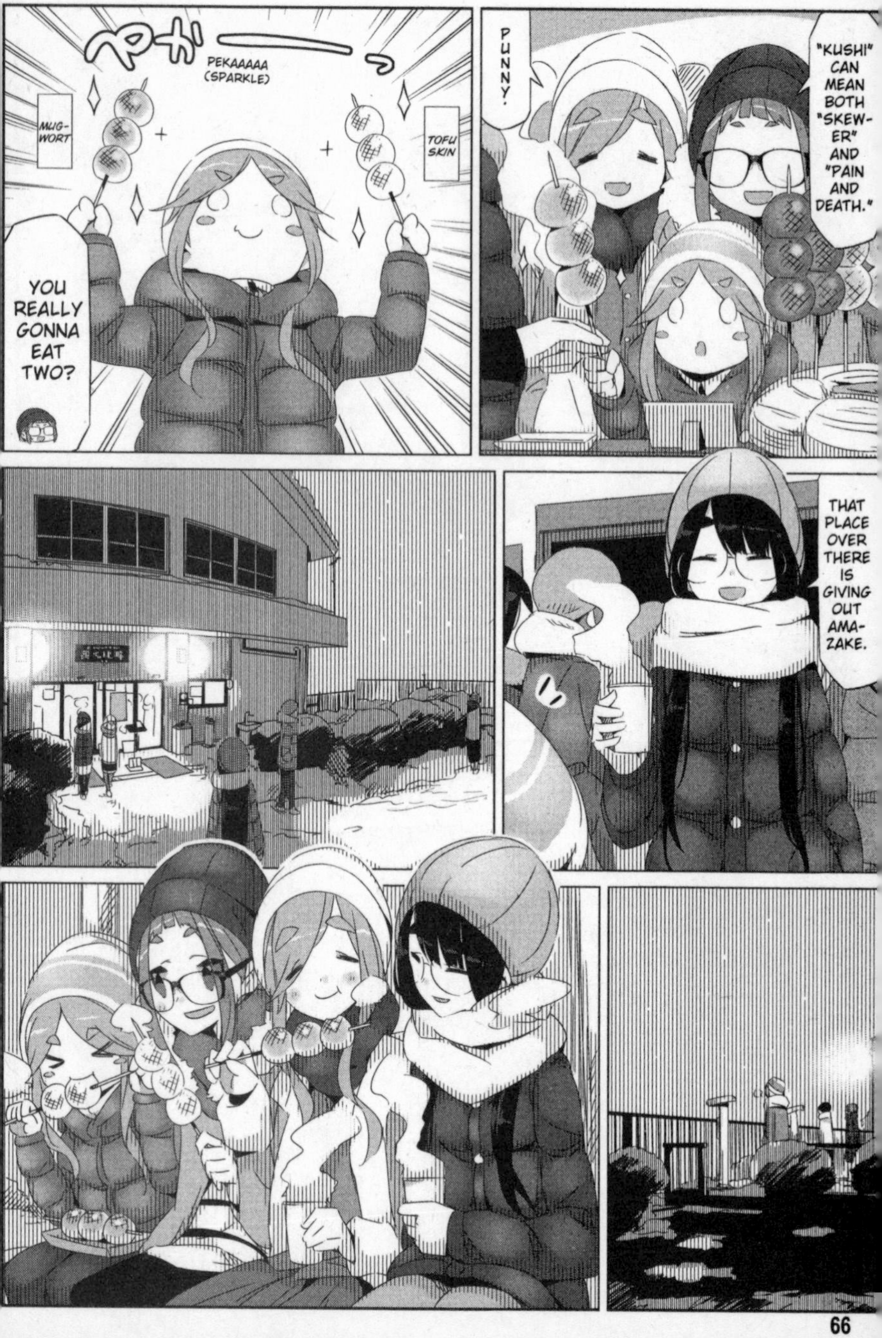
"KUSHI" CAN MEAN BOTH "SKEWER" AND "PAIN AND DEATH."
PUNNY.
PEKAAAAA (SPARKLE)
TOFU SKIN
MUGWORT
YOU REALLY GONNA EAT TWO?
THAT PLACE OVER THERE IS GIVING OUT AMAZAKE.

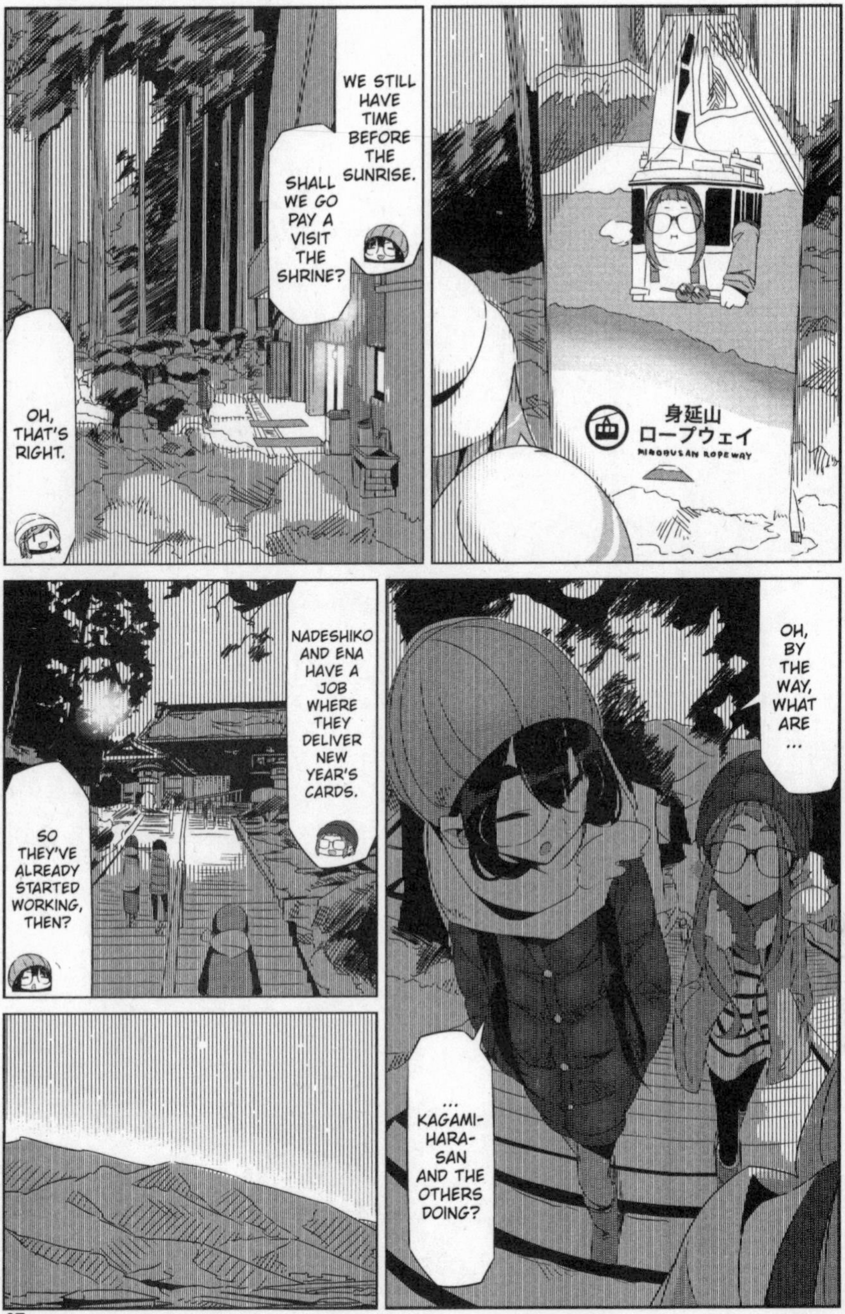
身延山
ロープウェイ
MINOBUSAN ROPEWAY
WE STILL HAVE TIME BEFORE THE SUNRISE.
SHALL WE GO PAY A VISIT THE SHRINE?
OH, THAT'S RIGHT.
OH, BY THE WAY, WHAT ARE ...
... KAGAMI-HARA-SAN AND THE OTHERS DOING?
NADESHIKO AND ENA HAVE A JOB WHERE THEY DELIVER NEW YEAR'S CARDS.
SO THEY'VE ALREADY STARTED WORKING, THEN?

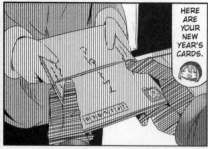

HERE ARE YOUR NEW YEAR'S CARDS.

HAPPY...

..NEW YEAR.

AND NEXT...

...IS FUJITA-SAN!

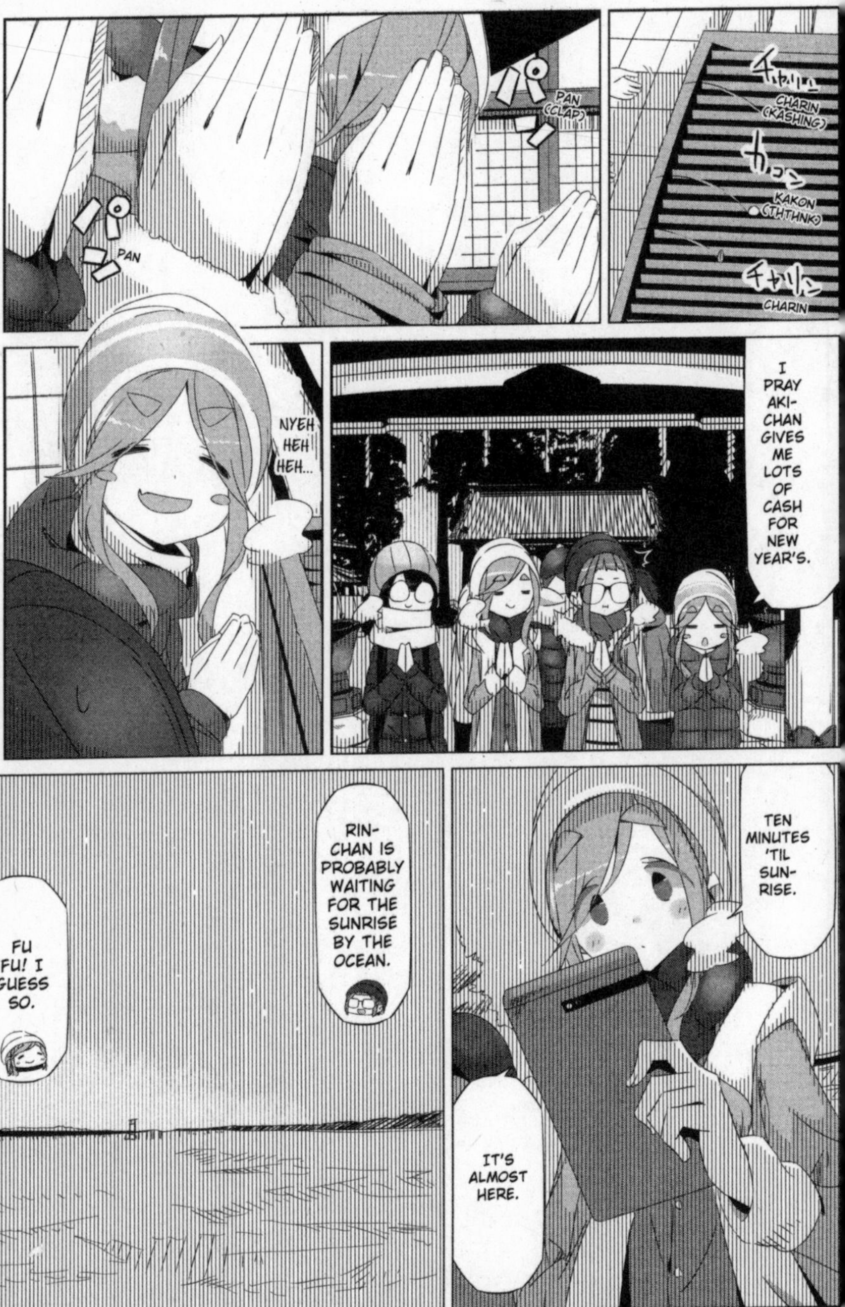
チャリン
CHARIN (KASHING)
カコン
KAKON (THTHNK)
チャリン
CHARIN
PAN (CLAP)
PAN
I PRAY AKI-CHAN GIVES ME LOTS OF CASH FOR NEW YEAR'S.
NYEH HEH HEH...
TEN MINUTES 'TIL SUNRISE.
IT'S ALMOST HERE.
RIN-CHAN IS PROBABLY WAITING FOR THE SUNRISE BY THE OCEAN.
FU FU! I GUESS SO.

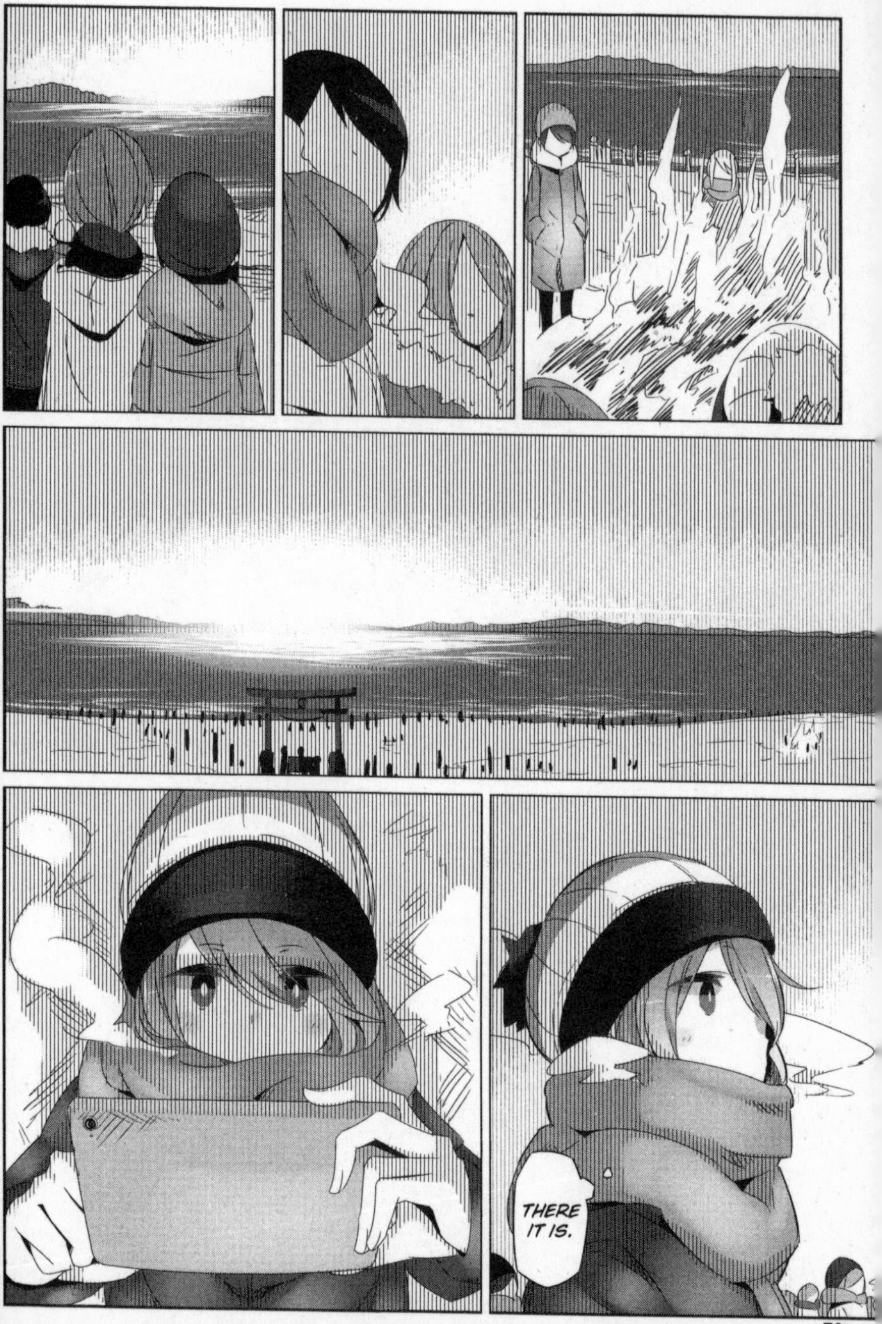
THERE IT IS.

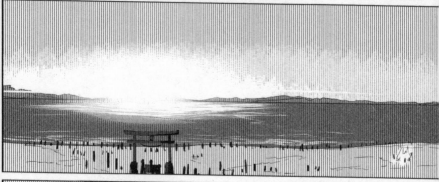

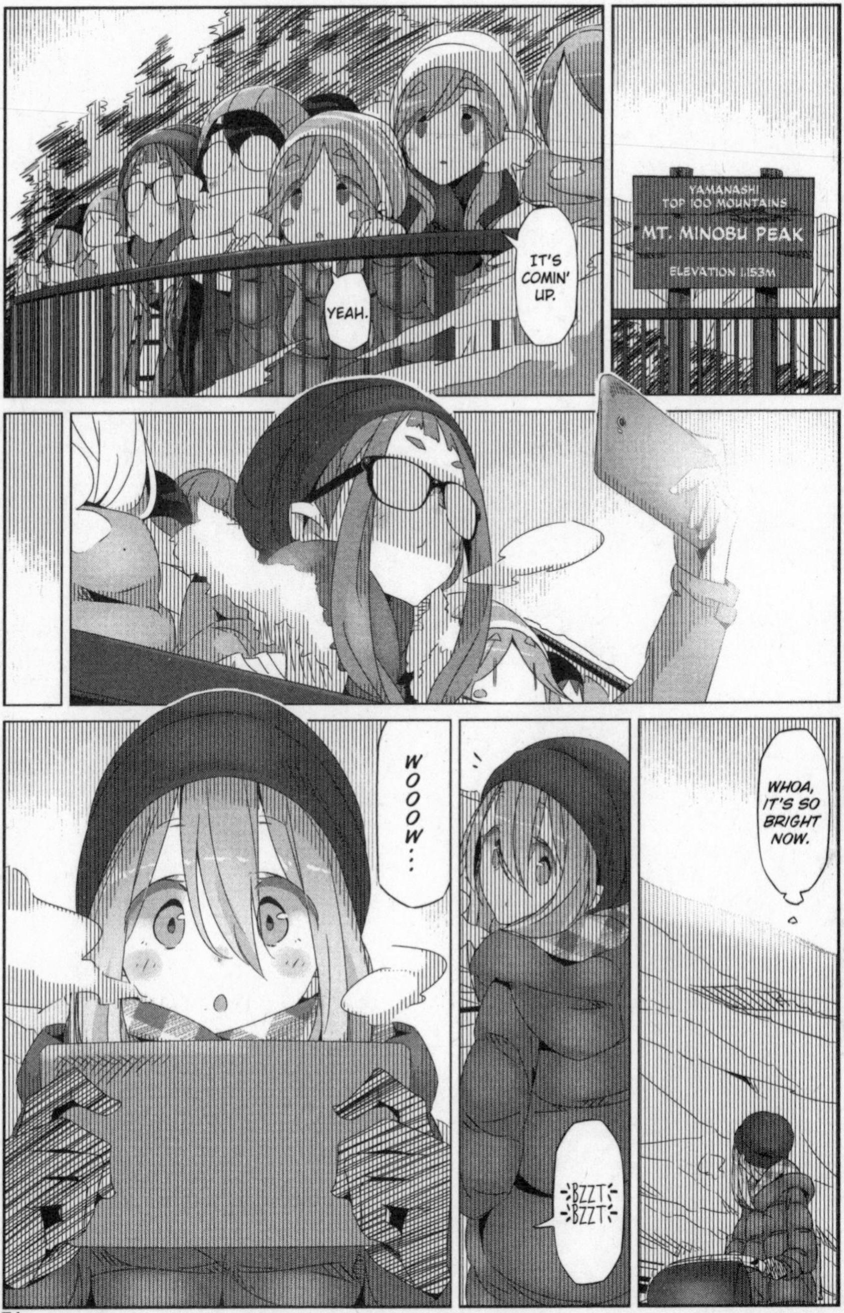
YAMANASHI TOP 100 MOUNTAINS
MT. MINOBU PEAK
ELEVATION 1,153M
IT'S COMIN' UP.
YEAH.
WHOA, IT'S SO BRIGHT NOW.
BZZT BZZT
WOOOW...

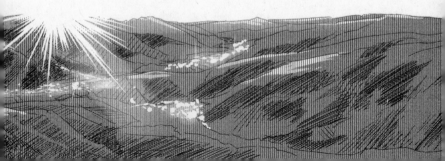

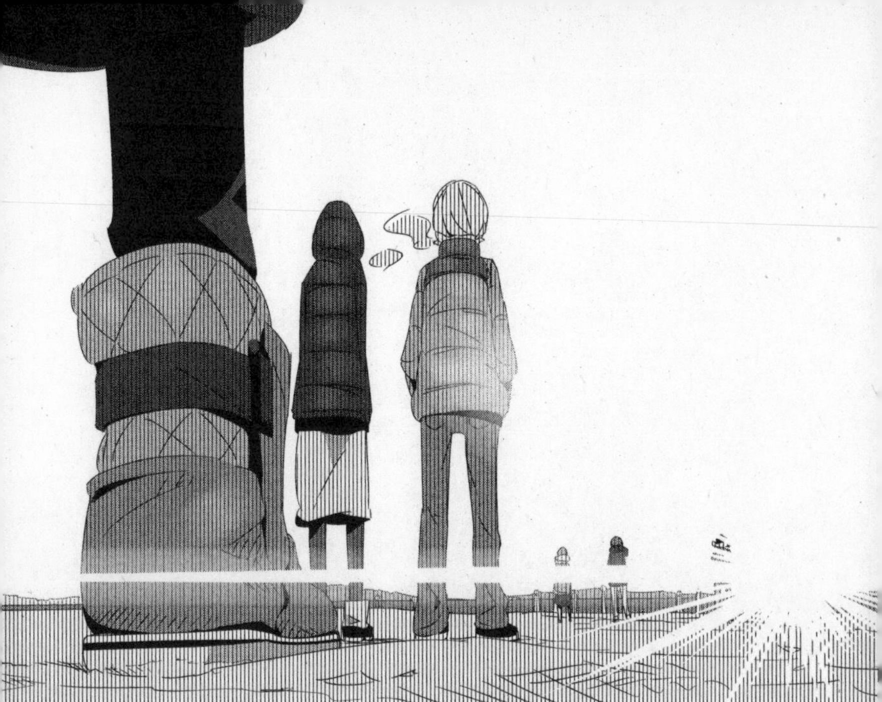
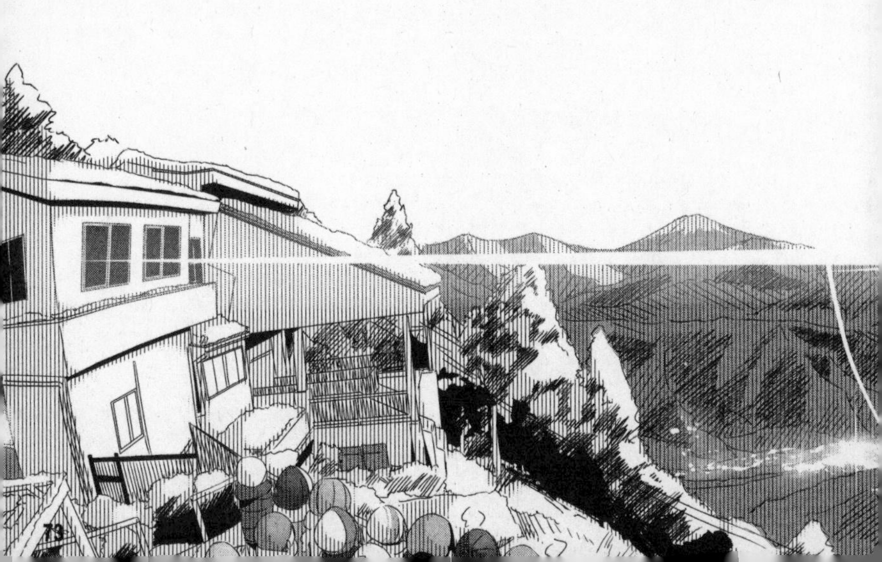

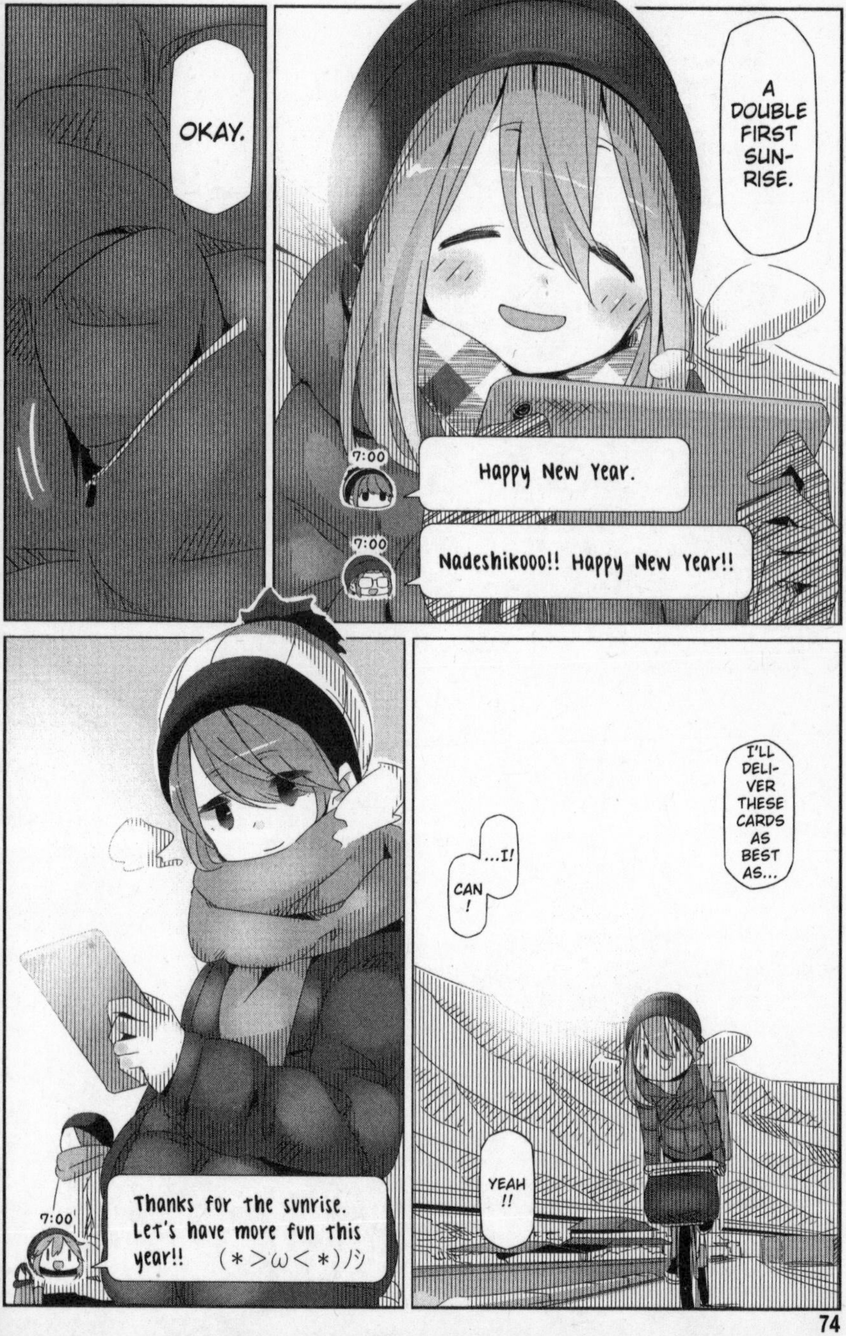
A DOUBLE FIRST SUN-RISE.
7:00
Happy New Year.
7:00
Nadeshikooo!! Happy New Year!!
OKAY.
I'LL DELI-VER THESE CARDS AS BEST AS...
...I!
CAN!
YEAH!!
7:00
Thanks for the sunrise. Let's have more fun this year!! (*>ω<*)ノシ

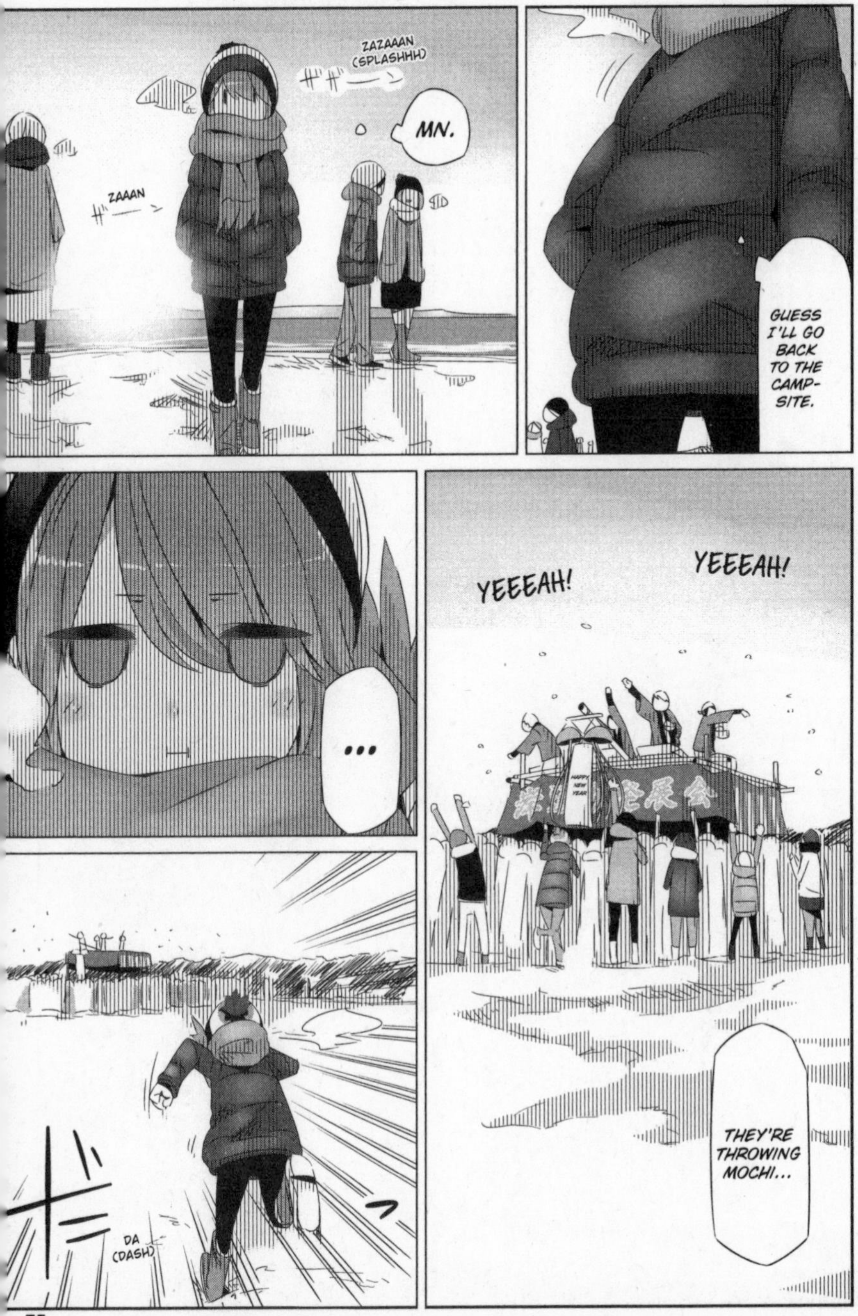
GUESS I'LL GO BACK TO THE CAMP-SITE.
ZAZAAAN (SPLASHHH)
MN.
ZAAAN
YEEEAH!
YEEEAH!
THEY'RE THROWING MOCHI...
...
DA (DASH)

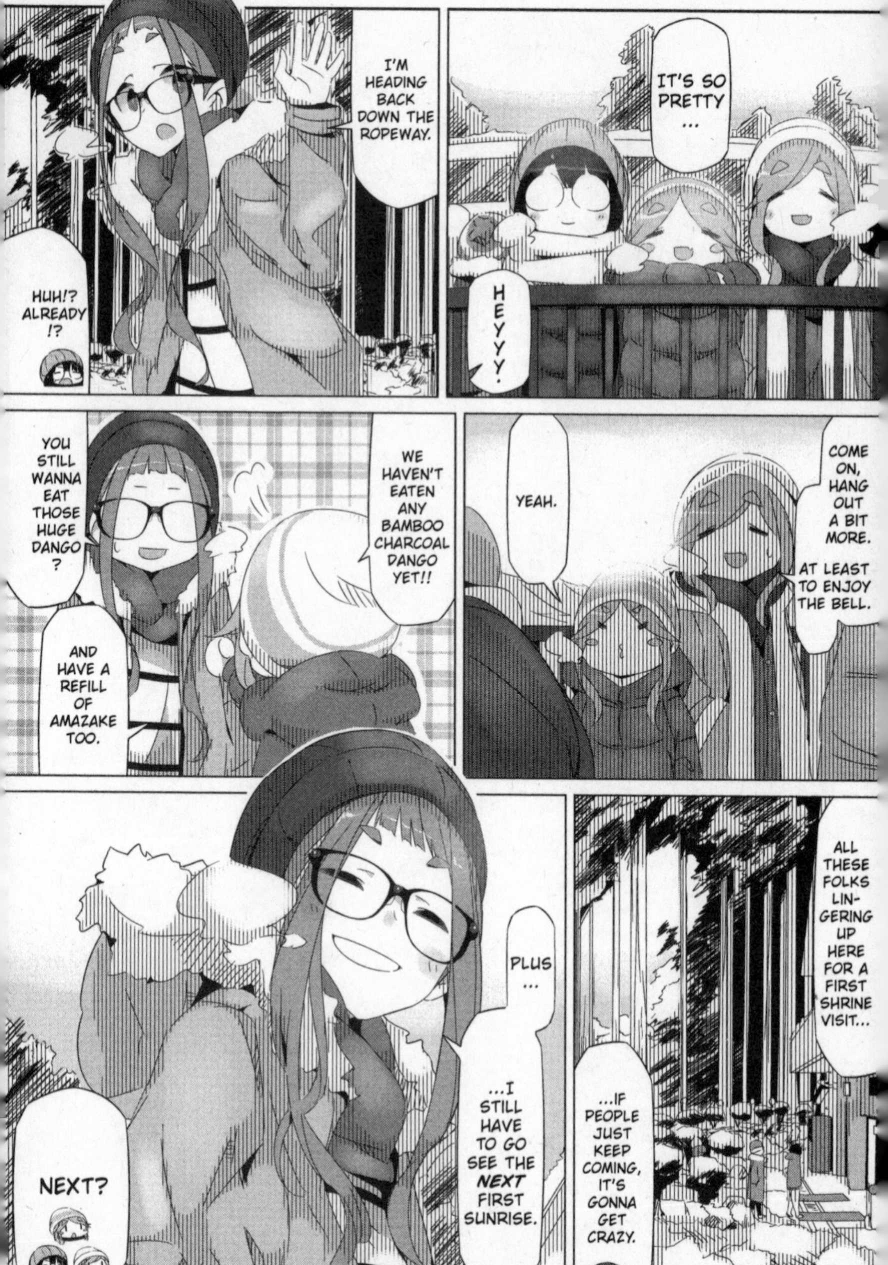
IT'S SO PRETTY ...
HEYYY.
I'M HEADING BACK DOWN THE ROPEWAY.
HUH!? ALREADY !?
COME ON, HANG OUT A BIT MORE.
AT LEAST TO ENJOY THE BELL.
YEAH.
WE HAVEN'T EATEN ANY BAMBOO CHARCOAL DANGO YET!!
YOU STILL WANNA EAT THOSE HUGE DANGO ?
AND HAVE A REFILL OF AMAZAKE TOO.
ALL THESE FOLKS LIN-GERING UP HERE FOR A FIRST SHRINE VISIT...
...IF PEOPLE JUST KEEP COMING, IT'S GONNA GET CRAZY.
PLUS ...
...I STILL HAVE TO GO SEE THE *NEXT* FIRST SUNRISE.
NEXT?

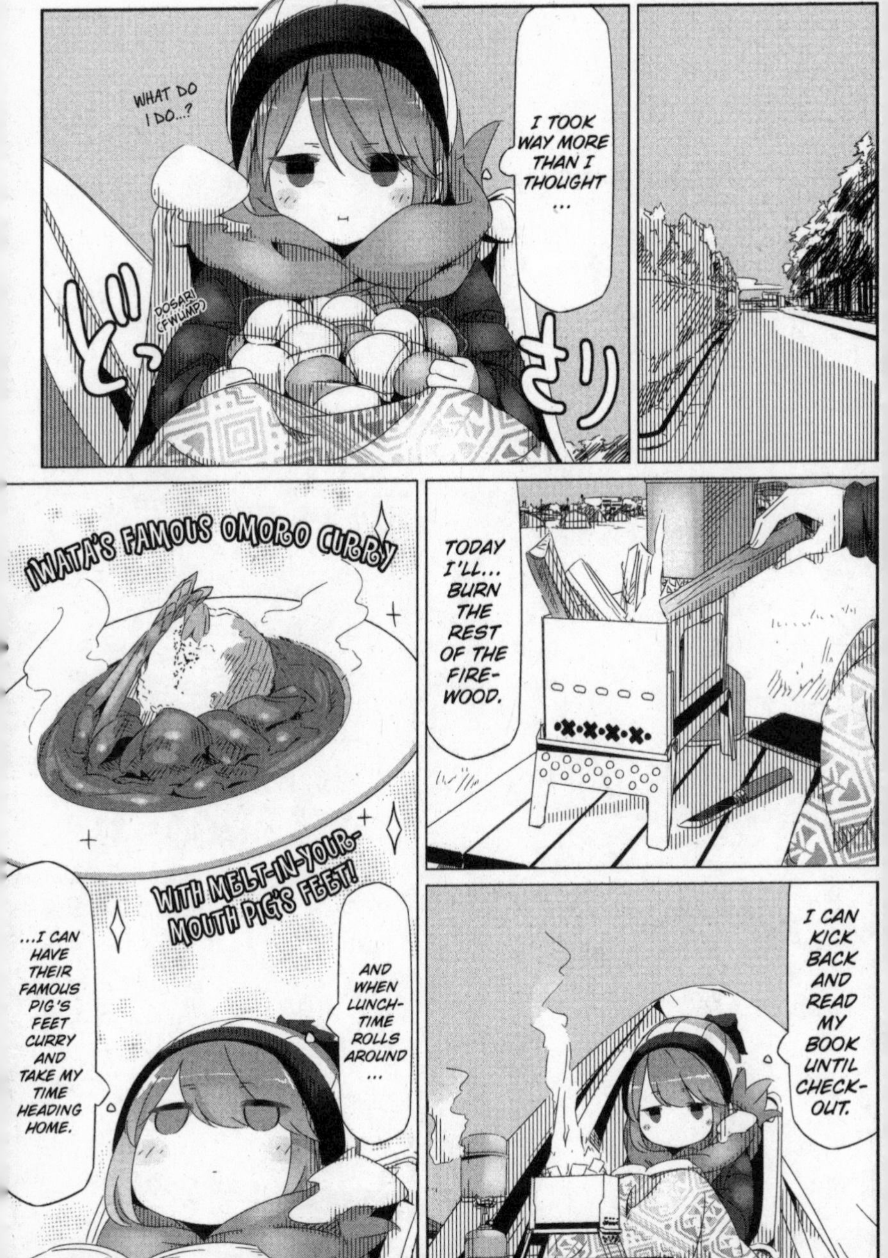
I TOOK WAY MORE THAN I THOUGHT...
WHAT DO I DO...?
どさり
DOSARI (FWUMP)
TODAY I'LL... BURN THE REST OF THE FIRE-WOOD.
I CAN KICK BACK AND READ MY BOOK UNTIL CHECK-OUT.
AND WHEN LUNCH-TIME ROLLS AROUND...
...I CAN HAVE THEIR FAMOUS PIG'S FEET CURRY AND TAKE MY TIME HEADING HOME.
IWATA'S FAMOUS OMORO CURRY
WITH MELT-IN-YOUR-MOUTH PIG'S FEET!

WHERE IS THAT FRAGRANT AROMA COMING FROM...?

FUWAAA (WAFT)

WOW...

OH, I GUESS A PIZZA FOOD TRUCK COMES HERE.

WE HAVE PIZZA FOR SALE. COME GET SOME!

GOKURI (GULP)

MARGHERITA... POT-AU-FEU...

LOTS O' CHEESE MARGHERITA

SMALL	800 YEN
HALF	450 YEN

LOCAL VEGETABLE POT-AU-FEU

350 YEN

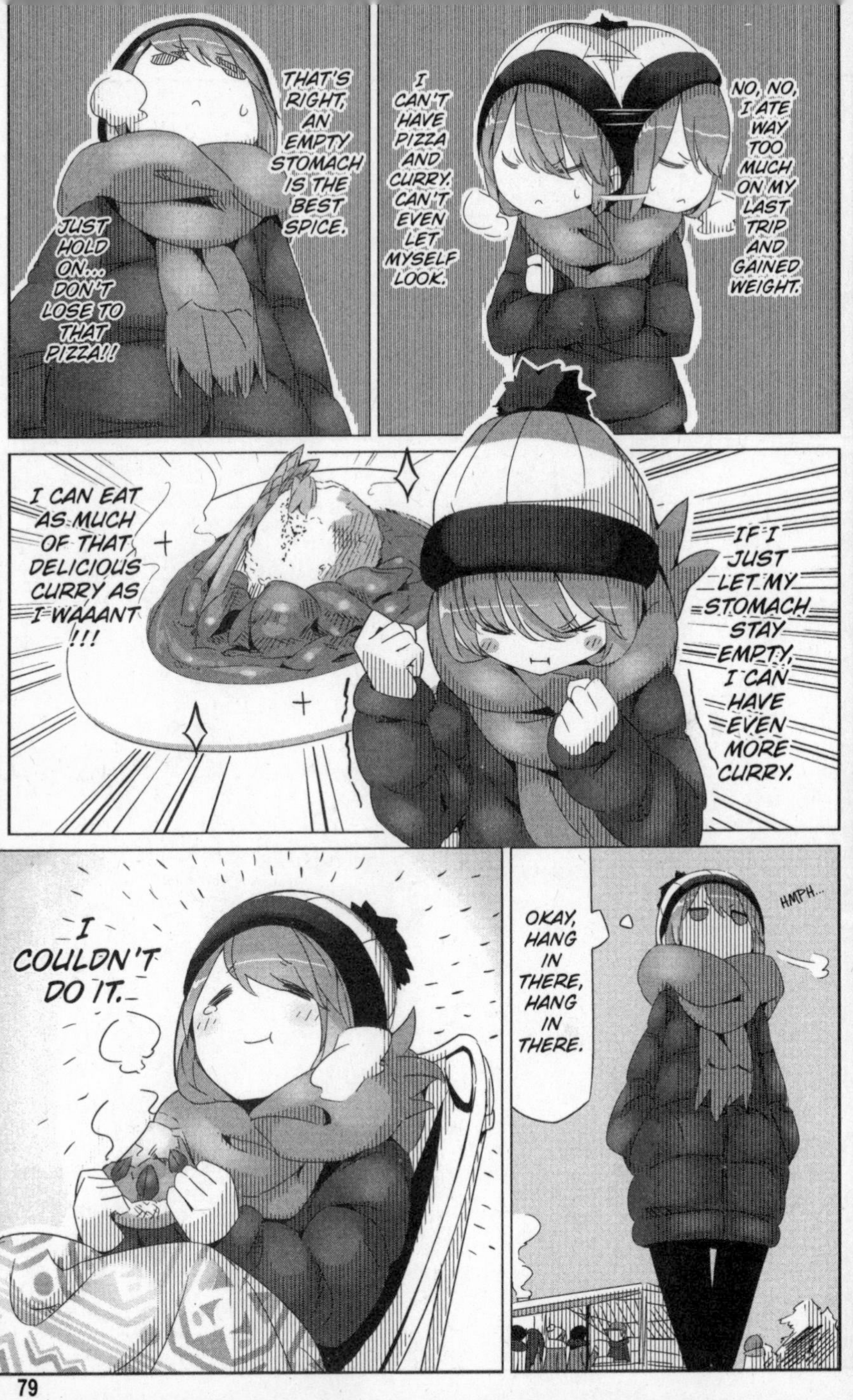
NO, NO, I ATE WAY TOO MUCH ON MY LAST TRIP AND GAINED WEIGHT.
I CAN'T HAVE PIZZA AND CURRY. CAN'T EVEN LET MYSELF LOOK.
THAT'S RIGHT, AN EMPTY STOMACH IS THE BEST SPICE.
JUST HOLD ON... DON'T LOSE TO THAT PIZZA!!
IF I JUST LET MY STOMACH STAY EMPTY, I CAN HAVE EVEN MORE CURRY.
I CAN EAT AS MUCH OF THAT DELICIOUS CURRY AS I WAAANT!!!
HMPH...
OKAY, HANG IN THERE, HANG IN THERE.
I COULDN'T DO IT.

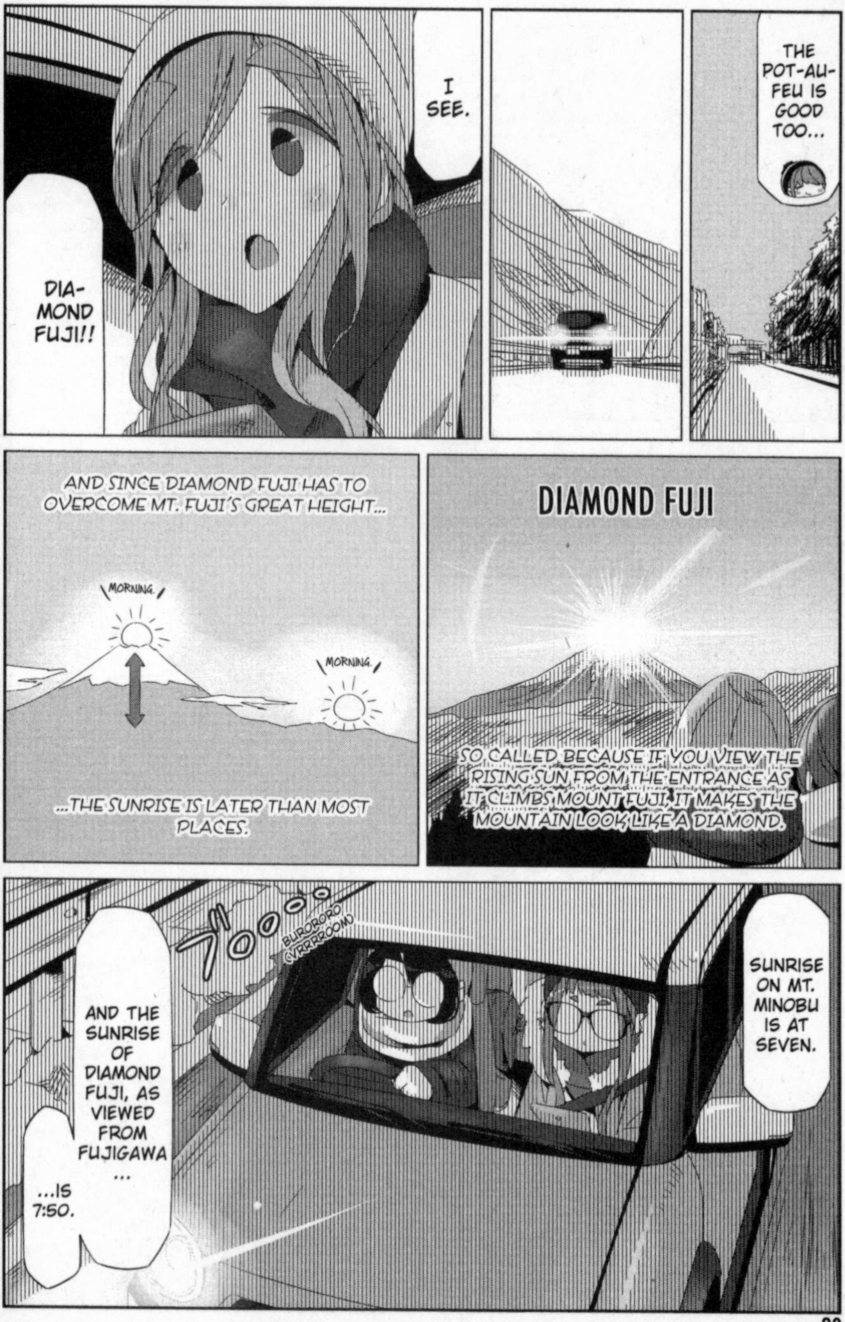
THE POT-AU-FEU IS GOOD TOO...
I SEE.
DIAMOND FUJI!!
DIAMOND FUJI
SO CALLED BECAUSE IF YOU VIEW THE RISING SUN FROM THE ENTRANCE AS IT CLIMBS MOUNT FUJI, IT MAKES THE MOUNTAIN LOOK LIKE A DIAMOND.
AND SINCE DIAMOND FUJI HAS TO OVERCOME MT. FUJI'S GREAT HEIGHT...
MORNING.
MORNING.
...THE SUNRISE IS LATER THAN MOST PLACES.
SUNRISE ON MT. MINOBU IS AT SEVEN.
BURORORO (VRRRROOM)
AND THE SUNRISE OF DIAMOND FUJI, AS VIEWED FROM FUJIGAWA...
...IS 7:50.

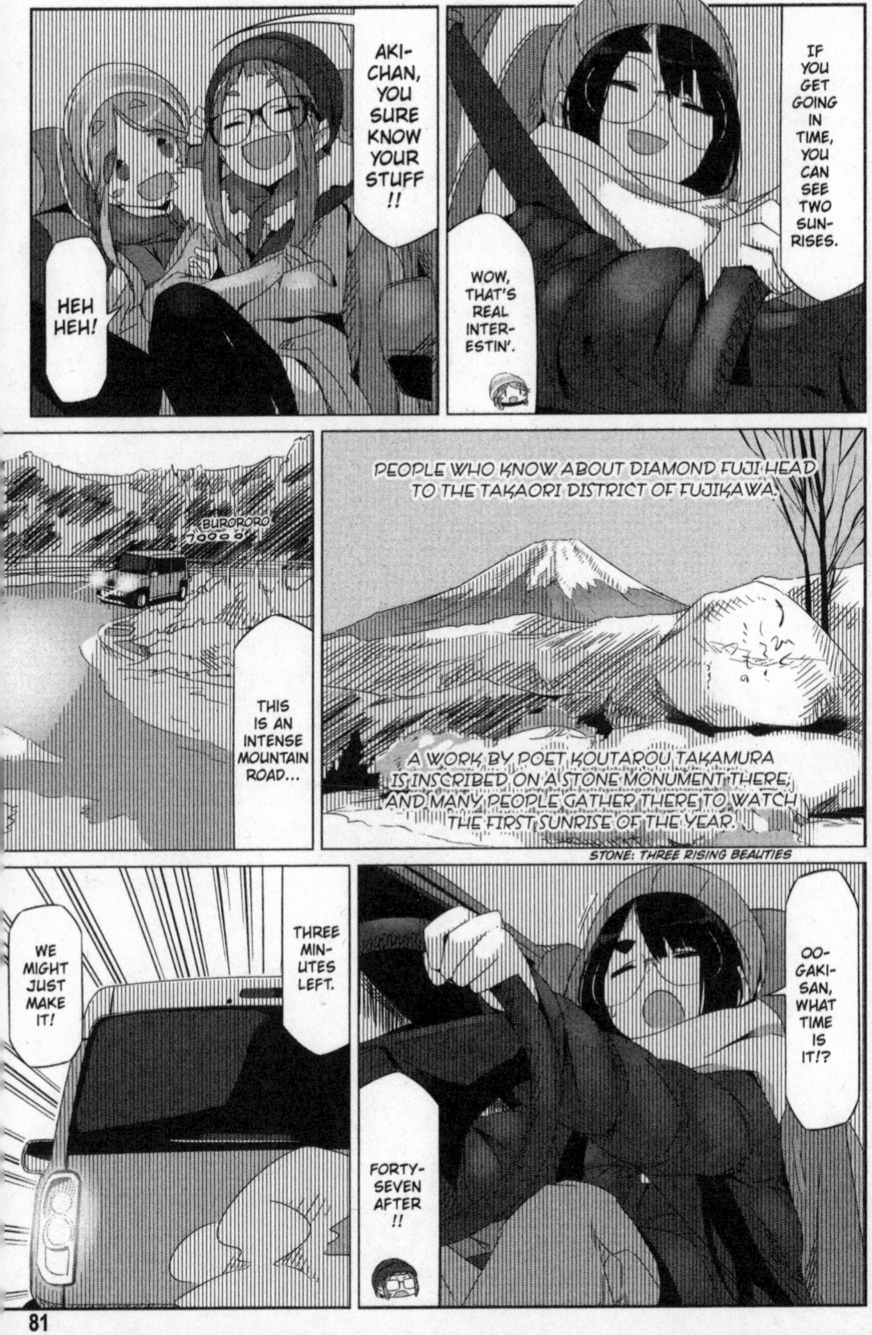
IF YOU GET GOING IN TIME, YOU CAN SEE TWO SUN-RISES.
WOW, THAT'S REAL INTER-ESTIN'.
AKI-CHAN, YOU SURE KNOW YOUR STUFF!!
HEH HEH!
PEOPLE WHO KNOW ABOUT DIAMOND FUJI HEAD TO THE TAKAORI DISTRICT OF FUJIKAWA.
A WORK BY POET KOUTAROU TAKAMURA IS INSCRIBED ON A STONE MONUMENT THERE, AND MANY PEOPLE GATHER THERE TO WATCH THE FIRST SUNRISE OF THE YEAR.
STONE: THREE RISING BEAUTIES
BURORORO
THIS IS AN INTENSE MOUNTAIN ROAD...
OO-GAKI-SAN, WHAT TIME IS IT!?
FORTY-SEVEN AFTER!!
THREE MIN-UTES LEFT.
WE MIGHT JUST MAKE IT!

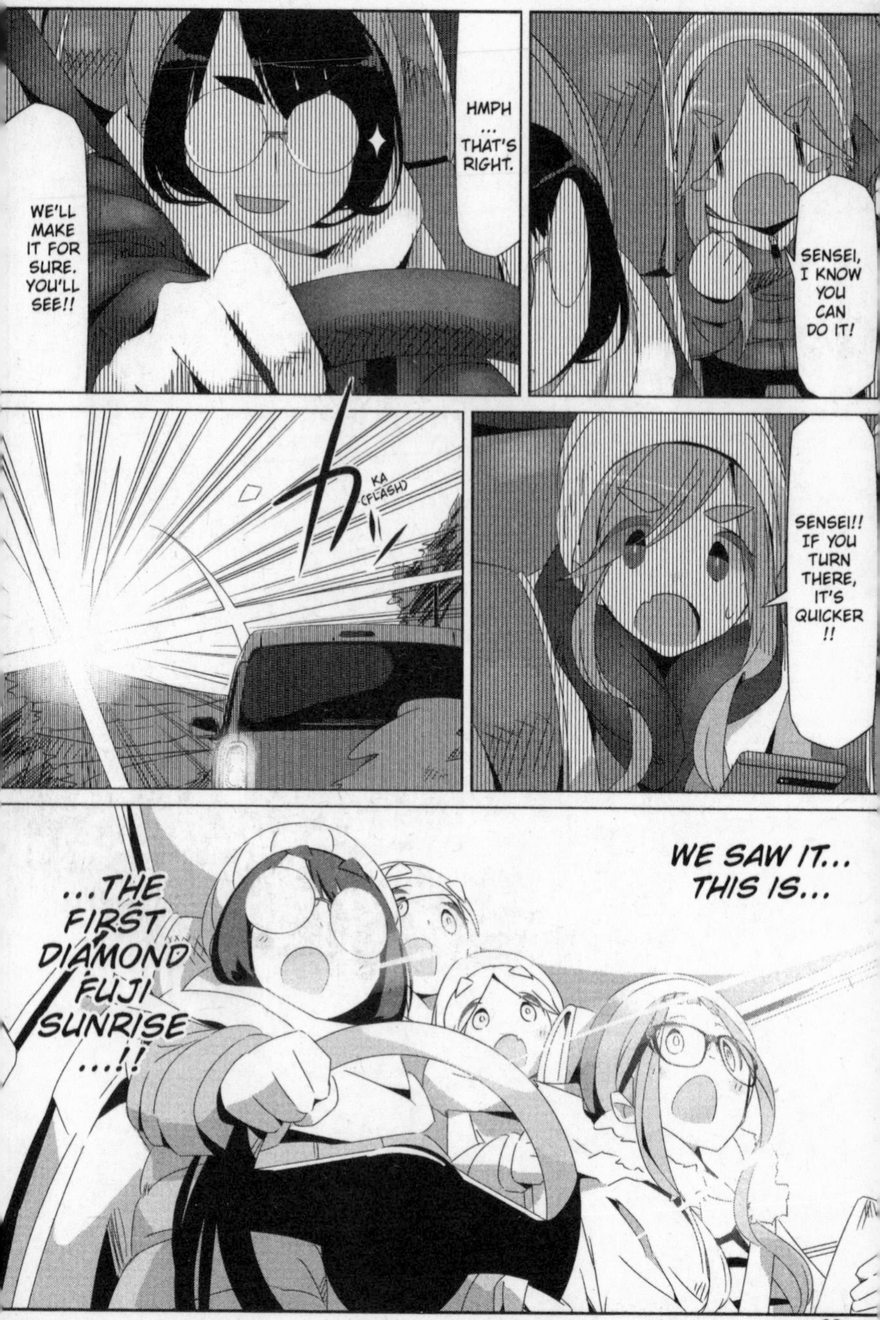
SENSEI, I KNOW YOU CAN DO IT!
HMPH ... THAT'S RIGHT.
WE'LL MAKE IT FOR SURE. YOU'LL SEE!!
SENSEI!! IF YOU TURN THERE, IT'S QUICKER!!
KA (FLASH)
WE SAW IT... THIS IS...
...THE FIRST DIAMOND FUJI SUNRISE ...!!

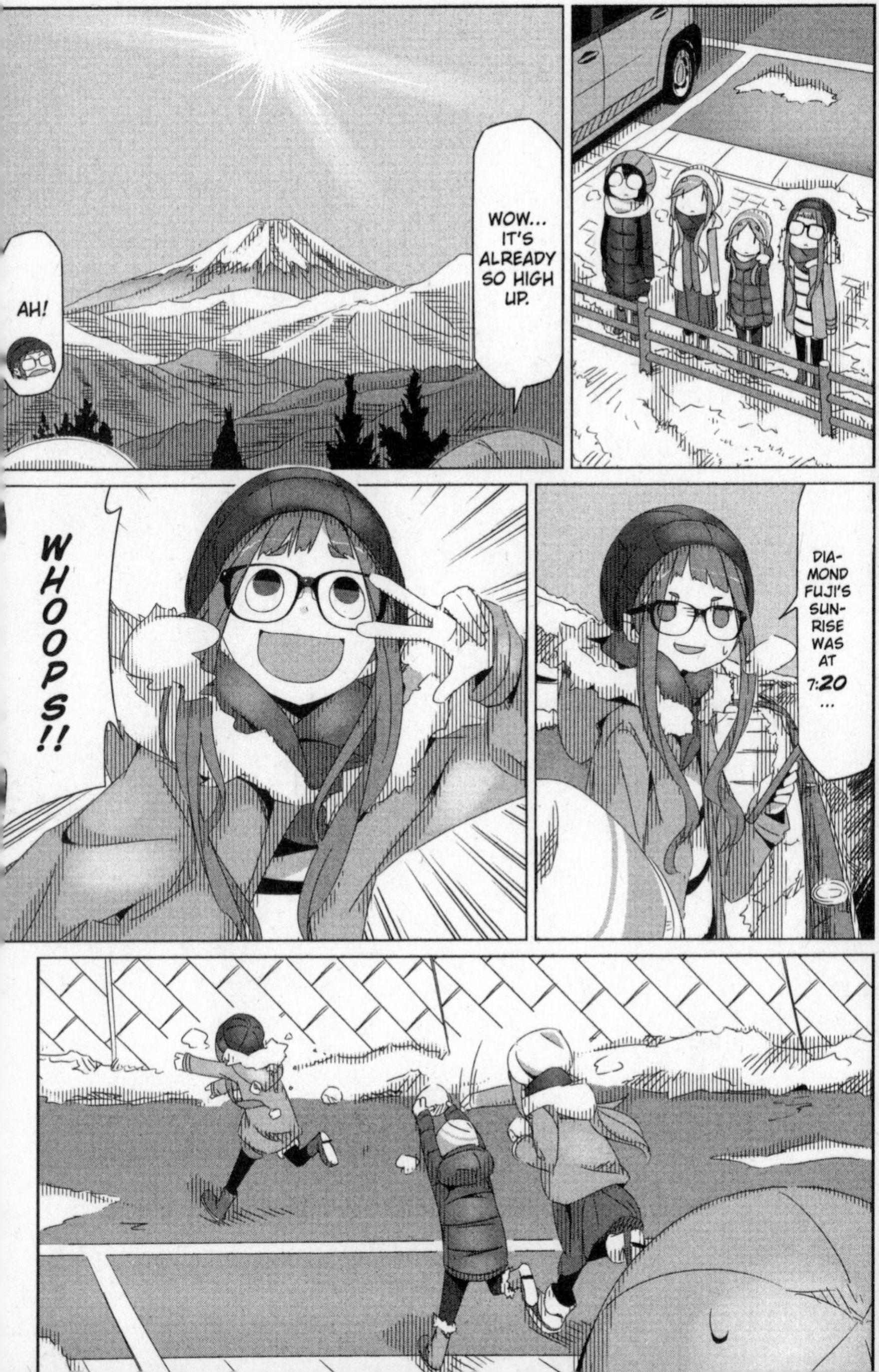
WOW... IT'S ALREADY SO HIGH UP.
AH!
DIAMOND FUJI'S SUNRISE WAS AT 7:20 ...
WHOOPS!!

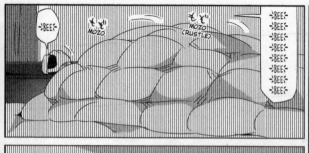

→BEE← →BEE←

ど ど
MOZO

ど ど
MOZO
(RUSTLE)

→BEE←
→BEE←
→BEE←
→BEE←
→BEE←
→BEE←
→BEE←
→BEE←

→BEE←
→BEE←
→BEE←
→BEE←
→BEE←
→BEE←
→BEE←
→BEE←

OH.

THE
FIRST
SUN-
RISE.

シャ
SHA
(SHFF)

84

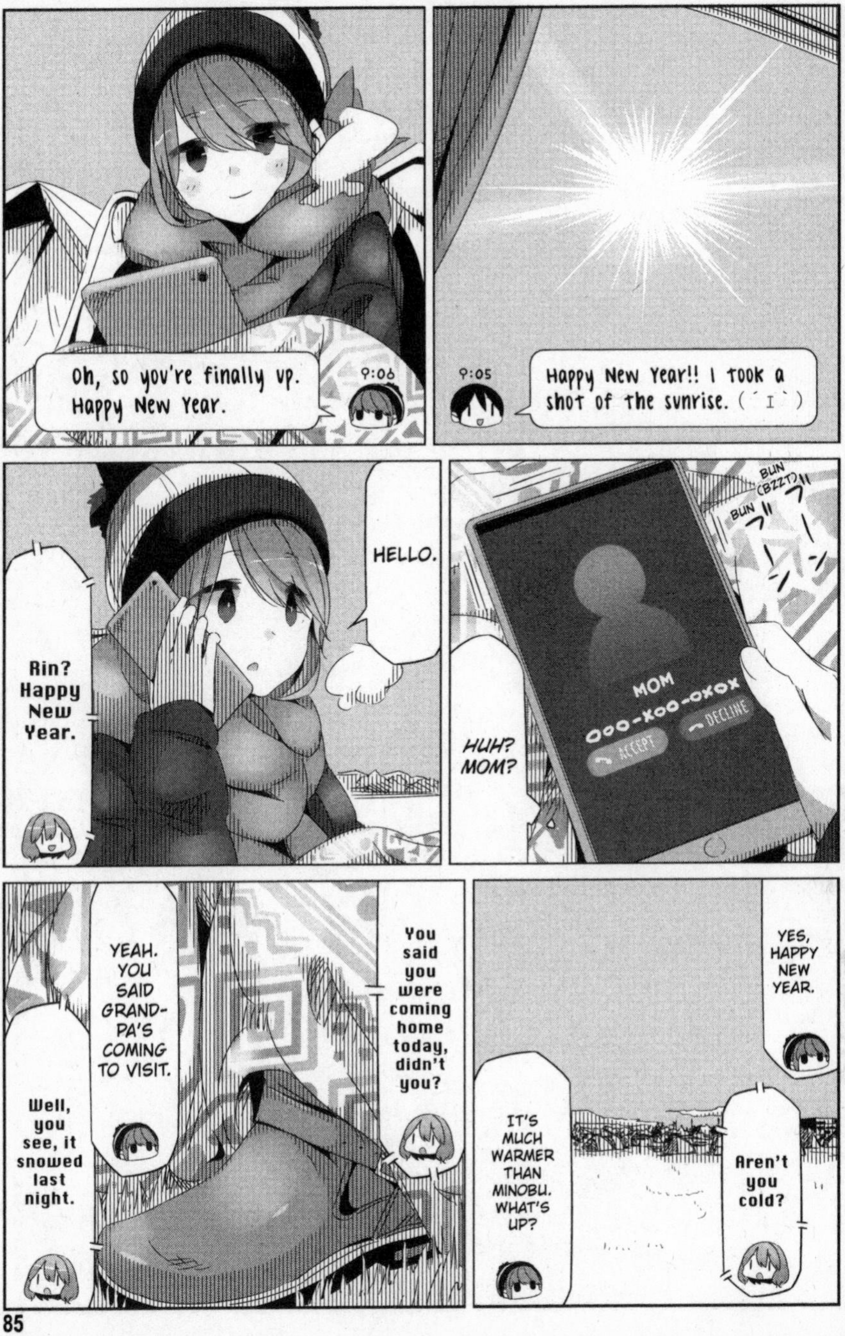
9:05
Happy New Year!! I took a shot of the sunrise. (´I`)
9:06
Oh, so you're finally up. Happy New Year.
BUN BUN (BZZT)
HUH? MOM?
MOM
OOO-XOO-OXOX
DECLINE
ACCEPT
HELLO.
Rin? Happy New Year.
YES, HAPPY NEW YEAR.
Aren't you cold?
IT'S MUCH WARMER THAN MINOBU. WHAT'S UP?
You said you were coming home today, didn't you?
YEAH. YOU SAID GRAND-PA'S COMING TO VISIT.
Well, you see, it snowed last night.

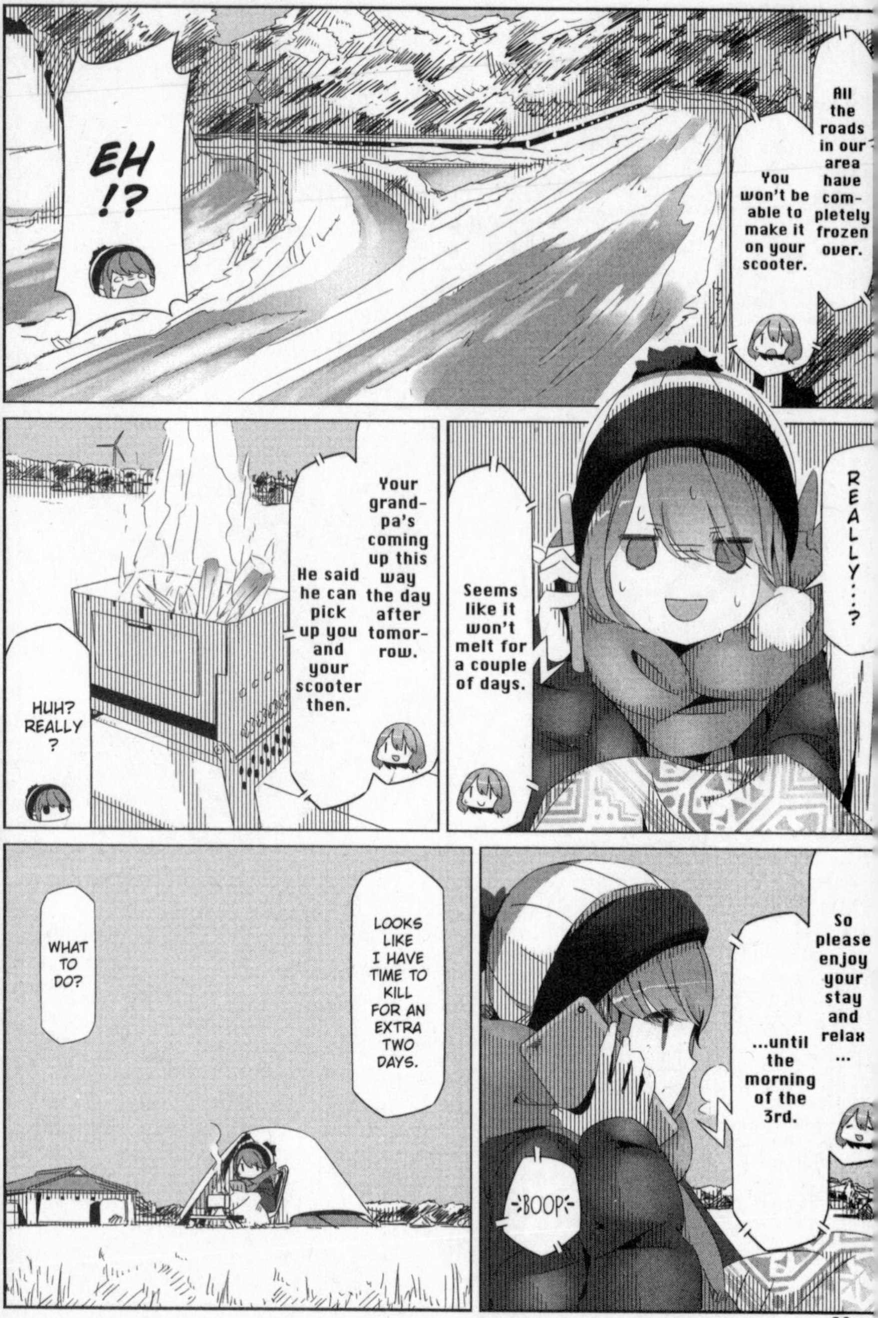
All the roads in our area have completely frozen over.
You won't be able to make it on your scooter.
EH!?
REALLY...?
Seems like it won't melt for a couple of days.
Your grandpa's coming up this way the day after tomorrow.
He said he can pick up you and your scooter then.
HUH? REALLY?
So please enjoy your stay and relax...
...until the morning of the 3rd.
BOOP
LOOKS LIKE I HAVE TIME TO KILL FOR AN EXTRA TWO DAYS.
WHAT TO DO?

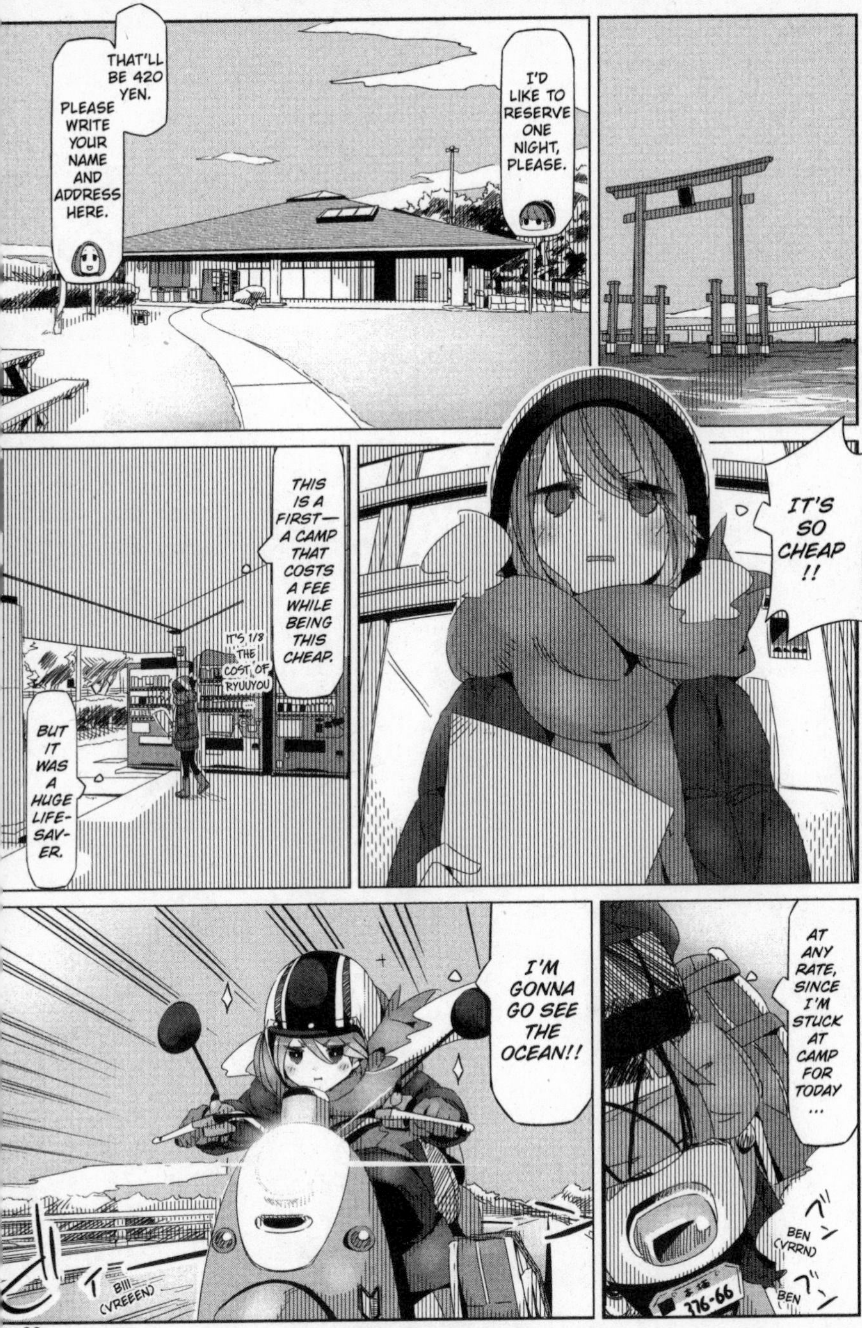
I'D LIKE TO RESERVE ONE NIGHT, PLEASE.
THAT'LL BE 420 YEN. PLEASE WRITE YOUR NAME AND ADDRESS HERE.
IT'S SO CHEAP!!
THIS IS A FIRST—A CAMP THAT COSTS A FEE WHILE BEING THIS CHEAP.
IT'S 1/8 THE COST OF RYUUYOU
...
BUT IT WAS A HUGE LIFE-SAVER.
AT ANY RATE, SINCE I'M STUCK AT CAMP FOR TODAY...
BEN (VRRN)
BEN
I'M GONNA GO SEE THE OCEAN!!
BIII (VREEEN)

11:06 I'm coming to Hamamatsu for the 2nd and 3rd.

11:07 If you like, wanna come stay at my grandma's place?

11:05 Rin-chan, you're stuck there until the 3rd, right?

11:08 It's in the Lake Okuhamana area. It's a really nice place. (´ ▽ `)

11:09 And one of my friends from the area is supposed to come by...

MNN.

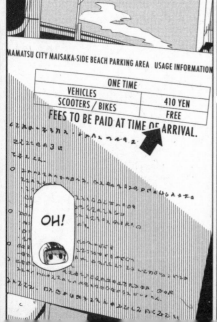

MAMATSU CITY MAISAKA-SIDE BEACH PARKING AREA USAGE INFORMATION

ONE TIME	
VEHICLES	410 YEN
SCOOTERS / BIKES	FREE

FEES TO BE PAID AT TIME OF ARRIVAL.

OH!

IT COSTS MONEY TO PARK HERE ...

THANK YOU, SCOOTER !!

BIII (VREEE)

HA-MANA BRIDGE IS HUGE.

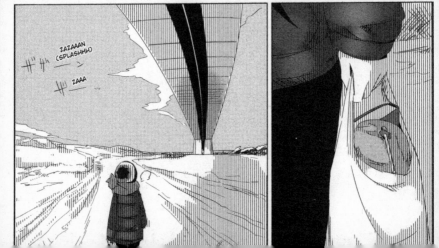

ZAZAAAN (SPLASHHH)

ZAAA

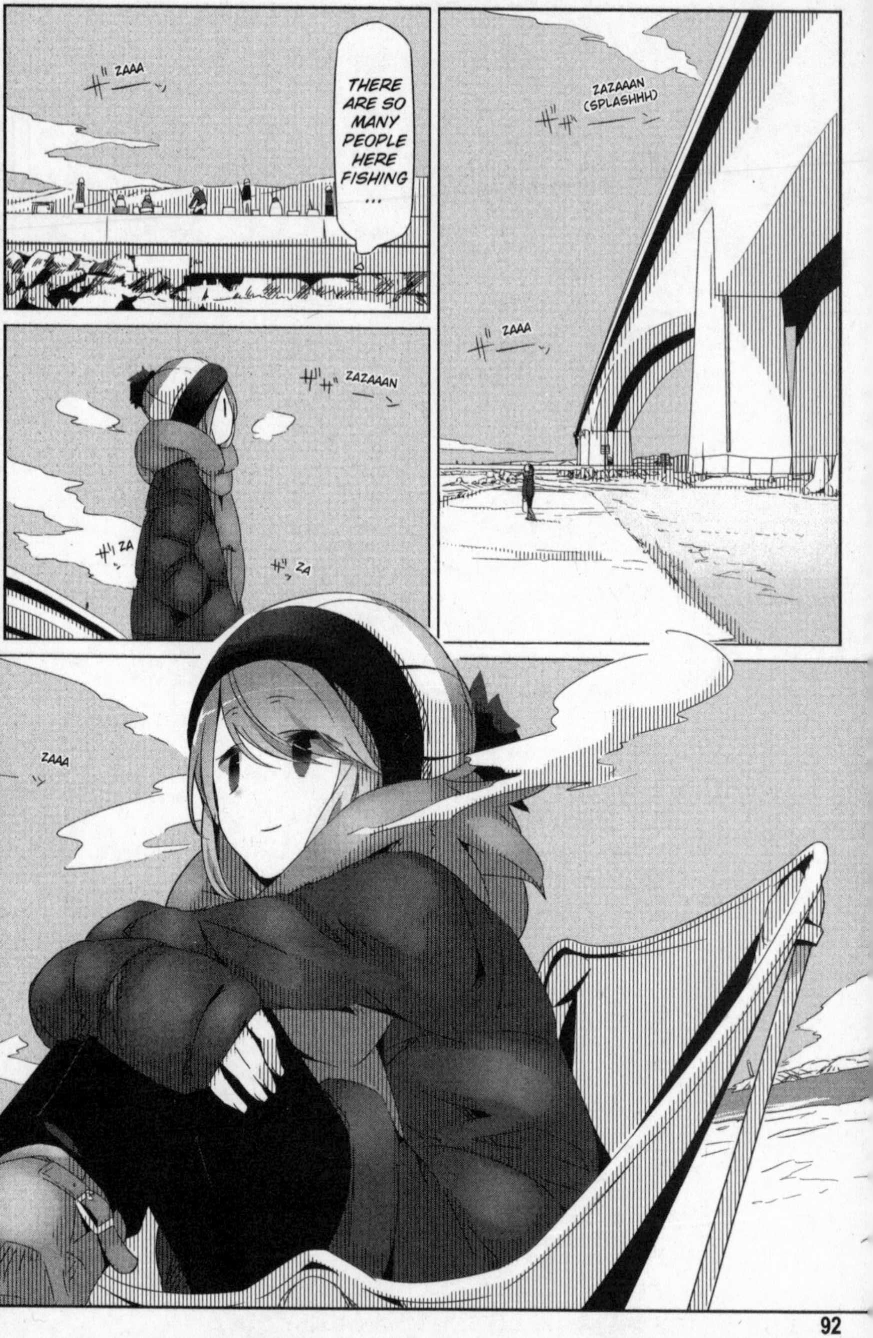
ZAZAAAN (SPLASHHH)
ZAAA
THERE ARE SO MANY PEOPLE HERE FISHING...
ZAAA
ZAZAAAN
ZA
ZA
ZAAA

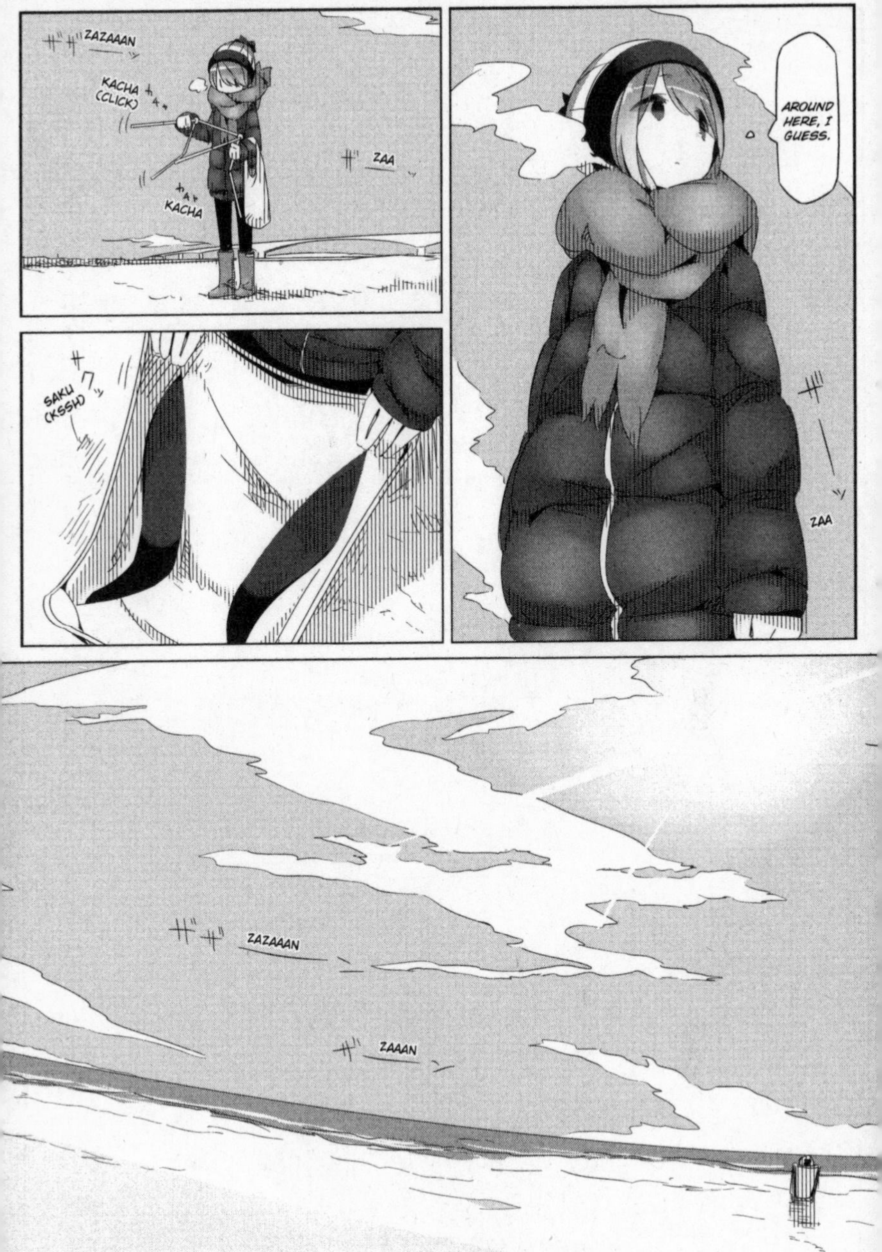
AROUND HERE, I GUESS.
ZAA
ZAZAAAN
KACHA (CLICK)
ZAA
KACHA
SAKU (KSSH)
ZAZAAAN
ZAAAN

CHAPTER 27 THE OCEAN, THE LAKE, AND SOME LUCKY CAMPING

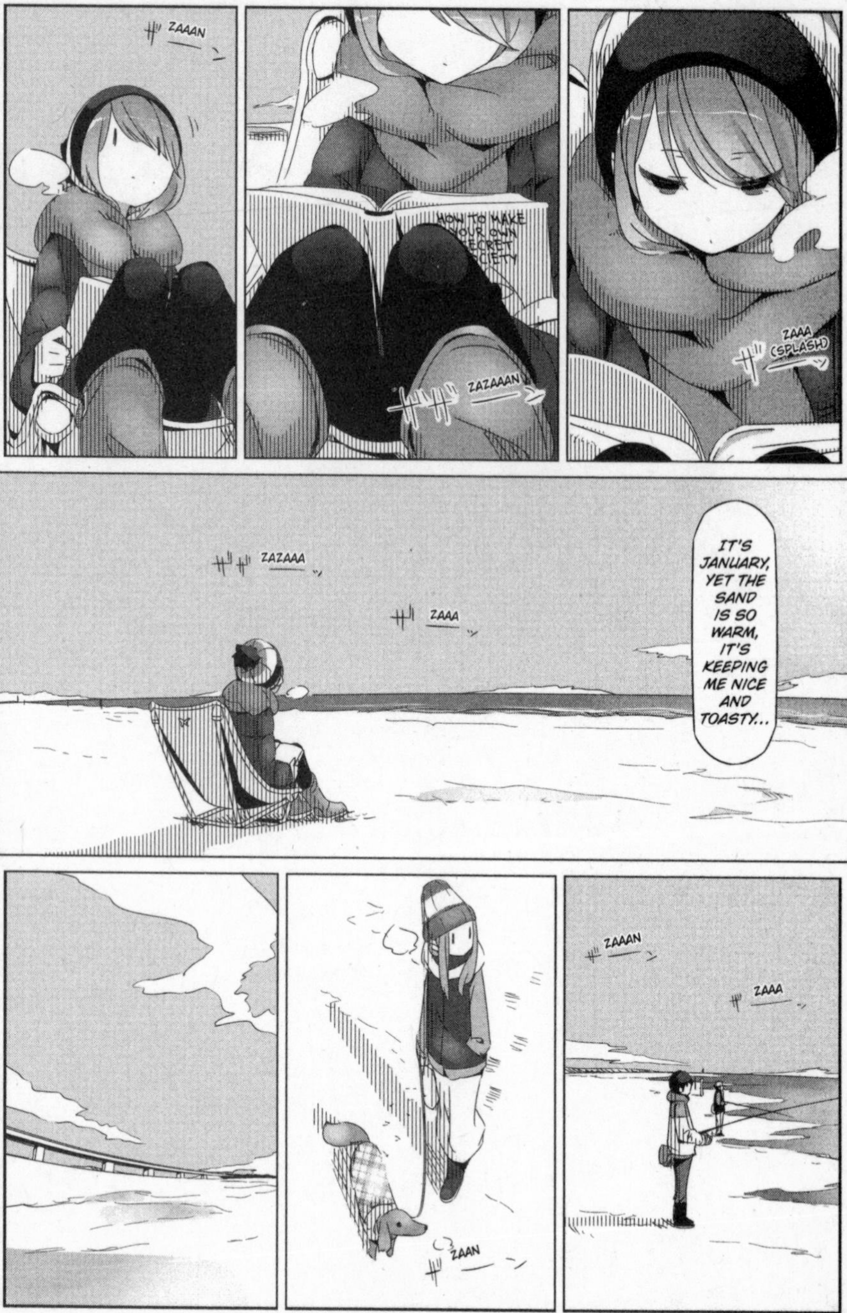
ZAAA (SPLASH)
HOW TO MAKE
OUR OWN
ECRET
CIETY
ZAZAAAN
ZAAAN
IT'S JANUARY, YET THE SAND IS SO WARM, IT'S KEEPING ME NICE AND TOASTY...
ZAZAAA
ZAAA
ZAAAN
ZAAA
ZAAN

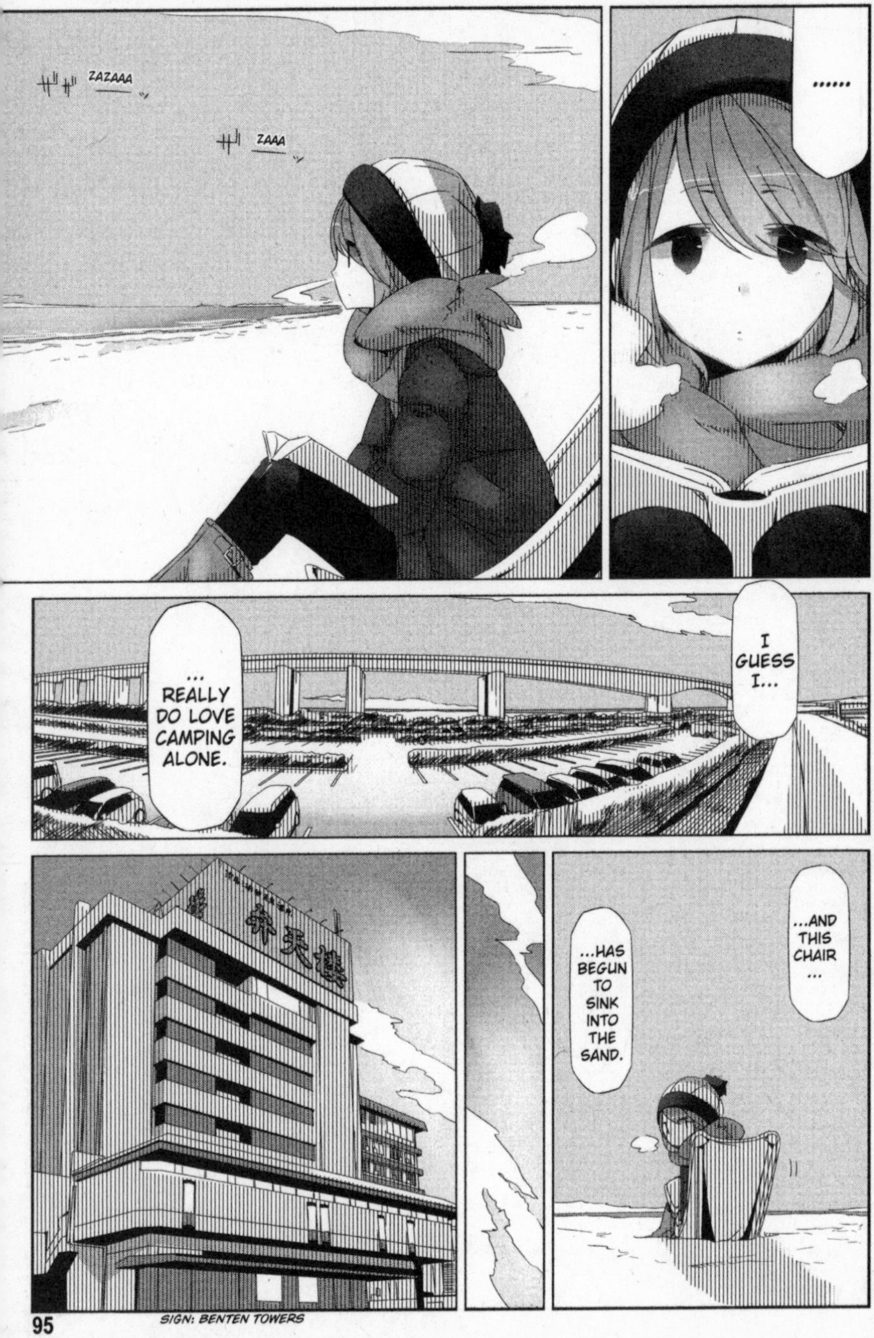
......
ザザ ZAZAAA
ザ ZAAA
I GUESS I...
... REALLY DO LOVE CAMPING ALONE.
...AND THIS CHAIR ...
...HAS BEGUN TO SINK INTO THE SAND.

SIGN: BENTEN TOWERS

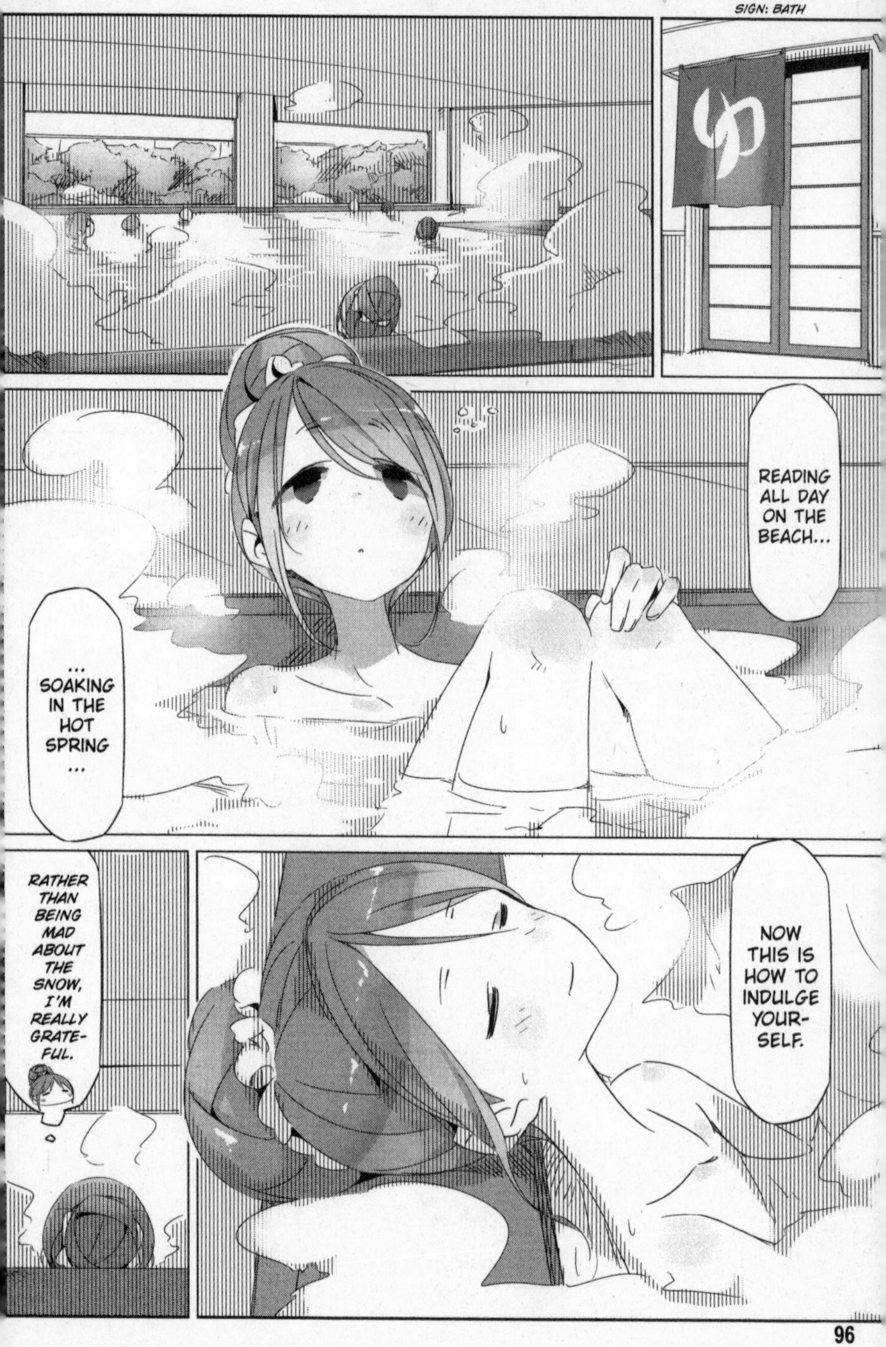
SIGN: BATH
READING ALL DAY ON THE BEACH...
...SOAKING IN THE HOT SPRING...
NOW THIS IS HOW TO INDULGE YOURSELF.
RATHER THAN BEING MAD ABOUT THE SNOW, I'M REALLY GRATEFUL.

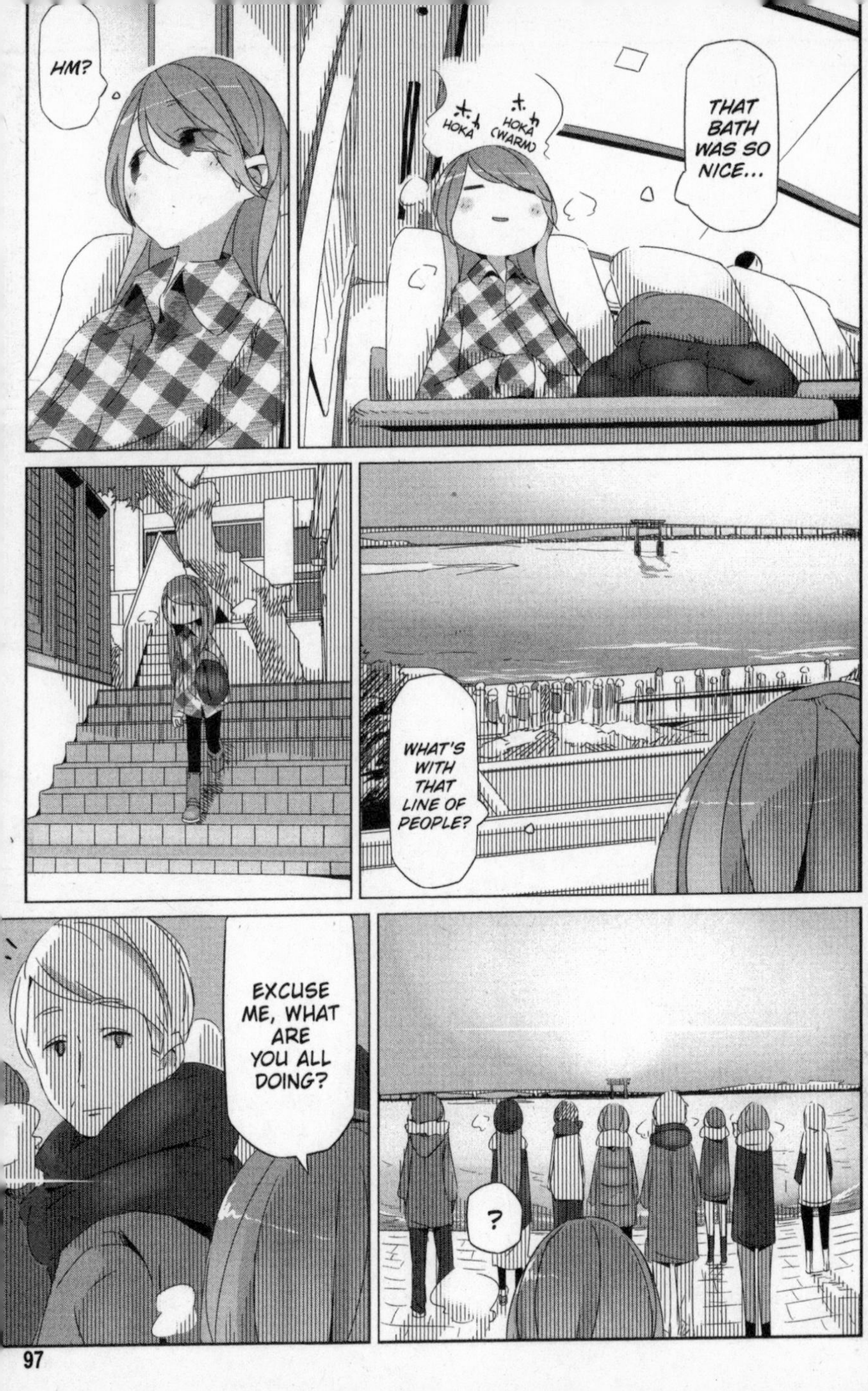
THAT BATH WAS SO NICE...
ホカ HOKA (WARM)
ホカ HOKA
HM?
WHAT'S WITH THAT LINE OF PEOPLE?
?
EXCUSE ME, WHAT ARE YOU ALL DOING?

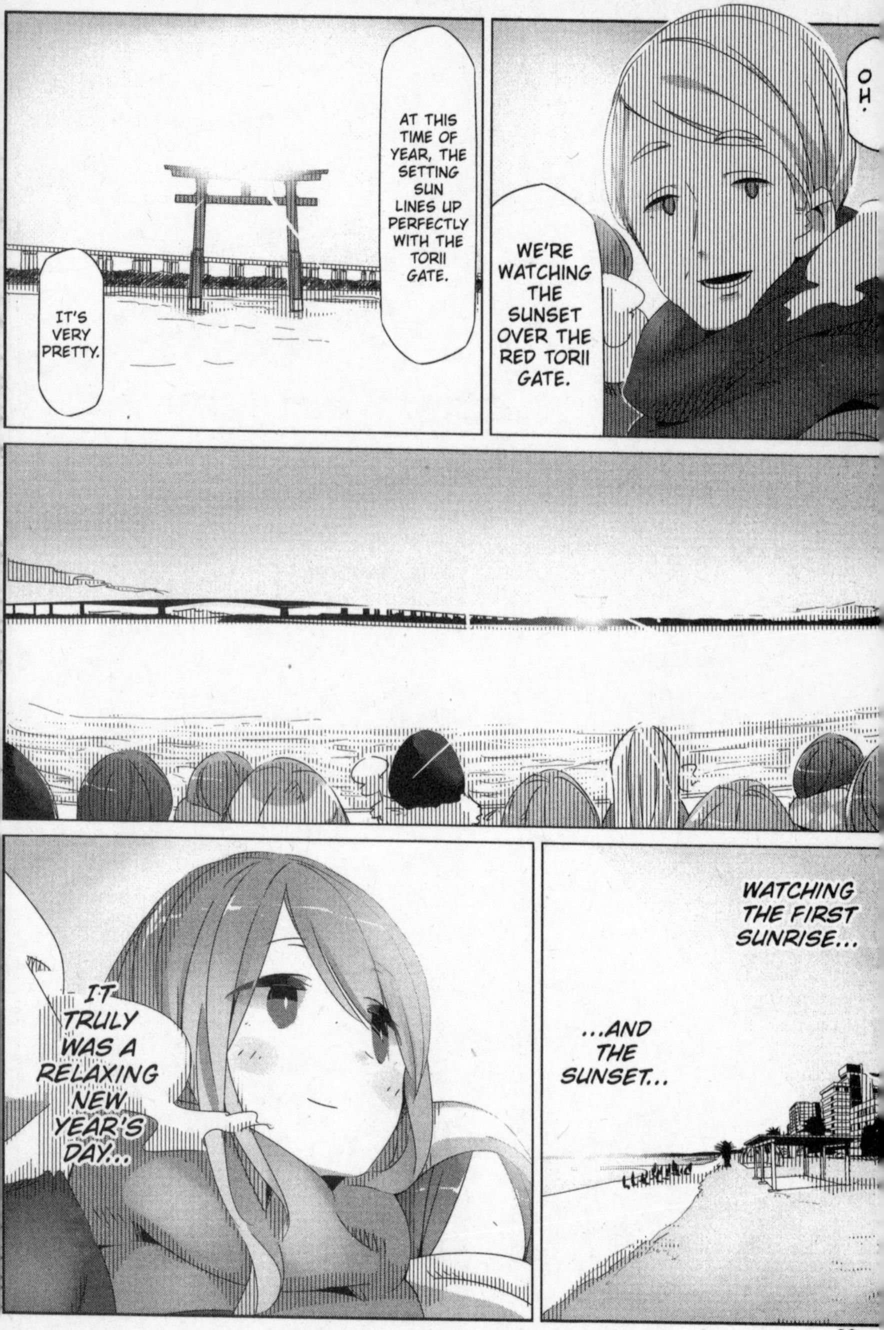
OH.
WE'RE WATCHING THE SUNSET OVER THE RED TORII GATE.
AT THIS TIME OF YEAR, THE SETTING SUN LINES UP PERFECTLY WITH THE TORII GATE.
IT'S VERY PRETTY.
WATCHING THE FIRST SUNRISE...
...AND THE SUNSET...
IT TRULY WAS A RELAXING NEW YEAR'S DAY...

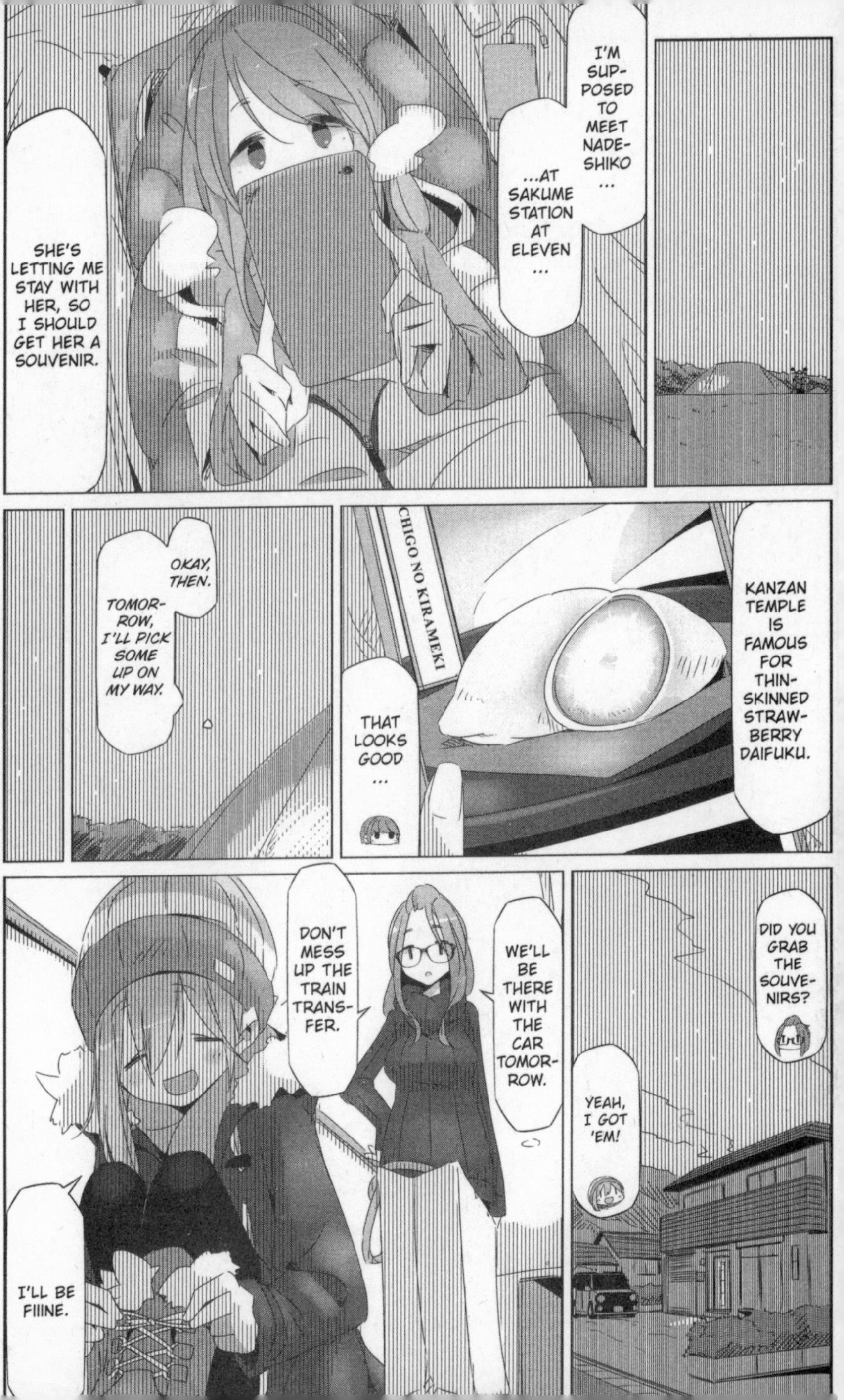
I'M SUPPOSED TO MEET NADESHIKO...
...AT SAKUME STATION AT ELEVEN...
SHE'S LETTING ME STAY WITH HER, SO I SHOULD GET HER A SOUVENIR.
KANZAN TEMPLE IS FAMOUS FOR THIN-SKINNED STRAWBERRY DAIFUKU.
CHIGO NO KIRAMEKI
THAT LOOKS GOOD...
OKAY, THEN.
TOMORROW, I'LL PICK SOME UP ON MY WAY.
DID YOU GRAB THE SOUVENIRS?
YEAH, I GOT 'EM!
WE'LL BE THERE WITH THE CAR TOMORROW.
DON'T MESS UP THE TRAIN TRANSFER.
I'LL BE FIIINE.

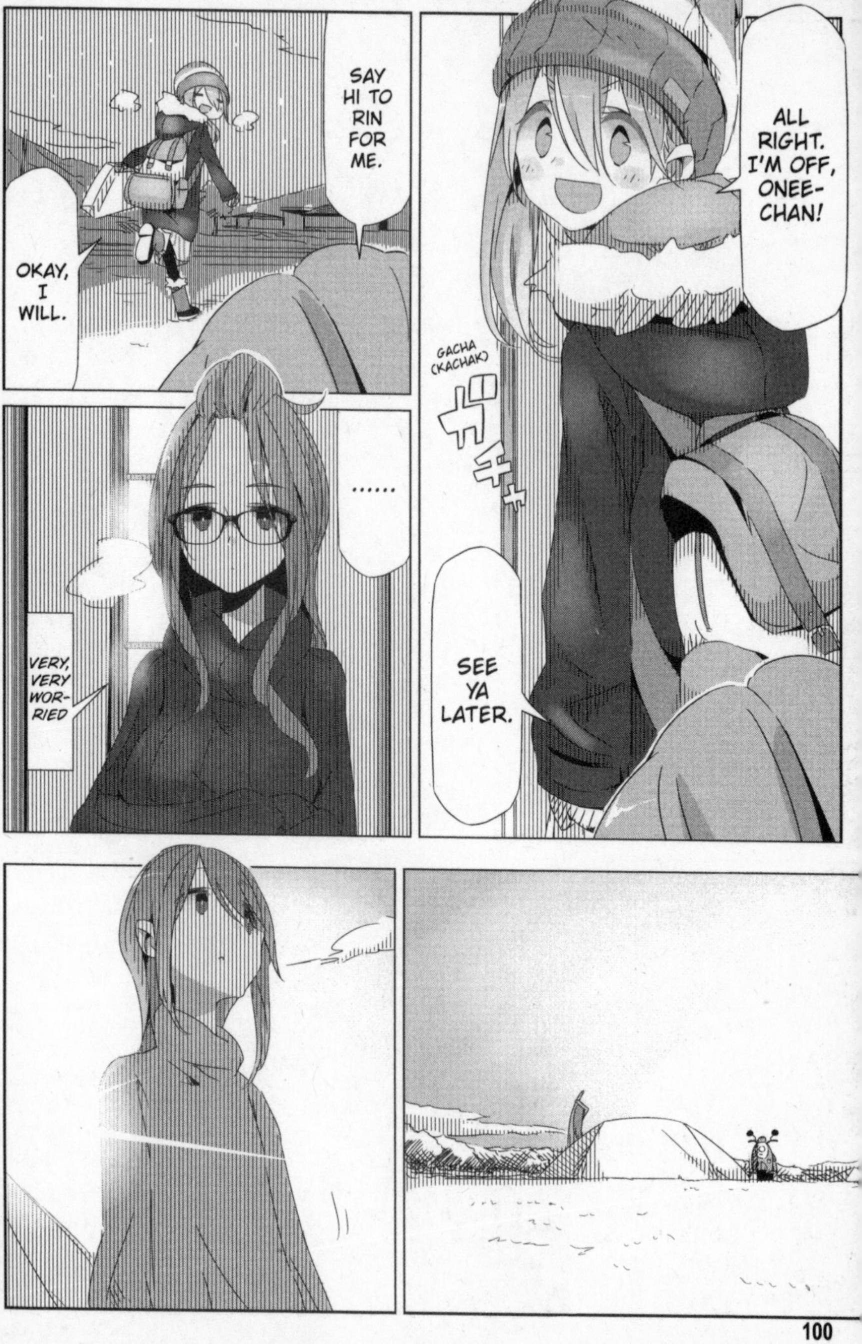
ALL RIGHT. I'M OFF, ONEE-CHAN!
GACHA (KACHAK)
SEE YA LATER.
SAY HI TO RIN FOR ME.
OKAY, I WILL.
......
VERY, VERY WOR-RIED

OKAY.

舘山寺温泉

門前通り

MADE IT TO KANZAN TEMPLE.

SIGN: KANZAN TEMPLE HOT SPRING GATE ENTRANCE STREET

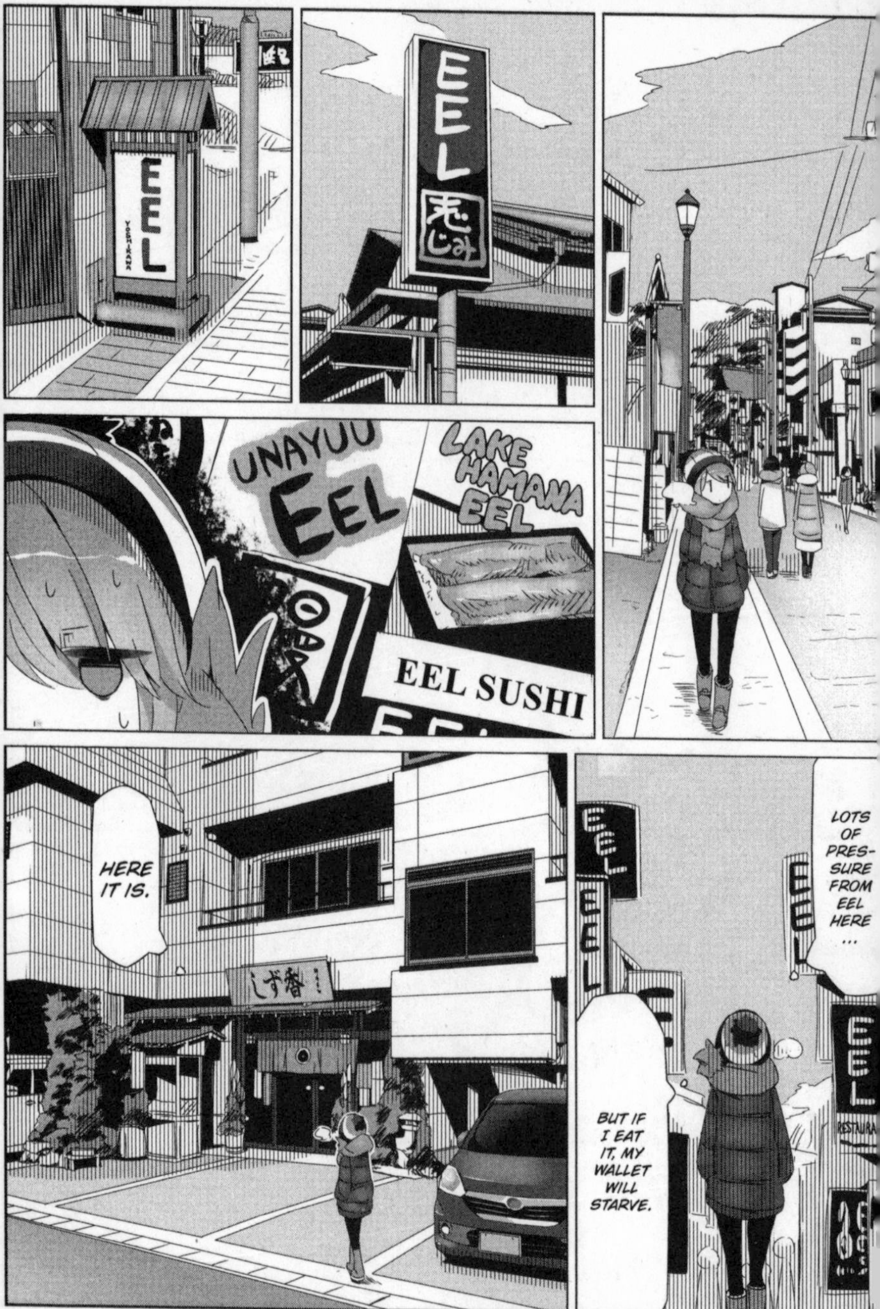
EEL
EEL
YOSHIKAWA
LAKE HAMANA EEL
UNAYUU EEL
EEL SUSHI
LOTS OF PRES-SURE FROM EEL HERE ...
EEL
EEL
BUT IF I EAT IT, MY WALLET WILL STARVE.
HERE IT IS.

SIGN: SHIZUKA

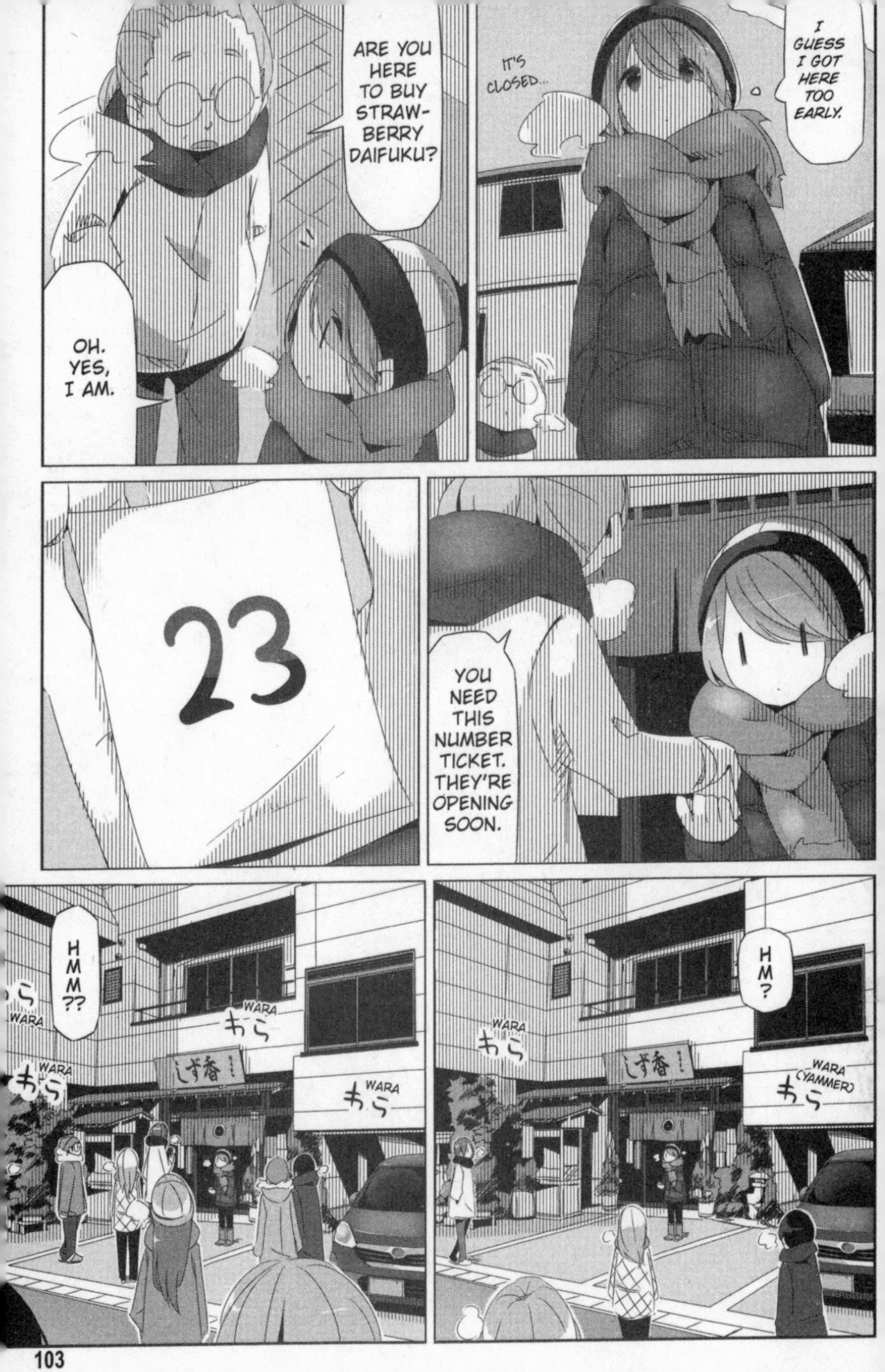
I GUESS I GOT HERE TOO EARLY.
IT'S CLOSED...
ARE YOU HERE TO BUY STRAWBERRY DAIFUKU?
OH. YES, I AM.
YOU NEED THIS NUMBER TICKET. THEY'RE OPENING SOON.
23
HM?
WARA (YAMMER)
わら
WARA
わら
しず香
HMM??
WARA
わら
しず香
WARA
わら
WARA
わら
WARA
わら

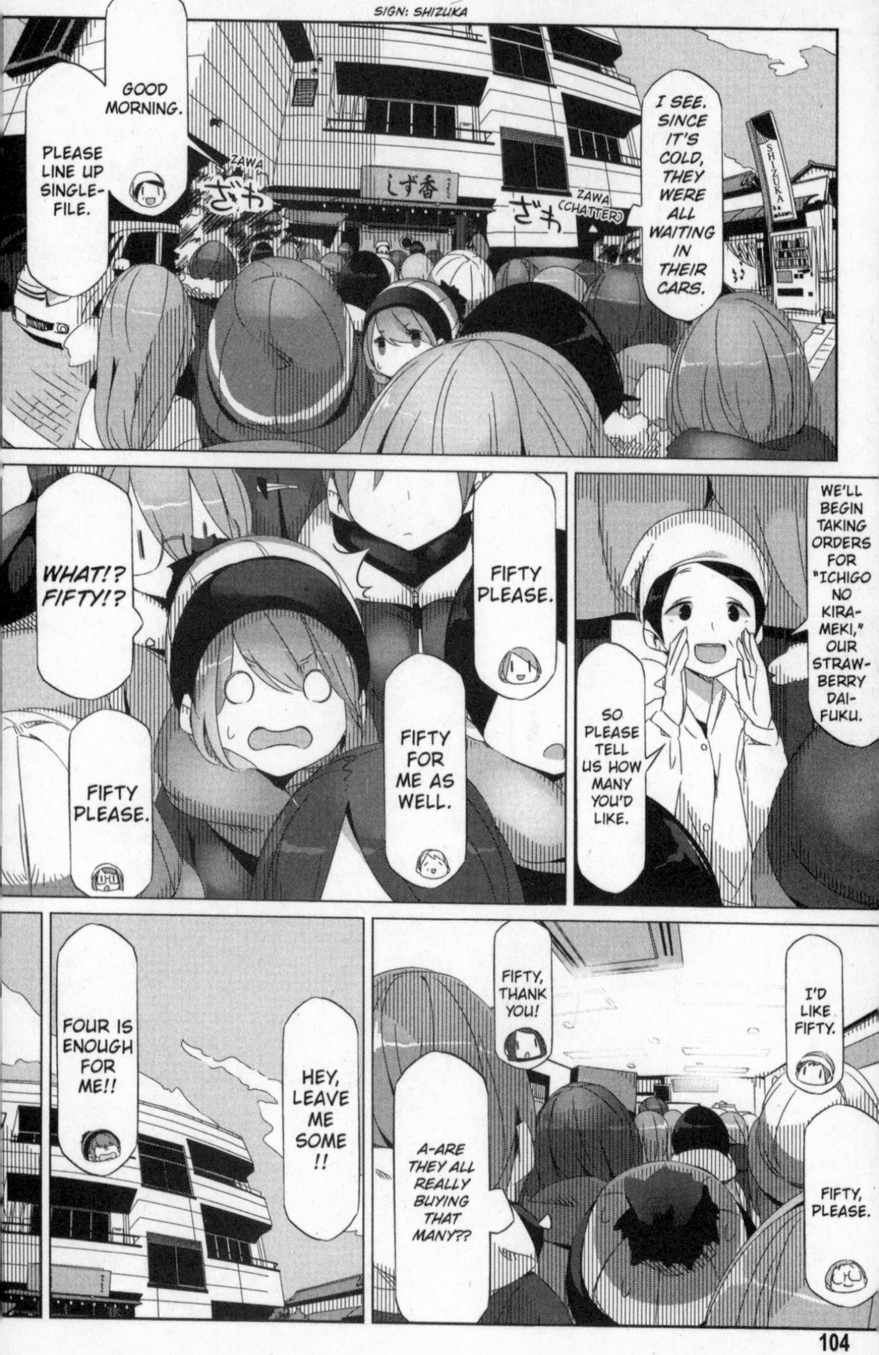
SIGN: SHIZUKA
I SEE. SINCE IT'S COLD, THEY WERE ALL WAITING IN THEIR CARS.
SHIZUKA
しず香
ざわ ZAWA
ざわ ZAWA (CHATTER)
GOOD MORNING.
PLEASE LINE UP SINGLE-FILE.
WE'LL BEGIN TAKING ORDERS FOR "ICHIGO NO KIRA-MEKI," OUR STRAW-BERRY DAI-FUKU.
SO PLEASE TELL US HOW MANY YOU'D LIKE.
FIFTY PLEASE.
FIFTY FOR ME AS WELL.
FIFTY PLEASE.
WHAT!? FIFTY!?
I'D LIKE FIFTY.
FIFTY, THANK YOU!
FIFTY, PLEASE.
A-ARE THEY ALL REALLY BUYING THAT MANY??
HEY, LEAVE ME SOME!!
FOUR IS ENOUGH FOR ME!!

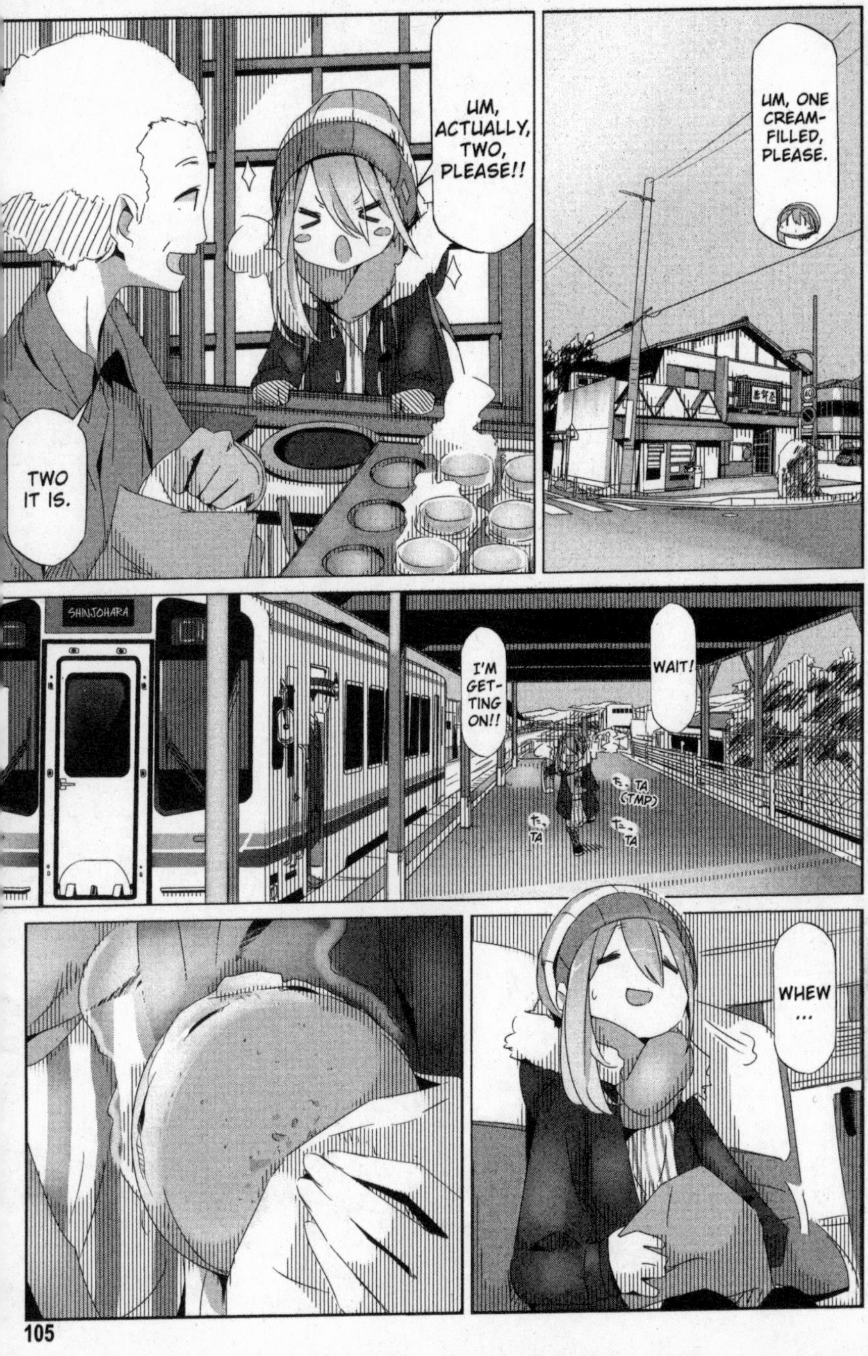
UM, ONE CREAM-FILLED, PLEASE.
UM, ACTUALLY, TWO, PLEASE!!
TWO IT IS.
SHINJOHARA
WAIT!
I'M GETTING ON!!
TA (TMP)
TA
TA
WHEW ...

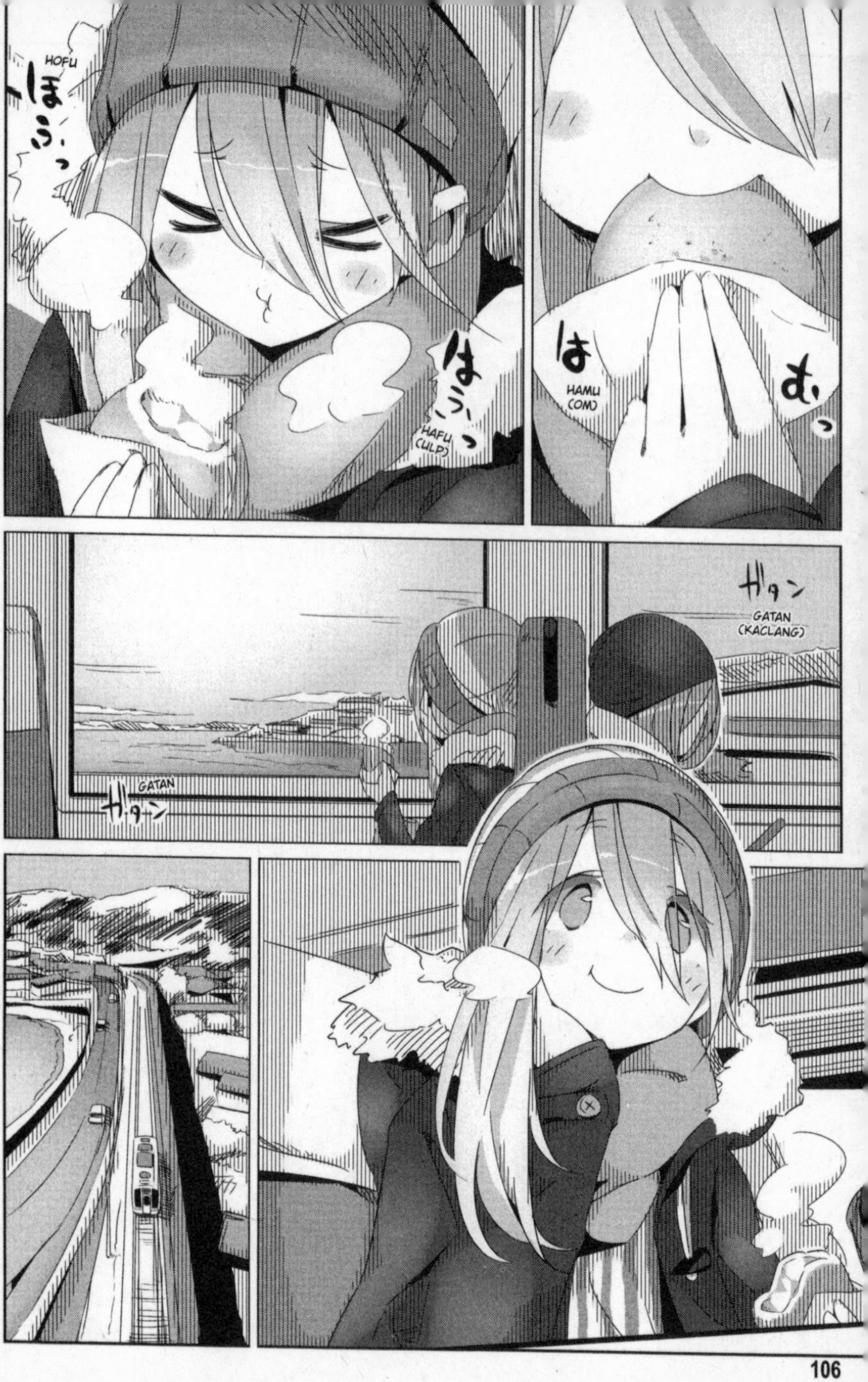
はむっ
HAMU (OM)
はふっ
HAFU (ULP)
ほふっ
HOFU
ガタン
GATAN (KACLANG)
GATAN
ガタン

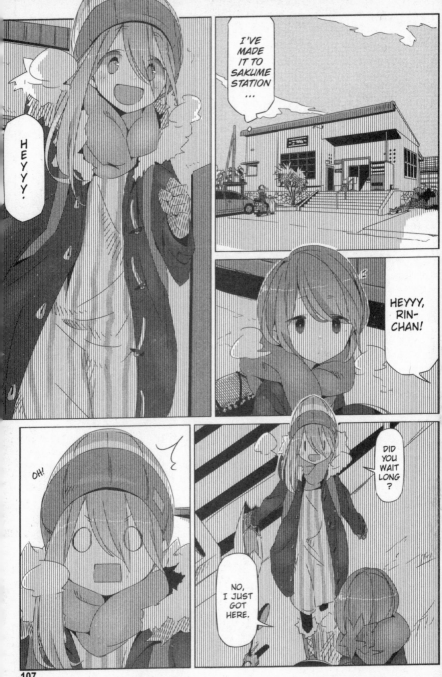

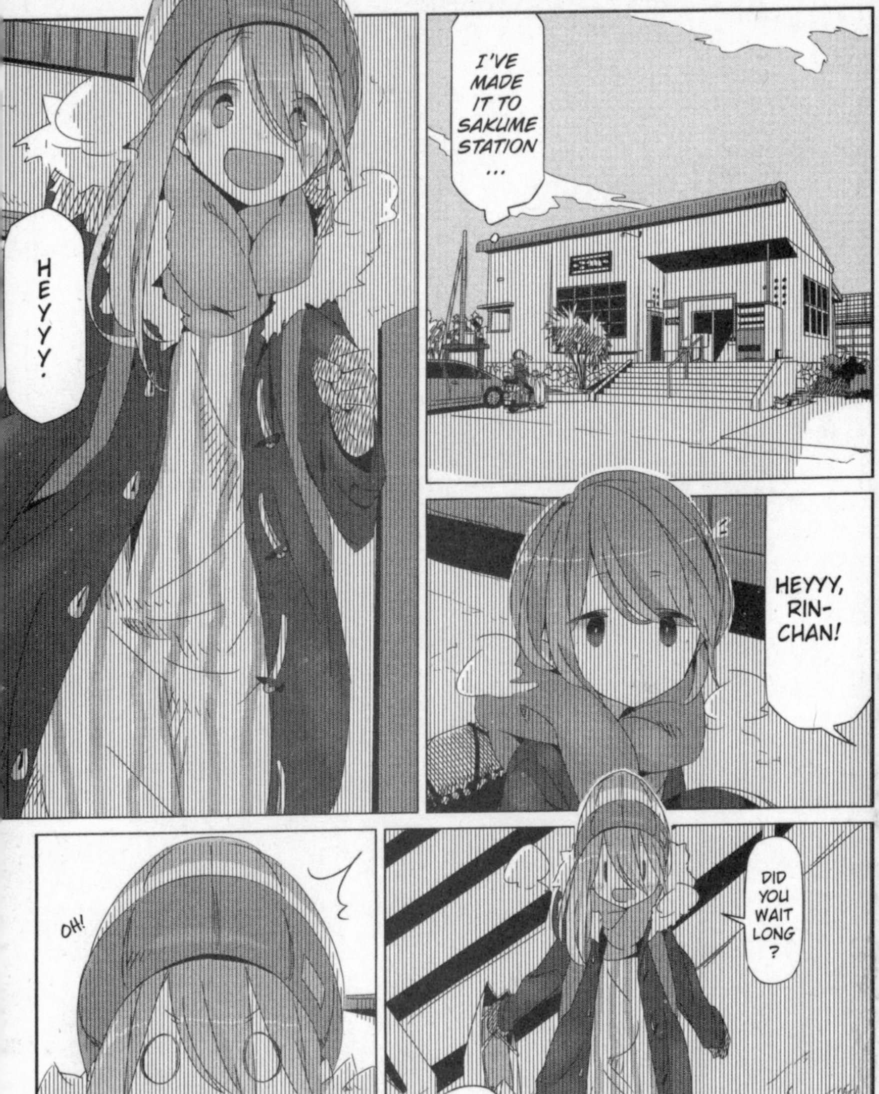
I'VE MADE IT TO SAKUME STATION...
HEYYY, RIN-CHAN!
HEYYY.
DID YOU WAIT LONG?
NO, I JUST GOT HERE.
OH!

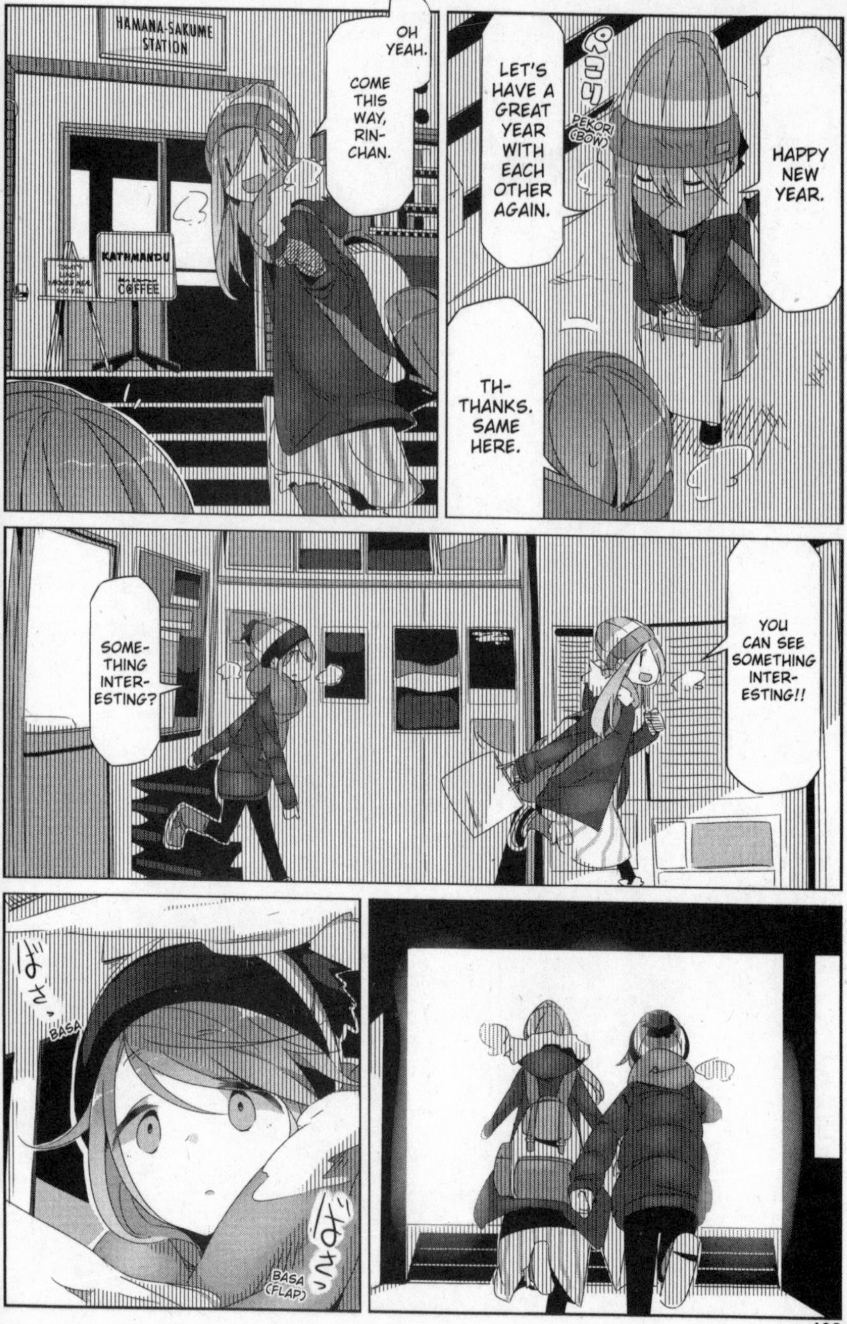
HAPPY NEW YEAR.
ぺこり
PEKORI (BOW)
LET'S HAVE A GREAT YEAR WITH EACH OTHER AGAIN.
TH-THANKS. SAME HERE.
HAMANA-SAKUME STATION
OH YEAH.
COME THIS WAY, RIN-CHAN.
KATHMANDU
C@FFEE
YOU CAN SEE SOMETHING INTER-ESTING!!
SOME-THING INTER-ESTING?
ばさ
BASA
ばさっ
BASA (FLAP)

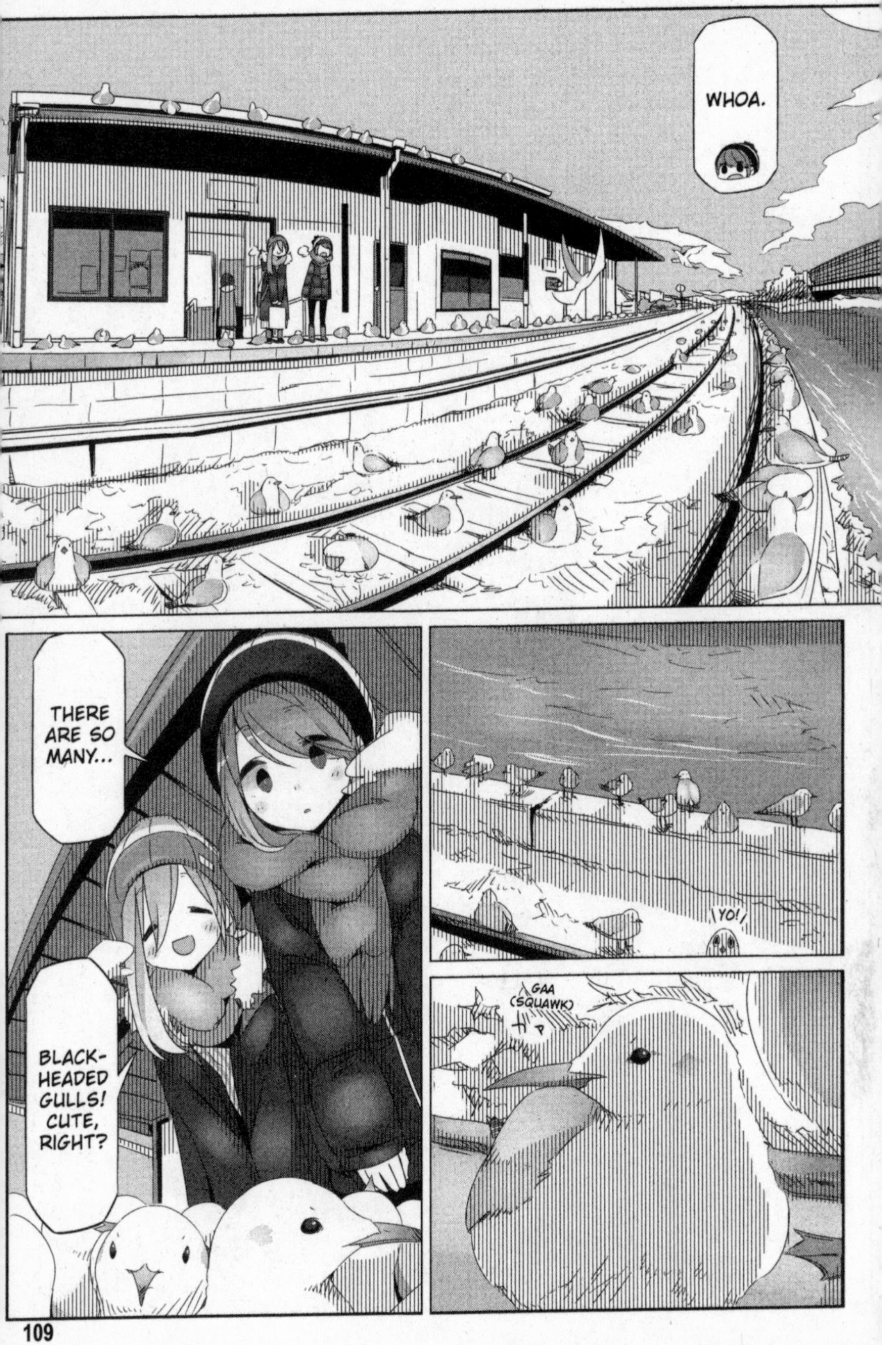
WHOA.
YO!
GAA (SQUAWK)
THERE ARE SO MANY...
BLACK-HEADED GULLS! CUTE, RIGHT?

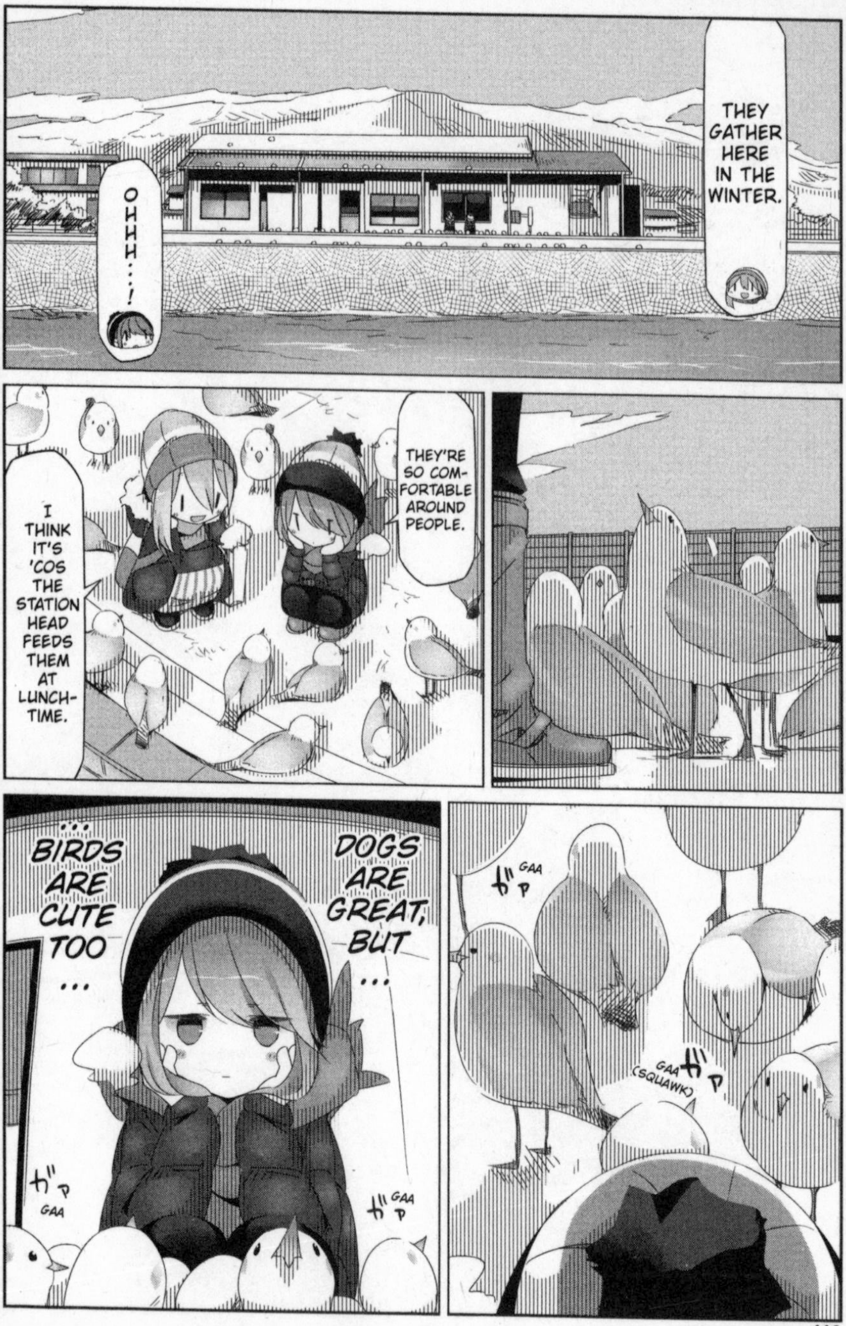
THEY GATHER HERE IN THE WINTER.
OHHH...!
THEY'RE SO COM-FORTABLE AROUND PEOPLE.
I THINK IT'S 'COS THE STATION HEAD FEEDS THEM AT LUNCH-TIME.
ガァ GAA
ガァ GAA (SQUAWK)
DOGS ARE GREAT, BUT ...
... BIRDS ARE CUTE TOO ...
ガァ GAA
ガァ GAA

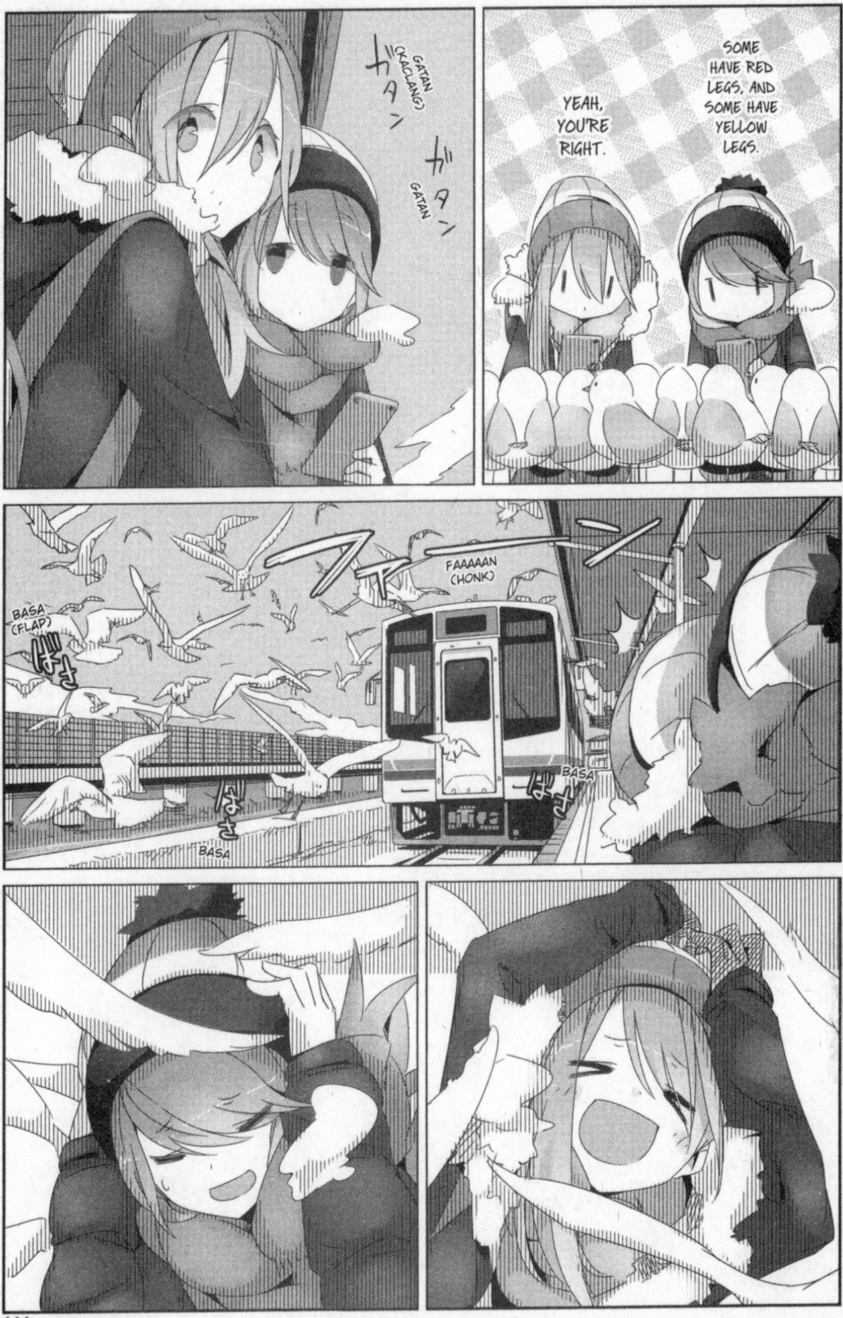
SOME HAVE RED LEGS, AND SOME HAVE YELLOW LEGS.
YEAH, YOU'RE RIGHT.
ガタン
GATAN
ガタン
GATAN (KACLANG)
ファーーン
FAAAAAN (HONK)
BASA
BASA (FLAP)
BASA

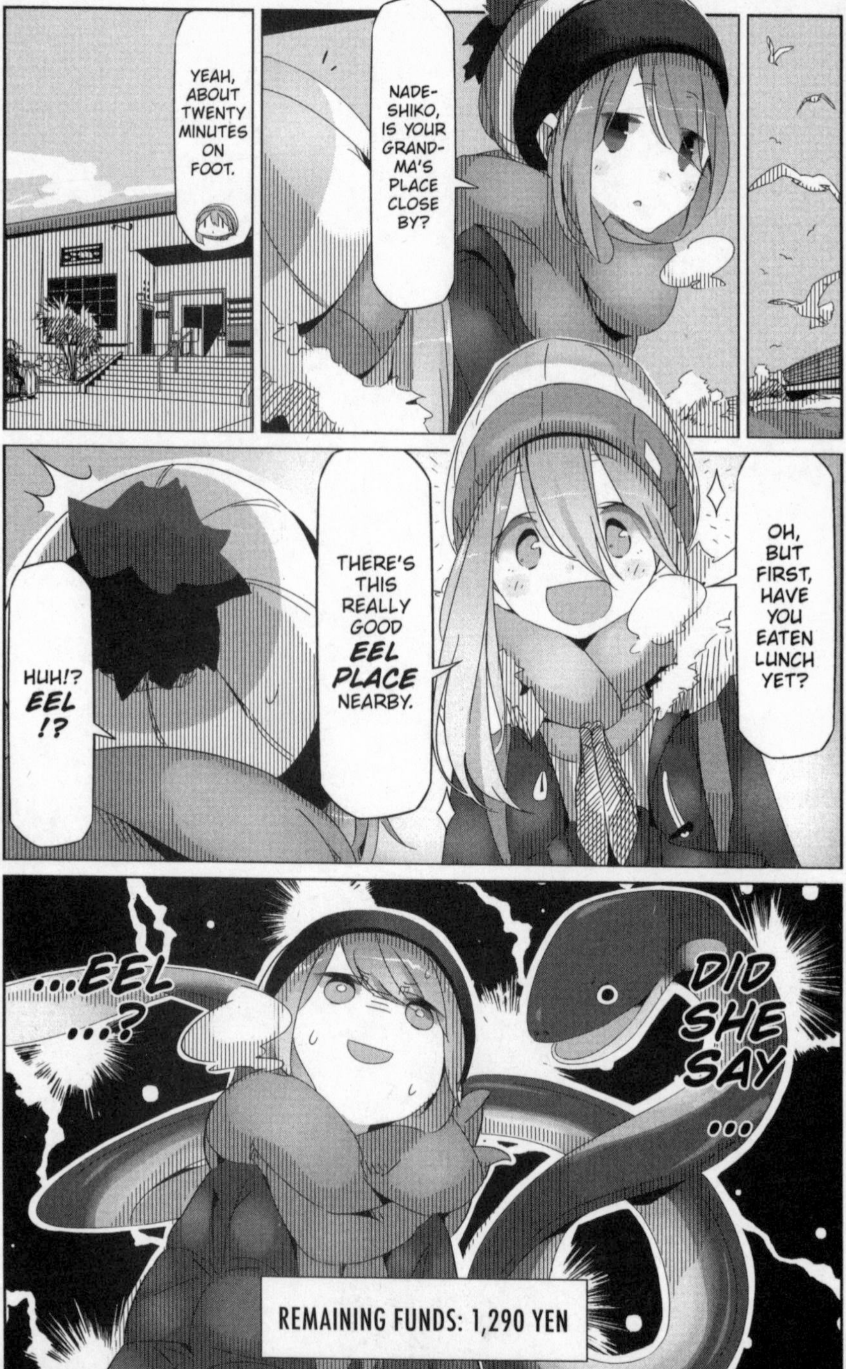
NADE-SHIKO, IS YOUR GRAND-MA'S PLACE CLOSE BY?
YEAH, ABOUT TWENTY MINUTES ON FOOT.
OH, BUT FIRST, HAVE YOU EATEN LUNCH YET?
THERE'S THIS REALLY GOOD EEL PLACE NEARBY.
HUH!? EEL!?
DID SHE SAY...
...EEL...?
REMAINING FUNDS: 1,290 YEN

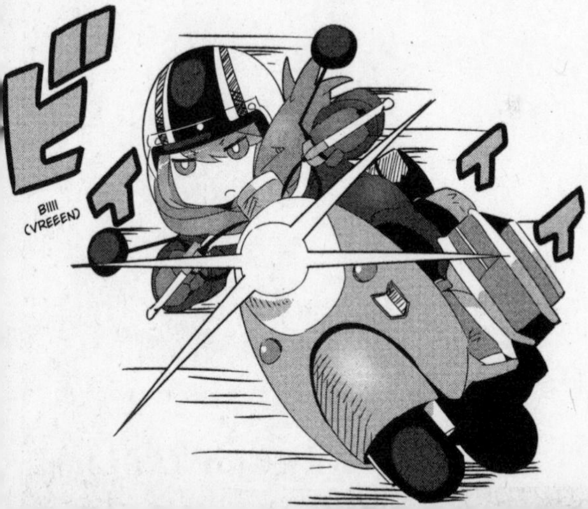
BIIII
(VREEEN)

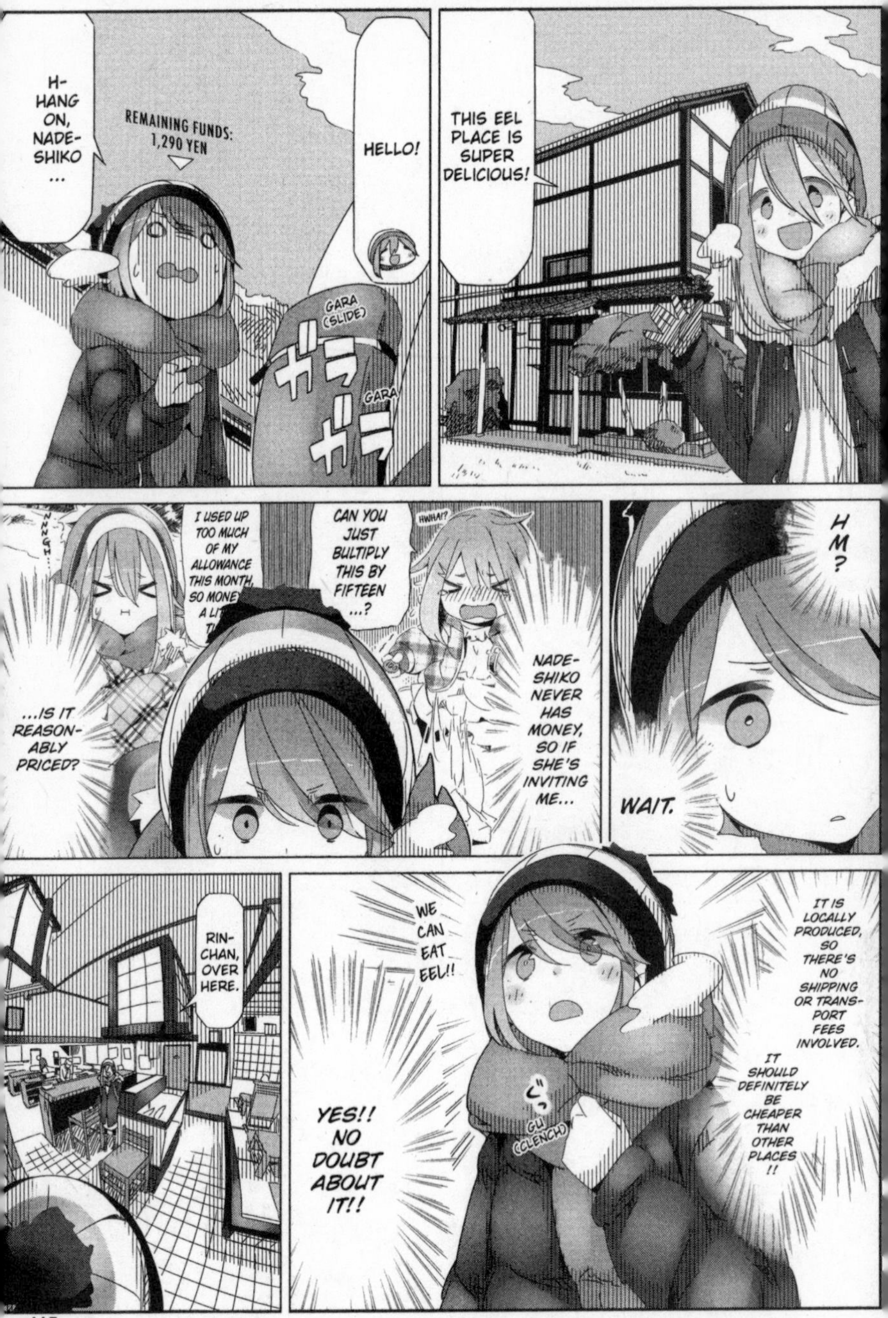
THIS EEL PLACE IS SUPER DELICIOUS!
HELLO!
GARA (SLIDE)
GARA
REMAINING FUNDS: 1,290 YEN
H-HANG ON, NADE-SHIKO ...
HM?
WAIT.
HWHA!?
CAN YOU JUST BULTIPLY THIS BY FIFTEEN ...?
I USED UP TOO MUCH OF MY ALLOWANCE THIS MONTH, SO MONE
NNNGH...
NADE-SHIKO NEVER HAS MONEY, SO IF SHE'S INVITING ME...
...IS IT REASONABLY PRICED?
IT IS LOCALLY PRODUCED, SO THERE'S NO SHIPPING OR TRANSPORT FEES INVOLVED.
IT SHOULD DEFINITELY BE CHEAPER THAN OTHER PLACES !!
WE CAN EAT EEL!!
GU (CLENCH)
YES!! NO DOUBT ABOUT IT!!
RIN-CHAN, OVER HERE.

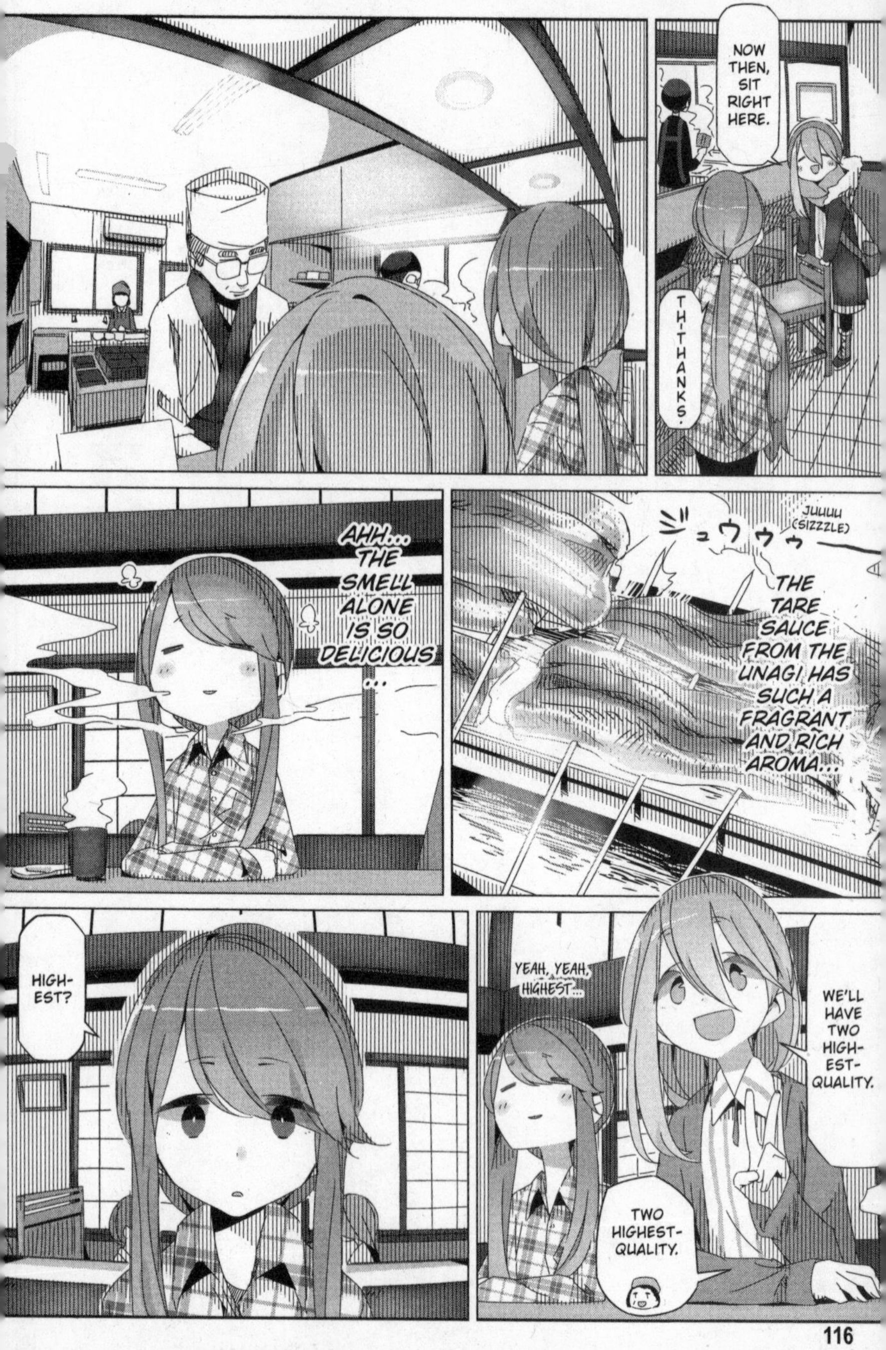
NOW THEN, SIT RIGHT HERE.
TH-THANKS.
JUUUU (SIZZZLE)
THE TARE SAUCE FROM THE UNAGI HAS SUCH A FRAGRANT AND RICH AROMA...
AHH... THE SMELL ALONE IS SO DELICIOUS...
WE'LL HAVE TWO HIGHEST-QUALITY.
YEAH, YEAH, HIGHEST...
TWO HIGHEST-QUALITY.
HIGHEST?

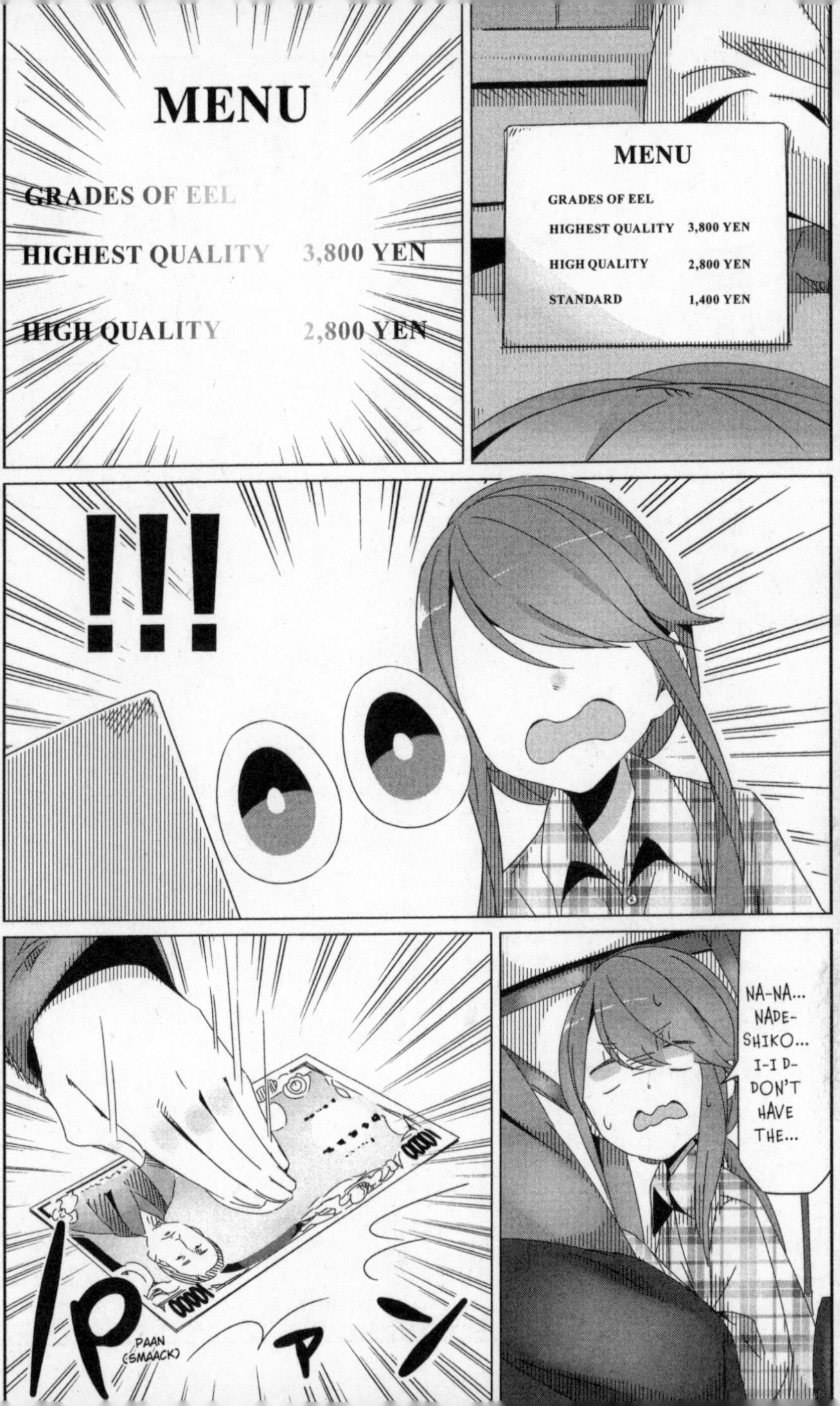
MENU
GRADES OF EEL
HIGHEST QUALITY 3,800 YEN
HIGH QUALITY 2,800 YEN
STANDARD 1,400 YEN
MENU
GRADES OF EEL
HIGHEST QUALITY 3,800 YEN
HIGH QUALITY 2,800 YEN
!!!
NA-NA... NADESHIKO... I-I D-DON'T HAVE THE...
PAAN (SMAACK)

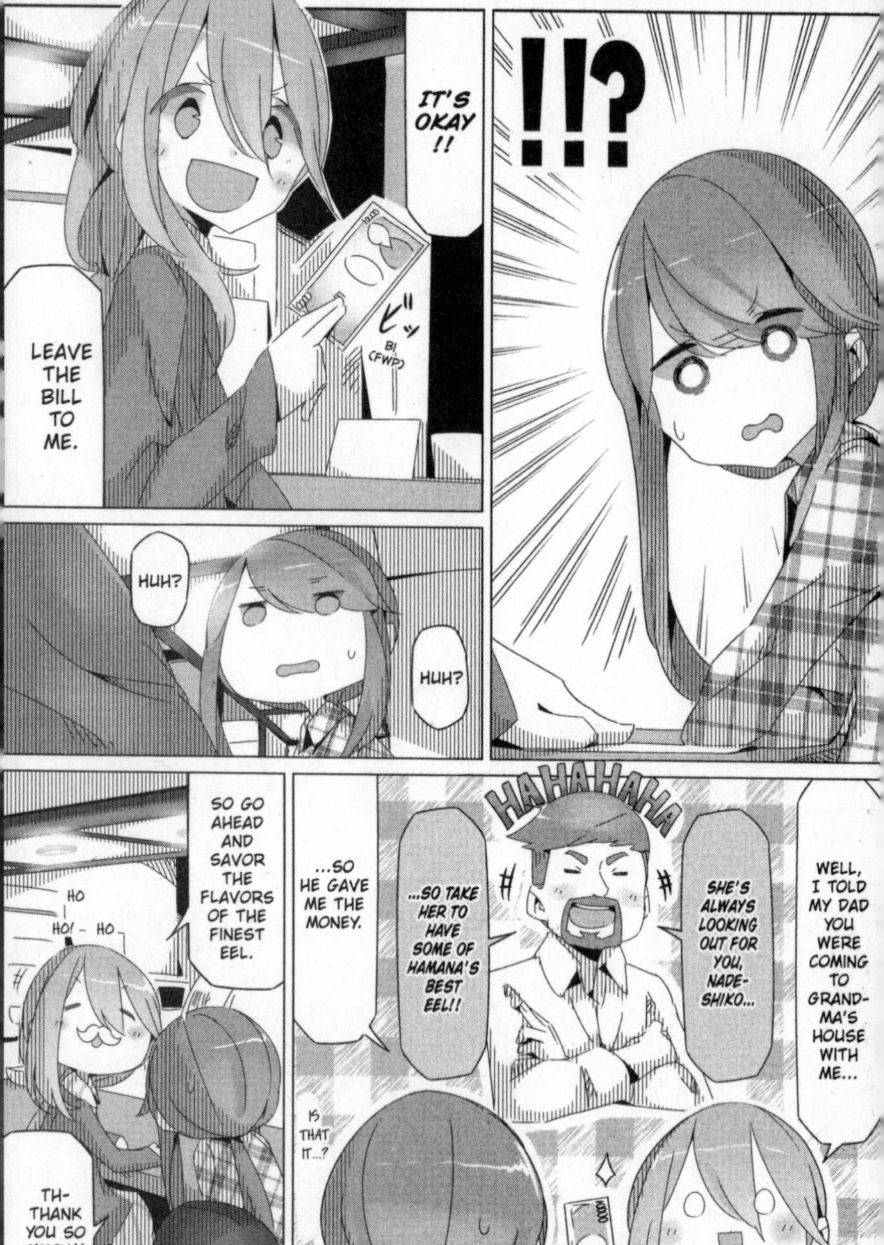
!!?
IT'S OKAY!!
LEAVE THE BILL TO ME.
ビッ
BI (FWP)
HUH?
HUH?
WELL, I TOLD MY DAD YOU WERE COMING TO GRANDMA'S HOUSE WITH ME...
SHE'S ALWAYS LOOKING OUT FOR YOU, NADESHIKO...
HAHAHAHA
...SO TAKE HER TO HAVE SOME OF HAMANA'S BEST EEL!!
...SO HE GAVE ME THE MONEY.
IS THAT IT...?
SO GO AHEAD AND SAVOR THE FLAVORS OF THE FINEST EEL.
HO-HO!-HO
TH-THANK YOU SO MUCH!!

CHAPTER 28 THINKING IT OVER AGAIN

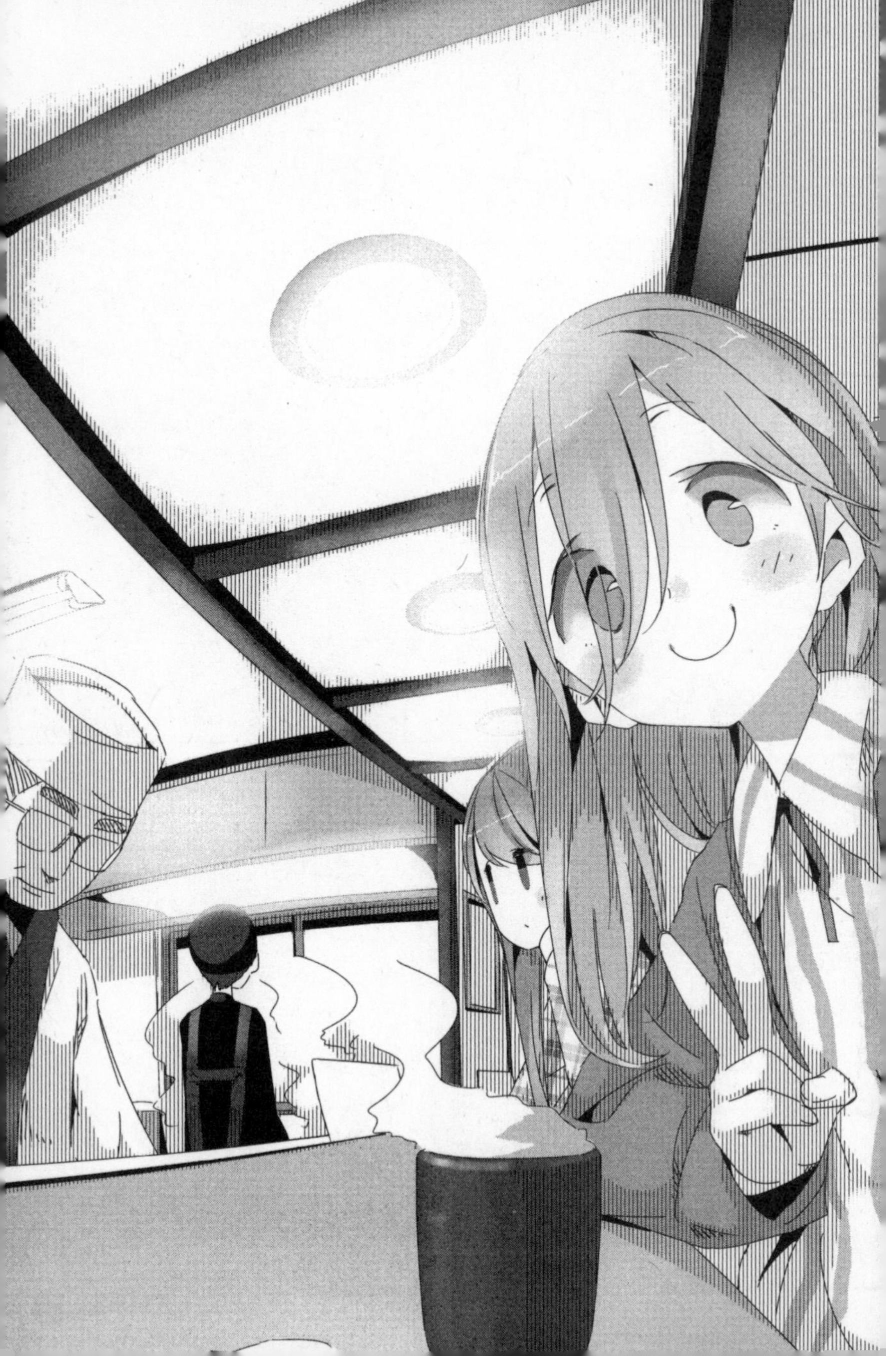

ZUZUUUU
(SLIIIIIDE)

トン
TON
(TAP)

ズ
ッ
ZU

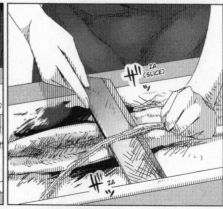

ザ
(SLICE)

ザ
ッ
ZA

HO
HOOO
...

OH...
SO
THIS
IS
HOW
THEY
PREP
IT.

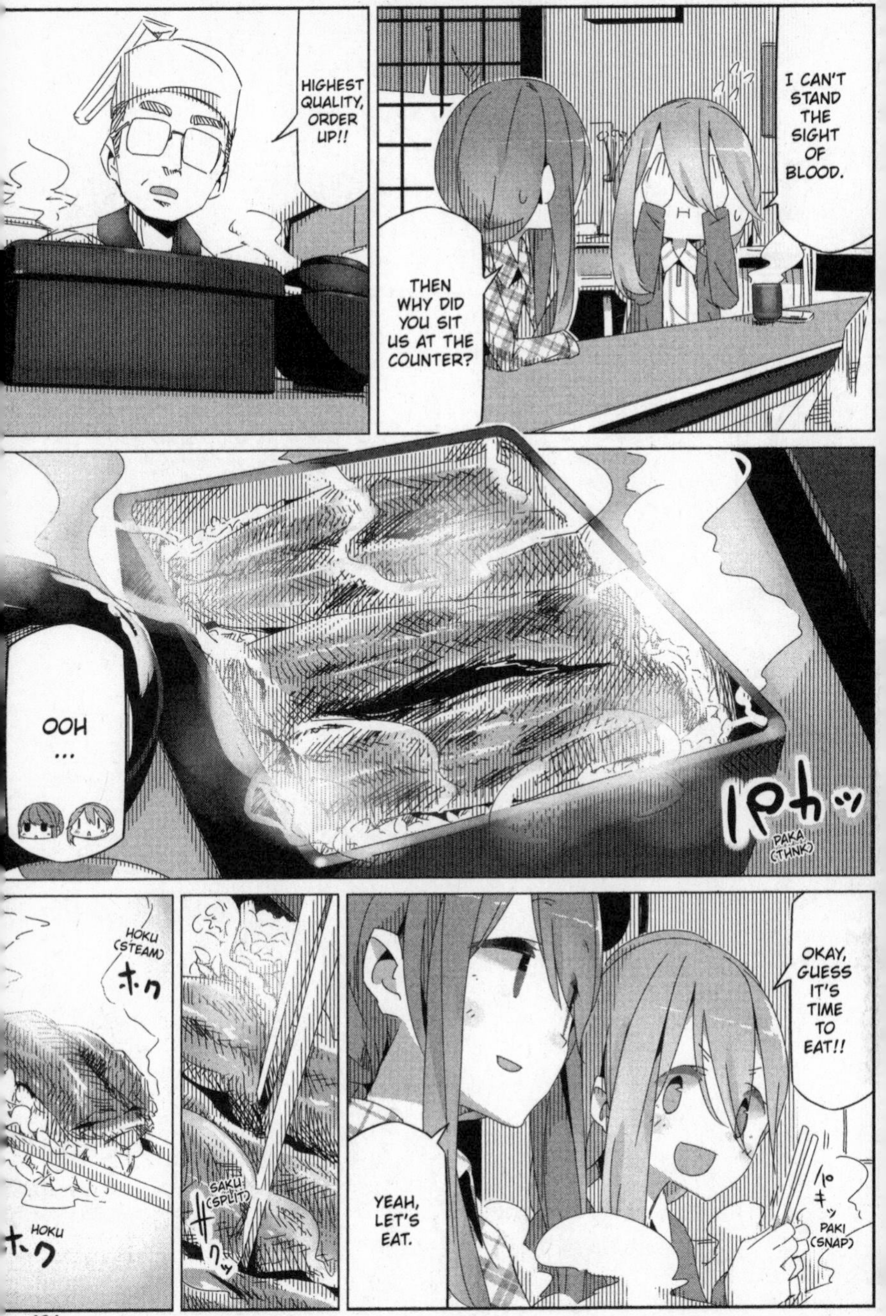
I CAN'T STAND THE SIGHT OF BLOOD.
THEN WHY DID YOU SIT US AT THE COUNTER?
HIGHEST QUALITY, ORDER UP!!
パカッ
PAKA (THNK)
OOH ...
OKAY, GUESS IT'S TIME TO EAT!!
パキッ
PAKI (SNAP)
YEAH, LET'S EAT.
サクッ
SAKU (SPLIT)
HOKU (STEAM)
ホク
ホク
HOKU

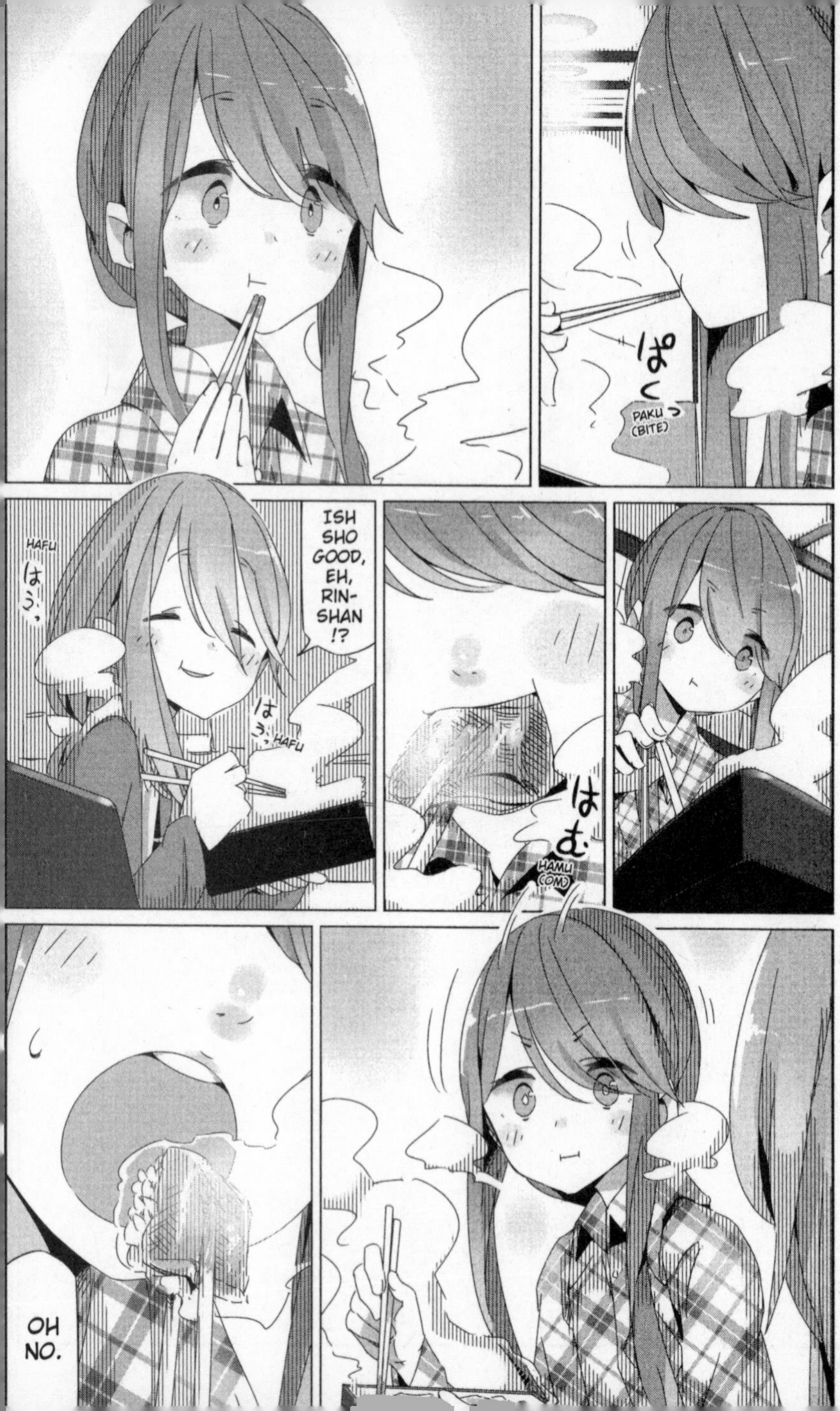
ぱくっ
PAKU (BITE)
はむ
HAMU (OM)
HAFU
はう
ISH SHO GOOD, EH, RIN-SHAN!?
はう
HAFU
OH NO.

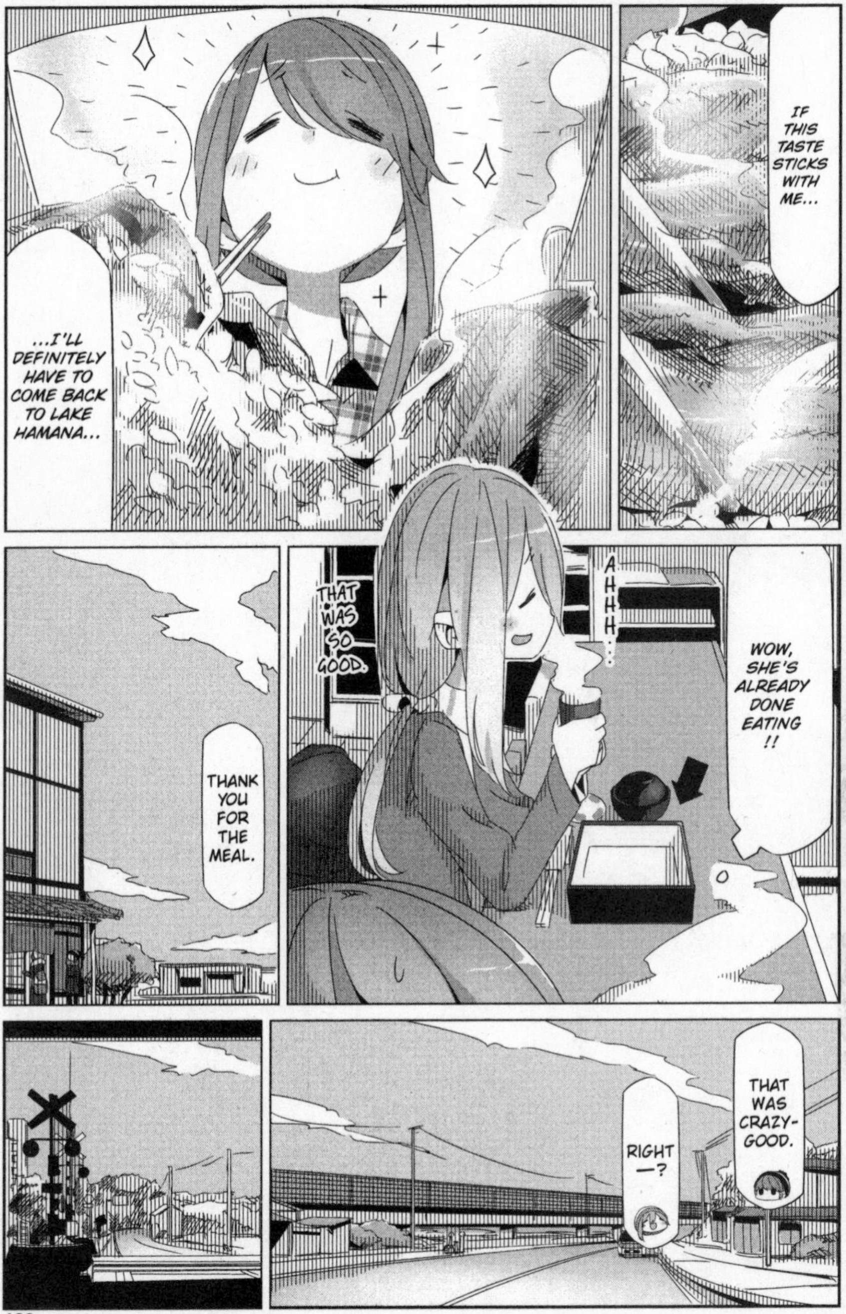
IF THIS TASTE STICKS WITH ME...
...I'LL DEFINITELY HAVE TO COME BACK TO LAKE HAMANA...
WOW, SHE'S ALREADY DONE EATING !!
AHHH...
THAT WAS SO GOOD.
THANK YOU FOR THE MEAL.
THAT WAS CRAZY-GOOD.
RIGHT—?

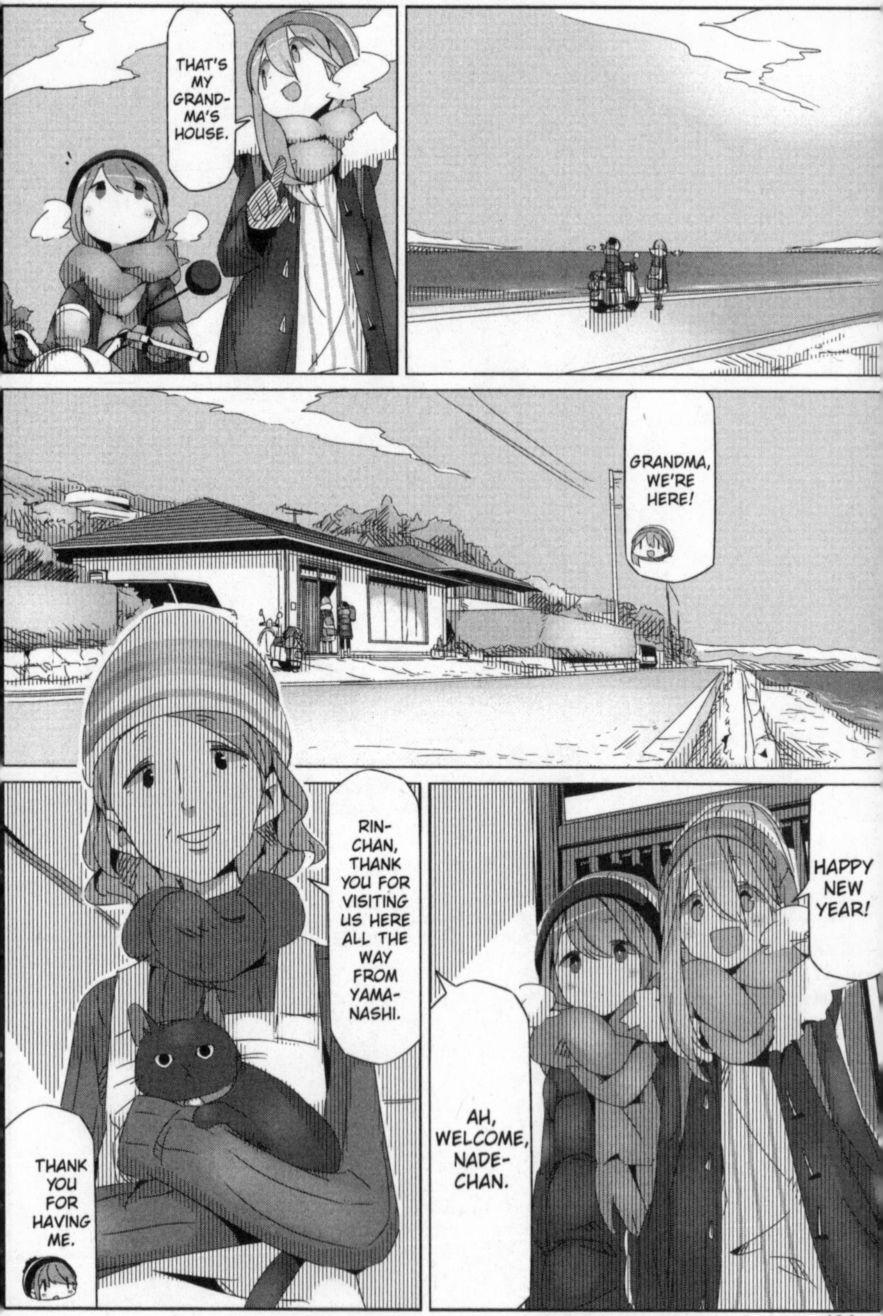
THAT'S MY GRAND-MA'S HOUSE.
GRANDMA, WE'RE HERE!
HAPPY NEW YEAR!
AH, WELCOME, NADE-CHAN.
RIN-CHAN, THANK YOU FOR VISITING US HERE ALL THE WAY FROM YAMA-NASHI.
THANK YOU FOR HAVING ME.

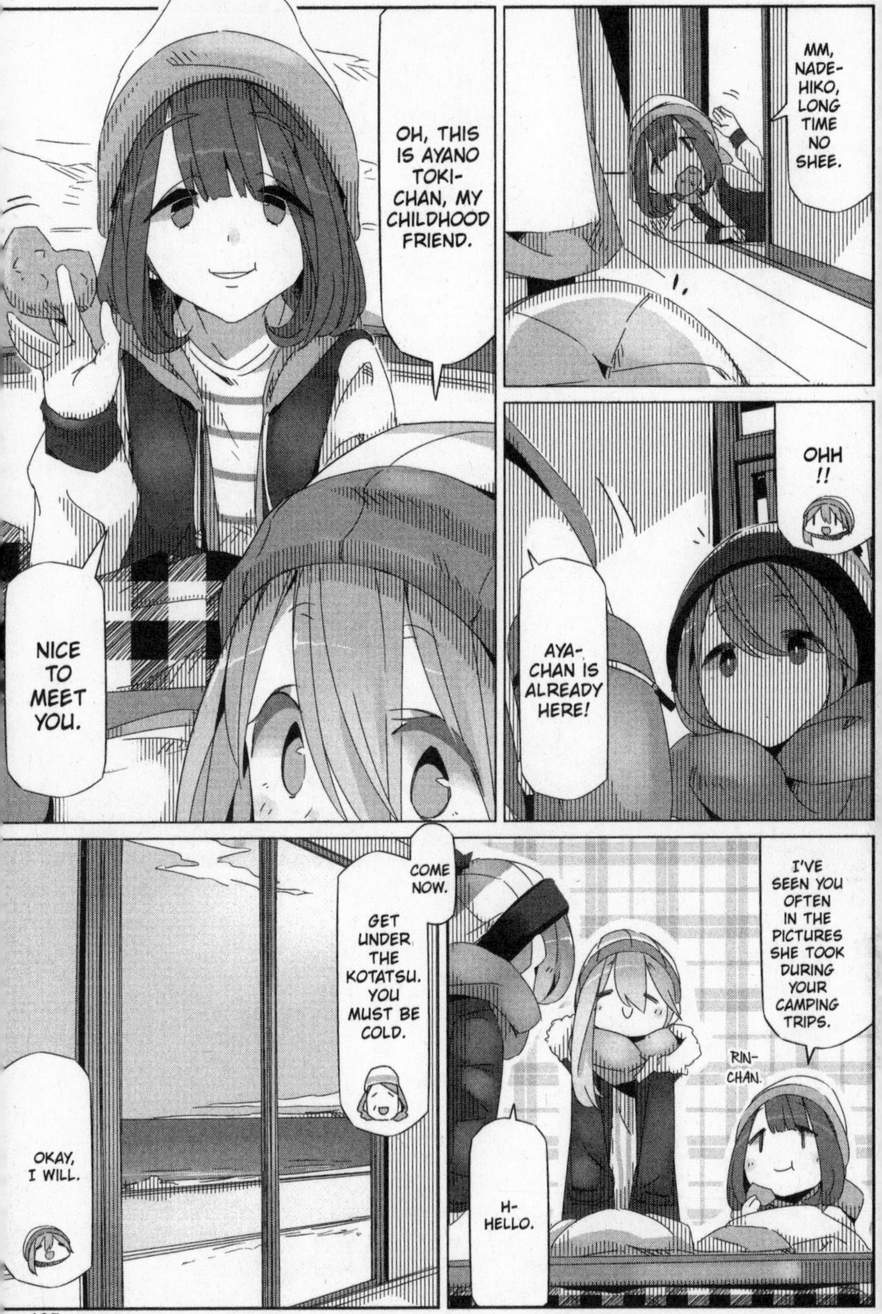
MM, NADE-HIKO, LONG TIME NO SHEE.
OHH !!
AYA-CHAN IS ALREADY HERE!
OH, THIS IS AYANO TOKI-CHAN, MY CHILDHOOD FRIEND.
NICE TO MEET YOU.
I'VE SEEN YOU OFTEN IN THE PICTURES SHE TOOK DURING YOUR CAMPING TRIPS.
RIN-CHAN.
COME NOW.
GET UNDER THE KOTATSU. YOU MUST BE COLD.
H-HELLO.
OKAY, I WILL.

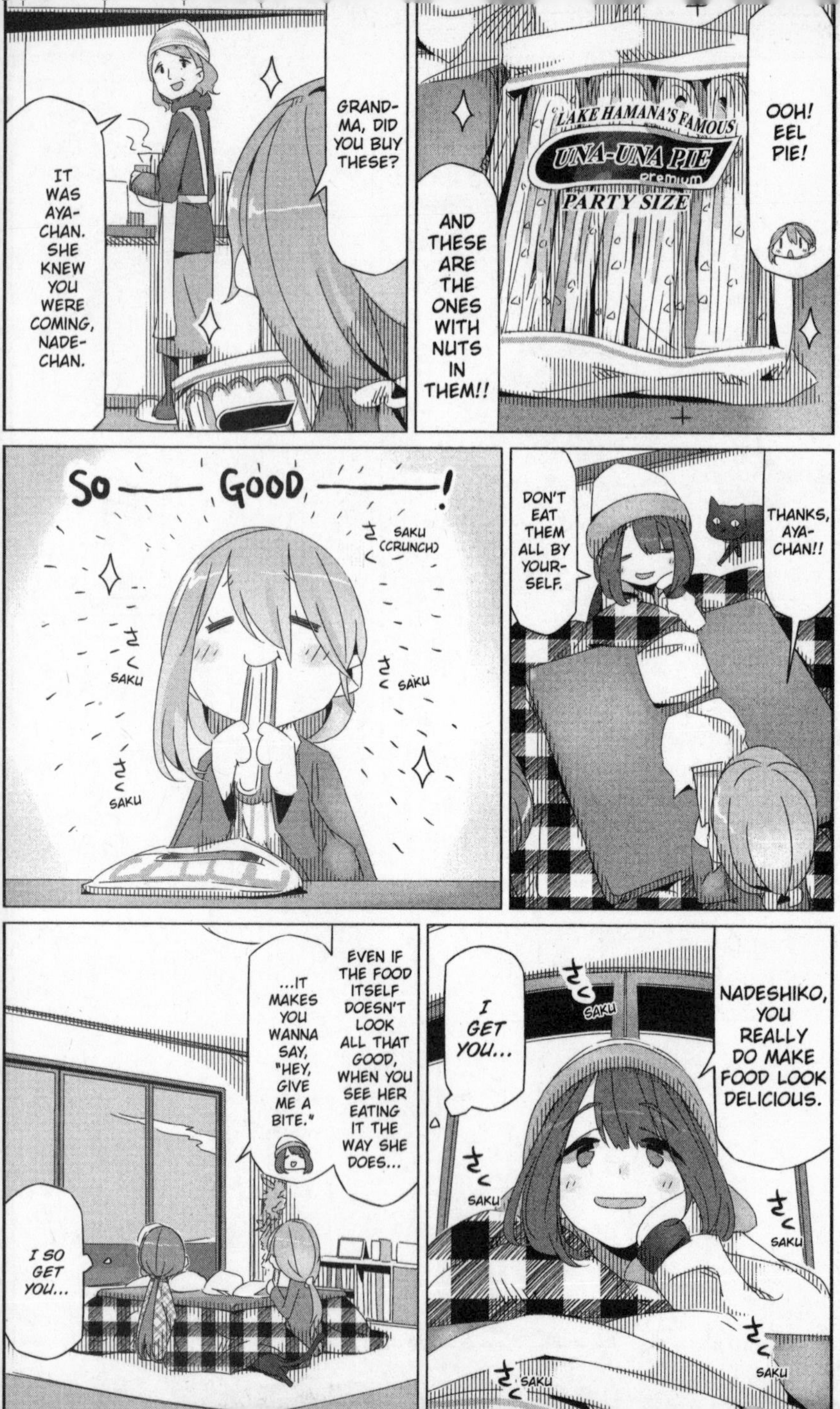
OOH! EEL PIE!
LAKE HAMANA'S FAMOUS
UNA-UNA PIE
premium
PARTY SIZE
AND THESE ARE THE ONES WITH NUTS IN THEM!!
GRAND-MA, DID YOU BUY THESE?
IT WAS AYA-CHAN. SHE KNEW YOU WERE COMING, NADE-CHAN.
THANKS, AYA-CHAN!!
DON'T EAT THEM ALL BY YOUR-SELF.
SO—GOOD—!
さく SAKU (CRUNCH)
さく SAKU
さく SAKU
さく SAKU
NADESHIKO, YOU REALLY DO MAKE FOOD LOOK DELICIOUS.
さく SAKU
I GET YOU...
さく SAKU
さく SAKU
さく SAKU
さく SAKU
EVEN IF THE FOOD ITSELF DOESN'T LOOK ALL THAT GOOD, WHEN YOU SEE HER EATING IT THE WAY SHE DOES...
...IT MAKES YOU WANNA SAY, "HEY, GIVE ME A BITE."
I SO GET YOU...

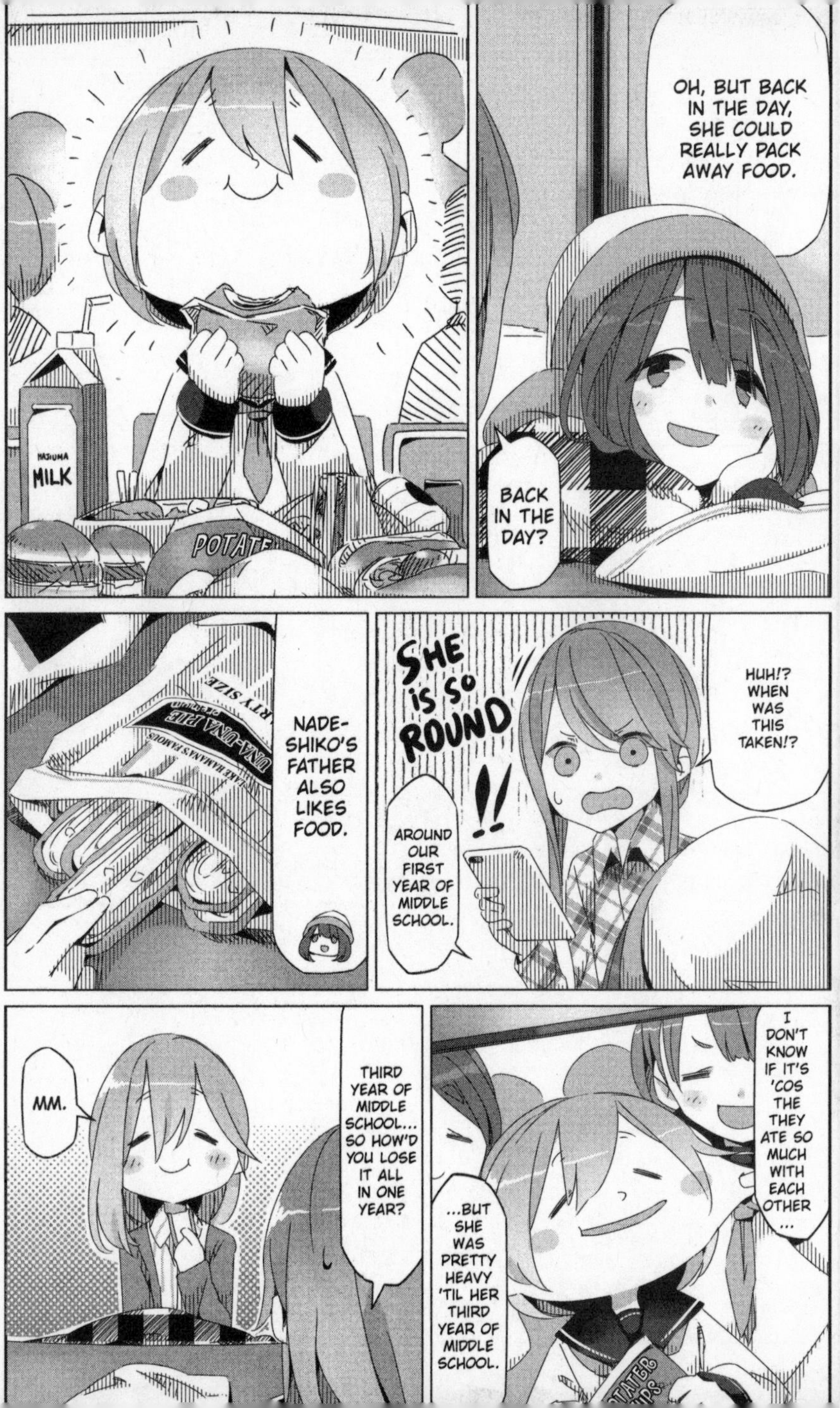

OH, BUT BACK IN THE DAY, SHE COULD REALLY PACK AWAY FOOD.
BACK IN THE DAY?
HAJIUMA MILK
POTATE
HUH!? WHEN WAS THIS TAKEN!?
SHE is so ROUND
AROUND OUR FIRST YEAR OF MIDDLE SCHOOL.
NADE-SHIKO'S FATHER ALSO LIKES FOOD.
LAKE HAMANA'S FAMOUS
UNA-UNA PIE
I DON'T KNOW IF IT'S 'COS THE THEY ATE SO MUCH WITH EACH OTHER...
...BUT SHE WAS PRETTY HEAVY 'TIL HER THIRD YEAR OF MIDDLE SCHOOL.
THIRD YEAR OF MIDDLE SCHOOL... SO HOW'D YOU LOSE IT ALL IN ONE YEAR?
MM.

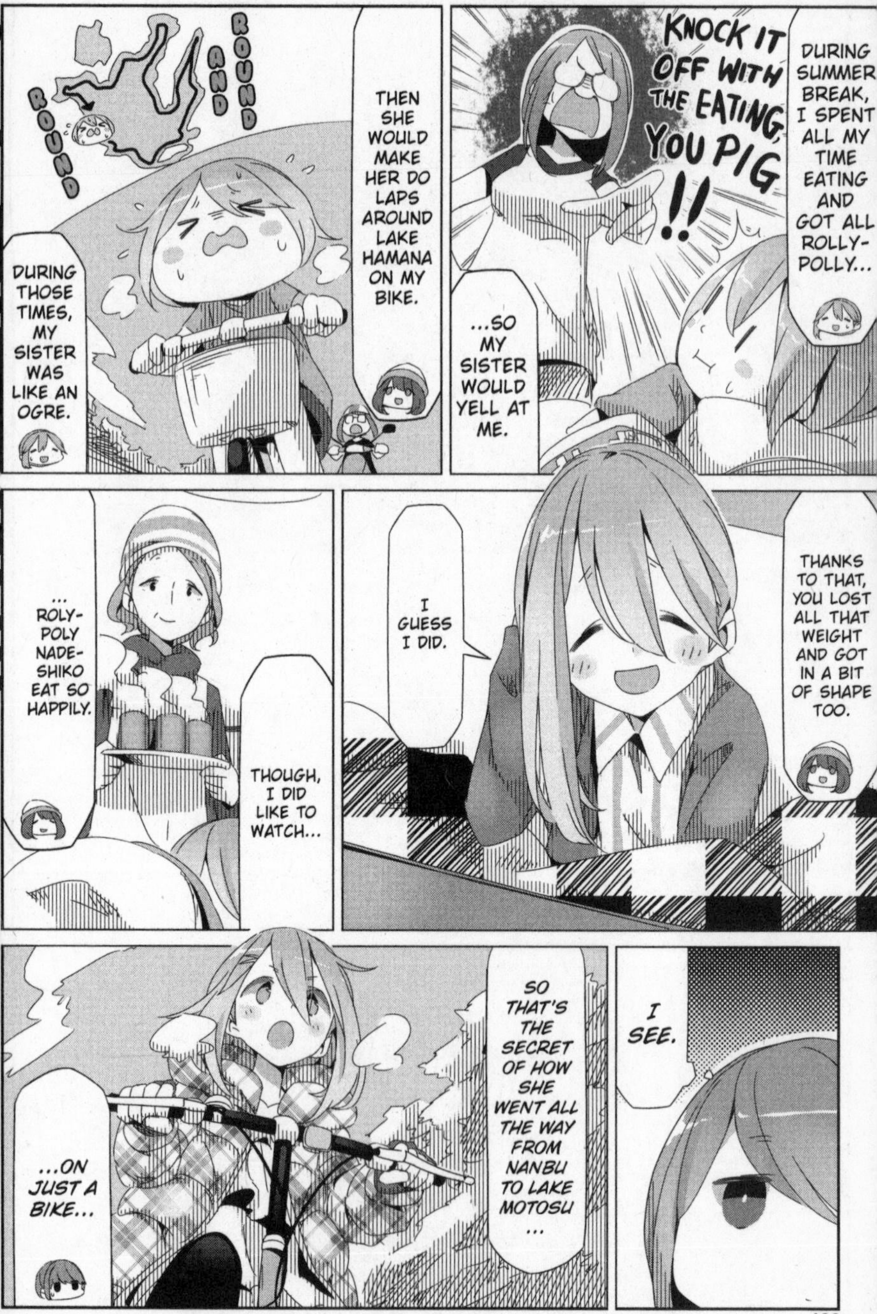
DURING SUMMER BREAK, I SPENT ALL MY TIME EATING AND GOT ALL ROLLY-POLLY...
KNOCK IT OFF WITH THE EATING, YOU PIG!!
...SO MY SISTER WOULD YELL AT ME.
THEN SHE WOULD MAKE HER DO LAPS AROUND LAKE HAMANA ON MY BIKE.
ROUND AND ROUND
DURING THOSE TIMES, MY SISTER WAS LIKE AN OGRE.
THANKS TO THAT, YOU LOST ALL THAT WEIGHT AND GOT IN A BIT OF SHAPE TOO.
I GUESS I DID.
THOUGH, I DID LIKE TO WATCH...
...ROLY-POLY NADE-SHIKO EAT SO HAPPILY.
I SEE.
SO THAT'S THE SECRET OF HOW SHE WENT ALL THE WAY FROM NANBU TO LAKE MOTOSU...
...ON JUST A BIKE...

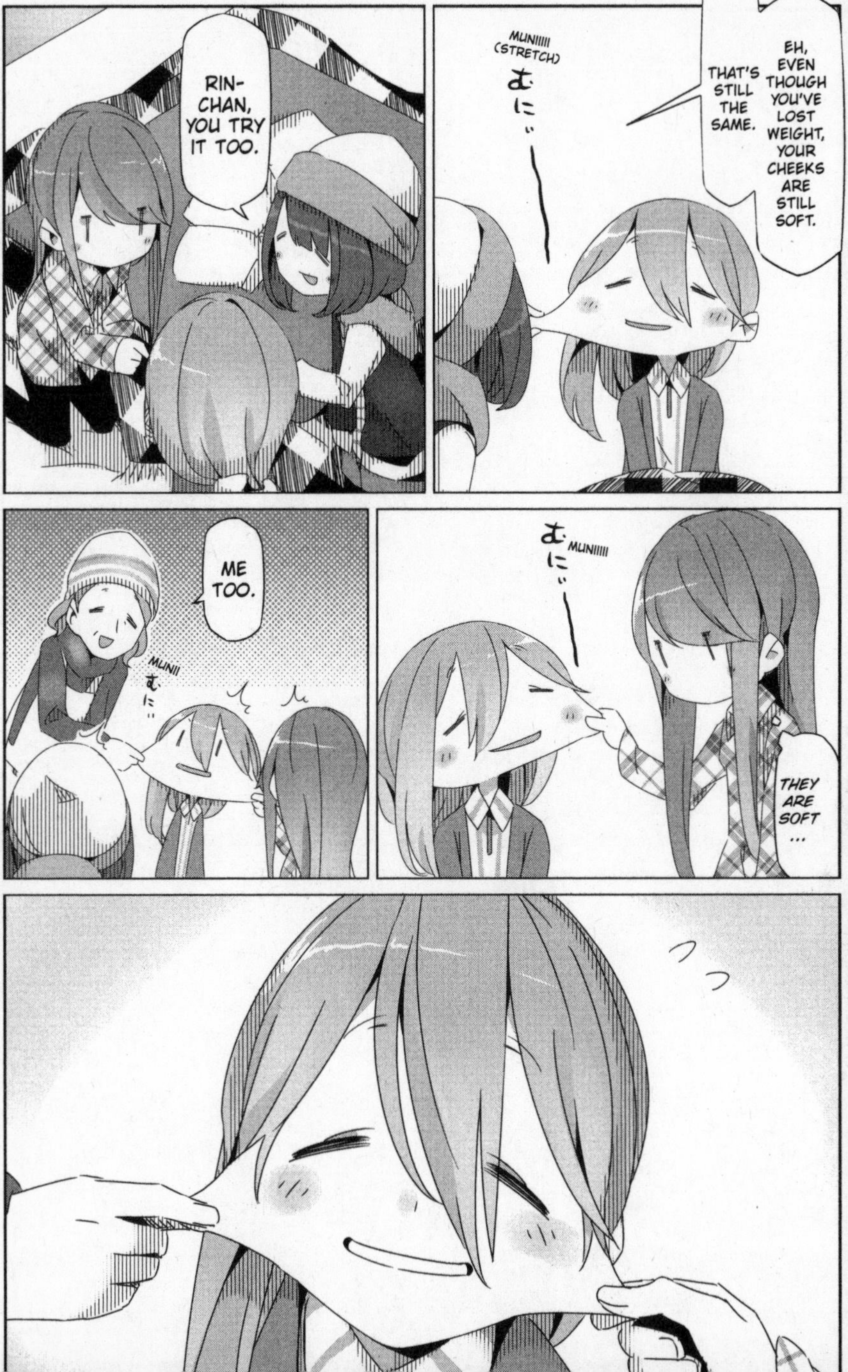
MUNIIIII (STRETCH)
むにぃー
EH, EVEN THOUGH YOU'VE LOST WEIGHT, YOUR CHEEKS ARE STILL SOFT.
THAT'S STILL THE SAME.
RIN-CHAN, YOU TRY IT TOO.
むにぃー
MUNIIIII
THEY ARE SOFT ...
ME TOO.
MUNII
むに..

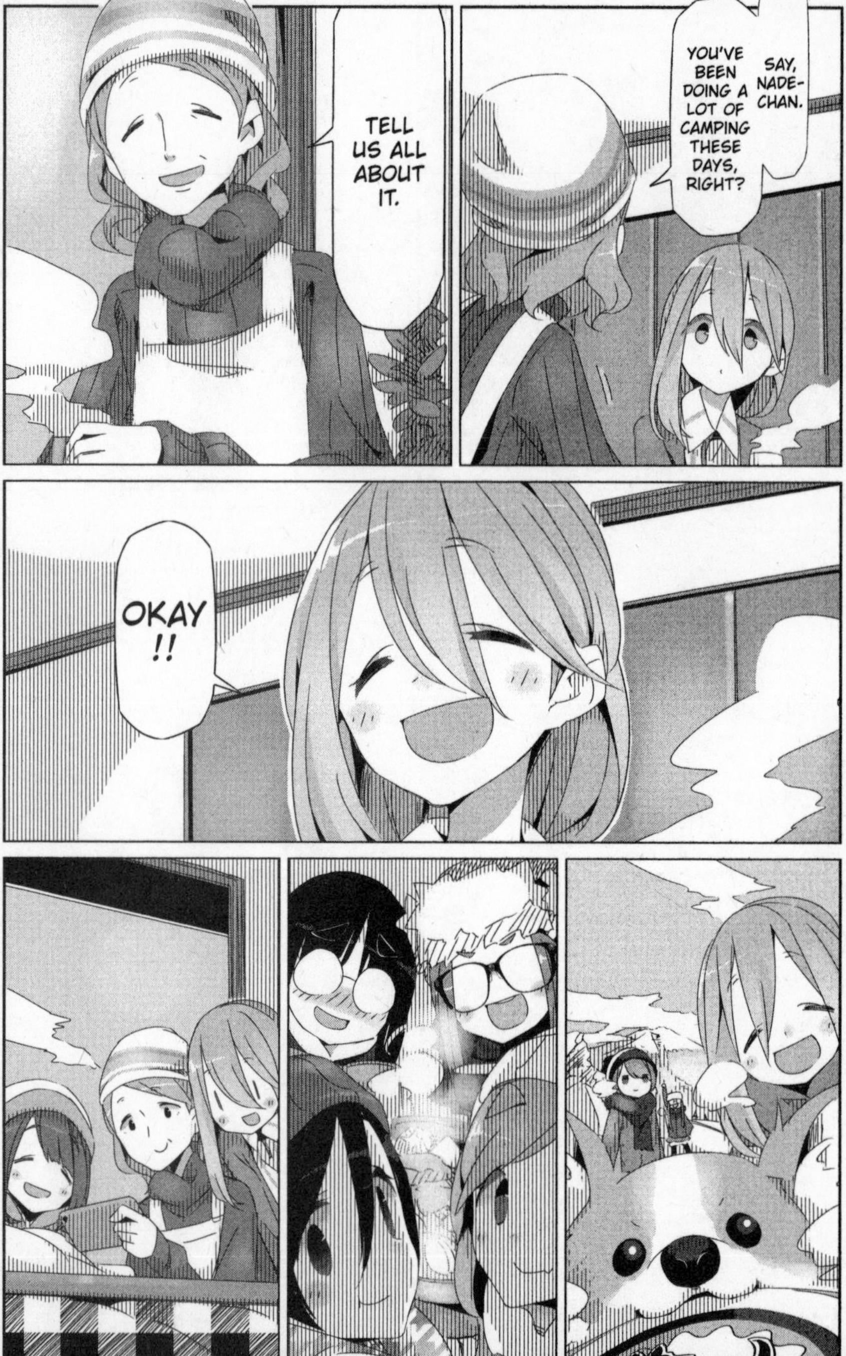
SAY, NADE-CHAN.
YOU'VE BEEN DOING A LOT OF CAMPING THESE DAYS, RIGHT?
TELL US ALL ABOUT IT.
OKAY!!

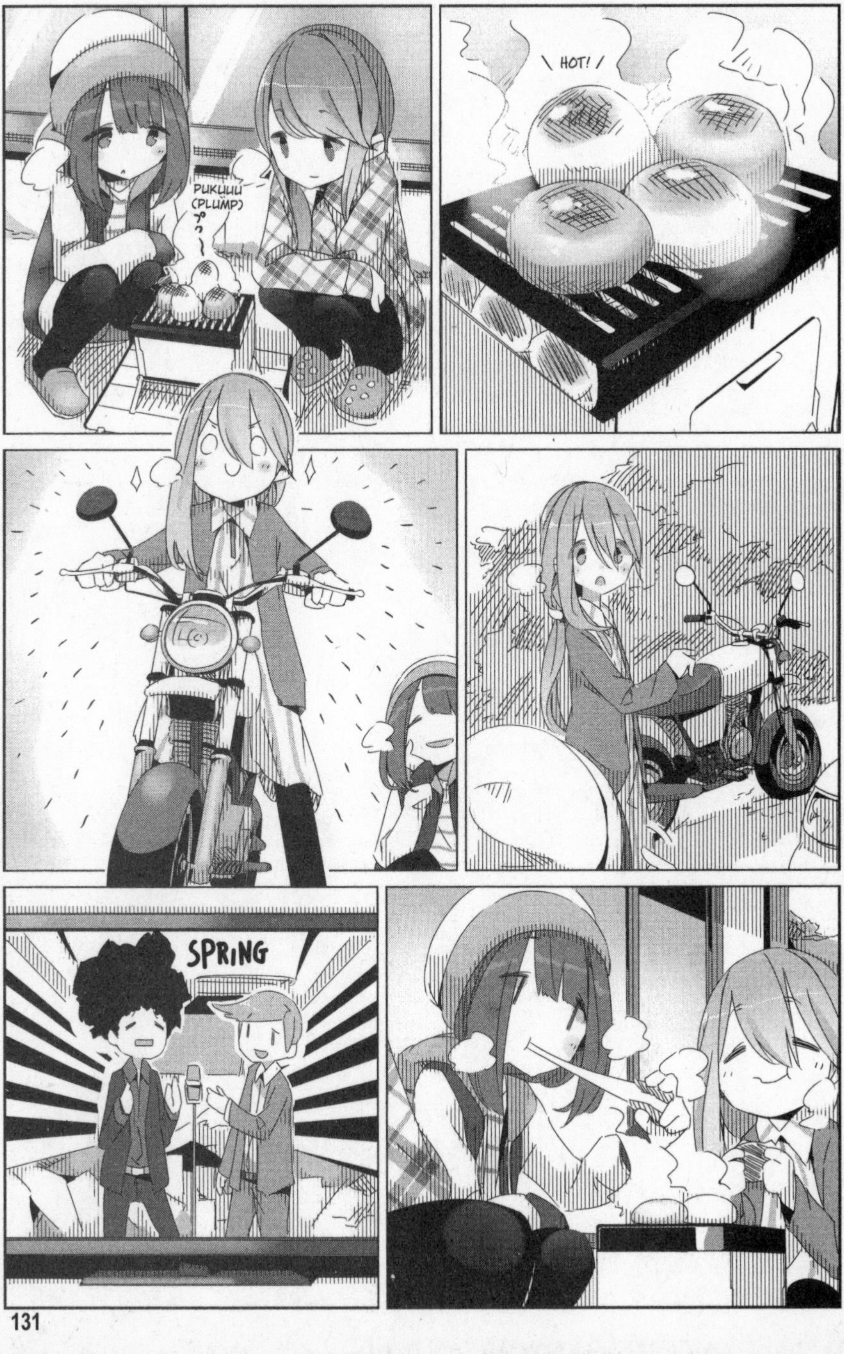
HOT!
PUKUUU (PLUMP)
SPRING

PACKAGING: KIRARA / ICHIGO NO KIRAMEKI

苺のきらめき
苺のきらめき
苺のきらめき

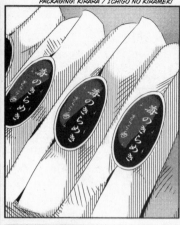

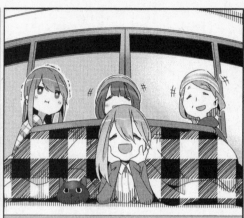

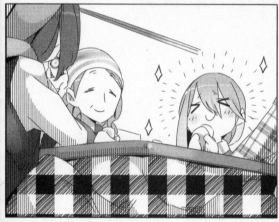

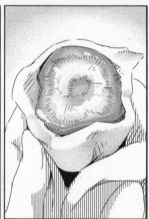

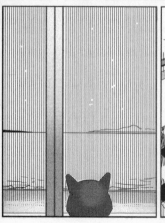

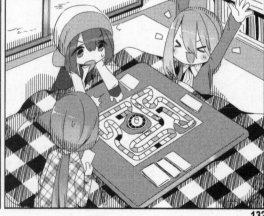

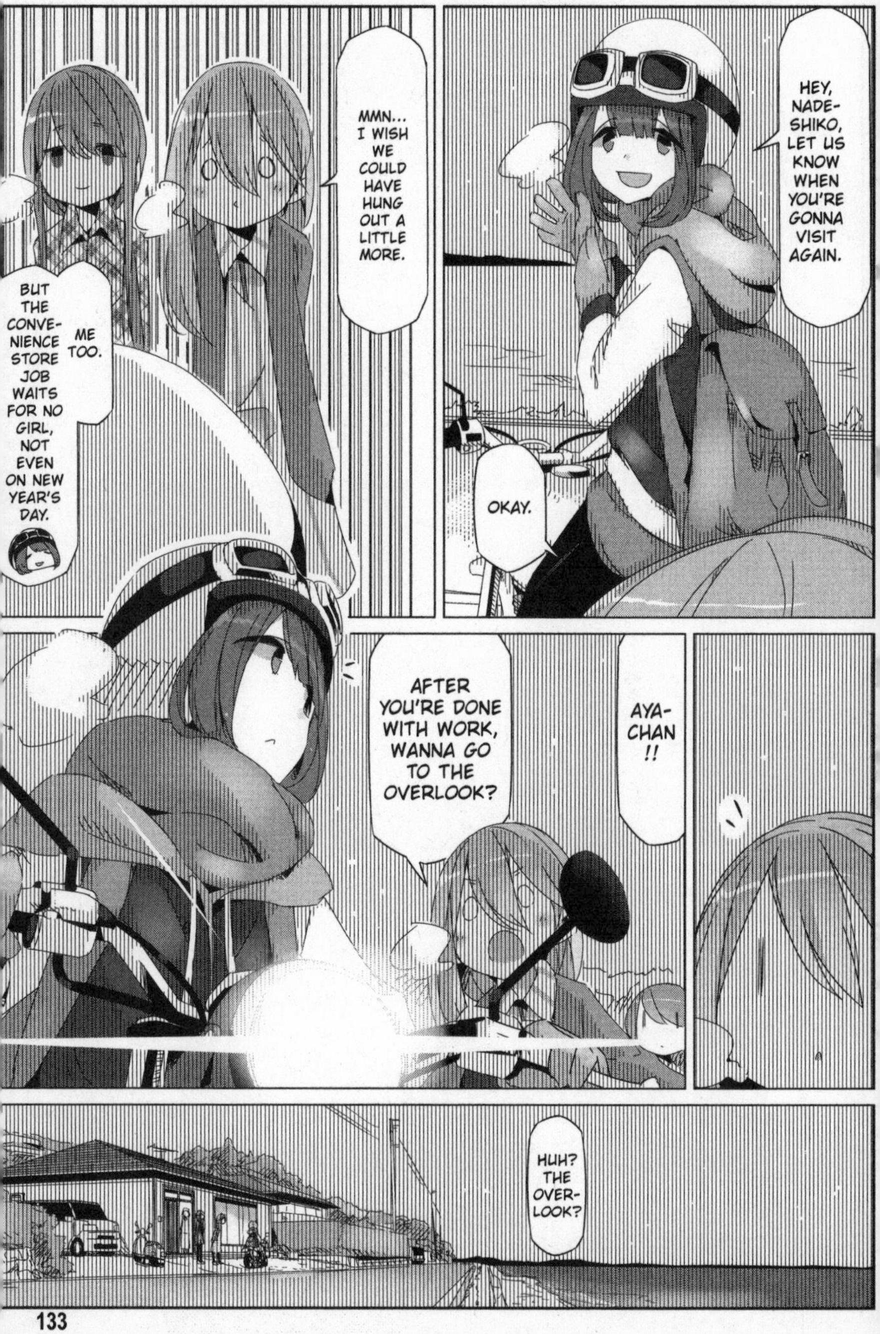
HEY, NADE-SHIKO, LET US KNOW WHEN YOU'RE GONNA VISIT AGAIN.
OKAY.
MMN... I WISH WE COULD HAVE HUNG OUT A LITTLE MORE.
ME TOO.
BUT THE CONVE-NIENCE STORE JOB WAITS FOR NO GIRL, NOT EVEN ON NEW YEAR'S DAY.
AYA-CHAN !!
AFTER YOU'RE DONE WITH WORK, WANNA GO TO THE OVERLOOK?
HUH? THE OVER-LOOK?

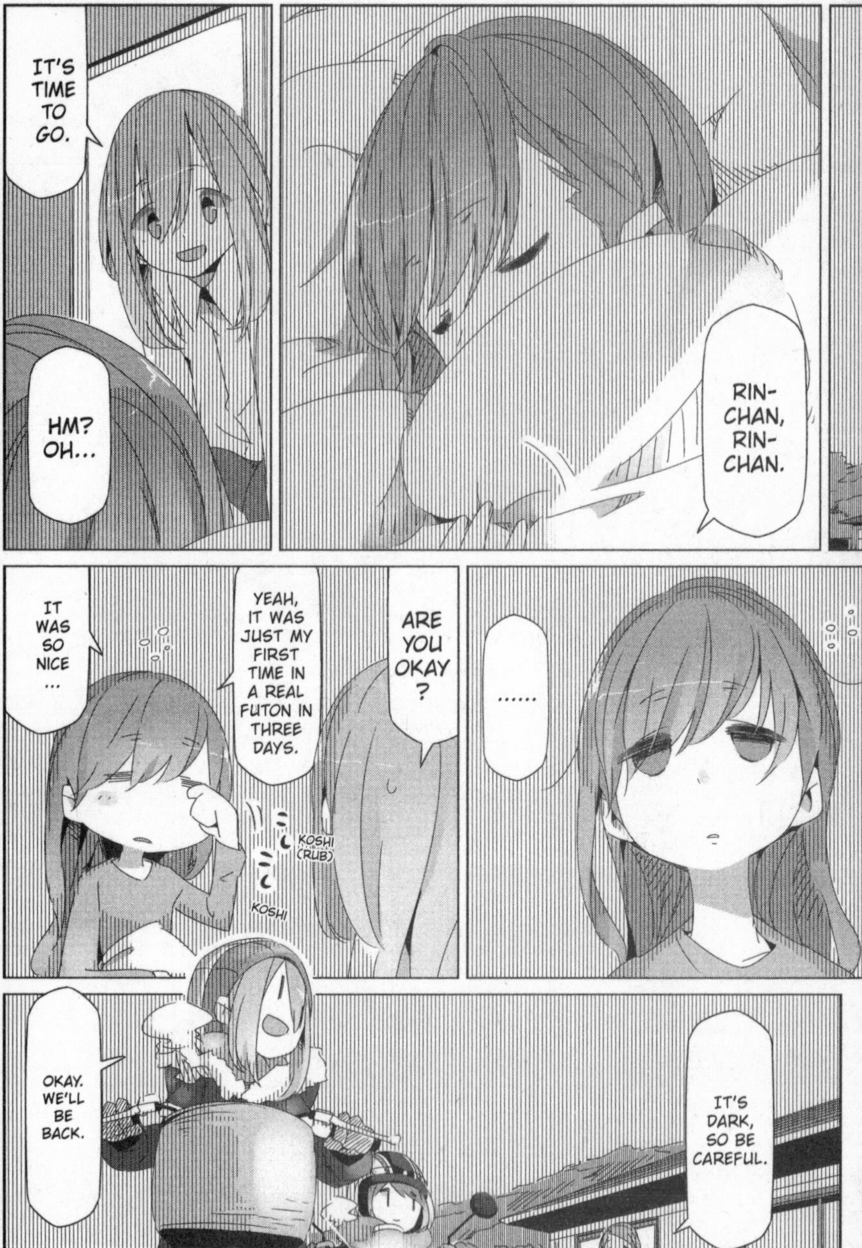
RIN-CHAN, RIN-CHAN.
IT'S TIME TO GO.
HM? OH...
......
ARE YOU OKAY?
YEAH, IT WAS JUST MY FIRST TIME IN A REAL FUTON IN THREE DAYS.
IT WAS SO NICE ...
KOSHI (RUB)
KOSHI
IT'S DARK, SO BE CAREFUL.
OKAY. WE'LL BE BACK.

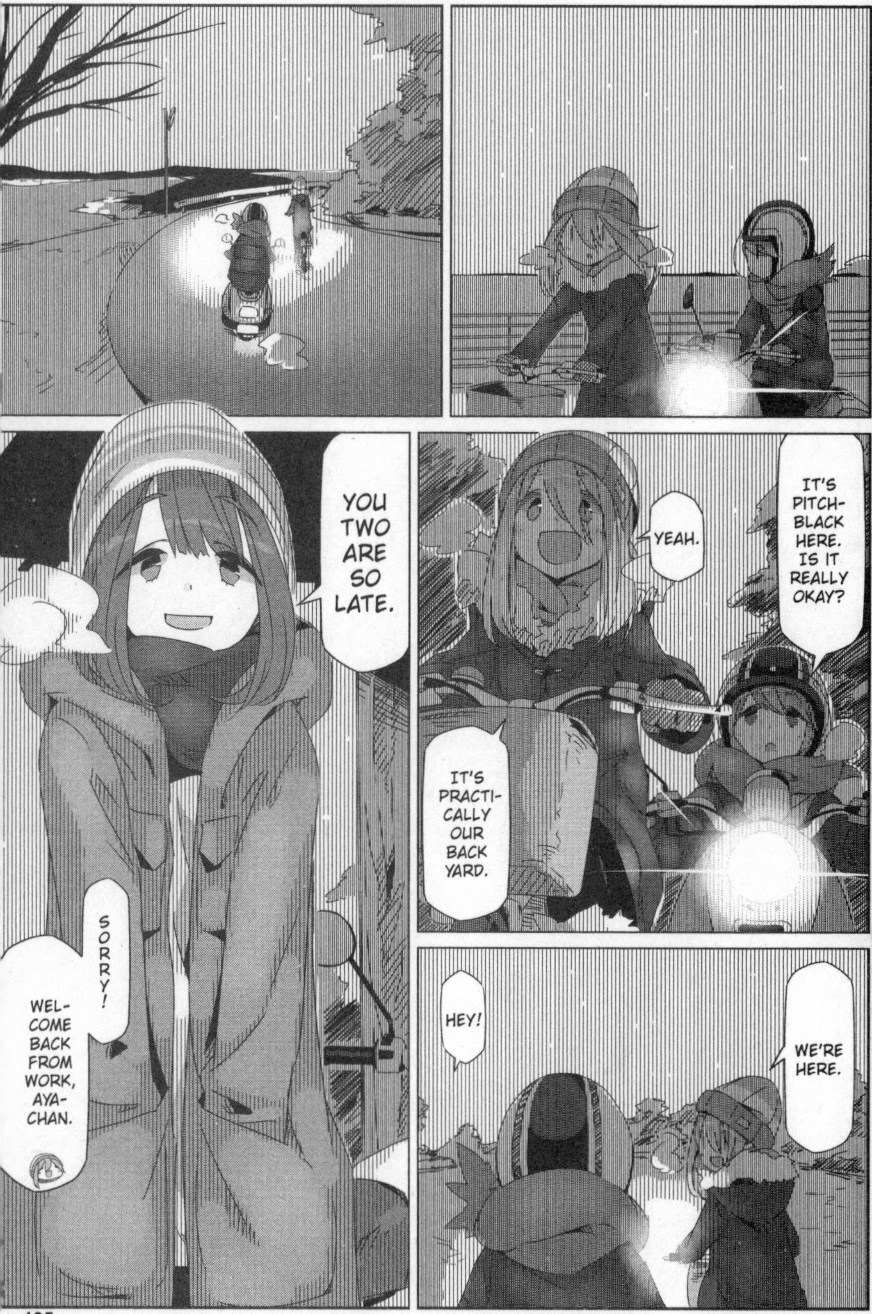
IT'S PITCH-BLACK HERE. IS IT REALLY OKAY?
YEAH.
IT'S PRACTICALLY OUR BACK YARD.
WE'RE HERE.
HEY!
YOU TWO ARE SO LATE.
SORRY!
WELCOME BACK FROM WORK, AYA-CHAN.

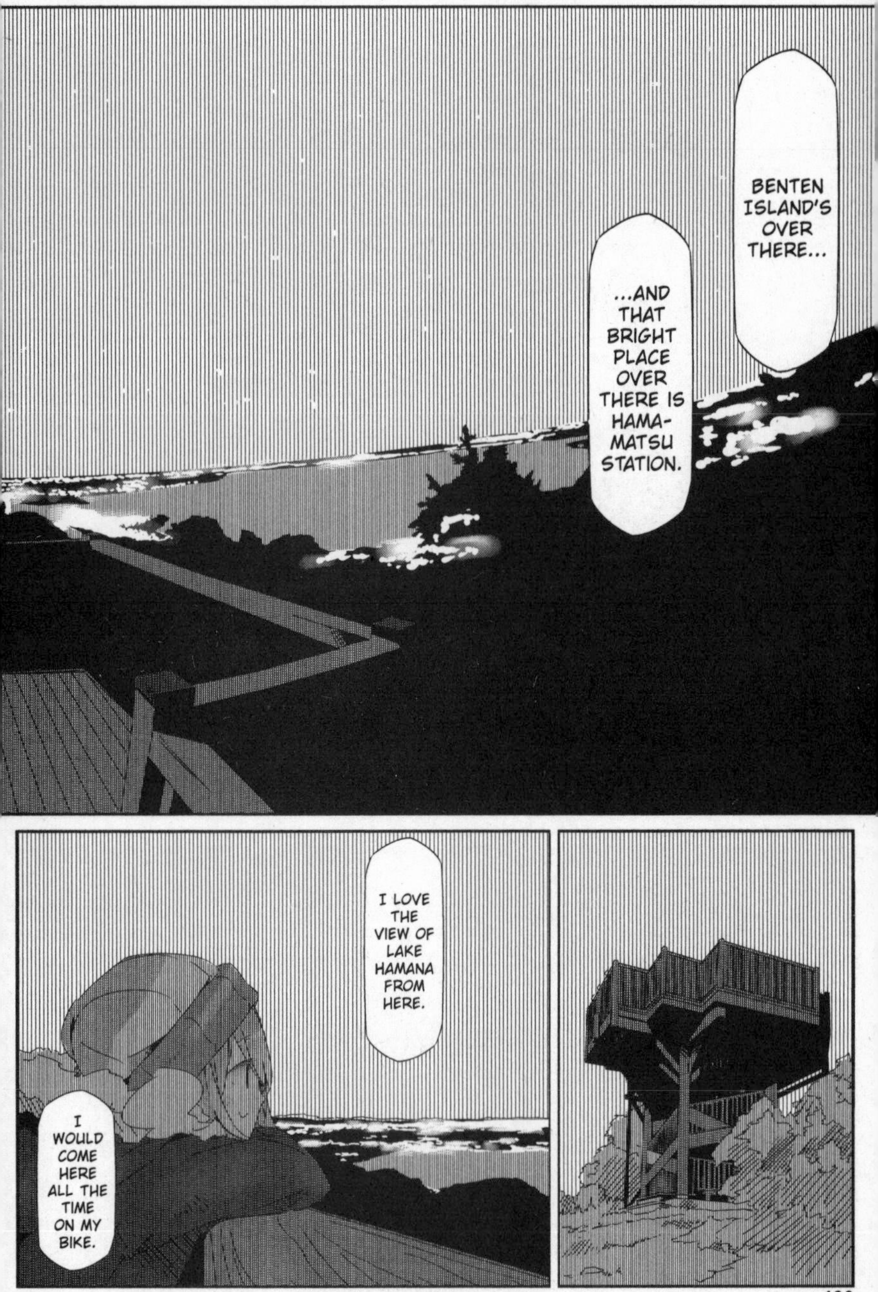
BENTEN ISLAND'S OVER THERE...
...AND THAT BRIGHT PLACE OVER THERE IS HAMA-MATSU STATION.
I LOVE THE VIEW OF LAKE HAMANA FROM HERE.
I WOULD COME HERE ALL THE TIME ON MY BIKE.

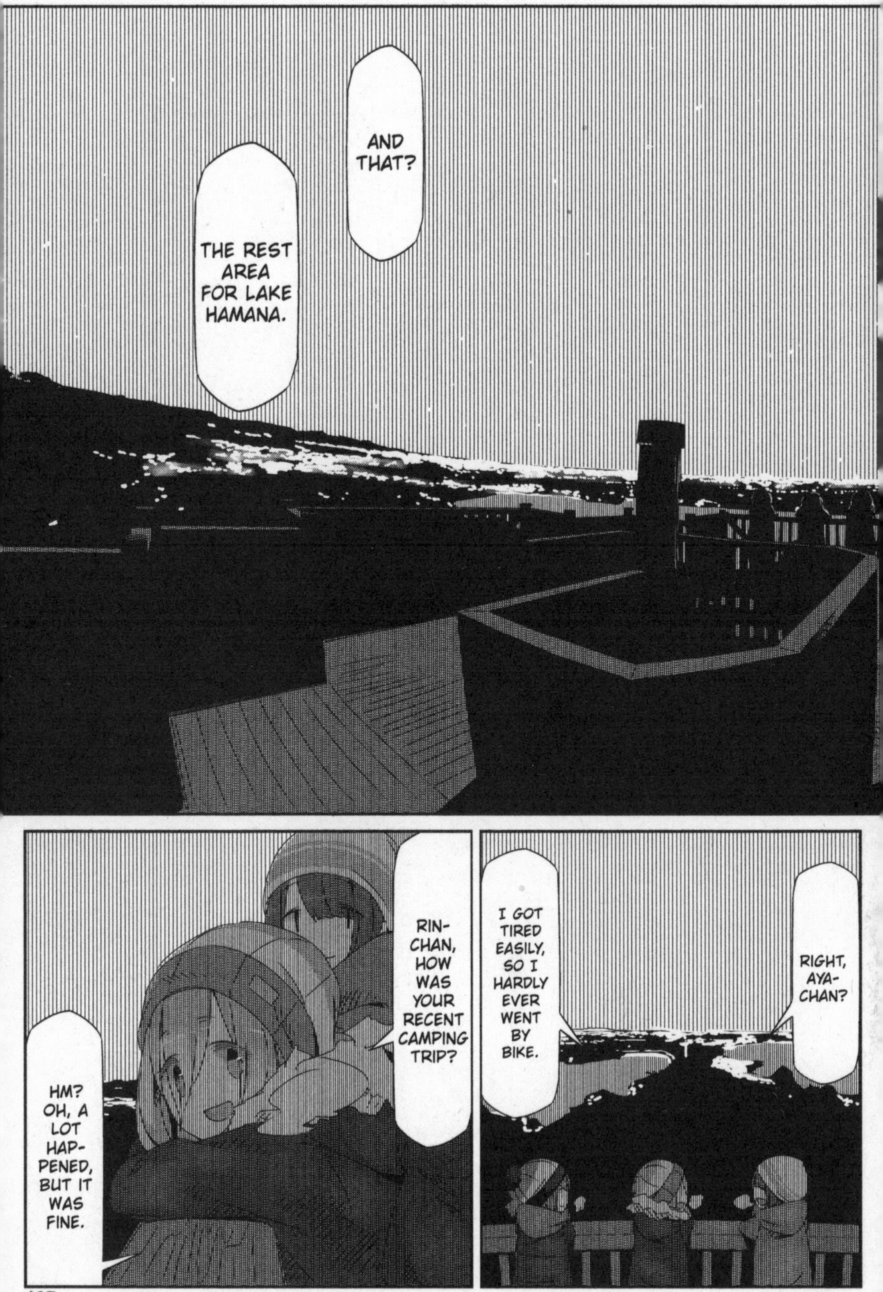
AND THAT?
THE REST AREA FOR LAKE HAMANA.
RIGHT, AYA-CHAN?
I GOT TIRED EASILY, SO I HARDLY EVER WENT BY BIKE.
RIN-CHAN, HOW WAS YOUR RECENT CAMPING TRIP?
HM? OH, A LOT HAP-PENED, BUT IT WAS FINE.

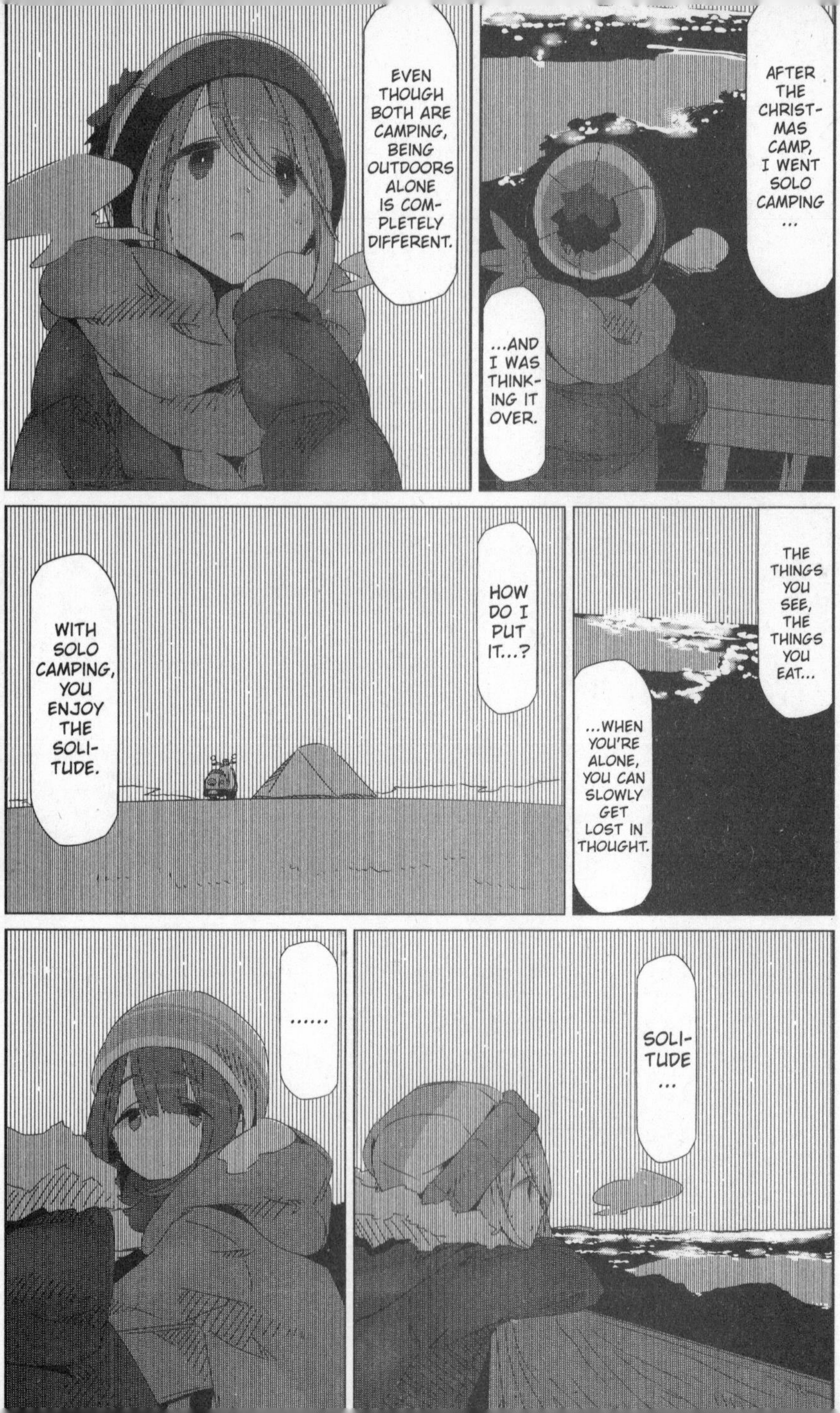
AFTER THE CHRISTMAS CAMP, I WENT SOLO CAMPING...
...AND I WAS THINKING IT OVER.
EVEN THOUGH BOTH ARE CAMPING, BEING OUTDOORS ALONE IS COMPLETELY DIFFERENT.
THE THINGS YOU SEE, THE THINGS YOU EAT...
...WHEN YOU'RE ALONE, YOU CAN SLOWLY GET LOST IN THOUGHT.
HOW DO I PUT IT...?
WITH SOLO CAMPING, YOU ENJOY THE SOLITUDE.
SOLITUDE...
......

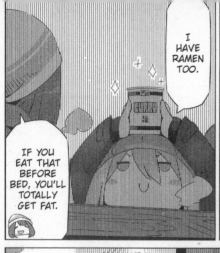

AYA-CHAN... WANT SOME COCOA?
OH, I DO.
I HAVE RAMEN TOO.
IF YOU EAT THAT BEFORE BED, YOU'LL TOTALLY GET FAT.
AFU COMO
あうっ
AFU
あうっ

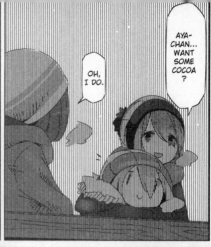

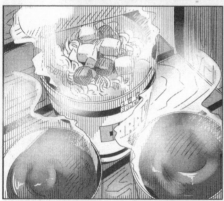

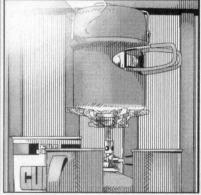

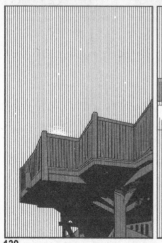

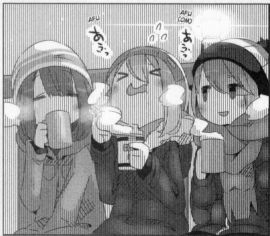

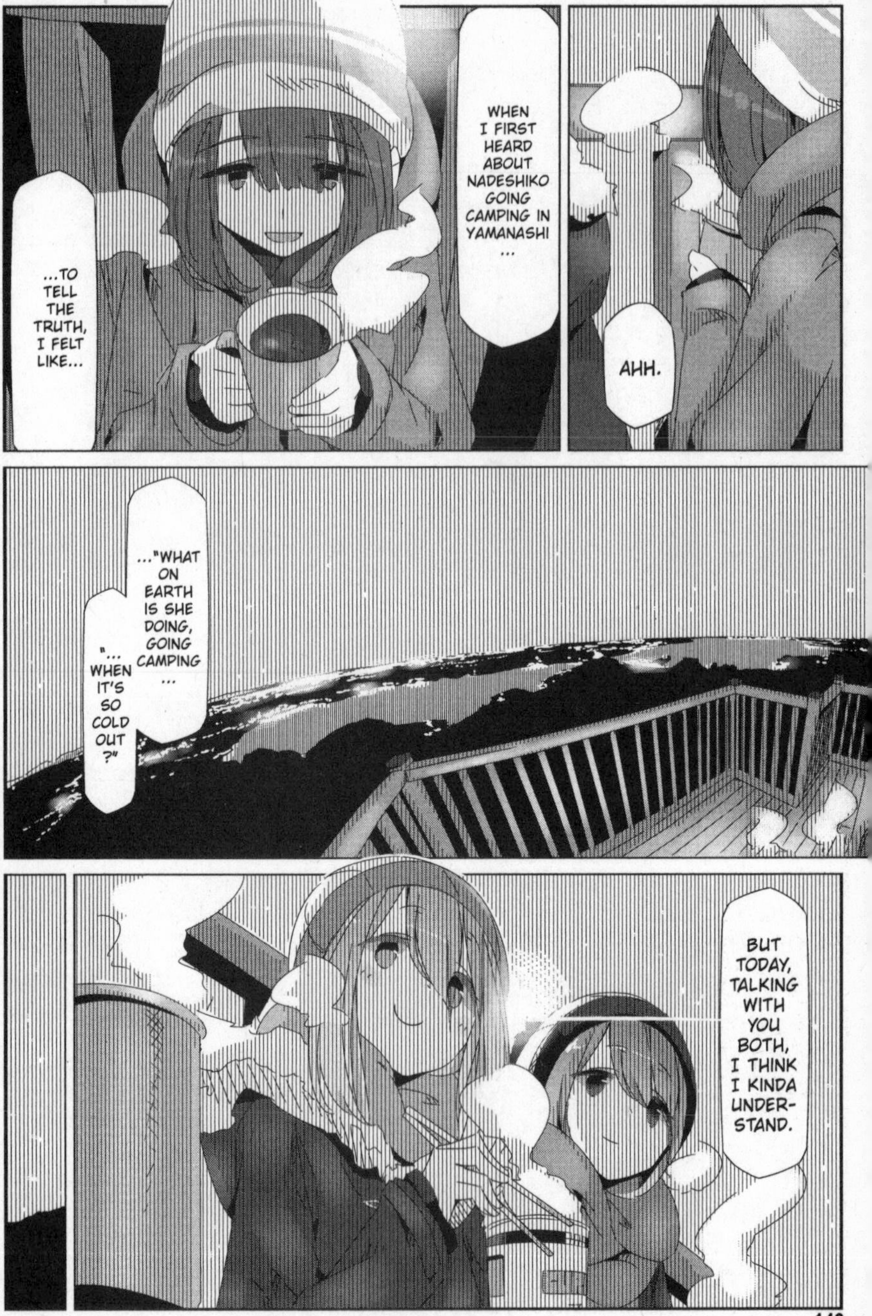
AHH.
WHEN I FIRST HEARD ABOUT NADESHIKO GOING CAMPING IN YAMANASHI...
...TO TELL THE TRUTH, I FELT LIKE...
..."WHAT ON EARTH IS SHE DOING, GOING CAMPING...
"...WHEN IT'S SO COLD OUT?"
BUT TODAY, TALKING WITH YOU BOTH, I THINK I KINDA UNDERSTAND.

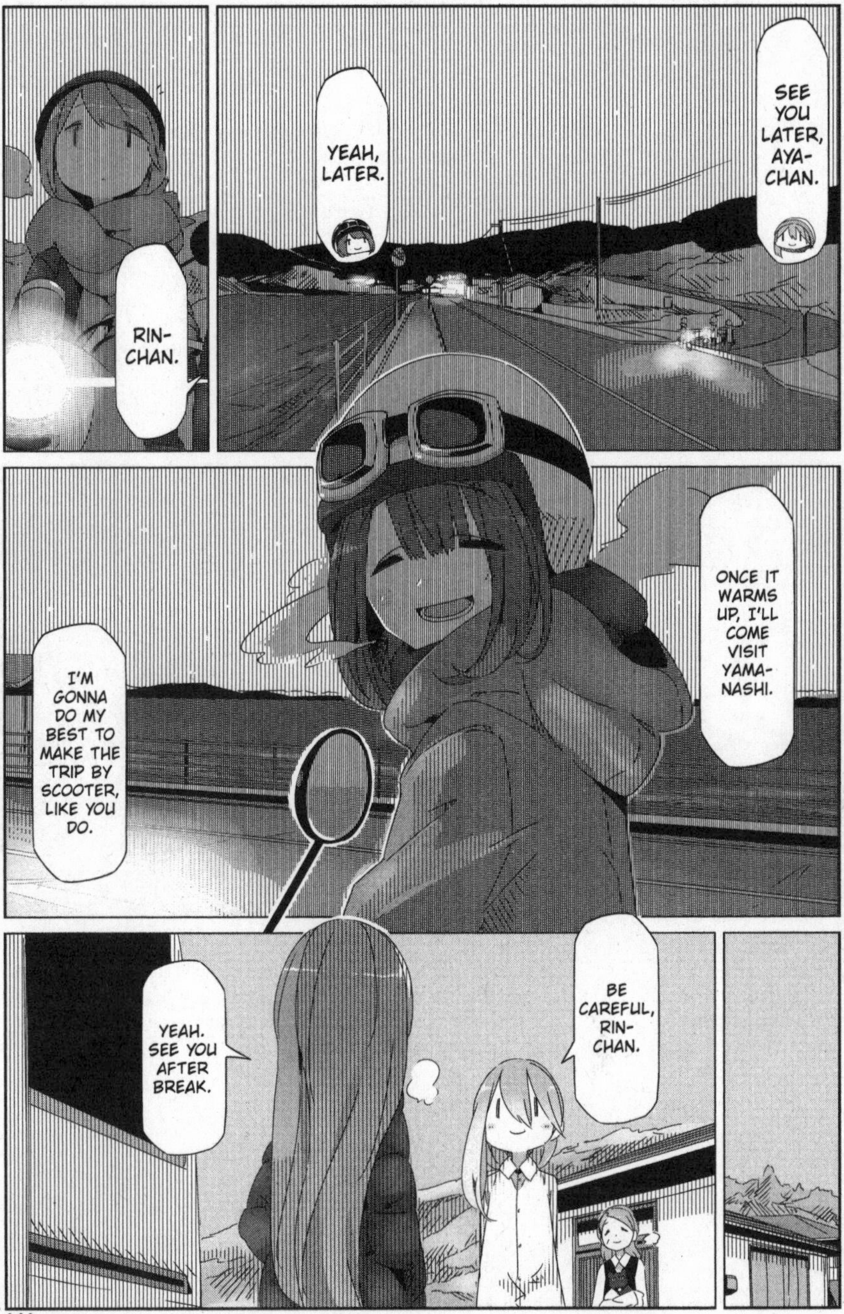
SEE YOU LATER, AYA-CHAN.
YEAH, LATER.
RIN-CHAN.
ONCE IT WARMS UP, I'LL COME VISIT YAMANASHI.
I'M GONNA DO MY BEST TO MAKE THE TRIP BY SCOOTER, LIKE YOU DO.
BE CAREFUL, RIN-CHAN.
YEAH. SEE YOU AFTER BREAK.

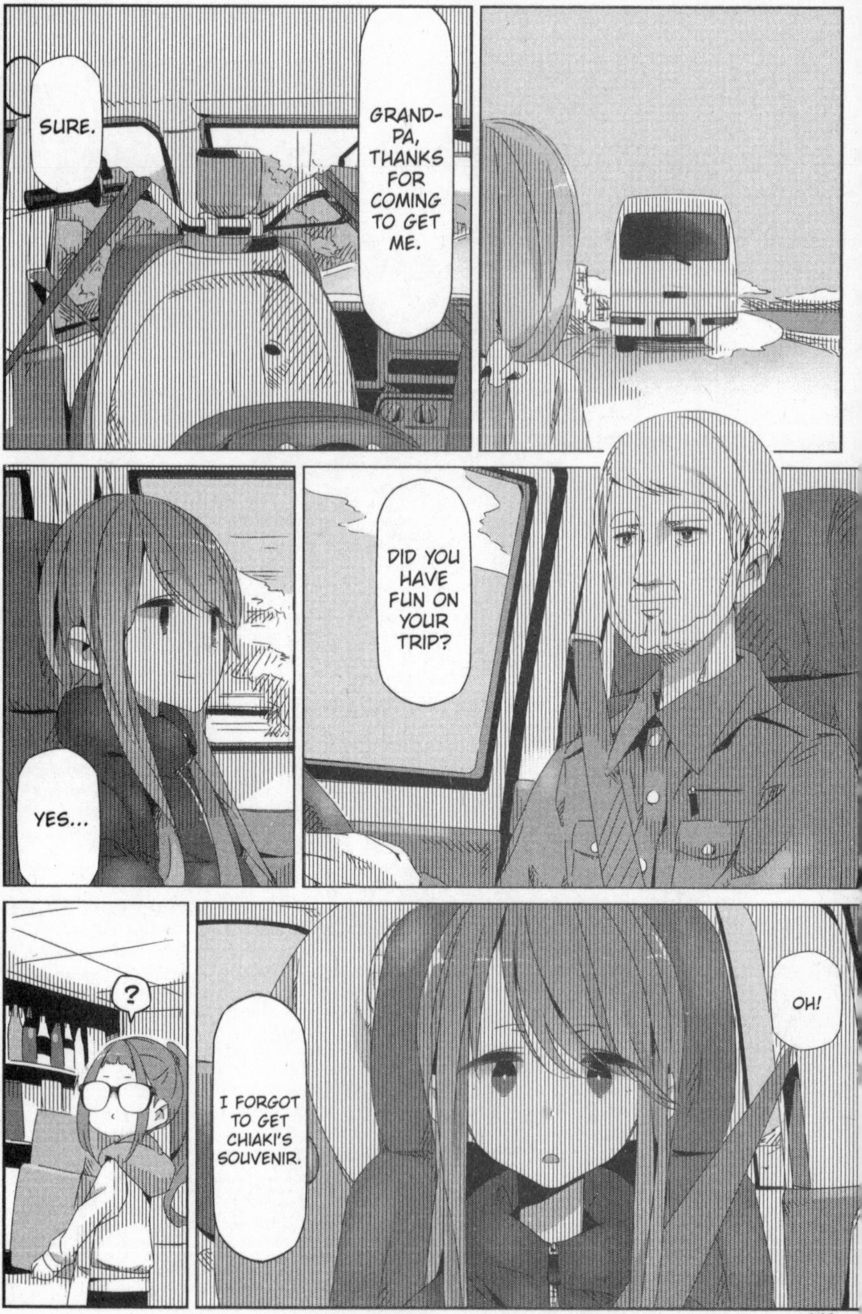
GRAND-PA, THANKS FOR COMING TO GET ME.
SURE.
DID YOU HAVE FUN ON YOUR TRIP?
YES...
OH!
I FORGOT TO GET CHIAKI'S SOUVENIR.
?

TRANSLATION NOTES

COMMON HONORIFICS

no honorific: Indicates familiarity or closeness; if used without permission or reason, addressing someone in this manner would constitute an insult.

-san: The Japanese equivalent of Mr./Mrs./Miss. If a situation calls for politeness, this is the fail-safe honorific.

-kun: Used most often when referring to boys, this indicates affection or familiarity. Occasionally used by older men among their peers, but it may also be used by anyone referring to a person of lower standing.

-chan: An affectionate honorific indicating familiarity used mostly in reference to girls; also used in reference to cute persons or animals of either gender.

-sensei: A respectful term for teachers, artists, or high-level professionals.

(o)nee: Japanese equivalent to "older sis."
(o)nii: Japanese equivalent to "older bro."

100 yen is approximately $1 USD.

PAGE 5
New Year's cards: In Japan, it's tradition to write and receive postcards congratulating friends, relatives, wishing a Happy New Year. It originally began as a way to inform those you couldn't see often that you were doing okay.

PAGE 9
House numbers in *kanji*: In Japanese, numbers can be written in *kanji*, or Chinese characters. However, there are no hard and fast rules for writing house numbers, so "11" could be seen as "eleven" or "one-one." Adding to the confusion is the fact that Japanese is commonly written vertically as well as horizontally; the *kanji* for one (一), two (二), and three (三) are somewhat similar and can cause confusion when written sloppily. For example, 三 could mean "three," or it could be a 一 and a 二 stacked really close together.

PAGE 17
First shrine visit of the year: *Hatsumoude* in Japanese; people go to pray for blessings in the new year. Major shrines like Meiji are often packed with people throughout the first few days of the new year.

Nigiri **sushi**: The most typical type of non-roll sushi, with a clump of rice on the bottom and a topping placed over it.

PAGE 23
Cross-year *soba*: Known as *toshikoshi soba* in Japanese ("crossing-into-the-next-year buckwheat noodles"), this dish is eaten on New Year's Eve because the long noodles symbolize longevity.

PAGES 25–26
Soumen: Thin wheat noodles.
Nyuumen: Hot *soumen*.
Pho: Vietnamese flat wheat noodle soup. Rice vermicelli is another common noodle in Vietnamese cuisine, hence Rin's comparison of the two.
Udon: Thick wheat flour noodles.
Harusame: Potato starch glass noodles.
Tokoroten: Thick seaweed noodles.
Himokawa udon: An *udon* that resembles thin sheets.
Udon youkai: This joke is based on a brand of *himokawa udon* called Oni Himokawa (ogre *himokawa*). *Youkai* are Japanese spirits.

TRANSLATION NOTES (continued)

PAGE 52
Nori: Dried seaweed sheets that are arguably most famously known for being used as wrappings for sushi rolls.

Shichimi: A spice mix usually made of seven ingredients. The main spice is usually red chili pepper while the rest of the recipe can vary.

PAGE 54
New Year's gift: Known in Japan as *otoshidama*, gifts are given to children on New Year's Day by older relatives and close family friends. They are usually monetary and presented in red envelopes.

PAGE 60
Chibi Inuko: Essentially means "Tiny Inuko" or "Mini-Inuko."

PAGE 63
Torii: The gateway of a Shinto shrine, it marks the entrance to a sacred area.

Charity, offertory: In the Japanese version, "charity" is written in *katakana*, the Japanese alphabet system most commonly used for foreign words.

PAGE 65
Dango: Chewy rice flour dumplings commonly eaten as dessert.

PAGE 66
Amazake: Literally "sweet sake," the drink actually usually contains little to no alcohol. It can be served hot or cold.

PAGE 75
Throwing *mochi*: A Japanese tradition for gatherings for special occasions such as weddings and religious events. Packages of *mochi* (chewy, glutinous rice balls) are thrown from up high, and the people below try to catch them. The act originally began as a way for people to show off their new houses as well as their prosperity.

PAGE 152
I Love to Ski Mount Fuji: The Japanese reads *Fuji-san sukiiiii*, a play on words between *suki* (like/love) and *sukii* (skiing).

PAGE 154
Arcadia: While this is the name of a region of Greece, its use here calls back to the idea of "Arcadia" as a kind of unspoiled, pastoral utopia, similar to irs presentation in ancient Greek mythology.

PAGE 156
"Hidebu!": A nonsensical cry of anguish from the manga *Fist of the North Star*. It's yelled by an enormously rotund villain named Heart when he is violently exploded by the hero Kenshiro's attacks. The strange yell is actually spposed to be "*Ittee-bu*" ("Ouch!"), but the act of having one's head forcibly burst apart causes some mispronunciation.

INSIDE COVER
Meiji Town, Little Planet, the Sweets Fortress, Fuji-P Land: All four places mentioned here are parodies of real-life attractions—Meiji Village architectural museum, Little World Museum of Man, the Sweets Castle, and Fuji-Q Highland, respectively.

◁ SIDE STORIES BEGIN ON THE NEXT PAGE ◁

AFTER-SCHOOL 27 EVER-GROWING TREEHOUSE

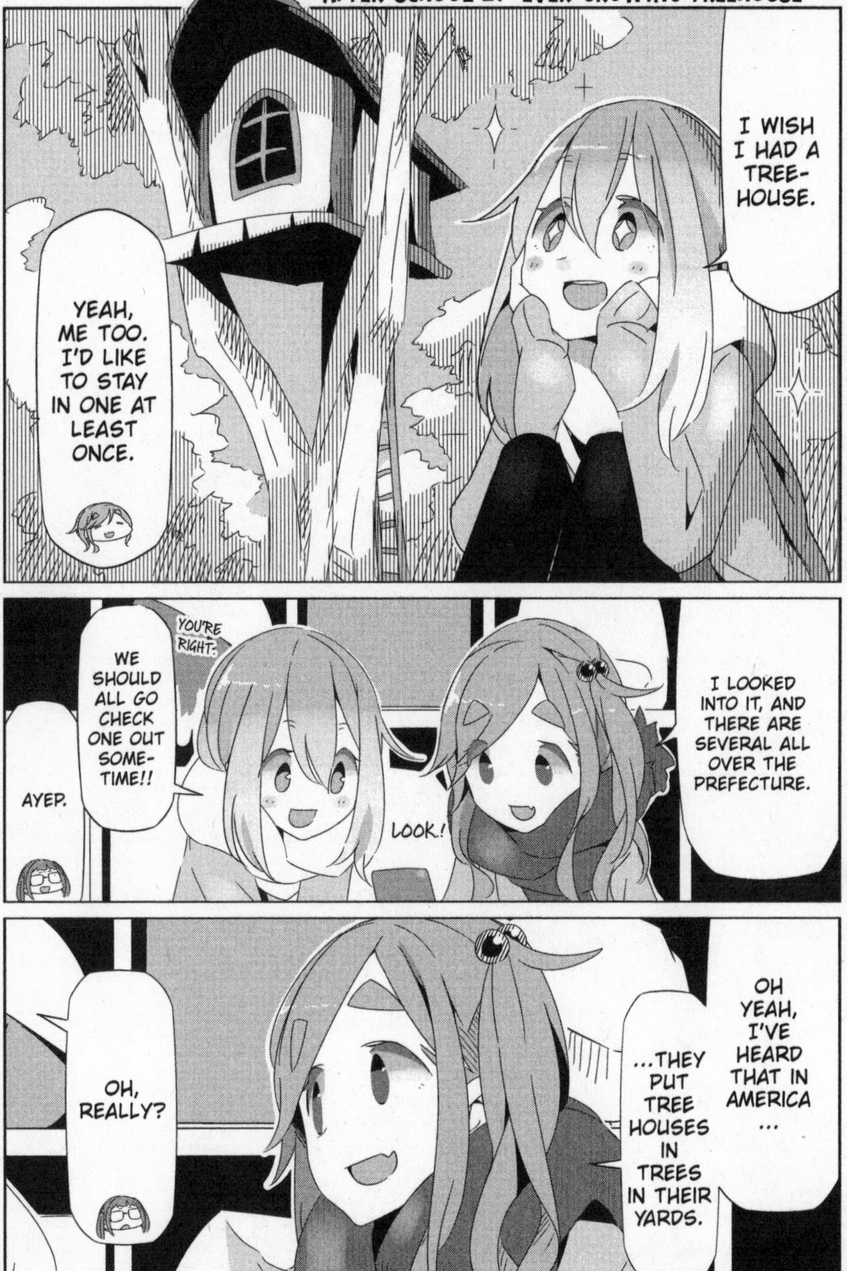
I WISH I HAD A TREE-HOUSE.
YEAH, ME TOO. I'D LIKE TO STAY IN ONE AT LEAST ONCE.
I LOOKED INTO IT, AND THERE ARE SEVERAL ALL OVER THE PREFECTURE.
LOOK.!
YOU'RE RIGHT.
WE SHOULD ALL GO CHECK ONE OUT SOME-TIME!!
AYEP.
OH YEAH, I'VE HEARD THAT IN AMERICA ...
...THEY PUT TREE HOUSES IN TREES IN THEIR YARDS.
OH, REALLY?

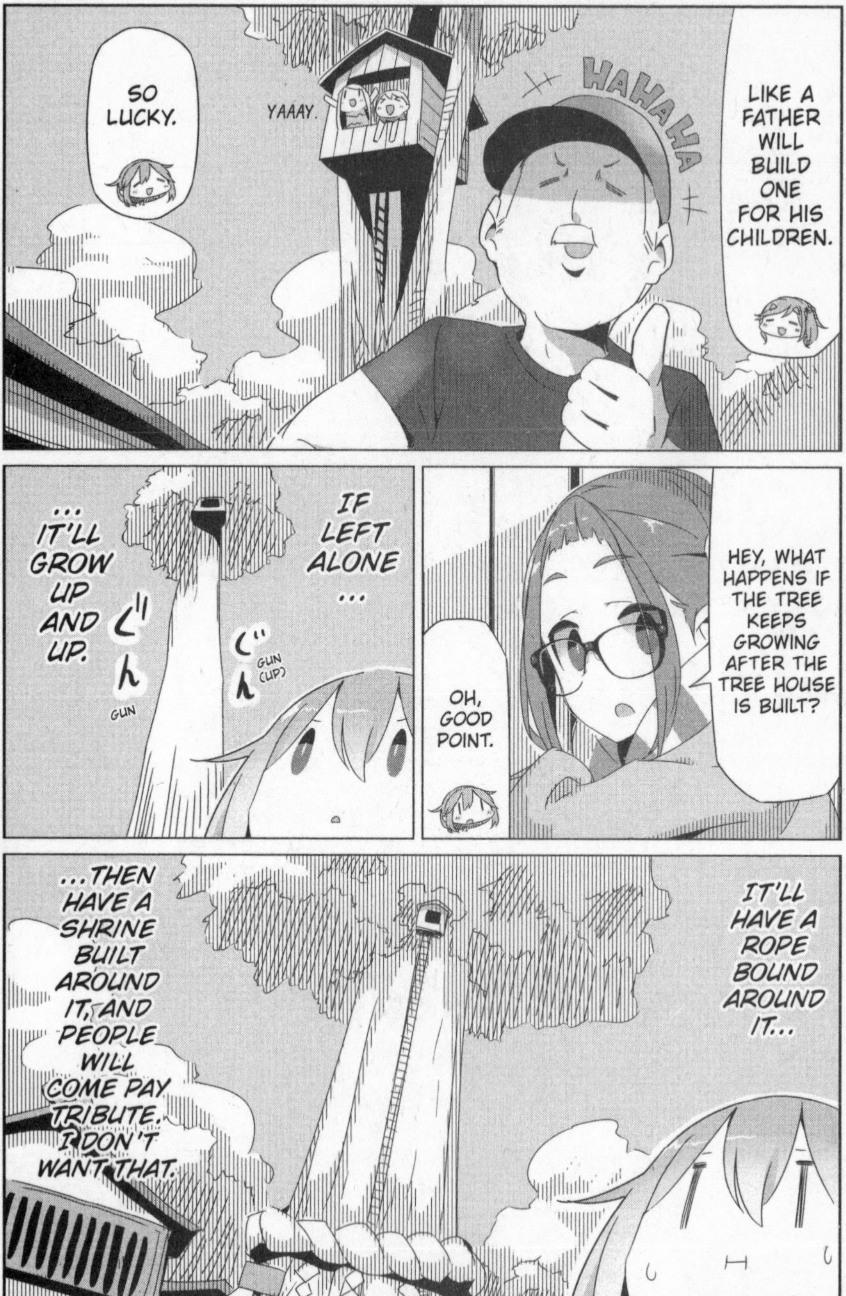
LIKE A FATHER WILL BUILD ONE FOR HIS CHILDREN.
HAHAHA
YAAAY.
SO LUCKY.
HEY, WHAT HAPPENS IF THE TREE KEEPS GROWING AFTER THE TREE HOUSE IS BUILT?
OH, GOOD POINT.
IF LEFT ALONE...
ぐん
GUN (UP)
...IT'LL GROW UP AND UP.
ぐん
GUN
IT'LL HAVE A ROPE BOUND AROUND IT...
...THEN HAVE A SHRINE BUILT AROUND IT, AND PEOPLE WILL COME PAY TRIBUTE. I DON'T WANT THAT.

AFTER-SCHOOL 28: HOW MANY PEOPLE CAN FIT IN YOUR TENT?

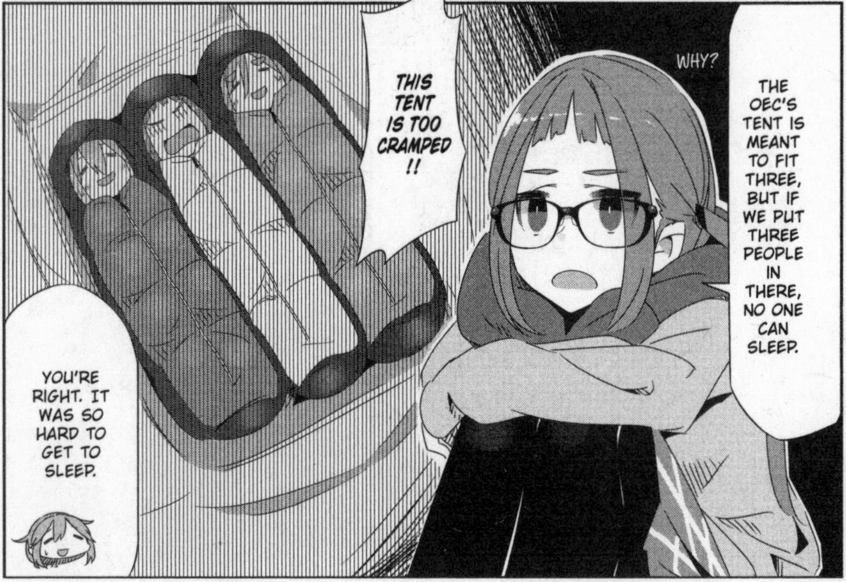
WHY?
THE OEC'S TENT IS MEANT TO FIT THREE, BUT IF WE PUT THREE PEOPLE IN THERE, NO ONE CAN SLEEP.
THIS TENT IS TOO CRAMPED!!
YOU'RE RIGHT. IT WAS SO HARD TO GET TO SLEEP.

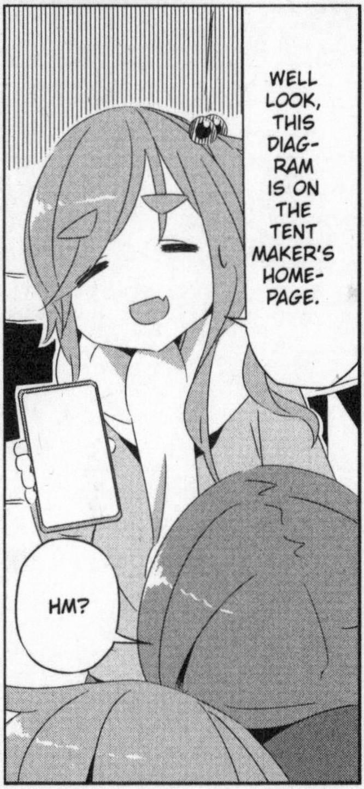
WELL LOOK, THIS DIAGRAM IS ON THE TENT MAKER'S HOMEPAGE.
HM?

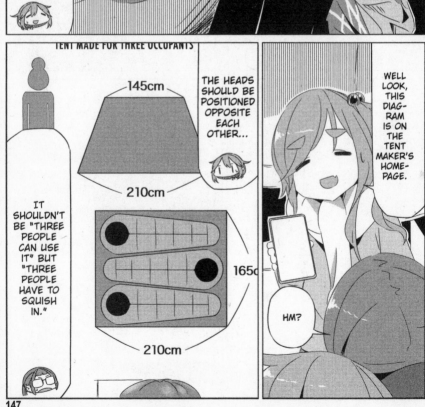

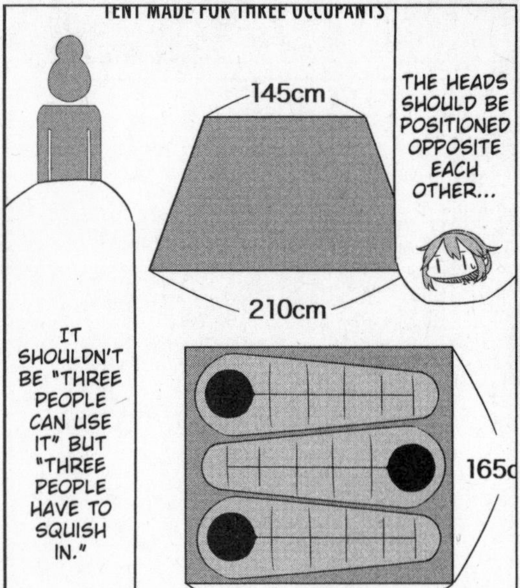
TENT MADE FOR THREE OCCUPANTS
145cm
210cm
THE HEADS SHOULD BE POSITIONED OPPOSITE EACH OTHER...
165c
210cm
IT SHOULDN'T BE "THREE PEOPLE CAN USE IT" BUT "THREE PEOPLE HAVE TO SQUISH IN."

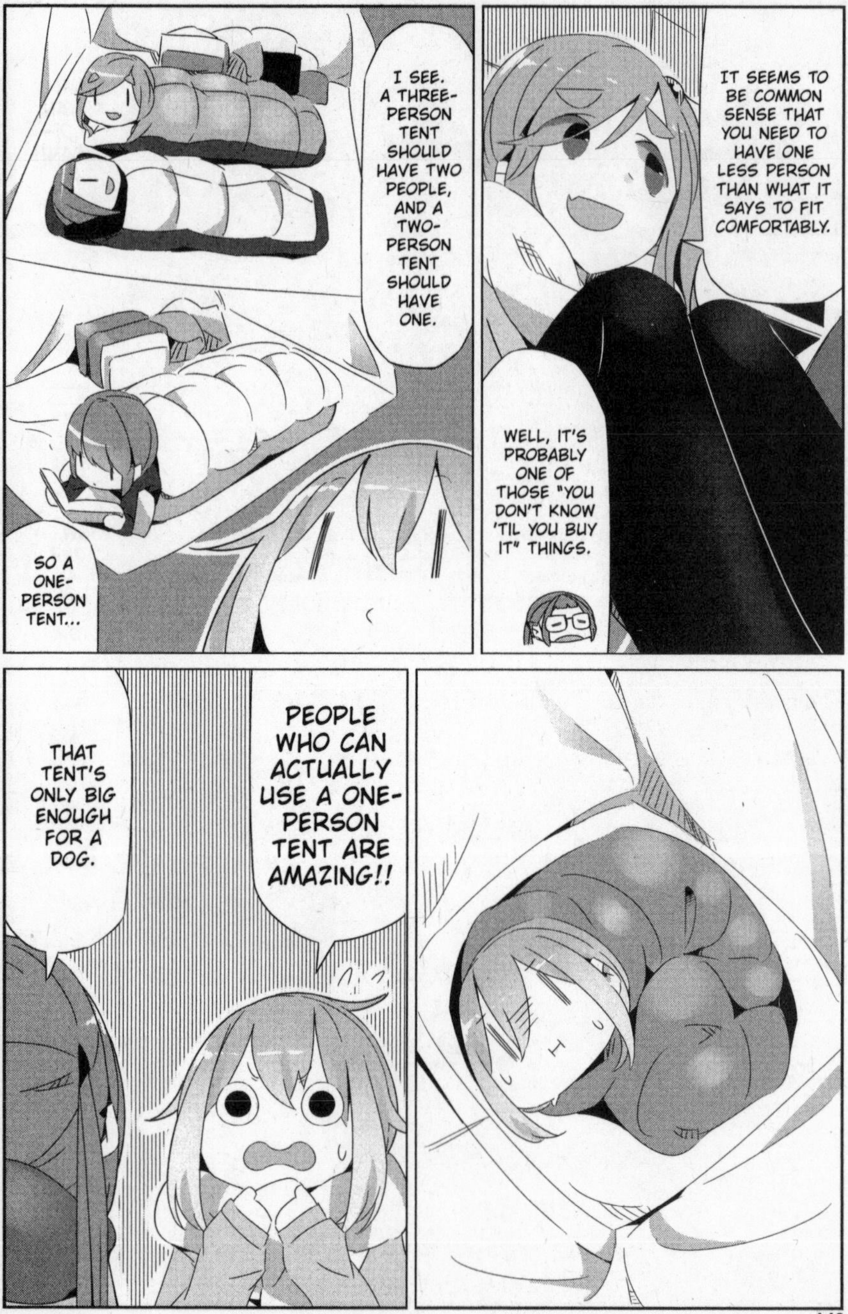
IT SEEMS TO BE COMMON SENSE THAT YOU NEED TO HAVE ONE LESS PERSON THAN WHAT IT SAYS TO FIT COMFORTABLY.
WELL, IT'S PROBABLY ONE OF THOSE "YOU DON'T KNOW 'TIL YOU BUY IT" THINGS.
I SEE. A THREE-PERSON TENT SHOULD HAVE TWO PEOPLE, AND A TWO-PERSON TENT SHOULD HAVE ONE.
SO A ONE-PERSON TENT...
PEOPLE WHO CAN ACTUALLY USE A ONE-PERSON TENT ARE AMAZING!!
THAT TENT'S ONLY BIG ENOUGH FOR A DOG.

AFTER-SCHOOL 29 FUN FACTORY TOUR

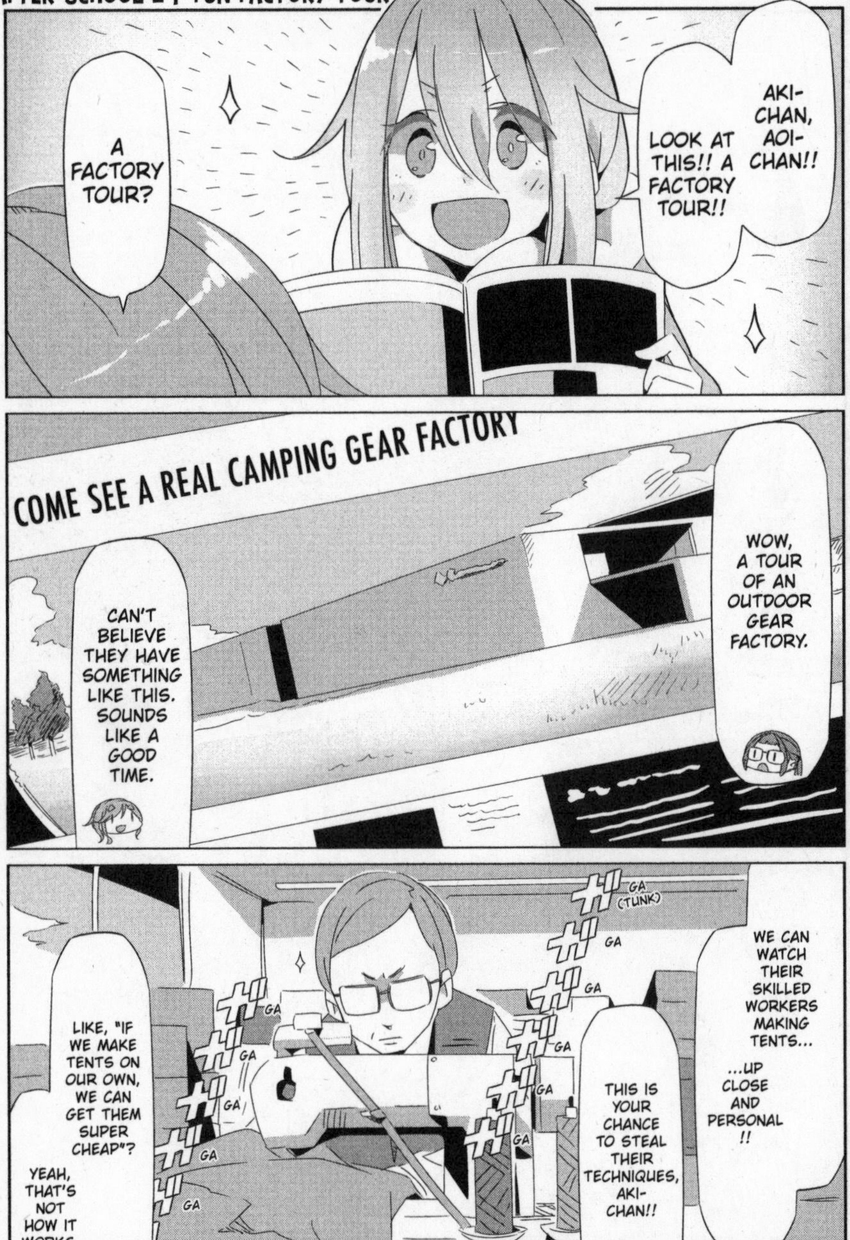
AKI-CHAN, AOI-CHAN!!
LOOK AT THIS!! A FACTORY TOUR!!
A FACTORY TOUR?
COME SEE A REAL CAMPING GEAR FACTORY
WOW, A TOUR OF AN OUTDOOR GEAR FACTORY.
CAN'T BELIEVE THEY HAVE SOMETHING LIKE THIS. SOUNDS LIKE A GOOD TIME.
WE CAN WATCH THEIR SKILLED WORKERS MAKING TENTS...
...UP CLOSE AND PERSONAL!!
GA (TUNK)
GA
GA
GA
GA
GA
GA
GA
GA
GA
THIS IS YOUR CHANCE TO STEAL THEIR TECHNIQUES, AKI-CHAN!!
LIKE, "IF WE MAKE TENTS ON OUR OWN, WE CAN GET THEM SUPER CHEAP"?
YEAH, THAT'S NOT HOW IT WORKS.

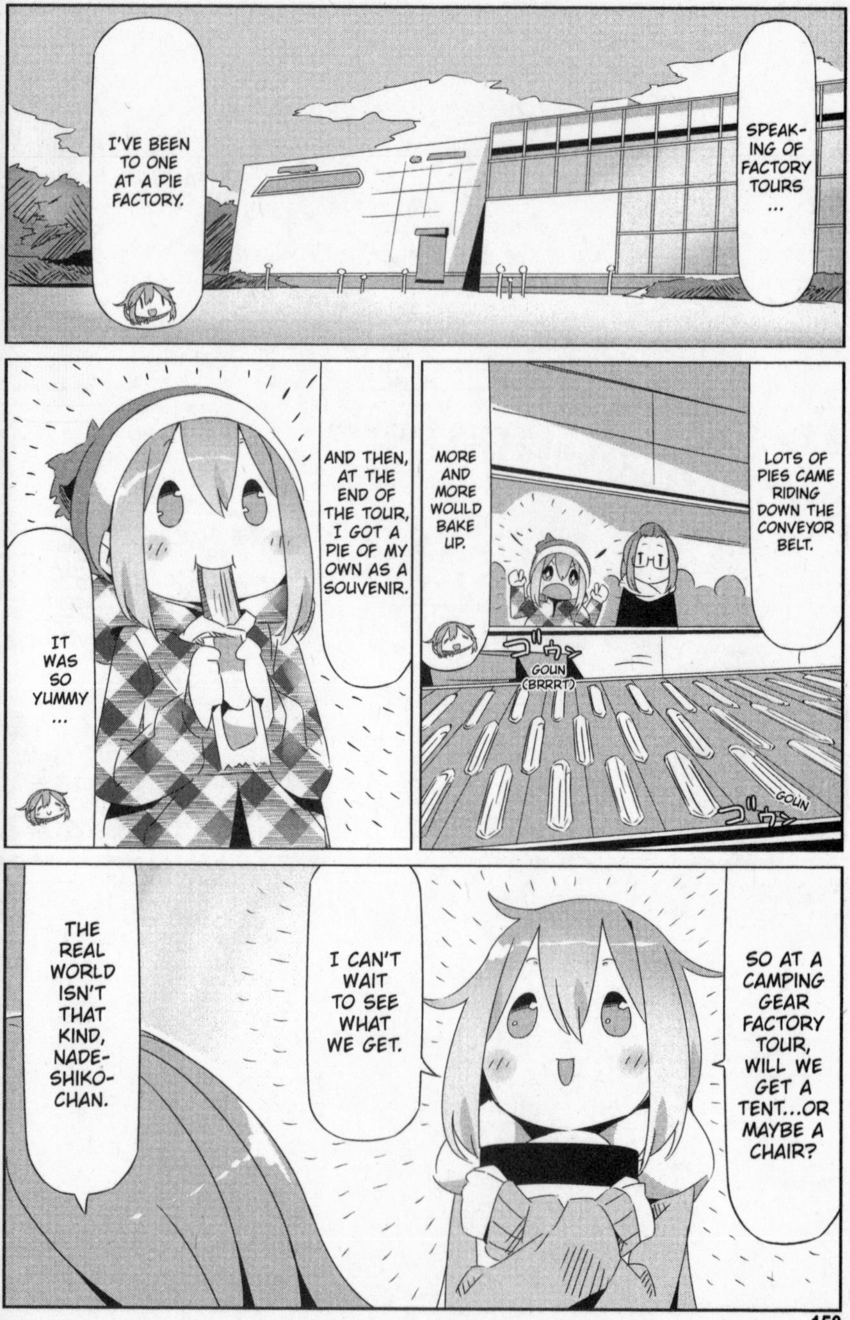
SPEAKING OF FACTORY TOURS...
I'VE BEEN TO ONE AT A PIE FACTORY.
LOTS OF PIES CAME RIDING DOWN THE CONVEYOR BELT.
MORE AND MORE WOULD BAKE UP.
ゴウン GOUN (BRRRT)
ゴウン GOUN
AND THEN, AT THE END OF THE TOUR, I GOT A PIE OF MY OWN AS A SOUVENIR.
IT WAS SO YUMMY...
SO AT A CAMPING GEAR FACTORY TOUR, WILL WE GET A TENT...OR MAYBE A CHAIR?
I CAN'T WAIT TO SEE WHAT WE GET.
THE REAL WORLD ISN'T THAT KIND, NADESHIKO-CHAN.

AFTER-SCHOOL 30 PLANS FOR NEXT SUMMER

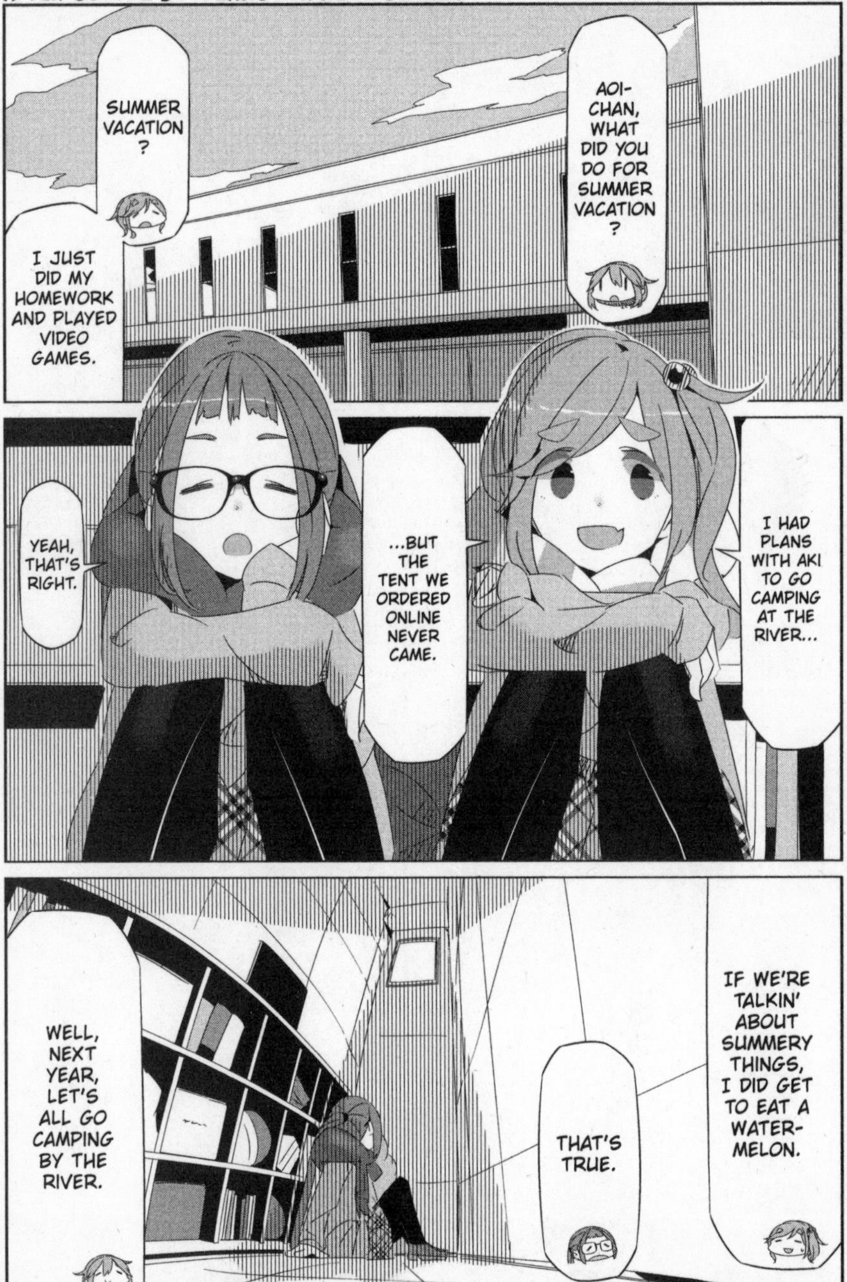
AOI-CHAN, WHAT DID YOU DO FOR SUMMER VACATION?
SUMMER VACATION?
I JUST DID MY HOMEWORK AND PLAYED VIDEO GAMES.
I HAD PLANS WITH AKI TO GO CAMPING AT THE RIVER...
...BUT THE TENT WE ORDERED ONLINE NEVER CAME.
YEAH, THAT'S RIGHT.
IF WE'RE TALKIN' ABOUT SUMMERY THINGS, I DID GET TO EAT A WATER-MELON.
THAT'S TRUE.
WELL, NEXT YEAR, LET'S ALL GO CAMPING BY THE RIVER.

T-SHIRT: I LOVE TO SKI MOUNT FUJI

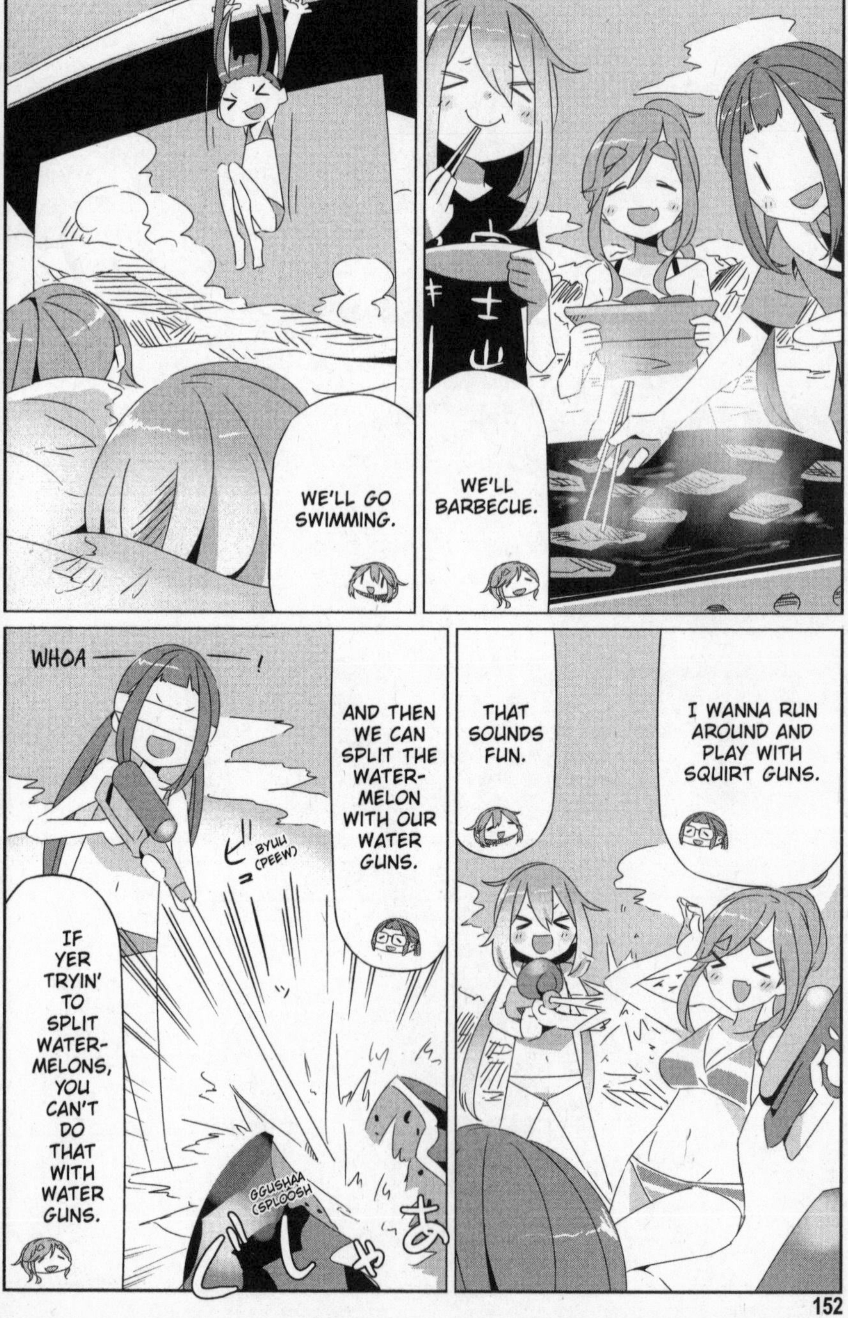
WE'LL BARBECUE.
WE'LL GO SWIMMING.
I WANNA RUN AROUND AND PLAY WITH SQUIRT GUNS.
THAT SOUNDS FUN.
AND THEN WE CAN SPLIT THE WATER-MELON WITH OUR WATER GUNS.
WHOA——!
BYUU (PEEW)
IF YER TRYIN' TO SPLIT WATER-MELONS, YOU CAN'T DO THAT WITH WATER GUNS.
GGUSHAA (SPLOOSH)

AFTER-SCHOOL 31 OEC, 1,000 YEARS ON

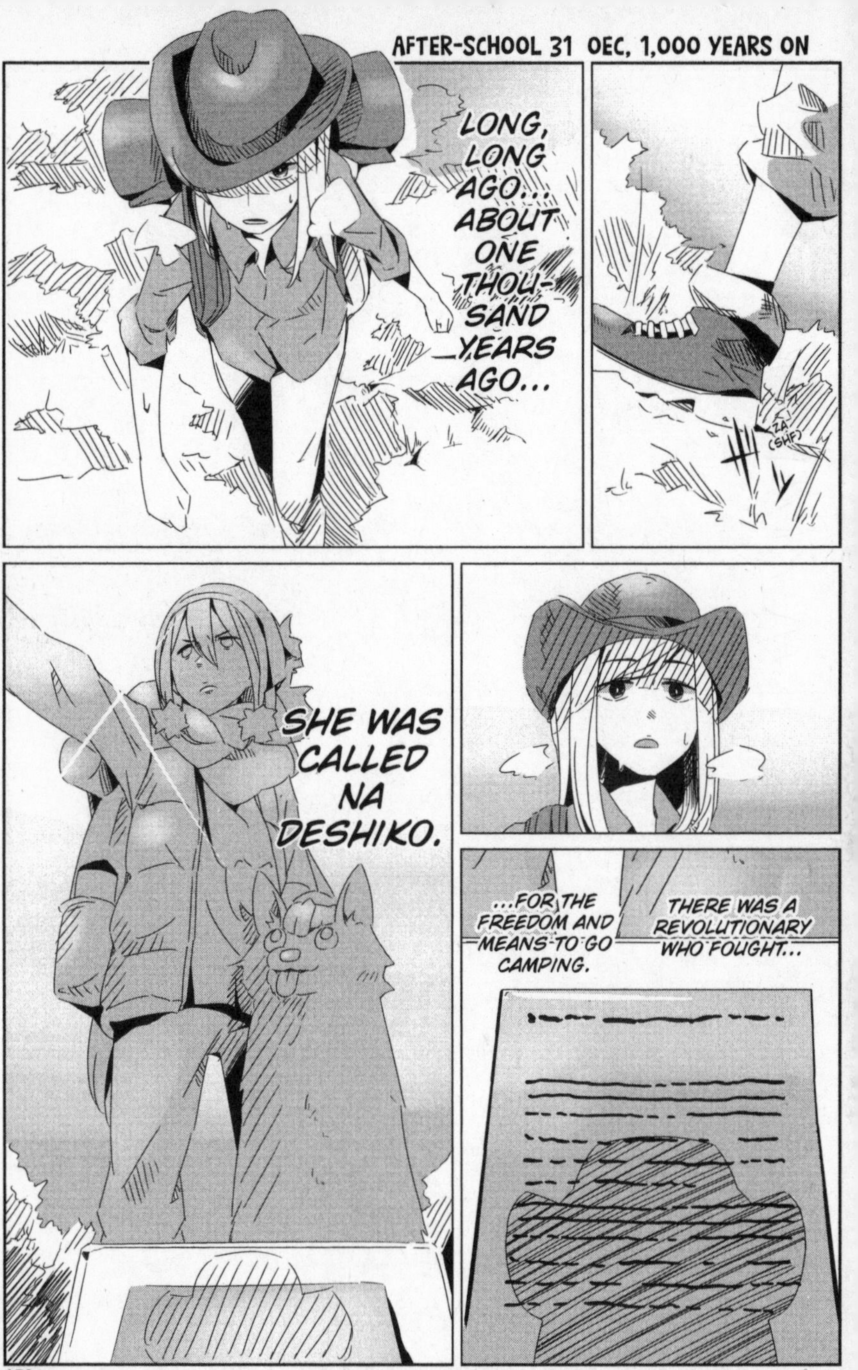
ZA (SHF)
LONG, LONG AGO... ABOUT ONE THOU-SAND YEARS AGO...
THERE WAS A REVOLUTIONARY WHO FOUGHT...
...FOR THE FREEDOM AND MEANS TO GO CAMPING.
SHE WAS CALLED NADESHIKO.

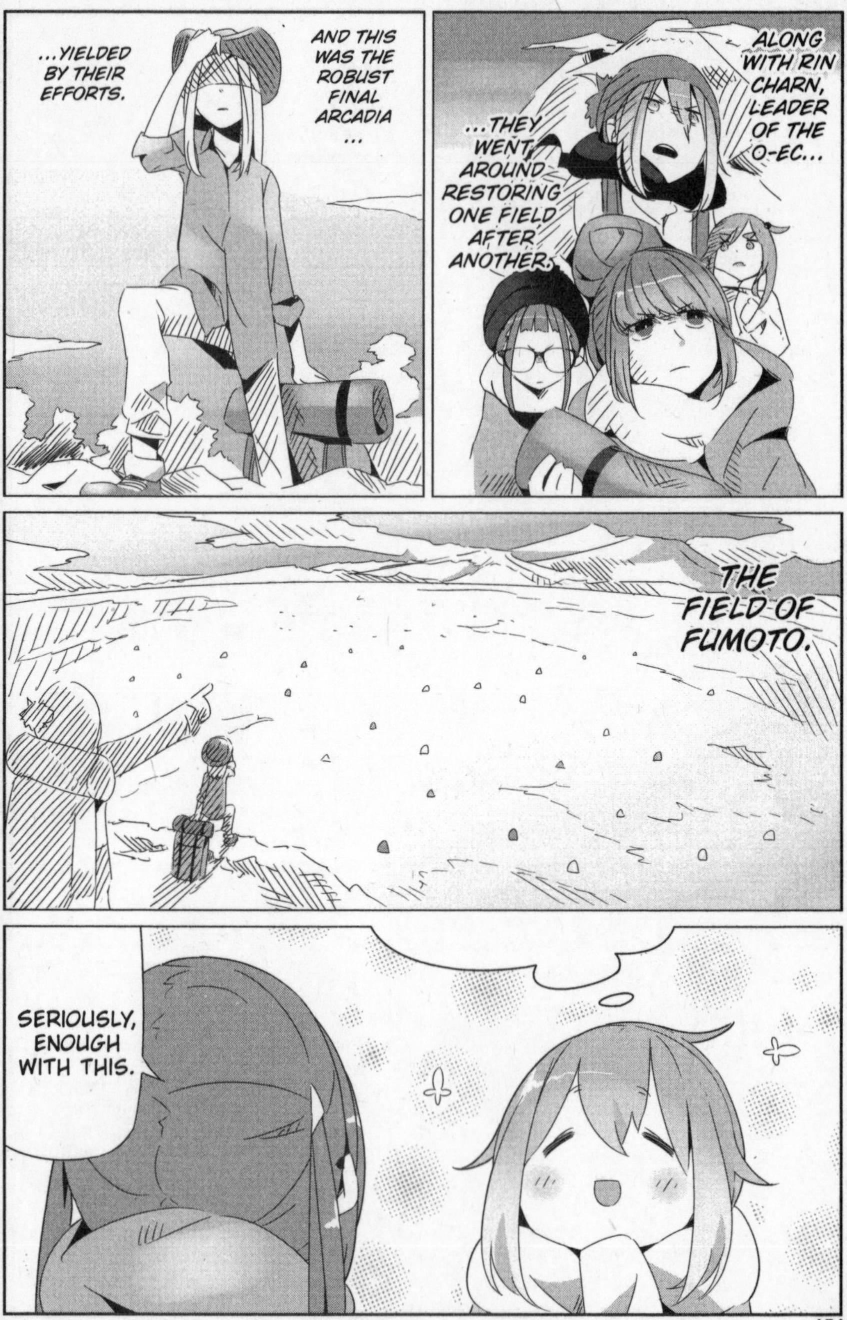
ALONG WITH RIN CHARN, LEADER OF THE O-EC...
...THEY WENT AROUND RESTORING ONE FIELD AFTER ANOTHER.
AND THIS WAS THE ROBUST FINAL ARCADIA ...
...YIELDED BY THEIR EFFORTS.
THE FIELD OF FUMOTO.
SERIOUSLY, ENOUGH WITH THIS.

AFTER-SCHOOL 32 GIRL OF NATURE SHIMARIN

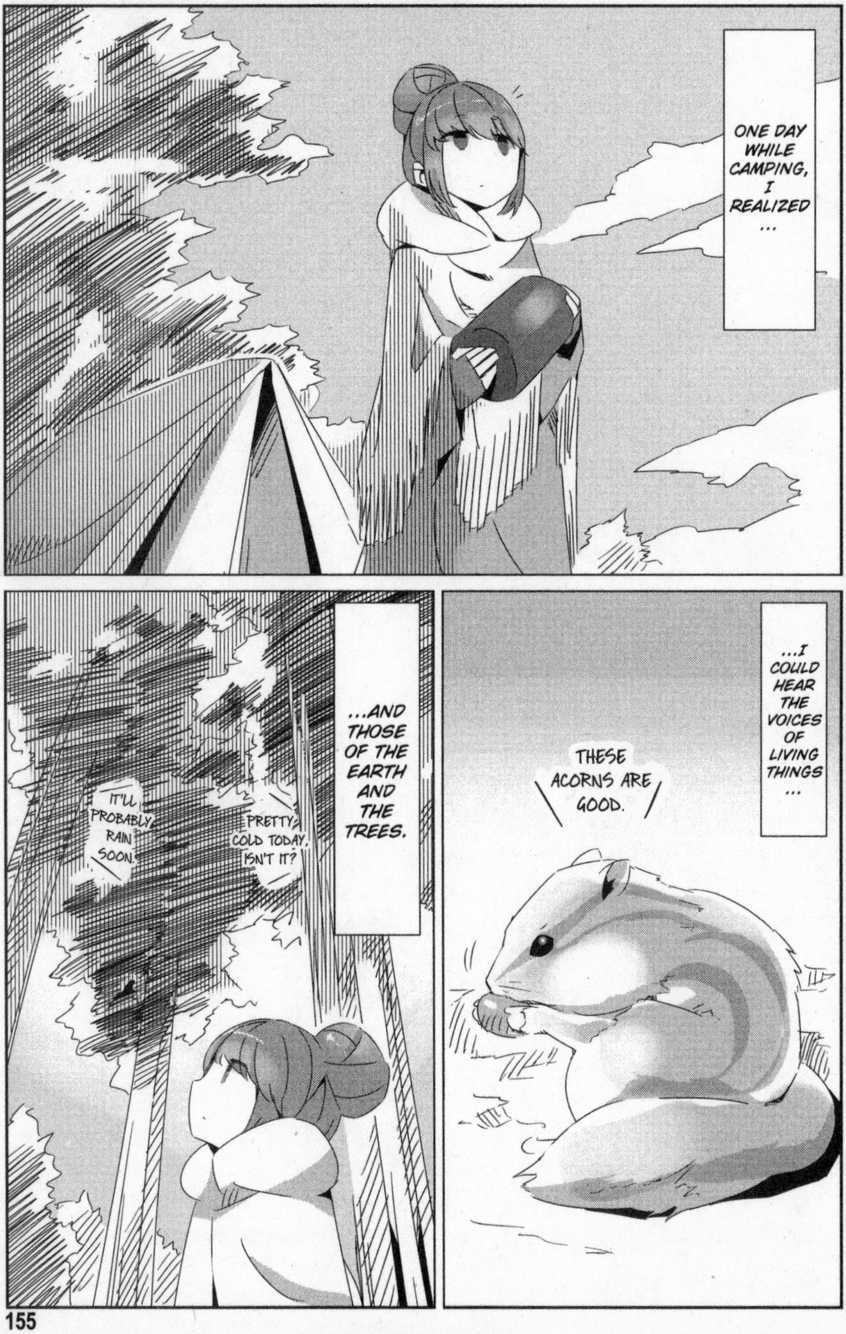
ONE DAY WHILE CAMPING, I REALIZED...
...I COULD HEAR THE VOICES OF LIVING THINGS...
THESE ACORNS ARE GOOD.
...AND THOSE OF THE EARTH AND THE TREES.
PRETTY COLD TODAY, ISN'T IT?
IT'LL PROBABLY RAIN SOON.

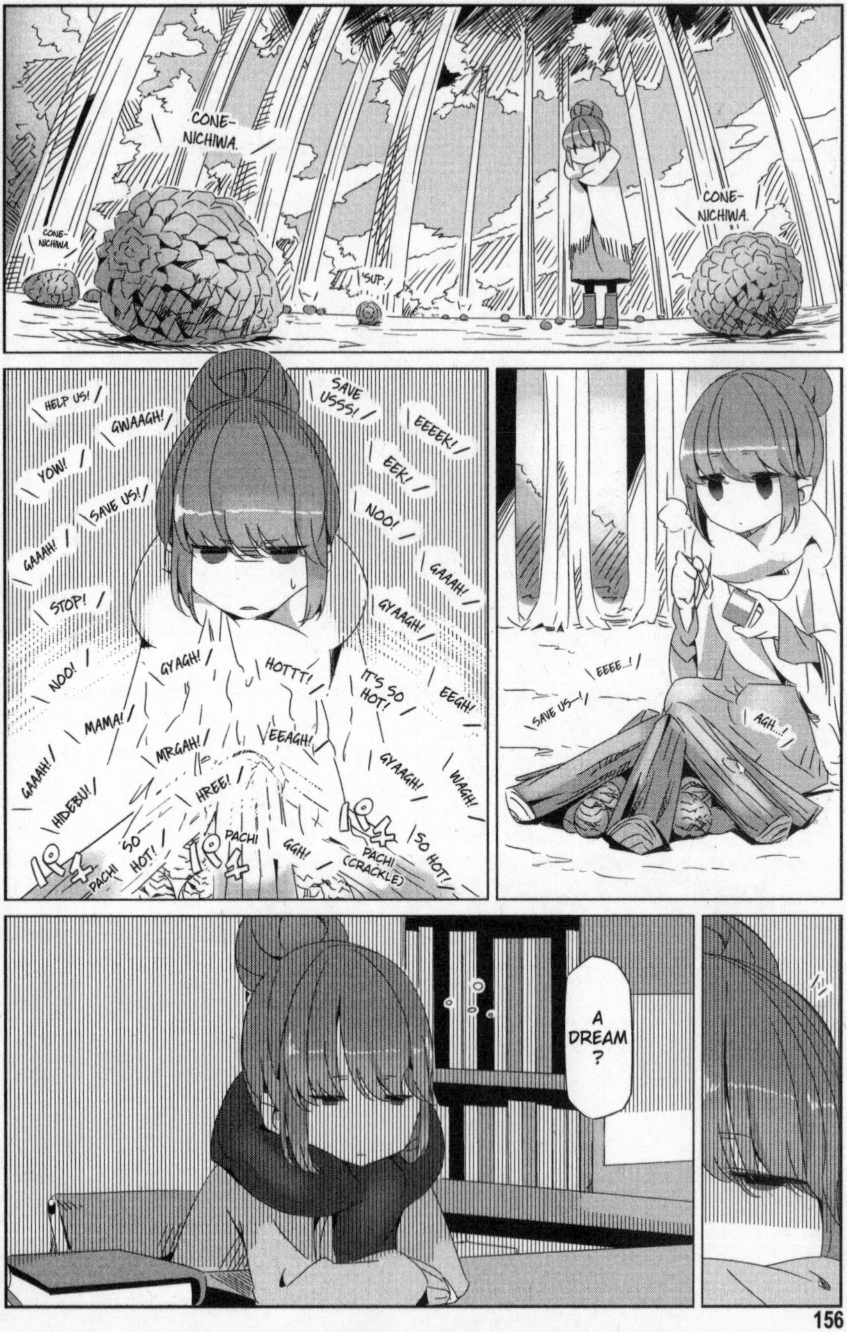
CONE-NICHIWA.
CONE-NICHIWA.
'SUP.
CONE-NICHIWA.
EEEE...!
AGH...!
SAVE US—!
SAVE USSSS!
EEEEK!
EEK!
NOO!
GAAAH!
GYAAGH!
HELP US!
GWAAGH!
YOW!
SAVE US!
GAAAH!
STOP!
EEGH!
IT'S SO HOT!
HOTTT!
GYAGH!
NOO!
WAGH!
GYAAGH!
EEAGH!
MRGAH!
MAMA!
GAAAH!
SO HOT!
PACHI (CRACKLE)
GGH!
PACHI
HREE!
SO HOT!
PACH!
HIDEBU!
A DREAM?

AFTER-SCHOOL 33 GIRL OF OUTER SPACE SHIMARIN

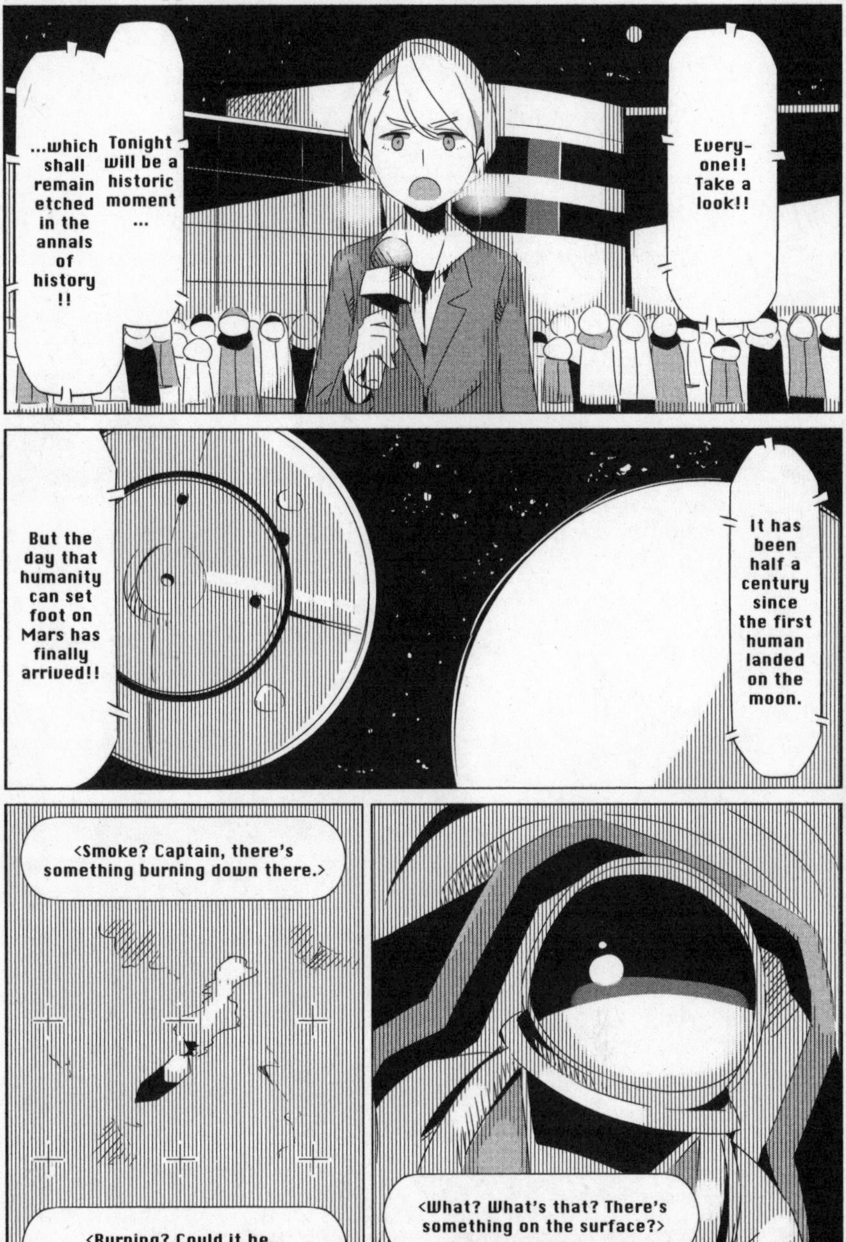
Every-one!! Take a look!!
Tonight will be a historic moment...
...which shall remain etched in the annals of history!!
It has been half a century since the first human landed on the moon.
But the day that humanity can set foot on Mars has finally arrived!!
<What? What's that? There's something on the surface?>
<Smoke? Captain, there's something burning down there.>
<Burning? Could it be... a Martian!!?>

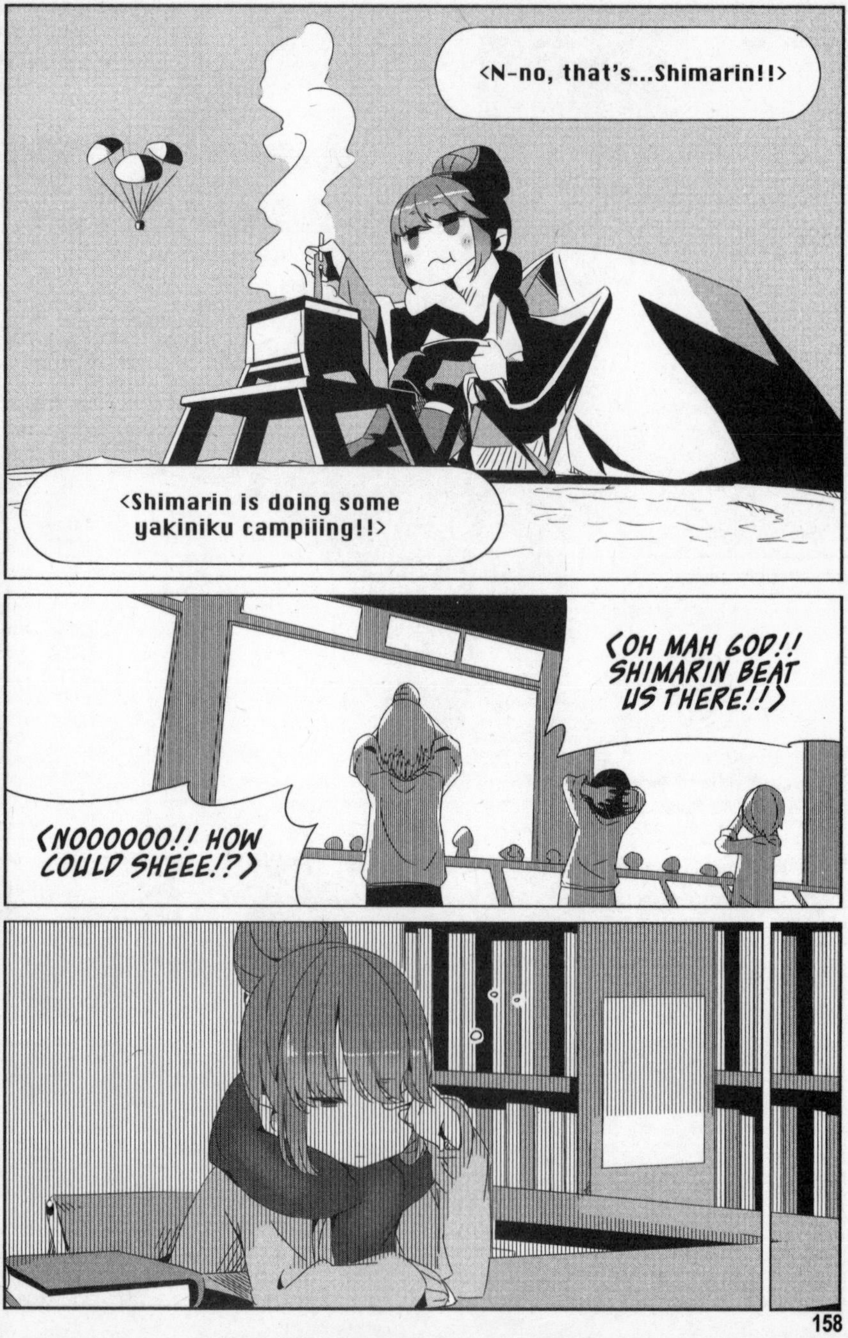
<N-no, that's...Shimarin!!>
<Shimarin is doing some yakiniku campiiing!!>
<OH MAH GOD!! SHIMARIN BEAT US THERE!!>
<NOOOOOO!! HOW COULD SHEEE!?>

AFTER-SCHOOL 34 THE SHIZU-'NASHI CONFLICT

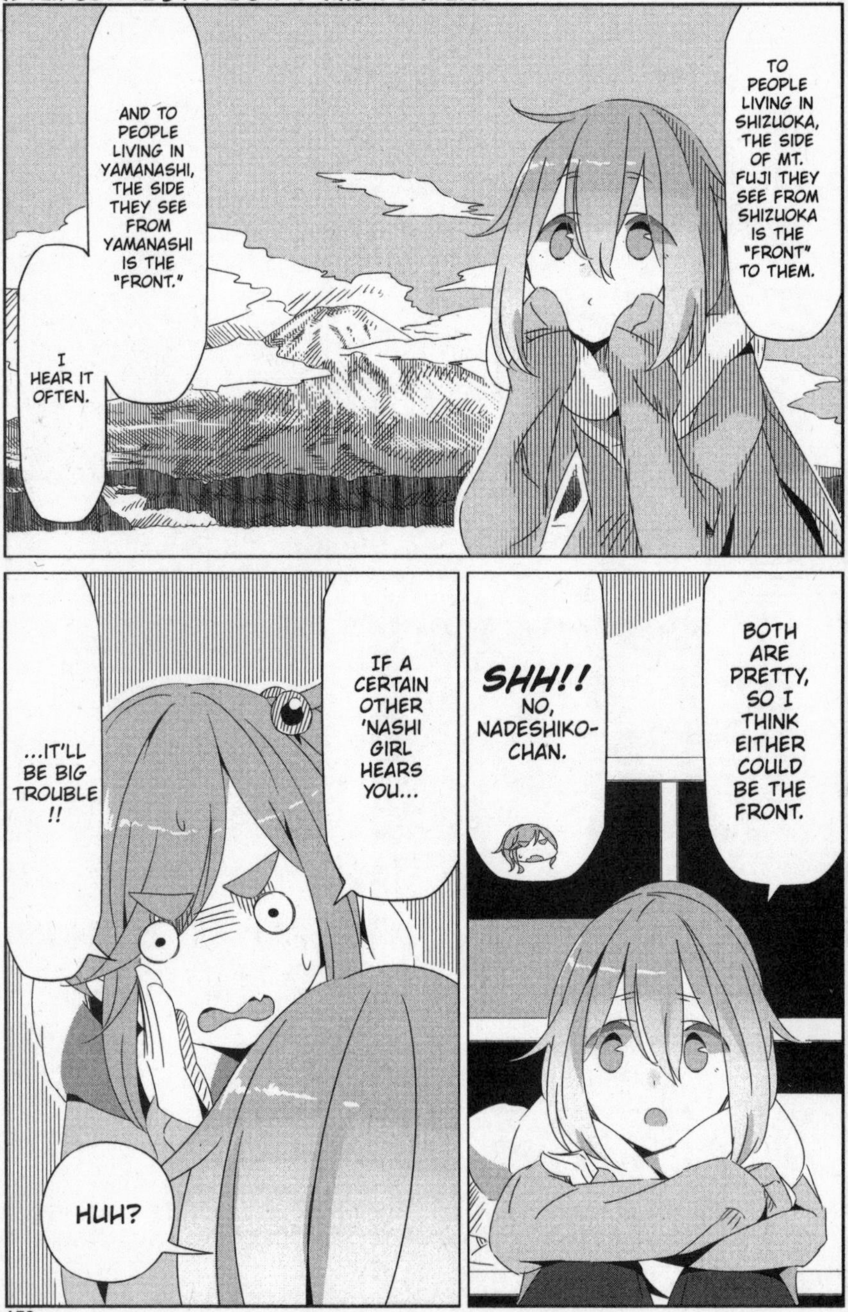
TO PEOPLE LIVING IN SHIZUOKA, THE SIDE OF MT. FUJI THEY SEE FROM SHIZUOKA IS THE "FRONT" TO THEM.
AND TO PEOPLE LIVING IN YAMANASHI, THE SIDE THEY SEE FROM YAMANASHI IS THE "FRONT."
I HEAR IT OFTEN.
BOTH ARE PRETTY, SO I THINK EITHER COULD BE THE FRONT.
SHH!!
NO, NADESHIKO-CHAN.
IF A CERTAIN OTHER 'NASHI GIRL HEARS YOU...
...IT'LL BE BIG TROUBLE!!
HUH?

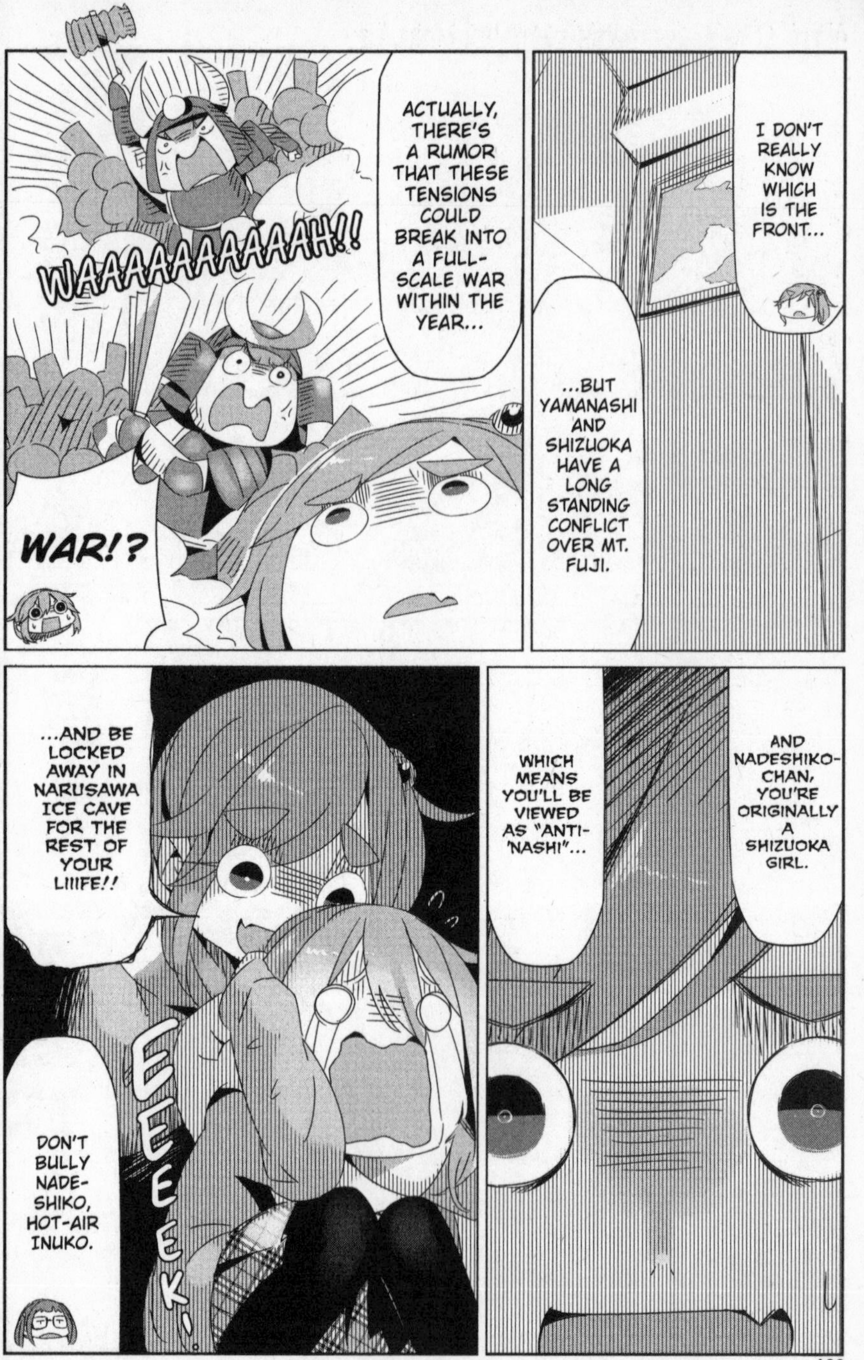
I DON'T REALLY KNOW WHICH IS THE FRONT...
...BUT YAMANASHI AND SHIZUOKA HAVE A LONG STANDING CONFLICT OVER MT. FUJI.
ACTUALLY, THERE'S A RUMOR THAT THESE TENSIONS COULD BREAK INTO A FULL-SCALE WAR WITHIN THE YEAR...
WAAAAAAAAAAAH!!
WAR!?
AND NADESHIKO-CHAN, YOU'RE ORIGINALLY A SHIZUOKA GIRL.
WHICH MEANS YOU'LL BE VIEWED AS "ANTI-'NASHI"...
...AND BE LOCKED AWAY IN NARUSAWA ICE CAVE FOR THE REST OF YOUR LIIIFE!!
EEEEK!
DON'T BULLY NADE-SHIKO, HOT-AIR INUKO.

AFTERSCHOOL 35 JAPANESE CAMPING FAIRY TALE

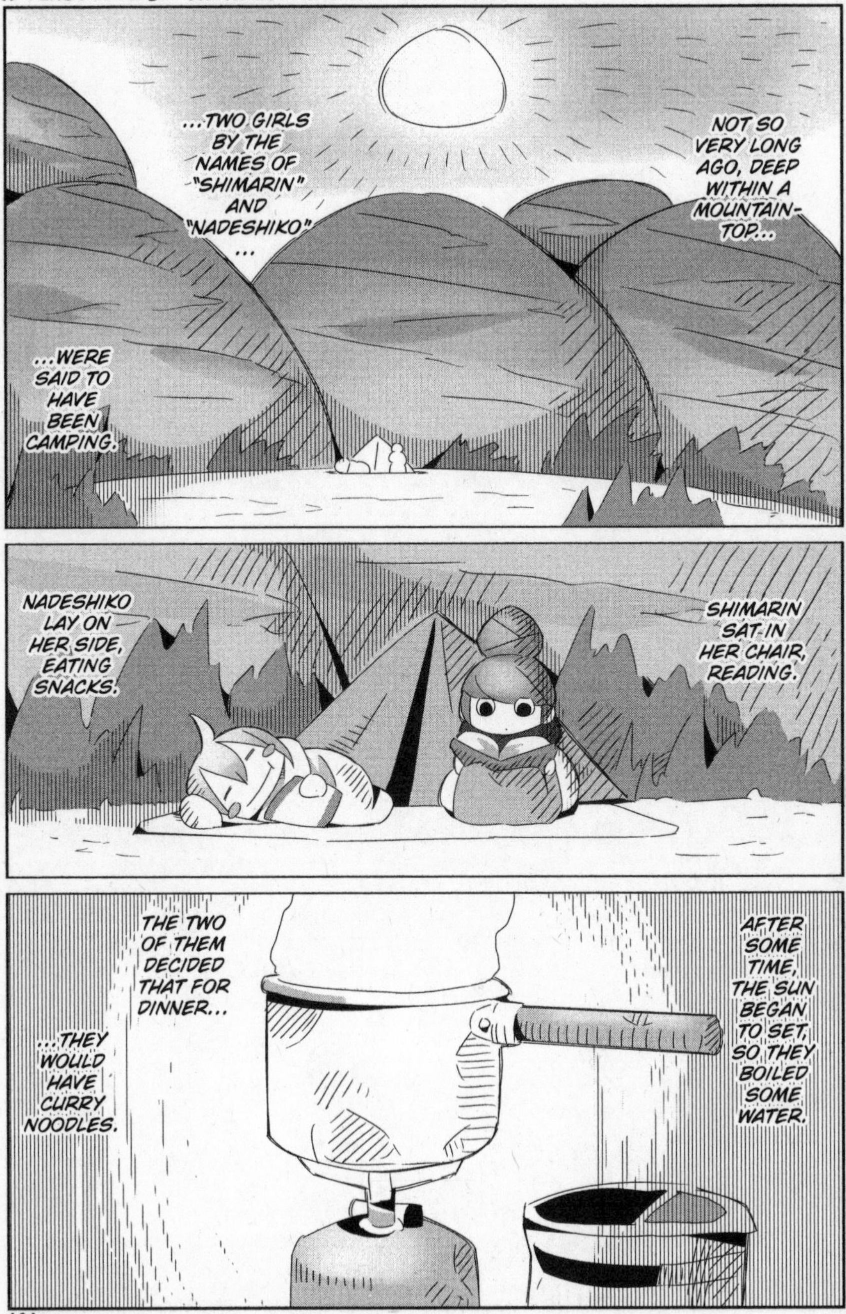
NOT SO VERY LONG AGO, DEEP WITHIN A MOUNTAIN-TOP...
...TWO GIRLS BY THE NAMES OF "SHIMARIN" AND "NADESHIKO"...
...WERE SAID TO HAVE BEEN CAMPING.
SHIMARIN SAT IN HER CHAIR, READING.
NADESHIKO LAY ON HER SIDE, EATING SNACKS.
AFTER SOME TIME, THE SUN BEGAN TO SET, SO THEY BOILED SOME WATER.
THE TWO OF THEM DECIDED THAT FOR DINNER...
...THEY WOULD HAVE CURRY NOODLES.

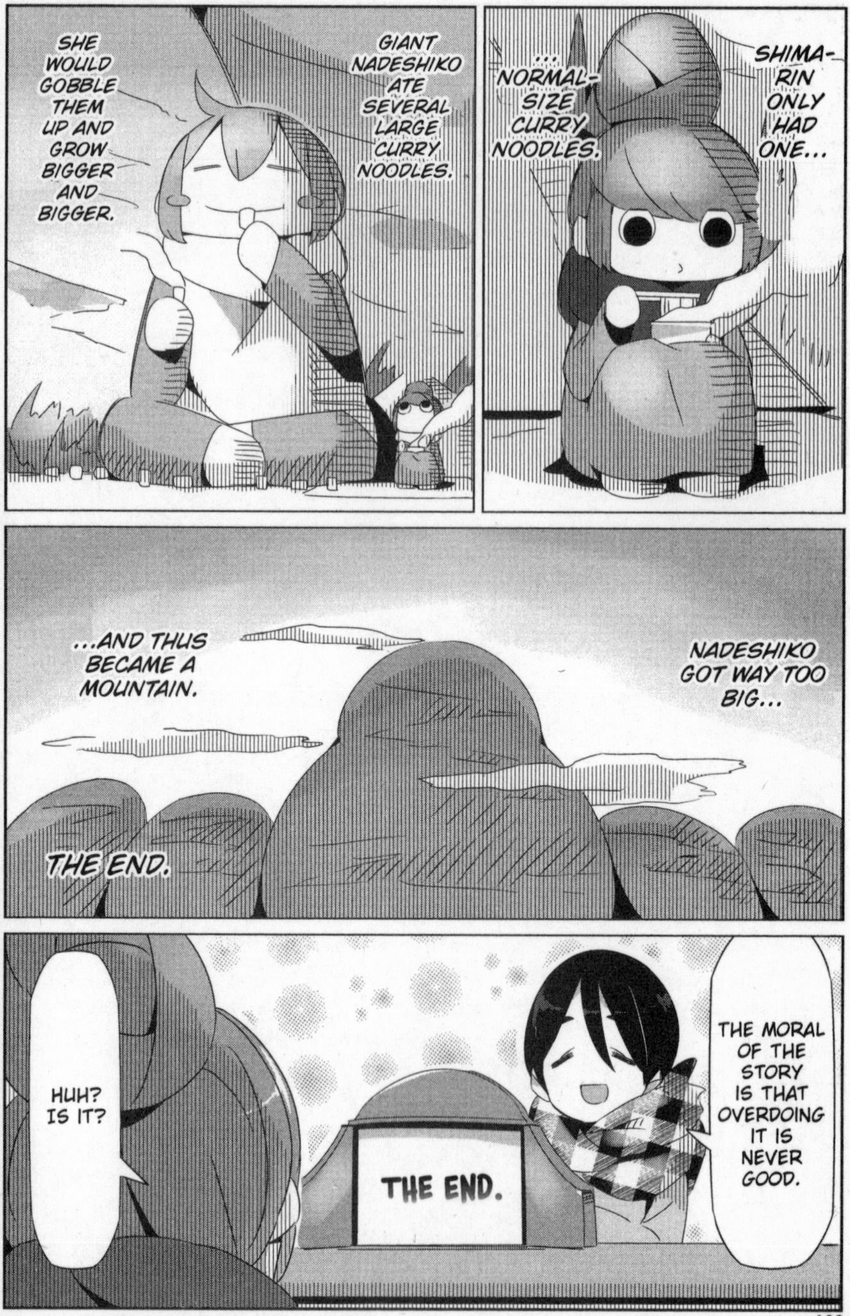
SHIMA-RIN ONLY HAD ONE...
...NORMAL-SIZE CURRY NOODLES.
GIANT NADESHIKO ATE SEVERAL LARGE CURRY NOODLES.
SHE WOULD GOBBLE THEM UP AND GROW BIGGER AND BIGGER.
NADESHIKO GOT WAY TOO BIG...
...AND THUS BECAME A MOUNTAIN.
THE END.
THE MORAL OF THE STORY IS THAT OVERDOING IT IS NEVER GOOD.
THE END.
HUH? IS IT?

AFTER-SCHOOL 36 TIGHTROPE FUN

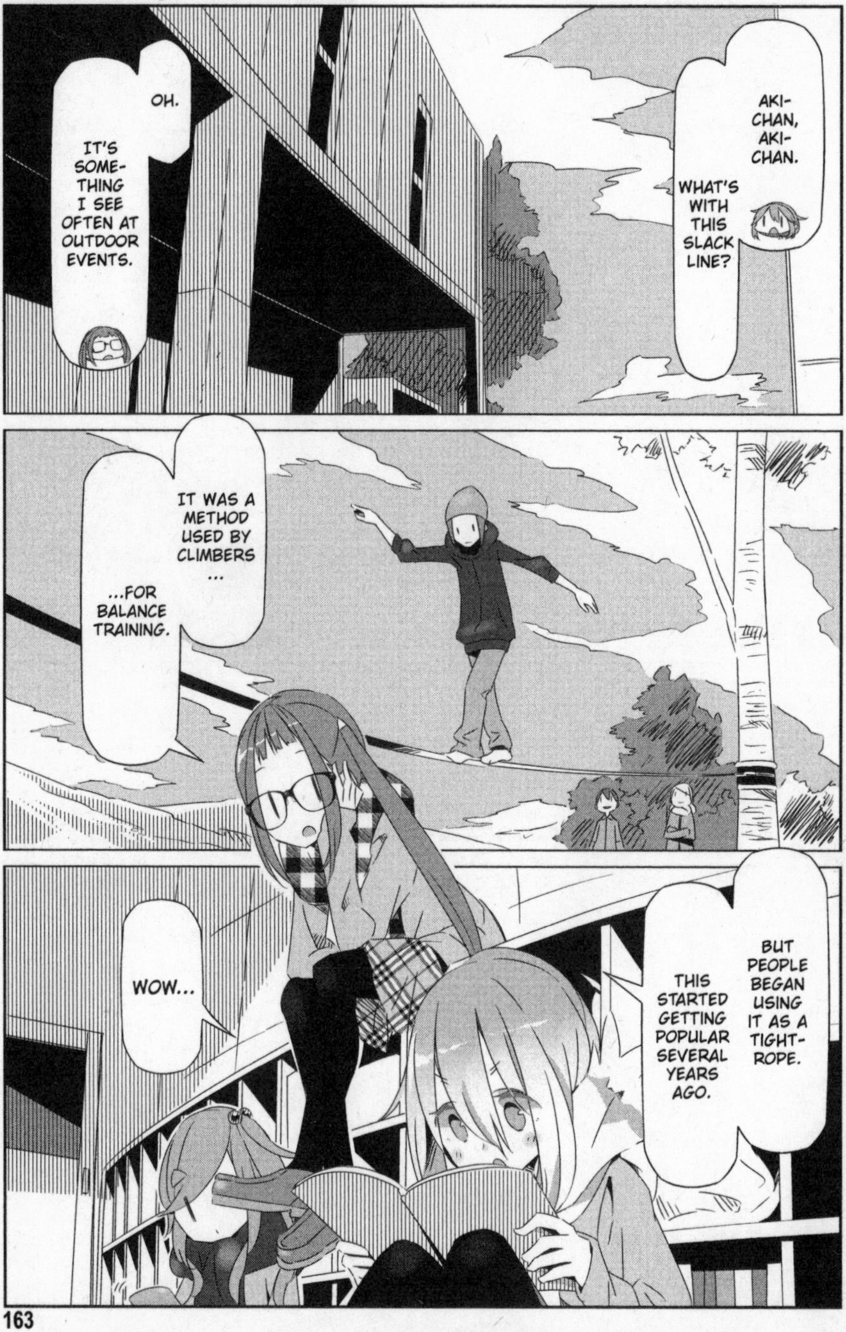
AKI-CHAN, AKI-CHAN.
WHAT'S WITH THIS SLACK LINE?
OH.
IT'S SOME-THING I SEE OFTEN AT OUTDOOR EVENTS.
IT WAS A METHOD USED BY CLIMBERS ...
...FOR BALANCE TRAINING.
BUT PEOPLE BEGAN USING IT AS A TIGHT-ROPE.
THIS STARTED GETTING POPULAR SEVERAL YEARS AGO.
WOW...

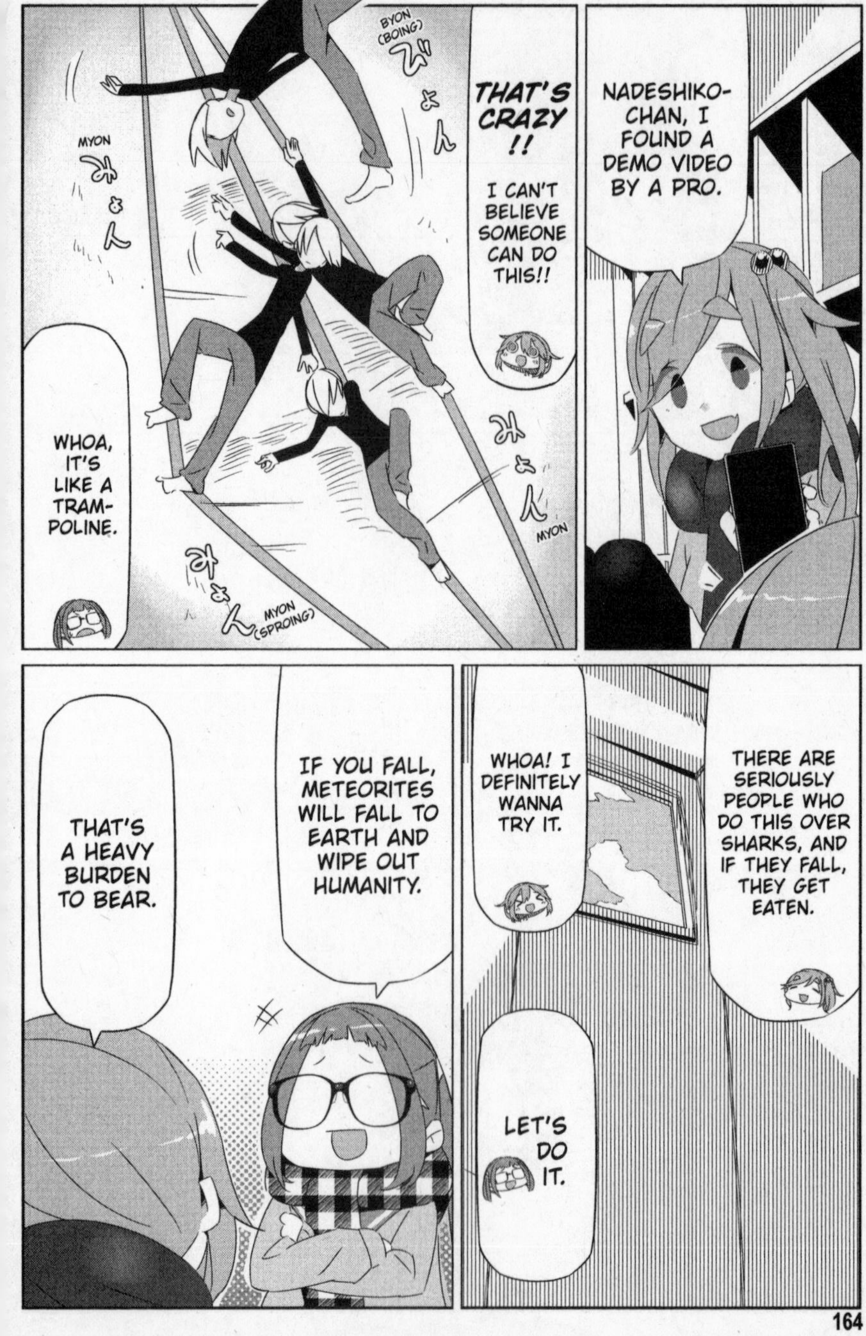
NADESHIKO-CHAN, I FOUND A DEMO VIDEO BY A PRO.
THAT'S CRAZY!! I CAN'T BELIEVE SOMEONE CAN DO THIS!!
BYON (BOING) びょん
MYON みょん
WHOA, IT'S LIKE A TRAMPOLINE.
みょん MYON
みょん MYON (SPROING)
THERE ARE SERIOUSLY PEOPLE WHO DO THIS OVER SHARKS, AND IF THEY FALL, THEY GET EATEN.
WHOA! I DEFINITELY WANNA TRY IT.
LET'S DO IT.
IF YOU FALL, METEORITES WILL FALL TO EARTH AND WIPE OUT HUMANITY.
THAT'S A HEAVY BURDEN TO BEAR.

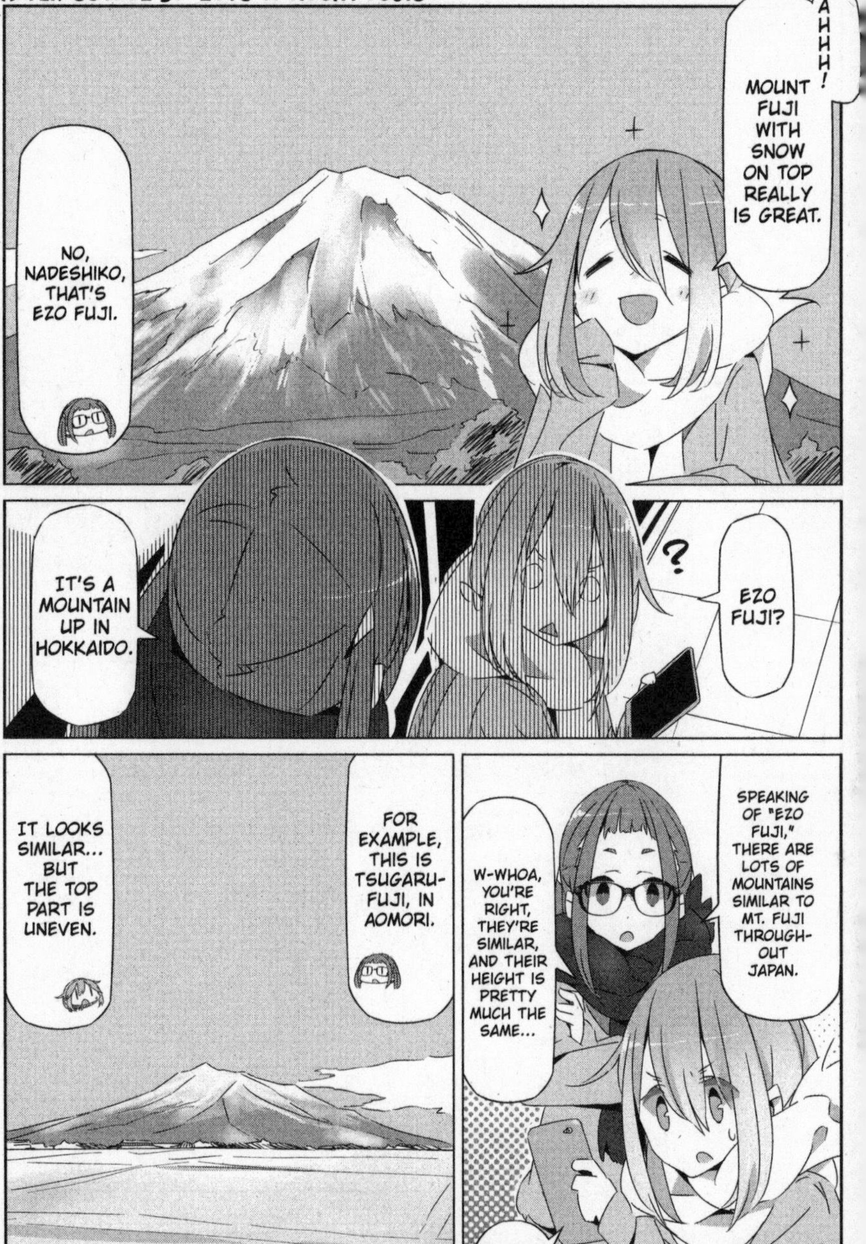
AHHHH! MOUNT FUJI WITH SNOW ON TOP REALLY IS GREAT.
NO, NADESHIKO, THAT'S EZO FUJI.
EZO FUJI?
?
IT'S A MOUNTAIN UP IN HOKKAIDO.
SPEAKING OF "EZO FUJI," THERE ARE LOTS OF MOUNTAINS SIMILAR TO MT. FUJI THROUGH-OUT JAPAN.
W-WHOA, YOU'RE RIGHT, THEY'RE SIMILAR, AND THEIR HEIGHT IS PRETTY MUCH THE SAME...
1,898 METERS.
FOR EXAMPLE, THIS IS TSUGARU-FUJI, IN AOMORI.
IT LOOKS SIMILAR... BUT THE TOP PART IS UNEVEN.

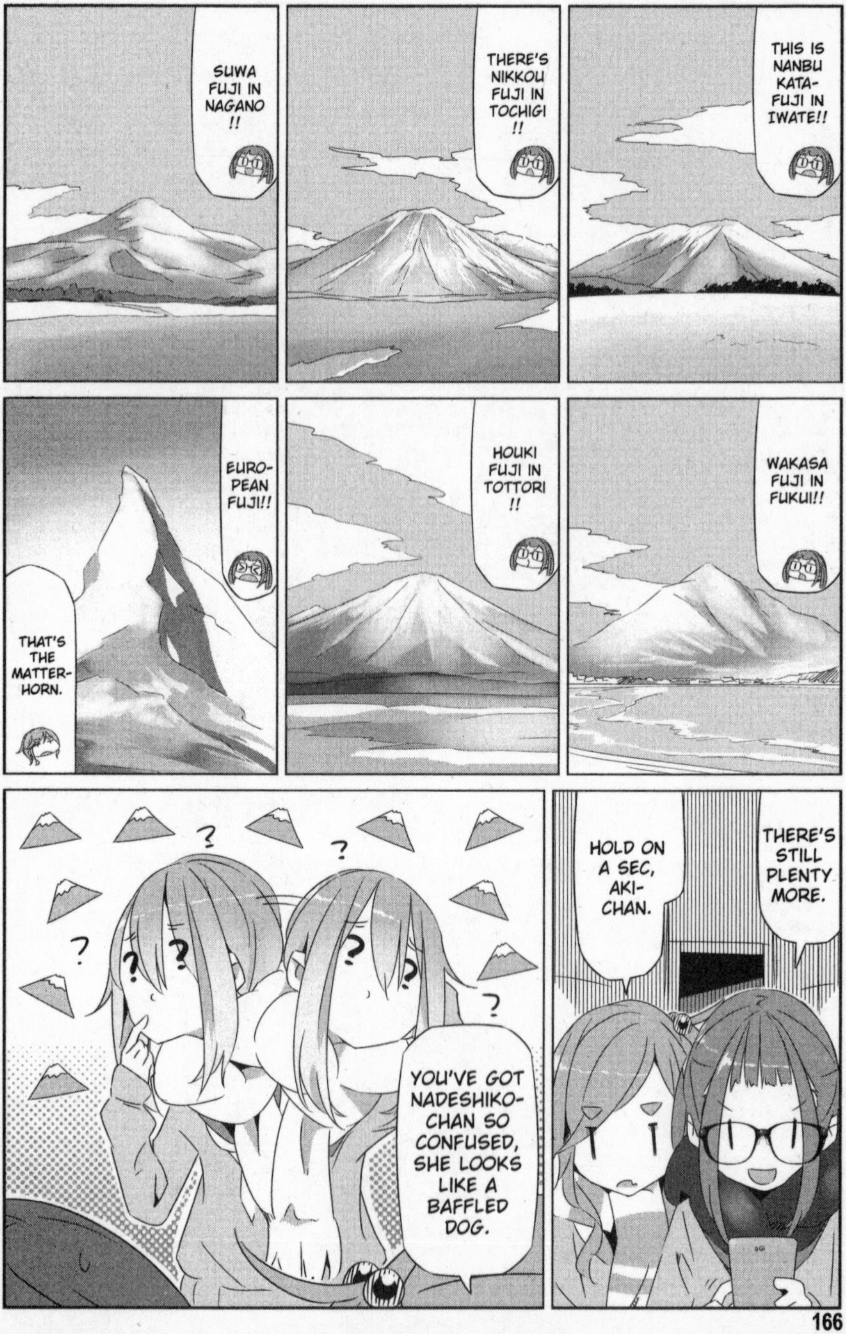
THIS IS NANBU KATA-FUJI IN IWATE!!
THERE'S NIKKOU FUJI IN TOCHIGI !!
SUWA FUJI IN NAGANO !!
WAKASA FUJI IN FUKUI!!
HOUKI FUJI IN TOTTORI !!
EUROPEAN FUJI!!
THAT'S THE MATTERHORN.
THERE'S STILL PLENTY MORE.
HOLD ON A SEC, AKI-CHAN.
YOU'VE GOT NADESHIKO-CHAN SO CONFUSED, SHE LOOKS LIKE A BAFFLED DOG.

AFTER-SCHOOL 38 SNOW HUT MEMORIES

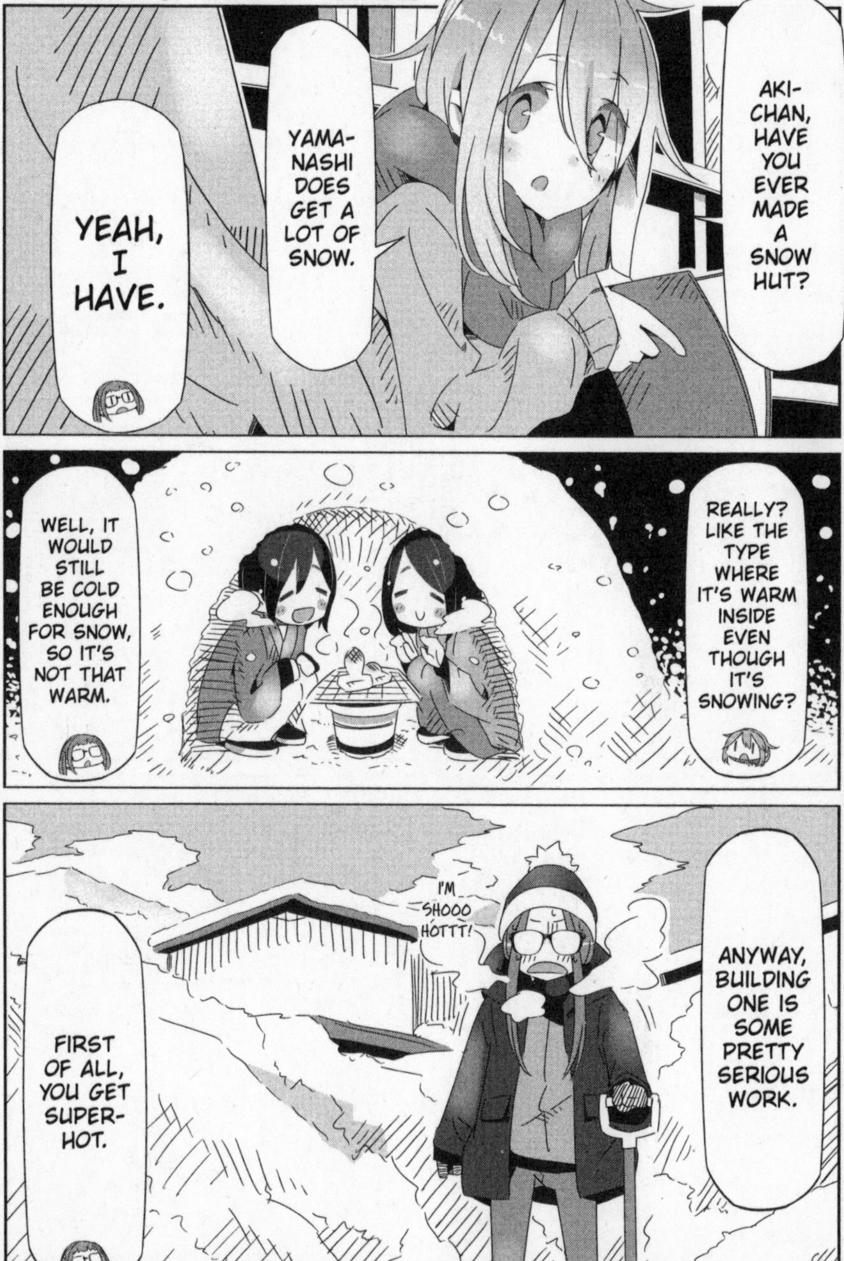
AKI-CHAN, HAVE YOU EVER MADE A SNOW HUT?
YAMANASHI DOES GET A LOT OF SNOW.
YEAH, I HAVE.
REALLY? LIKE THE TYPE WHERE IT'S WARM INSIDE EVEN THOUGH IT'S SNOWING?
WELL, IT WOULD STILL BE COLD ENOUGH FOR SNOW, SO IT'S NOT THAT WARM.
ANYWAY, BUILDING ONE IS SOME PRETTY SERIOUS WORK.
I'M SHOOO HOTTT!
FIRST OF ALL, YOU GET SUPER-HOT.

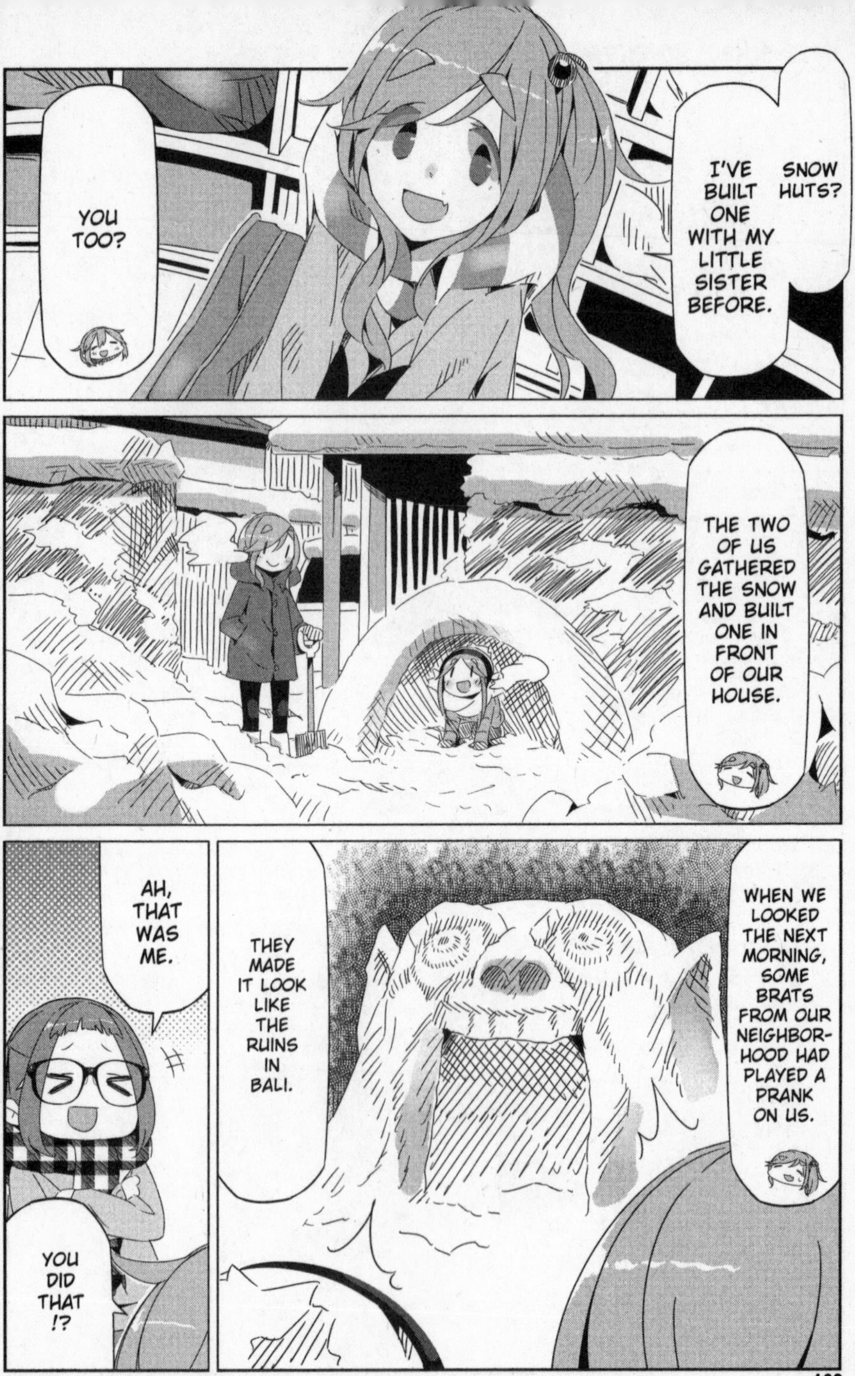
SNOW HUTS?
I'VE BUILT ONE WITH MY LITTLE SISTER BEFORE.
YOU TOO?
THE TWO OF US GATHERED THE SNOW AND BUILT ONE IN FRONT OF OUR HOUSE.
WHEN WE LOOKED THE NEXT MORNING, SOME BRATS FROM OUR NEIGHBOR-HOOD HAD PLAYED A PRANK ON US.
THEY MADE IT LOOK LIKE THE RUINS IN BALI.
AH, THAT WAS ME.
YOU DID THAT!?

THERE'S A TYPE OF CAMPING GEAR...

...KNOWN AS "ULTRA-LIGHT."

IT'S A TYPE OF PRODUCT PRIMARILY TARGETED AT MOUNTAIN CLIMBERS.

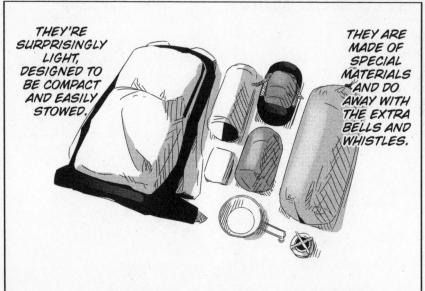

THEY ARE MADE OF SPECIAL MATERIALS AND DO AWAY WITH THE EXTRA BELLS AND WHISTLES.

THEY'RE SURPRISINGLY LIGHT, DESIGNED TO BE COMPACT AND EASILY STOWED.

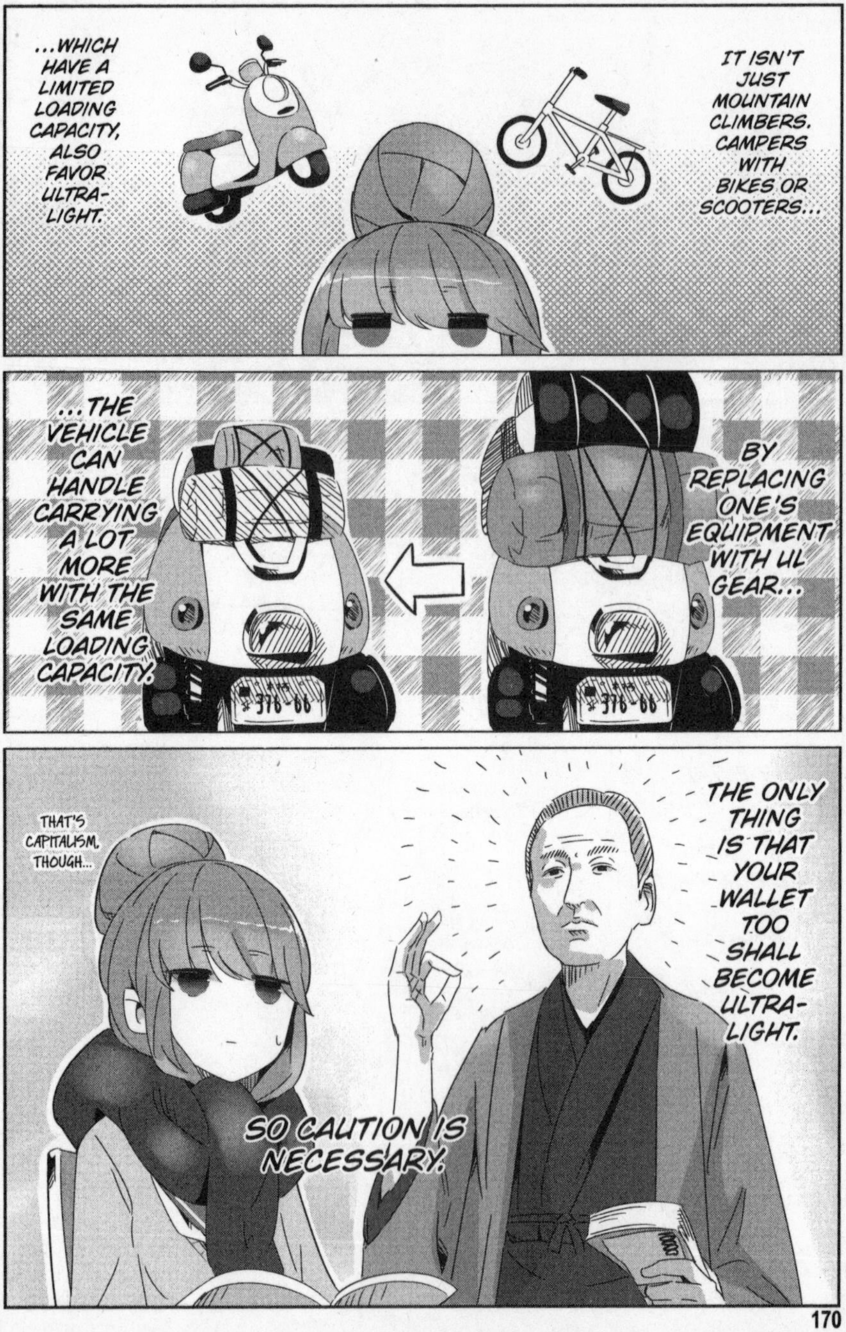
IT ISN'T JUST MOUNTAIN CLIMBERS. CAMPERS WITH BIKES OR SCOOTERS...
...WHICH HAVE A LIMITED LOADING CAPACITY, ALSO FAVOR ULTRA-LIGHT.
BY REPLACING ONE'S EQUIPMENT WITH UL GEAR...
...THE VEHICLE CAN HANDLE CARRYING A LOT MORE WITH THE SAME LOADING CAPACITY.
THE ONLY THING IS THAT YOUR WALLET TOO SHALL BECOME ULTRA-LIGHT.
SO CAUTION IS NECESSARY.
THAT'S CAPITALISM, THOUGH...

AFTER-SCHOOL 40 I HAVE A BLANKET

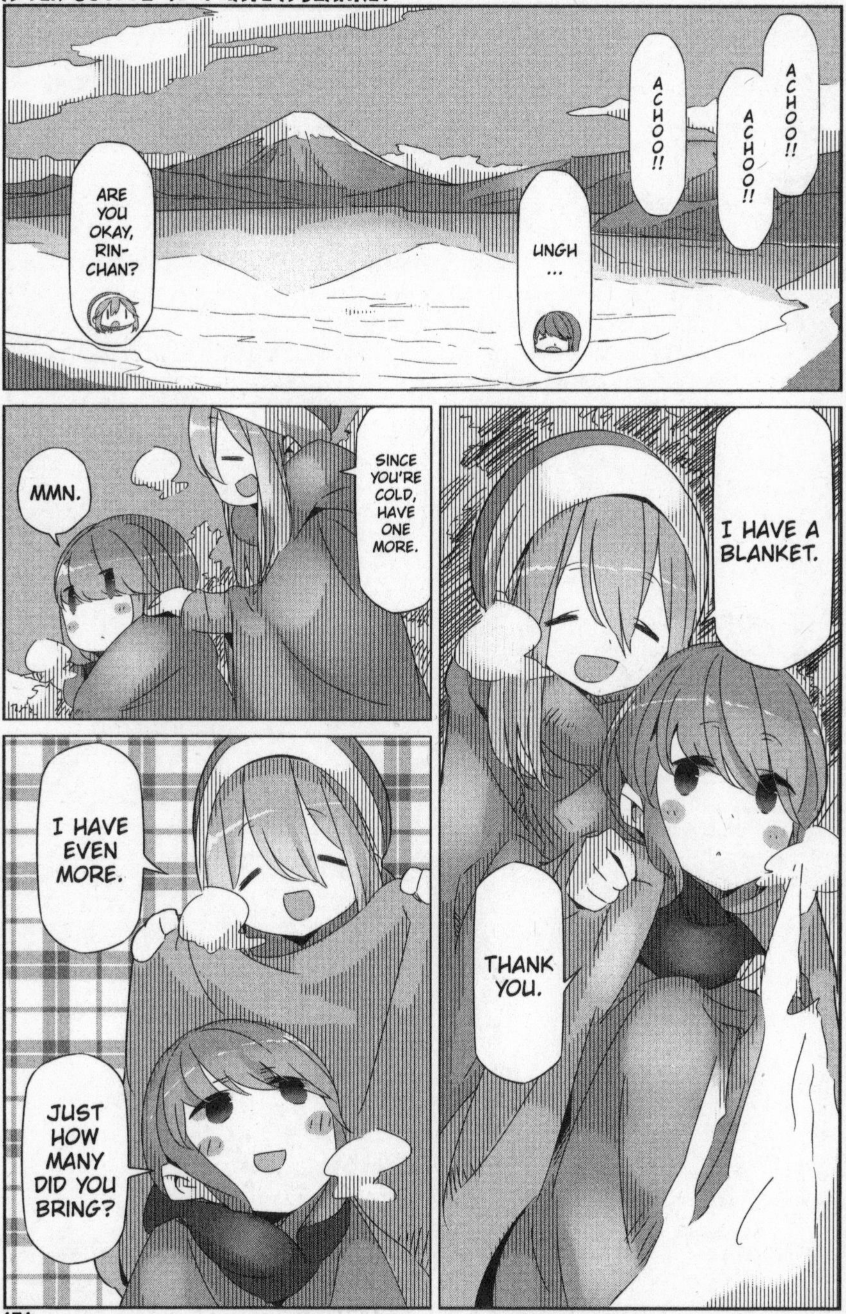

ACHOO!!
ACHOO!!
ACHOO!!
UNGH ...
ARE YOU OKAY, RIN-CHAN?
I HAVE A BLANKET.
THANK YOU.
SINCE YOU'RE COLD, HAVE ONE MORE.
MMN.
I HAVE EVEN MORE.
JUST HOW MANY DID YOU BRING?

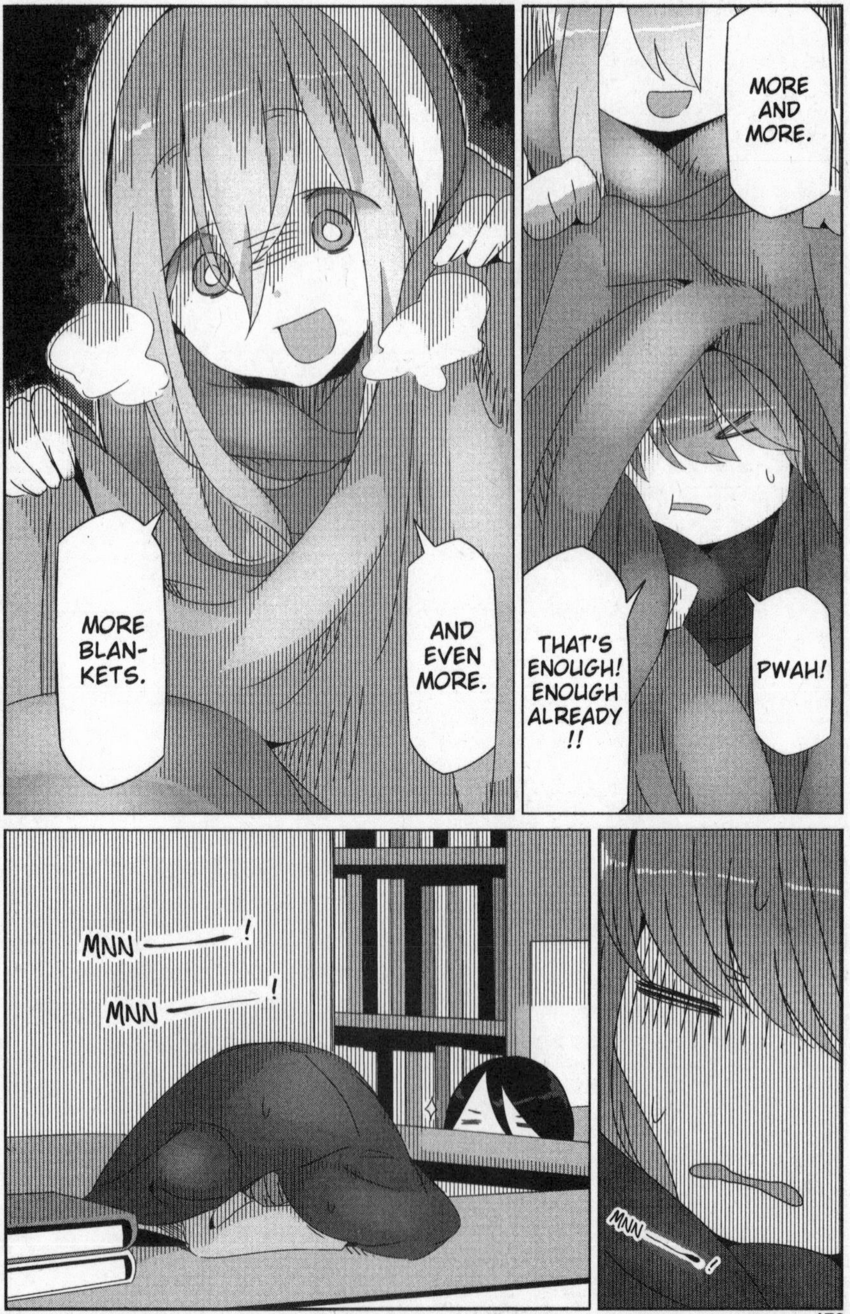
MORE AND MORE.
PWAH!
THAT'S ENOUGH! ENOUGH ALREADY!!
MORE BLAN-KETS.
AND EVEN MORE.
MNN——!
MNN——!
MNN——!

AFTER-SCHOOL 41 ****ING

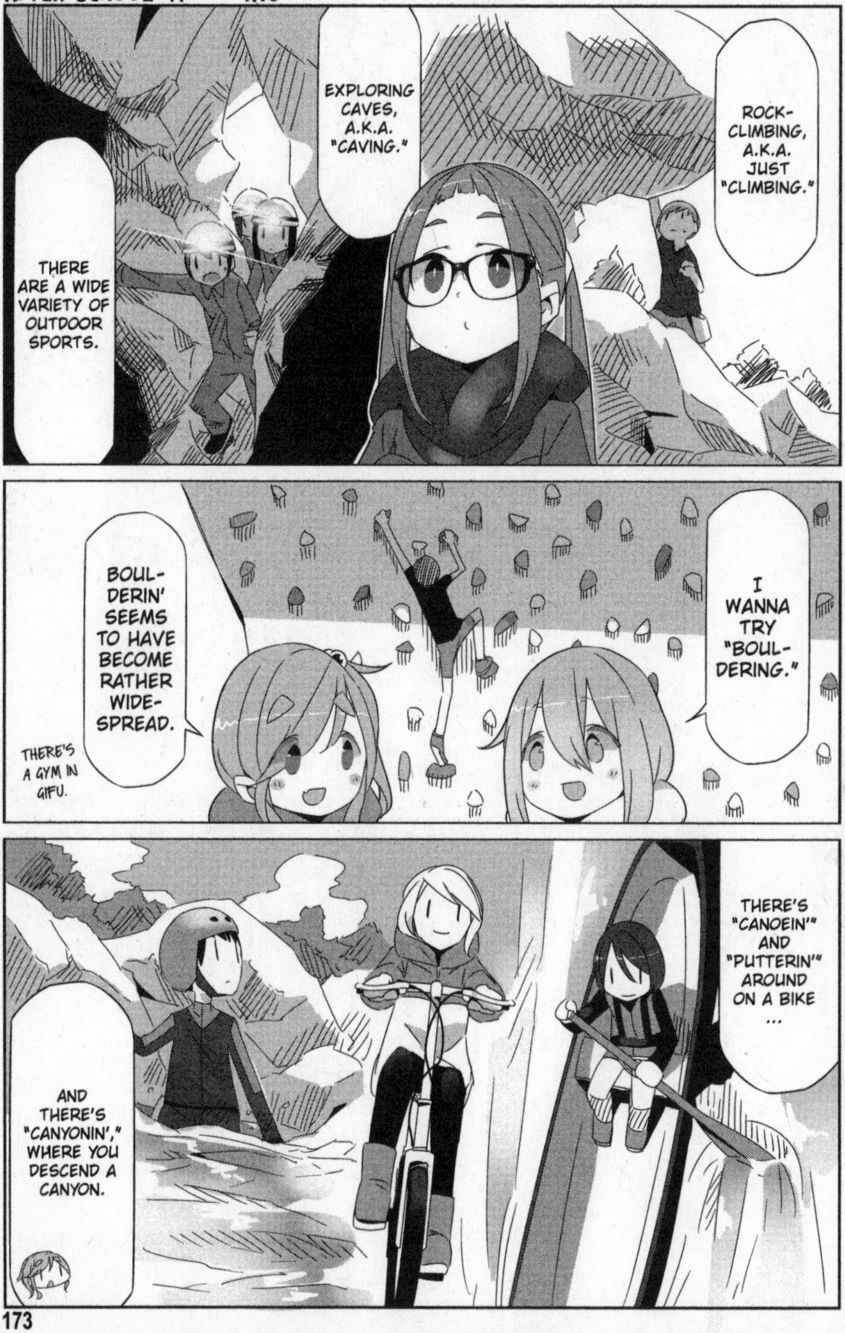
ROCK-CLIMBING, A.K.A. JUST "CLIMBING."
EXPLORING CAVES, A.K.A. "CAVING."
THERE ARE A WIDE VARIETY OF OUTDOOR SPORTS.
I WANNA TRY "BOULDERING."
BOULDERIN' SEEMS TO HAVE BECOME RATHER WIDESPREAD.
THERE'S A GYM IN GIFU.
THERE'S "CANOEIN'" AND "PUTTERIN'" AROUND ON A BIKE ...
AND THERE'S "CANYONIN'," WHERE YOU DESCEND A CANYON.

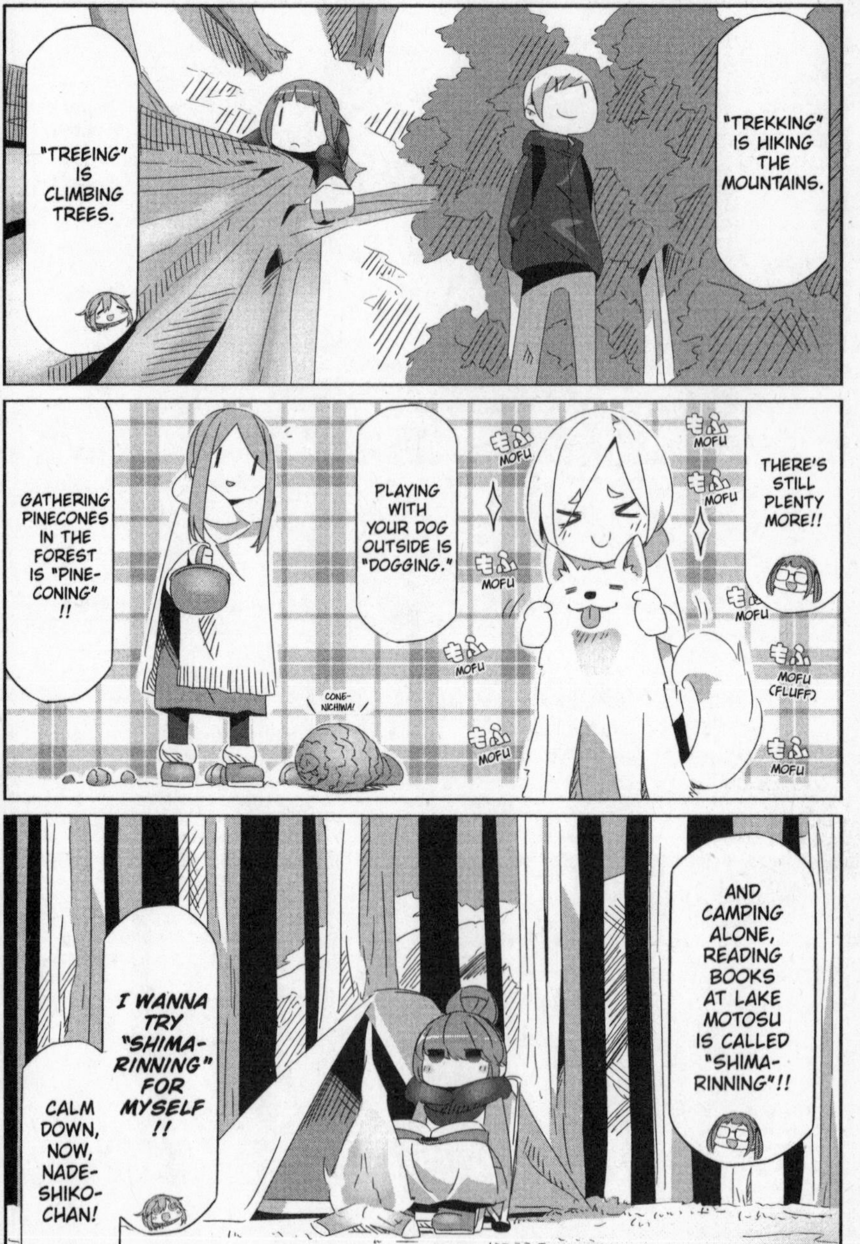
"TREKKING" IS HIKING THE MOUNTAINS.
"TREEING" IS CLIMBING TREES.
THERE'S STILL PLENTY MORE!!
もふ MOFU
もふ MOFU
もふ MOFU
もふ MOFU (FLUFF)
もふ MOFU
もふ MOFU
PLAYING WITH YOUR DOG OUTSIDE IS "DOGGING."
もふ MOFU
もふ MOFU
もふ MOFU
CONE-NICHIWA!
GATHERING PINECONES IN THE FOREST IS "PINE-CONING"!!
AND CAMPING ALONE, READING BOOKS AT LAKE MOTOSU IS CALLED "SHIMA-RINNING"!!
I WANNA TRY "SHIMA-RINNING" FOR MYSELF!!
CALM DOWN, NOW, NADE-SHIKO-CHAN!

AFTER-SCHOOL 42 UNUSED TREASURE

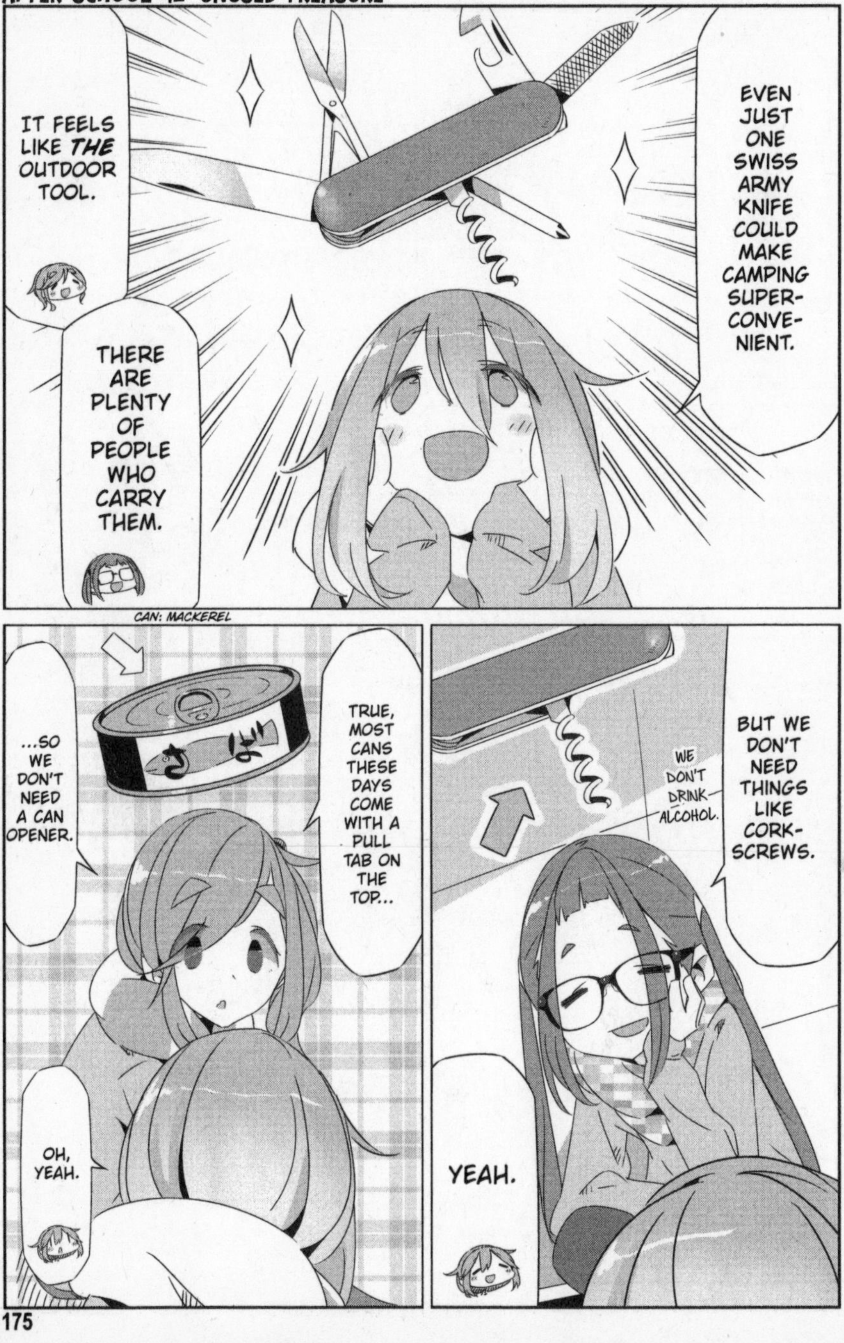
EVEN JUST ONE SWISS ARMY KNIFE COULD MAKE CAMPING SUPER-CONVENIENT.
IT FEELS LIKE *THE* OUTDOOR TOOL.
THERE ARE PLENTY OF PEOPLE WHO CARRY THEM.
BUT WE DON'T NEED THINGS LIKE CORK-SCREWS.
WE DON'T DRINK ALCOHOL.
YEAH.
TRUE, MOST CANS THESE DAYS COME WITH A PULL TAB ON THE TOP...
CAN: MACKEREL
...SO WE DON'T NEED A CAN OPENER.
OH, YEAH.

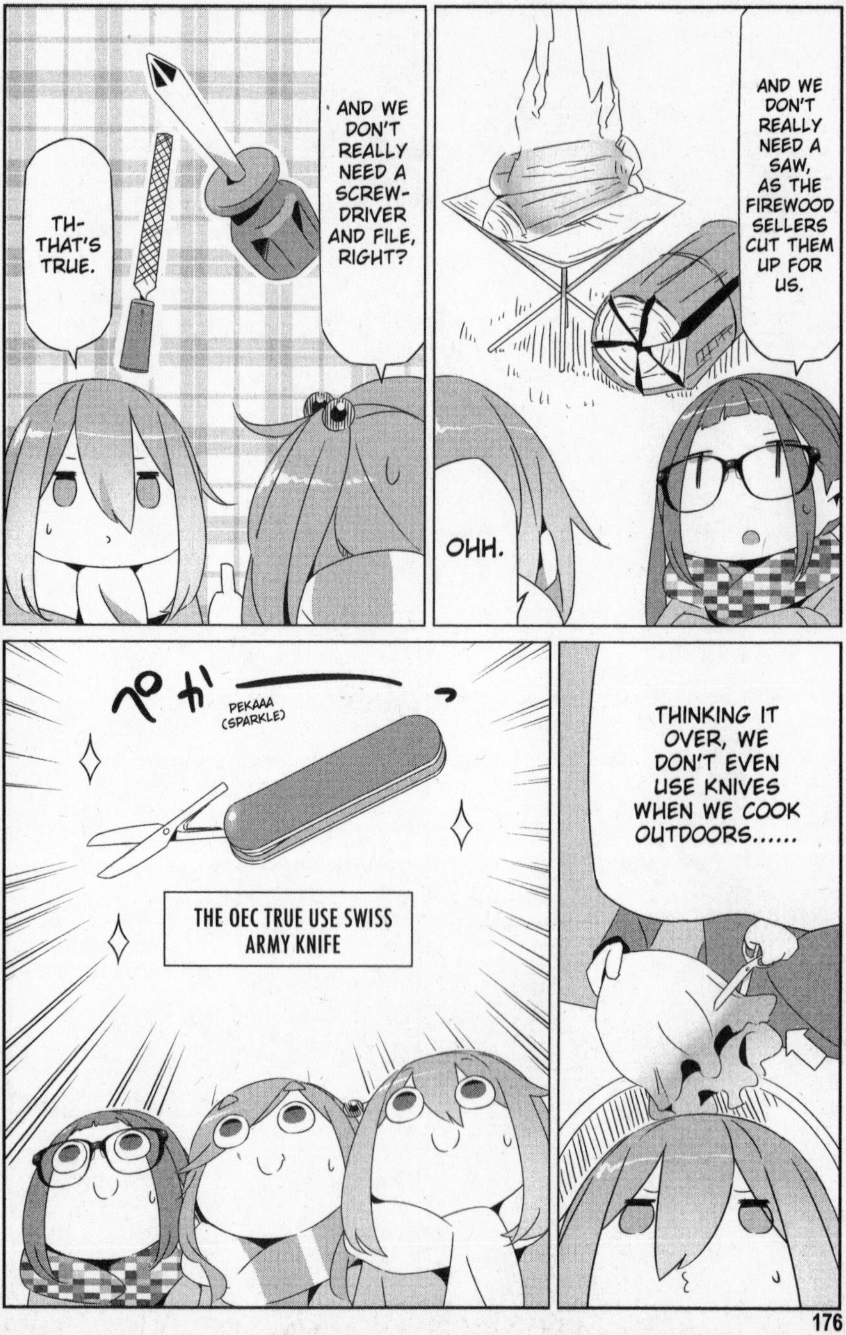
AND WE DON'T REALLY NEED A SAW, AS THE FIREWOOD SELLERS CUT THEM UP FOR US.
OHH.
AND WE DON'T REALLY NEED A SCREW-DRIVER AND FILE, RIGHT?
TH-THAT'S TRUE.
THINKING IT OVER, WE DON'T EVEN USE KNIVES WHEN WE COOK OUTDOORS......
ぺか――っ
PEKAAA (SPARKLE)
THE OEC TRUE USE SWISS ARMY KNIFE

HOW DID YOU LIKE VOLUME 5 OF *LAID-BACK CAMP*?
THIS TIME COVERED THE END OF ONE YEAR AND THE BEGINNING OF ANOTHER, PLUS RIN'S SOLO CAMPING.

IN THIS WORK, I DEPICTED A SCENE WHERE A CHARACTER COULDN'T GET HOME DUE TO ICY ROAD CONDITIONS.
IT OFTEN HAPPENS WHEN CAMPING IN WINTER. THE FIRST DAY OF CAMP IS SUNNY AND WARM, BUT THE TEMPERATURE DROPS OVERNIGHT AND CREATES FREEZING CONDITIONS THE NEXT MORNING.
SO EVERYONE, PLEASE BE CAREFUL.

THIS HAS BEEN AFRO.

[FIRST PUBLICATION]
***MANGA TIME KIRARA FORWARD* JUNE–OCTOBER 2017 ISSUES
***KIRARA BASE* JULY 19TH, OCTOBER 14TH 2016–MARCH 7TH 2017 ISSUES (UPDATED)
*ONE-SHOT (DRAWN FOR THIS BOOK)
THE MATERIALS IN THIS VOLUME WERE COLLECTED FROM THE ABOVE SOURCES.

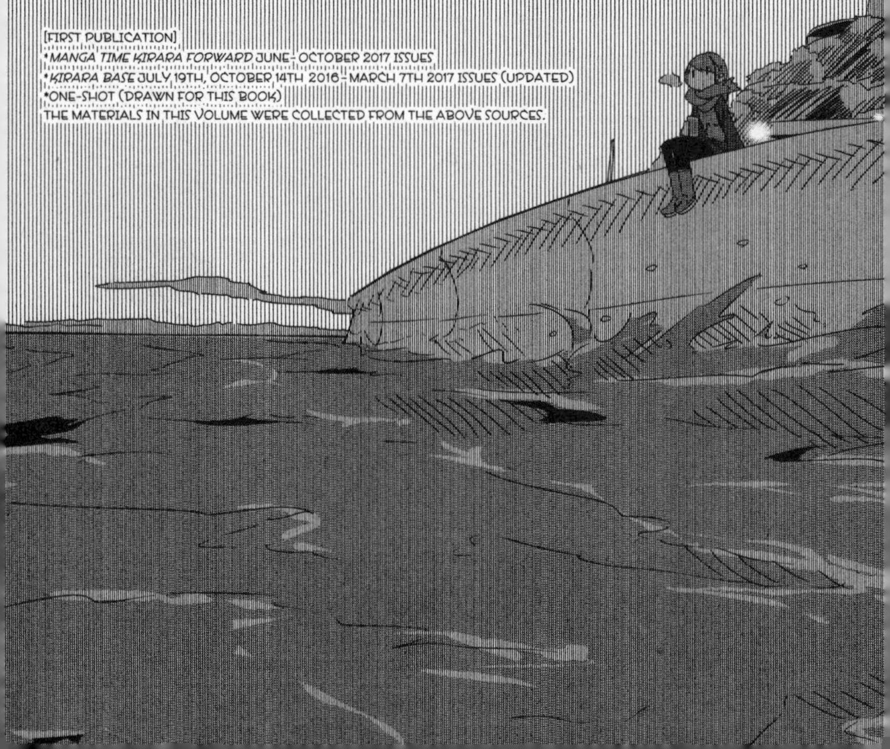

LAID BACK CAMP ⑤

Afro

Translation: **Amber Tamosaitis** ✳ Lettering: **DK**

YURUCAMP Vol. 5
© 2017 afro. All rights reserved. First published in Japan in 2017 by HOUBUNSHA CO., LTD., Tokyo. English translation rights in United States, Canada, and United Kingdom arranged with HOUBUNSHA CO., LTD. through Tuttle-Mori Agency, Inc., Tokyo.

English translation © 2019 by Yen Press, LLC

Yen Press
1290 Avenue of the Americas
New York, NY 10104

Visit us at yenpress.com
facebook.com/yenpress
twitter.com/yenpress
yenpress.tumblr.com
instagram.com/yenpress

First Yen Press Edition: February 2019

Yen Press is an imprint of Yen Press, LLC.
The Yen Press name and logo are trademarks of Yen Press, LLC.

The publisher is not responsible for websites (or their content) that are not owned by the publisher.

Library of Congress Control Number: 2017959206

ISBNs: 978-1-9753-0192-7 (paperback)
       978-1-9753-2882-5 (ebook)

10 9 8 7 6 5 4 3 2 1

WOR

Printed in the United States of America